THE HEADLOCK OF DESTINY

TITAN WARS

SAMUEL GATELY

THE HEADLOCK OF DESTINY

Edited by Mike Myers
Cover Illustration by Dominik Mayer
Cover Typography by Humble Nations

Other Books by Samuel Gately

<u>Open, Fire Eye, Close Series</u>

The Fire Eye Refugee

The Fire Eye Chosen

<u>Spies of Dragon and Chalk Series</u>

Night of the Chalk

Rise of the Falsemarked

Alliance of the Sunken

For more information visit samuelgately.com

Contents

Prologue...1

Chapter 1 15

Chapter 2 24

Chapter 3 29

Chapter 4 34

Chapter 5 44

Chapter 6 52

Chapter 7 60

Chapter 8 71

Chapter 9 77

Chapter 10 83

Chapter 11 94

Chapter 12 100

Chapter 13 108

Chapter 14 114

Chapter 15 122

Chapter 16 128

Chapter 17 134

Chapter 18 140

Chapter 19 147

Chapter 20 154

Chapter 21 158

Chapter 22 169

Chapter 23 179

Chapter 24 184

Chapter 25 193

Chapter 26 206

Chapter 27 213

Chapter 28 227

Chapter 29 237

Chapter 30 247

Chapter 31 253

Chapter 32 258

Chapter 33 263

Chapter 34 267

Chapter 35 273

Chapter 36 284

Chapter 37 297

Chapter 38 305

Chapter 39 312

Chapter 40 320

Chapter 41 330

Chapter 42 335

Chapter 43 340

Author's Notes 347

Author's Bio 347

Prologue

The watching crowd held its breath as the Savage circled Troll-Blooded Thom, waiting to pounce. Cold mountain air wove between the two titans. The mat below them creaked and whispered with their heavy steps. The long fight was nearly done. The mighty titans stared at each other, moving in slow circles, until one showed the slightest downturn of the eyes, a glimmer of fear. The Savage smiled. Troll-Blooded Thom was his.

The Savage leapt across the ring and caught Troll-Blooded Thom's chin with a hard cross, stunning him. The Savage picked up the smaller ten-man and hoisted him over his head. Thom struggled, kicking, pleading. The Savage smiled wider, his muscles tensed, as he raised Thom over the crowd. Slowly, the Savage circled the ring, driving the crowd to a frenzy, ignoring the struggles of the desperate titan in his grasp. When he finished the circle, his face tightened, his smile curled into a grimace. As the crowd surged to their feet, the Savage let out a roar that carried through the town and echoed off the distant mountain peaks. A titan's roar. The fight might be over, but the show had just begun.

...

"He slammed Troll-Blooded Thom practically through the mat! The whole town shook! Everyone lost their minds!" Darren's eyes shot wildly around the gathered group of ten- to twelve-year-old boys. "It was, no fooling, the most insane fight I've ever seen."

1

Alec, the only other in the bunch who'd been at the match, scoffed at Darren's commentary. "It's the only fight you've ever seen, dumbass."

"Not true." Darren's brow furrowed. "My dad took me to one of the Friday night bouts in Landing Point."

"The only *real* fight." Alec smirked and shook his head. "Not some rinky-dink pretenders. Real titans." Alec was taller than any of the boys, aside from Van, and he wore a permanent sneer on his thin, angular face. Van could tell he wished he was the only one who'd seen the fight and could recap it for the others.

"I've seen titans before," Darren said, but he fell quiet momentarily, which gave Alec the chance to jump in and take over the description of the match.

As the boys wrestled over the story, the traffic on the only major street in Headwaters had slowed to a crawl, horse-drawn wagons fighting for space amongst throngs of festival goers armed with mugs full of beer. The usually quiet town, resting in the foothills of the mountains to the north, was hosting its Annual Headwaters Beer Festival. And it was that festival that had brought the match to town. It was a rare occurrence for Headwaters to host a match featuring two real titans, even if one of them was only Troll-Blooded Thom. The boys huddled in a shadowy corner between two buildings where the adults wouldn't bother them. Their eyes bounced back and forth between Darren and Alec, as the tale of the fight unwound in a typically chaotic manner.

"So, Troll-Blooded Thom enters the ring first," Alec said, "and the crowd boos. Everybody's waiting for the Savage. Thom looked like he was going to piss his stupid, yellow shorts. And when the Savage showed up, I bet he did."

Darren wasn't about to sit the whole story out. "Yeah, he came charging down the aisle, just huge. I almost touched him when he went past—"

"You aren't supposed to grab at them, you asshole," Alec said, looking unhappy with the interruption.

Van listened attentively; the rest of the world had fallen away as the boys clustered tight around Darren and Alec. Titans were rumored to be descendants of the giants who once roamed the Open Nations, stomping on stuff and shoving down castle walls just for fun. Modern titans were called ten-men, because they were supposed to have the strength of ten men. Sometimes twice as tall as a full-grown man, they towered over the crowds just as Van towered over most of the boys around him. But Van was nowhere near full-grown yet. Thus far his titan blood had done him few favors other than singling him out. He was bigger and stronger than the other boys, though Alec was older and nearly as strong. But it was just a matter of time before Van left him in the dust. Van muttered the word *asshole* under his breath, impressed with how easily swearing came to Alec. Whenever Van tried it, he sounded like a dick.

"So, the Savage comes flying in, dives under the bottom rope. Man, he just started wailing on Thom. Didn't even hesitate, just pounded him into the mat. I wouldn't be surprised if Thom's dead."

Another boy, Regis, piped up with a high voice, "He's not dead—he's drinking over at Tyler's Pub."

Alec laughed. "Probably drinking the dregs of that batch of porter that turned sour, thinking he'll never come back to this shitty town."

"No," Regis said, excited to share his insight. His dad was a regular at Tyler's, one of only three real bars in Headwaters, not counting the brewery's tap room for employees. "Tyler's pouring Foundation. Got it special for the festival. My da went down early to get a seat at the bar."

The boys all turned and stared down the rutted street at Tyler's. The warped wooden sign bearing its name sagged over the door on rusty chains. A line of grumbling men waited to get in, no doubt hoping to land a stool next to the titan.

Alec took advantage of the distraction and leapt on Darren. The other boys shouted and whistled as the pair rolled in the dirt. Alec quickly gained the upper hand, forcing Darren into a headlock. Seeing the smaller boy restrained, Alec's various toadies jumped into the fray and rained weak punches on the hapless Darren.

Van took a step back from the wrestling mass of boys. He didn't want to roll in the dirt, getting unfairly piled on by the others, to endure Alec's pinches and slaps. He wanted to be tough, a proper titan, but thus far it hadn't come easily. Van was a constant target in the impromptu wrestling matches that broke out among boys his age. The bragging rights that came from besting a titan, even one as young and embarrassingly soft as Van, were too much of a temptation to the others. Those few times Van had come out on top, it usually resulted in a lecture from whichever adult ended the fight about how it was unfair for him to be involved in the first place, beating on these poor boys, the same boys who laughed behind the back of the lecturer and mocked Van's flailing arm movements. It seemed like every time he raised his hands he lost, one way or another. Lately he'd been far more focused on something other than finding glory in the squared circle, the kind the Savage earned every time he squared off with another ten-man. Van knew what he wanted today.

"I want to get my hands on some of the Kingsland," he said. It was the beer Headwaters was most renowned for. Van intended the words only for his friend Cormac,

4

but the fight had unexpectedly lulled and everyone's eyes landed on him. Van's voice was far deeper than the others', though he spoke with the same unstable mix of boldness and worry. His skin was dark brown, his curly hair darker still, and his brow had a pinched look to it, making him appear mean or slow, though he was neither.

Alec smirked from his position on the ground, arm still locked around the red-faced Darren's neck. "Yeah, right, Van. I'm *sure* you're gonna get some Kingsland."

Van looked out over the crowd on the main street as the boys struggled to their feet, a few parting shoves thrown in for good measure. It would definitely be a challenge. The festival was nearing full swing, and that meant that the women who charged themselves with maintaining the town's decorum would be out in spades as well. The boys were probably being watched right now by the militant, self-appointed peacekeepers, though it was a good sign the short fight hadn't drawn one of them over.

Miss Briggs was the worst. She was the one who had scheduled a special mandatory session at school last night, preventing all but Alec and Darren from seeing the best wrestling match Headwaters had hosted in ten years. Alec's dad was the only one with the guts to stand up to her, and that was because Alec's mom was dead and Miss Briggs couldn't shame his dad into complying. Darren's dad had probably been too drunk to remember his son was supposed to be someplace else. Van and the others were locked in the schoolhouse and forced to suffer through a lecture on the history of Headwaters while they tried to ignore the delighted cries of the crowd down the street. Van was sure Miss Briggs deliberately selected the most boring lecture she could find, which featured no mention of titans or beer.

Which was crazy because, even though Headwaters wasn't a large town, it hosted the largest and best brewery in all the Open Nations. Van overheard Alec's dad bragging it up one day. Everyone knew beers brewed in the Headwaters Brewery were the best, and they sent out six times as many barrels as their closest competitor. That didn't even count the sludge they sent to the orcs west of the Uplands.

Beer was everything in Headwaters, and the most frequent pour in the town was Foundation, a heavy stout. Van had swiped several abandoned half-full mugs of the stuff and developed a taste for it. But the prize of the day would be a Kingsland, the most hyped ale of every brewing season. Closely guarded and jealously distributed, the much touted and frightfully expensive brew would be coveted by everyone at the festival. The brewmaster would open a few barrels later in the day, probably more than a few, but it wasn't the kind of drink anyone would leave lying around. No one would sell the boys a pour, and the beer gardens would be patrolled by Miss Briggs's army of enforcers, who apparently thought the best use of their time during the annual festival was preventing the boys from enjoying themselves.

Alec was dusting himself off, staring spitefully at Van for the transgression of interrupting. "Anyway, who's telling this story?" he said. "Do you want to hear about the match or not?"

"Yeah, shut up, Van." This was from one of the other boys, emboldened by Alec's presence. Van scowled but kept his mouth shut. He did want to hear about the fight. It was only the exciting prospect of a Kingsland that made him forget himself and speak in a group that included the likes of Alec Durheed.

Alec launched into a lengthy description of the fight, occasionally interrupted by Darren. To hear it from them, there had been thousands of historic moments. Troll-Blooded Thom got in a lucky shot and took the Savage to the mat with a chokeslam. When the Savage got loose, Thom nearly took his head off with a clothesline. The Savage got all charged up then, waving his arms to rally the crowd and coming back with a flurry of fists to Thom's face. He beat Thom down until the match finally ended with a bodyslam, followed by a flying elbow drop from the top rope. Thom didn't get up after that.

Van wondered how much Alec was just making up. To hear him tell it, it was the longest and most awesome match of the year. Van doubted that was the case. Two real titans wouldn't waste their best moves on a local beer festival in the sticks. Not to mention it wasn't even a fair fight. The Savage was much better known than Troll-Blooded Thom for a reason. "The Savage used to be called the Spider, right?" he asked.

Alec shot him an annoyed look, but before he could answer, the crowd along the main thoroughfare burst into cheers. The boys all saw the unmistakable towering presence in the middle of the knot of approaching people. In unspoken agreement they raced towards it and began weaving through the crowd to get closer.

On the crowded street Van struggled to keep up with the other boys. He earned dark looks as he slid past, bumping festival goers on either side of the gaps the other boys, slimmer and more fleet of foot, shot through with ease. He plastered an apologetic smile on his face and worked his way forward. He caught sight of Miss Briggs watching the boys, lips pursed tightly as she waited for someone to dare step out of line. Maybe *her* name should be the Spider, he thought with a grin.

The Savage stood over the group of town leaders as they led him towards the raised platform that marked the town square. The hot afternoon sun baked the dusty square, but the draw of last night's winning titan persuaded the townsfolk to surrender their shade and gather in a crowd in front of the platform.

As the group took the stage, Van squinted up at the Savage. The tallest of the people surrounding him came up roughly to his armpits. His toned muscles were on full display in his thin, ropy top; its bright colors stood out amongst the somber blacks and blues of the men around him. He was deeply tanned, with flowing brown hair and a thick, wild beard and wore dark-tinted glasses with brightly colored rims that matched his shirt.

Not to be outdone, Mayor Holmes wore her finest hat, a shade of red rarely seen in the mountain town. In addition to the mayor, two other women mixed into the mostly male crowd pressed around the Savage. Miss Briggs shot them disapproving looks for their tight clothes and flirty laughter as the Savage whispered something to them.

Alec and Darren did well leading the boys in close. They'd found a pack of smaller boys, who'd probably been holding their spot in front of the platform since early in the morning, and drove them away with cruel pinches and whispered threats. Only one had the audacity to cry, but his tears dried quickly when he saw how little attention it drew in the wake of a titan. And not just any titan, the Savage. His name was known to everyone in the town, at least everyone who mattered. Folks were saying he'd be in the Headlock of Destiny Tournament soon, representing the nation of Peakfall, once the aging Hellhound had the sense to get out of his way before he got hurt.

Van murmured his last apologies to the unfortunates in his elbow range as he took his place at the rear of the boys, shifting to avoid blocking the view of the shorter adults behind him. He fingered the coins in his pocket, making sure they were still there. He had maybe enough for a lemon ice. Definitely not enough for a beer. He'd pretended not to notice that his latest foster mother had given her real children a lot more spending money for the festival.

Van stared up at the Savage. It was exciting to see a real titan. Van would be one someday, in a way the others couldn't. Titans were born of titans. There were some men outside the titan bloodlines who made it into the ring, but they universally fell before the might of a true ten-man. Van's titan blood was no guarantee of success, though. There were weaklings among the titans and, as Alec and the others liked to remind him every chance they got, Van seemed to land more on the weak than the mighty side of things. He hated wrestling. He hated fighting. But that didn't mean he couldn't dream of himself up there, basking in adulation rather than being shoved out of the way.

On the platform, the Savage turned to face the crowd, raising a beer-fueled roar. Hardly a single soul stood without a glass mug in hand, and the dirt of the town square became a frothy mire beneath their muddy shoes. The mayor took her place on one side of the titan, the president of the Headwaters Brewery stood on the other. With the practiced glare of a politician, Mayor Holmes subtly cleared the others back, all except the two women whom the Savage had locked into place by flinging his arms over their shoulders. The Savage slouched over them and nodded at the crowd, acknowledging the cheers.

Mayor Holmes started her practiced speech, but Van stopped paying attention as Brewmaster Hayes approached the rear of the platform with three men behind him, carefully transporting a heavy barrel of ale on a wheeled cart. The mayor and the brewery president might be the richest people in Headwaters, but Brewmaster Hayes was the most respected. The

Headwaters Brewery lived and died on his reputation, and he never failed to deliver. He was like a titan in his own way.

Van's eyes were glued to the barrel. It had no visible markings: no dates, notes, or branding. Which meant it was one of the few the brewmaster tended entirely by himself. It was not just Kingsland, it was a batch of ale he'd use to model the rest of the production after.

As the men hoisted the barrel onto the stage and the mayor blathered on, the Savage lazily gazed around the crowd. Van suddenly wished he weren't standing so close. He was too big to blend in, and he didn't want the Savage to recognize him as a young titan by the contrast between his size and youthful appearance. It seemed he didn't need to worry. The speech droned on and the Savage seemed only to be paying attention to the two ladies in his arms, quietly teasing them with bicep flexes. When one let out a loud giggle, the mayor seemed to get the point and wrapped up her remarks.

"And with that," the mayor said at last, "we are pleased to present to you, the mighty Savage, the Headwaters Annual Beer Festival Championship Belt." She paused and looked around, confusion on her face. "We also have a belt for the runner-up."

"You won't be seeing him around here, not after last night's beating!" the Savage called out loudly. The crowd burst into laughter and more cheers.

Mayor Holmes smiled. "Before we present you with the belt, there is one other gift we have for you." At a motion from her, the brewmaster quickly hammered the tap into the large barrel's stopper. "One of the finest brews from the finest brewery in the Open Nations, Kingsland Ale."

Van had no idea if the Savage knew anything about beer, or particularly cared. But when the mayor and brewmaster together drew a large glass from the

Kingsland Ale barrel, there was no mistaking the solemnity of the occasion. The whole town waited breathlessly as they carefully topped off an enormous, titan-sized glass mug with the golden beverage.

The Savage was no rookie when it came to being the center of attention. He seemed to understand that, in the minds of the gathered crowd, this was the true trophy. The belt was an afterthought. He let go of his companions and straightened out of his slouch, his full height raising him even higher above the crowd. He accepted the mug from the mayor with a respectful nod and made a show of inspecting the beer, peering into the glass and then lowering it under his nose. He took his time, building the crowd's tension. Van felt himself drawn in by the titan. Kingsland Ale was the crown jewel of Headwaters, its greatest achievement, its claim to fame. It seemed as though the fate of the town hung in the balance as the titan gripped the glass mug.

Finally, the Savage raised the mug to his lips and took a huge gulp of the beer, his throat pulsing as he swallowed it down. When he lowered the mug, silence gripped the crowd. Everyone held their breath as he gazed at them from the platform and wiped his mouth with his gigantic forearm. Then he raised his mug to the crowd. "Damn if that isn't the best beer I've ever tasted."

The crowd exploded. Beer spilled and splashed everywhere as the delirious townspeople hollered, circling up to clink their heavy mugs together. The Savage looked out on the crowd, clearly enjoying the rapture he'd caused and momentarily ignoring even the pretty women by his side. Van's heart pounded as he realized the Savage's eyes had stopped roaming, and the titan was staring right at him. The Savage flashed a curious smile and turned to the mayor.

"What's this?" he asked her, pointing at Van. "Is that a little two-man?"

Van had never been called a two-man before. It would be an insult to call a fully grown titan anything less than a ten-man, but for young titans, *two-man* was a term of affection, a sign that they would grow mighty one day. He felt a smile threatening to break out on his face.

"What?" the mayor said, seemingly confused. Then she followed the titan's pointed finger. "Oh, yes." She beckoned impatiently, "Get over here, Van."

Van initially resisted but there were hands pushing on his back. The crowd eyed him darkly as he was guided closer to the platform. They'd just enjoyed a victory with the Savage's endorsement of the Kingsland. They didn't want Van to screw it up. He felt Miss Briggs's eyes on him. If he said the wrong thing here, he'd be in line for a lot of extra lectures. And he'd never be allowed close to another visiting titan. Or another festival.

As Van walked the few stairs, he looked up at the gigantic Savage, feeling smaller than he ever had before. Would he really one day be that size?

"Hey, two-man." The Savage stepped across the platform and held out his hand. Van grasped it and was wrestled through a complex handshake he couldn't quite follow. He felt stupid when the Savage grinned knowingly at his clumsiness. "No need to be shy. Always good to meet a fellow titan."

Van simply nodded. The Savage looked like he wanted to make their meeting into a bit of a show, but Van wasn't giving him much to work with, so the titan simply smiled again and turned back to the mayor. "You all treating the two-man right?"

The mayor rushed to assure him that they regarded Van as a special member of their community, which struck Van as a bit of a half-truth. Magical bloodlines behaved strangely in the Open Nations, and titans ran exclusively male, just as other species like valkyrie and sprites ran exclusively female. Titans crossed all variety of races and colors and even some blends of magical creatures and animals. But one thing the eclectic titans all seemed to share was that they were pretty shitty dads. They rarely stuck around for the birth of their children, always heading to the next match or adventure. Bearing a titan's child was hard on its mother and often led to death in childbirth, as had happened to Van's mom. He never knew which titan had been his dad. With so many titans abandoned or orphaned, communities took them on and raised them together. Van had been through several foster homes, most run by kind women who treated him well, if a bit distantly. Communities like Headwaters, which volunteered to raise titans, were rewarded for their efforts by having homegrown champions to wrestle on their behalf. And if Van couldn't deliver in the ring, they would probably just have him work in the brewery. Which was fine by him.

Mayor Holmes was passed a large belt bearing the words *Headwaters Annual Beer Festival Champion*. It was a nice bit of black leather and gold-plating, but Van suspected the Savage had a hundred more just like it or nicer. As the mayor held it out towards the Savage, the titan hesitated a moment and then turned to Van. "Here, two-man. Hold my beer."

Van took the heavy glass mug awkwardly with both hands. The Savage grabbed the belt from the mayor, raised it over his head, and held it glistening in the bright sun. The crowd cheered and a chant of "Savage! Savage!" broke out. The titan nodded along, clearly enjoying himself.

Then the chant abruptly broke off in a collective gasp. The crowd shouted in outrage. Van was holding the giant mug over his head, chugging the Kingsland down as quickly as he could. The glorious, foamy beer slid down his throat; his eyes teared as he desperately gulped it down. He had just finished off the titan-sized portion when he felt hands grasping at his shirt. He sprinted down the stairs and off into the crowd.

Van cleared the clutching hands, empty glass mug still pressed to his chest. He let out a laugh and a long victory whoop. Despite the sounds of furious pursuit behind him, he had no regrets. After all, titans were titans, but *beer was beer*. He shot a quick look back. The Savage was staring at him, mouth agape, looking, for a moment, impossibly dumbstruck above the sea of angry faces. The last words Van heard from the mighty titan as he left him behind were "That little fucker stole my beer."

12 YEARS LATER

Chapter 1

An excited crowd had gathered in the modest arena on the outskirts of Shelby for one of the Uplands regional matches. The afternoon sun beat down on rickety, tiered wooden benches. The men and women, mostly drunk, who occupied them surrounded the ring. Two titans warmed up and stretched in their corners, preparing for what should be a mismatch, at least Larvell Winslow hoped it would be.

It seemed as though everyone in the crowd was more excited about the match than Larvell, which was not unusual. He spat nervously onto the floor of the private executive box that sat behind and above the bleachers and glared off his neighbors. The introductions had almost finished and the titans were squared off in the ring below. Everyone else could go ahead and be thrilled at the sunny day, bearing just enough breeze to carry off the heat and stench from the gathered masses. Larvell wanted this over and done. His gut churned. That was his titan down there, and the only good one he had.

Larvell was a thin, dark-skinned man who prided himself on his style. He wore a white, brimmed hat that matched his suit of expensive Valley of Sevens cotton.

Even in the private boxes, packed with the most important people on this side of the Uplands, he still stood out. And that was the way he liked it. It made it less likely the idiots who surrounded him would speak to him. He hated the fucking regional matches. With the Headlock of Destiny Tournament just a week away, his only goal was to make sure his titan made it there intact.

When Larvell had been offered the job as the head of the Uplands Wrestling Coalition, he hadn't realized quite what an enormous ass-ache it would be. It was the highest position a promoter or manager, really anyone in the business who wasn't himself a titan, could land in the Uplands. The pay was good and the idea of standing in private boxes and getting greased by locals had sounded enticing at the time. The Uplands had had a strong showing at recent tournaments, mostly due to the presence of Owen Grit, the titan who was right now flexing his muscles for the crowd below. With Owen firmly on board for the Uplands, it had looked like a good deal. Larvell took the job.

Unfortunately, there was always someone up the chain. When Governor Crowell finally took the time to meet with Larvell, the point had been made early and often that she expected Larvell to deliver tournament wins. Or he'd find his ass on the street. So the worry started. Each non-tournament match ground down his nerves. He could barely watch the tournament matches, never mind this regional garbage.

Even now he could feel the eyes of the others in the box. The mayor and local promoters didn't hold any weight. But a party had traveled from Rockton, the capital city of the Uplands, for the late-stage regional. And among them was a quiet duo, standing dour-faced at the edge of the gathering, who reported directly to the governor.

Larvell spat again and looked out over the ring where the titans waited for the bell. Owen Grit was a little taller than average for a titan. His enormous shoulders rumbled out wide and tapered down to a thin waist. His chin-length red hair fell across his pale face as he smirked at his challenger. Grit was an expert tactician. He'd grown up in a family of titans, a rare occurrence in the Open Nations, and had learned the sport from infancy. It was that or starve, stampeded under the feet of his older brothers and cousins. There were bigger titans, and there were faster titans, but Owen made the most of his size and strength. He had notched up numerous tournament victories. At the last Headlock of Destiny Tournament he'd made the round of eight before being brutalized by the Landshaker, and the solid showing for the Uplands meant Larvell had had two blissful weeks free of the agonizing uncertainty that dominated his life. If only the last go-round's results mattered this time. But they didn't. Every year the new tournament bracket was set, the clock started over, and Larvell's ass was back on the line.

Across from Owen, his challenger shambled into a fighting stance. Golem Jones was an ugly titan with long limbs and thick, clumsy features, all wrapped in flaky skin of grey and pink. The bright sun did him no favors. Rumor put the titan as the son of the old wrestler Axeman Goreth. According to said rumor, a sorcerer of dubious sanity had created a female golem, molded with extra clay in the parts that would catch the eye of a titan. He sent this animated creation out to a tournament in Urdesta. Axeman took the bait and, with the usual tenacity of a titan, his seed took hold. The golem returned to the sorcerer.

The sorcerer had hoped the resulting offspring, which came out a chalky mix of clay and flesh, would show the same obedience as his golem. It had worked that way for a time, as the growing Golem Jones took direction from the only father he knew. But soon after coming into his strength, he tired of playing bodyguard and servant to the sorcerer. So he twisted off his master's head and set out for the nearest tavern in search of a manager.

The wrestling career he launched that day was enviable. Golem Jones even fought in the Headlock once. He didn't win, of course. He was always a little too slow and deliberate, always having the look in his blank eyes as though waiting for someone else to tell him what to do. Still, he'd had strength, endurance, and a single-minded drive to crush his opponent.

Then time drew on, as it always did, and the Golem grew old and crusty. Now he left clay crumblings with every step as he marched between shitty regional matches, shedding more of himself each passing day. Larvell might have been tempted to feel sad for the titan, if he hadn't been renowned as one of the dirtiest fighters of his era. Now Larvell just wanted Owen to put him down, and quickly.

The bell pealed out over the crowd and the titans closed on each other. Owen wasted no time establishing an upper hand. He twisted out of a grapple and ducked behind Golem Jones. Then he locked his massive arms around Jones's chest, hoisted him up in the air, twisted, slammed him down on the mat, and landed his full weight on top of him. Golem Jones roared in anger and flung his elbows at Owen's head, missing, as he extracted himself.

Owen jumped up but didn't retreat far. Jones was only halfway to his feet when Owen came thundering back with a dropkick that sent Jones to the edge of the ring. But Jones bounced off the ropes while Owen was still on the mat, and pounced on Owen, roaring, snarling and punching at anything and everything. The titans toiled in a squirming mass.

Larvell rolled his eyes. He'd known this would be an ugly fight. It looked as though Golem Jones had already shed a few fingers onto the mat. Owen would get this mess under control soon, but that didn't stop Larvell from fretting. One of the liaisons from Rockton stepped next to him at the railing and gestured at Golem Jones, who had just been driven back by Owen's fists. "Who'd he clear out to get here?"

Larvell kept his voice low as he answered, sliding his white, brimmed hat into his hands as he did so. Even with worry gnawing at his gut he wasn't foolish enough be overheard insulting a local favorite within earshot of the mayor. "Jones beat a couple other contenders, barely titans. And he's not much better. Practically falling apart out there. He shouldn't be in the ring with Owen. Regionals are a waste of damn time. This year especially."

Governor Crowell and most bureaucrats down the chain understood that the Uplands, and Larvell by extension, could only send one titan to the Headlock of Destiny. And this year they only had one titan who had a chance in hell of winning on behalf of their nation. That was Owen. Yet Larvell had been unable to get them to build any slack into the regionals schedule. If anything, he was being pressured to trot his only asset around to every damn town large enough to hold a ring. The promoters loved it. The beer vendors loved it. Everybody loved it. Today. They wouldn't love it tomorrow when their only representation at the tournament was a bruised and tired titan facing a slate of better-prepared, pampered opponents. The Landshaker sure as shit wouldn't have more than one or two cakewalk matches in his runup to the tournament.

And mercy on them all if Owen got hurt. The drop-off in talent behind him, at least among any titan who would champion the Uplands, was severe. Two years ago the last of the Grit brothers had found another nation to fight for. Giant Tequa had retired, then moved to an island for good measure. The other native titans were nothing more than the usual meat to be ground up by anyone of reasonable talent. So it was Larvell's neck if Owen didn't make it to the tournament. If they lost him they'd have to scour the region for some local sacrifice. That or absorb the cost of hiring an outsider, who would then immediately be bribed to throw his first tournament match when they arrived in Empire City.

Larvell tried to imagine Golem Jones, whose slab-like face grew more and more frustrated as Owen continued to duck his slow advances, stepping into a tournament match with the likes of Scott Flawless, or Judge Cage, or Billy Blades. The Uplands contingent would be laughed out of Empire City. On his return Larvell would be marched straight into the governor's office. She would take his house and everything else he owned and send him packing. Maybe let him keep his suit so he could wander out in the Open Nations with his hat in hand, searching for a new job.

In the ring, Owen had the match solidly in control, but he was playing to the crowd, mounting the ropes for an elbow drop as Jones lay twitching in the center of the mat. Larvell pushed the man yapping at him out of the way and scanned the box for Kyle, the only one he trusted among the collection of idiots. She broke off her conversation as she caught his eye. She stood by his side a moment later. Larvell gestured towards the ring. "You told him to keep it short and safe, right?"

Kyle nodded, her shoulder-length blonde hair bouncing. "He was listening, but you know how he gets when he hears that crowd..." As she looked off with concern on her face, Larvell's glance lingered on her a moment too long, his eyes running up and down her lithe frame. She was pretty, sometimes distractingly so when he should be focused on business, though the lines of worry around her eyes showed she wasn't new to the game. Just like him.

Larvell was sure Kyle worked for the governor, though he'd never gotten a straight answer from her. Whoever she worked for, it was abundantly clear the tournament put her career and wellbeing on the line just like his. She'd been around before him, and she materialized by his side a few weeks before the tournament every year. She would join the contingent as they traveled to Empire City and stay throughout the matches. She wanted the Uplands to win just as much as he did, though her work carried on past the Uplands matches. Larvell had the feeling she was far more valuable to the governor than he was. Some sort of diplomat or, more likely, a spy. Not that he'd ever verbalize that. Larvell was no fool, unlike his titan in the ring below, who had landed his elbow drop and was currently spinning Golem Jones over his head, showering the front row of fans with clumps of dried clay.

Whatever her role, she seemed to get the stakes. The Headlock of Destiny Tournament had become far more than a chance to pit the Open Nation's best titans against each other every year. The tournament had grown to shape international policy, trade agreements, everything. Nations that did well were rewarded with prosperity, economic investment, tourism. Nations that fared poorly invited disaster. In many ways, the tournament had come to replace the Titan Wars, which originally carved out the Open Nations borders, with a less costly substitute. All while preserving the pecking order. The largest nations, like the Vantages, the Valley of Sevens, and Dunham North, had the resources to consistently bring in the best talent. The tenth-best titan in the Valley of Sevens could easily throttle the best that smaller nations like Kohler and the Dustbowl put up. The Uplands had avoided falling into that category of perennial losers through sheer luck. Sheer luck first named Grand Tequa and then named Owen Grit.

The crowd was cheering Owen on, the match reaching its dramatic peak, when Larvell felt a sharp pain in his gut, as though some part of him knew exactly what was coming. Golem Jones was thrashing wildly, Owen was spinning rapidly, and Owen lost his grip. Rather than throwing Jones across the ring, Owen fumbled and dropped Jones, who twisted and landed, with all his mass of muddy flesh, on the side of Owen's bent knee. It folded up under the weight of both titans, and a sickening crack was heard as far away as the executive box before the renewed roars of the crowd swallowed it up. Golem Jones leapt to his feet as Owen lay on the ground, thrashing in pain and holding his knee.

Larvell clutched the railing of the box. Someone was talking to him, but he couldn't hear anything over the pounding blood in his ears. He couldn't move, couldn't breathe. At last, he turned to Kyle to send her to find out how bad it was, but she was already gone. He scanned below him and saw a flash of blonde hair and a trim body sliding through the crowd as she raced towards the ring.

Golem Jones, oblivious or unconcerned, sealed the match with a kick to Owen's undefended face, laying him flat. As the referee verified the titan was down, Jones rumbled around the ring, arms in the air. The Shelby crowd was going wild at the upset. They didn't understand what they'd done, how they may have fucked the entire Uplands by cheering this chump to a win. Owen was twitching on the mat, still clutching his knee.

"When will you leave for the tournament?" one of the local politicians asked Larvell.

His question was so out of place, so ill-timed that Larvell just stared at him, wide-eyed in disbelief. The box fell into an awkward silence, giving Larvell the chance to grip the railing in both hands and imagine what it would feel like to have his arms broken by the governor's bodyguards. He took his hat off and put it back on again. Would they stop at the arms? Or move on to his legs next? Should he get out of the Uplands tonight? Whatever he did next, no need to tip his hand. He plastered an unconvincing smile on his face as conversation resumed in the box. The locals were too excited about the unexpected upset to let one grouch hold them back from mimicking the revelry below them.

Maybe Owen would be okay. Titans healed fast. Owen had been hurt before and come back. He'd dislocated a shoulder tossing Bearhugger into a lake. He'd twinged his other knee in the cage fight with the Brute Squad. He might be okay. Some ice, a couple bottles of wine, an abrupt end to any lingering regionals on the schedule...and Larvell would find a way to get Golem Jones disqualified. The governor would back him. They'd get Owen stood up.

And then Kyle was back at his elbow, her expression grave, her normally bright and inviting face ashen. "We've got a huge problem," she said.

Chapter 2

"Van, where the hell have you been?"

Van gave a start. Normally, he'd have had his ears open for the sounds of his foreman's approach. Bastard must have crept from the back. Van was on his ass, waiting for the early morning to find its way to lunchtime. He lamely picked up the clipboard next to him from the dirt floor of the brewery warehouse, looked up at Alec, then decided it was pointless to pretend he hadn't been caught red-handed.

"I've been on my ass." He looked up and smiled. The twelve long years since his infamous run-in with the Savage had smoothed his brow and given him a dark beard to go with his mop of dark, curly hair. He had enormous arms and an ample gut. He stood taller than most titans, not that he lined up next to them often.

"That's great, Van. What a place to be. Do you think there's a chance you could get off of it? Your ass, I mean? We've got three shipments leaving for Empire City this morning and one for Rockton." Alec pointed at Van's clipboard. "What's that?"

"Regis asked me to check the backlog." Van gestured lamely at the hundreds of stacked barrels behind him.

"Four shipments headed out this morning and you're fucking around with the backlog? You're killing me. Get up front and see what Garret needs." He looked down at his own clipboard. Van could see the neat notations in orderly rows, a contrast to the one Van held, which was close to illegible. Van was reasonably certain Regis was illiterate. "And take two barrels of Foundation with you," Alec said.

Van rose to his feet when it was clear Alec intended to watch him on his way. As Van plodded past him, his heavy, shoeless feet dragging in the packed dirt, the foreman added, "And one of Old Man Johan's hounds is loose in the back. I saw him between warehouses six and seven. Take care of him if you see him."

Van had his back to Alec so he didn't have to hide his smirk. Alec was scared of dogs, all animals really, especially the lanky black hounds kept around for the brewery's security. The creatures didn't like him. Probably could sense evil. "What, take care of him, like…?" Van turned back and mimed snapping a neck.

Alec's reaction was exactly what he'd hoped for: his eyes bugged out. "What?! No, you giant moron, chase him back to the watchhouse before he attacks someone. Or whatever. I don't care. Get those barrels first. Daylight is wasting."

Van stopped and feigned pondering a great question. "How can daylight waste, Alec?"

"I don't know, smartass. But if something wants to figure out how to get wasted, it can always look to you as an example. Now get the fucking barrels."

Van grinned as he ducked through the warehouse side door, blinking at the bright sunlight slanting across the brewery yard. He straightened to his full height and rocked back on his heels, cracking his back and groaning. The yard was bustling as everyone hustled around, pulling barrels on carts, waving clipboards at each other, and generally making themselves useful. Van sighed and set out to do the same. He was the only titan at the brewery so people tended to notice when he sluffed off too hard. Garret's Foundation barrels would be back in warehouses three or eight, and eight was closer.

Van was almost to warehouse eight when one of Johan's hounds ran up, tail wagging, tongue hanging out in the heat. Van knelt down next to the creature and gently petted it while he admired its glowing red eyes. It was a graveyard hound. Rumor had it that their bark was meant to drive one backwards into their worst fears. It was straight bullshit. Their primary contribution to security was that they were very loud and very curious.

After a glance around the yard, Van reached into his pocket and gave the hound a piece of dried beef, which it wolfed down. "Good girl," he said. He stood, then bent close over the dog and whispered, "I think Alec was headed back to the front office. If you get his clipboard, I'll give you more tomorrow."

Van held his breath as he passed warehouse seven. All the beer slated for distribution to trolls, orcs, and ogres was housed there, and it smelled awful. They preferred it sour and rotten and the brewmasters had perfected every trick of the trade to get it to that state quickly. The magic that helped keep the other warehouses cool and prevent the beer from spoiling in the heat of the sun wasn't in place here. The brewers tossed all sorts of junk into the mix, everything from spider webs to rotten leaves. Even then sometimes the beer wasn't sour enough for the orcs. Rumor was if the brewery didn't make it strong enough, the orcs would piss in it to add more flavor. Van gave a shudder at the thought and ducked into warehouse eight, letting out his held breath.

Warehouse eight was dark and cool after the yard. Sunlight crept through gaps in the boards to fall on stacks of barrels twice as tall as Van. He could see a few others loading up near the front of the stacks and loped over in their direction.

"Where you been, Van?" asked Rawly, a good-natured veteran of the brewery. He was even more averse to hard work than Van was, but he knew the story of every barrel they'd produced. And, perhaps more importantly, where they were.

"I have been on my ass, good sir."

"And a lovely ass it is," Rawly replied, pretending to scope out the titan's hindquarters, nearly level with the short man's face.

"Save it for the festival, you two," one of the others called as he left, pulling a cart behind him.

Van took a second to help another group of men struggling with a heavy barrel. As he loaded it onto their cart, they tossed him grateful looks. "Where am I grabbing two Foundation from?" he asked Rawly.

"Where they bound?"

"Either Empire City or Rockton."

"You don't know which?"

"No." Van shifted uncomfortably. "But they need 'em quick."

"Okay, grab those two." Rawly pointed at two barrels in stack sixteen. "If it was definitely Empire City, I'd have you grab the swill in stack eighteen instead. Can't risk our pristine reputation amongst our good customers in Rockton."

"No doubt," Van said, reaching up to grab the barrels. He tucked one under each arm and stood there a moment, not quite ready to go back out into the sun.

"You going to the match tomorrow night?" Rawly asked.

"Wouldn't miss it for the world."

Rawly unleashed an eager smile which showcased his many missing teeth. "Should be a pretty good one. Richard the Living Portrait will mop the floor with High-Flying Hank—never heard a less true name—maybe earn himself a spot at the regional finals. Course everybody knows Richard will get spanked by Owen Grit. That's a real titan, there." Rawly was staring upwards as if he were in Owen Grit's mighty shadow. He emerged from his revelry to peer up at Van. "Look at you, standing there holding them barrels like it's nothing. How come you never tried wrestling?"

"I tried it a bit. Not my thing."

Rawly didn't appear satisfied. "A titan who don't wrestle. I don't know, Van. Seems like a shame."

Van fought a surge of irritation. He liked Rawly, but this conversation? Not so much. "I gotta run these up. Alec's been on me already once today. You be careful, Rawly, I heard there's wasting daylight around here. Sounds dangerous."

It was a short walk to the loading docks. As Van approached the rows of wagons, he was forced to pay attention to his feet and avoid the piles of horse droppings. His mood had soured a bit. Rawly's question would be on everyone's lips as the furor over the festival match consumed Headwaters. Why wasn't Van, who was just as big and just as strong as the titans who traveled in to put on the annual show, in the ring? What was the point of being a titan if you didn't smash the heads of other titans, show the world your sweaty armpits as you raised your hands in victory, then grab a pretty girl to come back to your luxury hotel? Spend your whole life in the center of attention, trapped doing what everyone else wanted you to do?

"Van, where have you been?" someone called out from the men gathered around a nearly loaded wagon.

Van opened his mouth to tell them he'd been on his ass when his foot slid into a pile of horse shit. He settled for a sigh instead.

Chapter 3

The town square was brightly decorated for the Annual Headwaters Beer Festival. Headwaters's one and only elevated wrestling ring had been set up in the center of converging rows of wooden chairs. As Van took a place in the back row along the aisle, carefully distributing his weight across two chairs placed closely together, the seats were already mostly full. The buzz of the excited crowd was topped by the yells of beer vendors hurrying to beat the opening bell.

The lamps had been lit as the cool evening settled over the foothills. Everyone in town had been drinking all day, and their finest clothes had long since fallen victim to the stains of spilled beer. Dignity was as rare amongst the crowd as a clean shirt, just the way it should be. Van saw the few men he considered friends lurking near the back rows. He had a proper buzz going and was nursing half a large Foundation he'd bought with the last of his coin. Payday wasn't until next week, so this was probably his dinner as well.

"Hi, Van," came a quiet voice at his elbow.

Van took a deep breath. He felt his face flush, as it always did whenever Annie was nearby. He bought himself some time by taking a long drink of his beer before answering. "Hi, Annie." He turned slowly to look at her. He hadn't seen her since he'd embarrassed himself, and her, at her wedding. A painful memory he quickly dispelled. She was radiant as usual. Thin, pale face with sharp features. Deep eyes and long, curly hair twining over her shoulders, falling down across…a baby cradled in her arms. *That* was new.

Van stared at the baby so long that Annie finally said, "Van?"

"Sorry," he said, meeting her eyes. "Nice to see you. Have you been enjoying the festival?"

She smiled and suddenly the bright lights of the town square seemed dim by comparison. "It's been lovely. Lizzy slept most of the day, for a change. It gave me a chance to catch up. I haven't seen anyone in forever, been trapped in the house." She gently swayed to keep the baby calm.

Van racked his mind for something to say. The gap between them seemed to have grown insurmountable. Seemed that was a side effect of making a fool of yourself during someone else's special day. "Um, can I get you a beer?"

She frowned. "No, not while I'm…well, not right now. It makes the baby upset."

It took Van a long moment to follow what she'd said, why her drinking a beer would bother the baby. He found himself hoping they'd ring the bell to start the fight. Maybe he could just vanish, anything to get out of this conversation. Was he supposed to compliment the baby? Offer to hold it? No, no one in their right mind would want a titan so close to their child.

His discomfort must have been obvious, because Annie looked down at her child self-consciously. "Surely Alec told you about her?"

"Oh, yeah, I just forgot…er, I mean, I just haven't seen you. Or her." Alec may or may not have told him. When Alec had first started seeing Annie, he'd brought her up relentlessly whenever Van was nearby. Rubbing it in. Eventually he'd grown tired of the game. Or he'd sensed he was toeing close to the line where Van might stuff him headfirst into a barrel and worry about the consequences later. Van may have even said something to that effect as he was drunkenly dragged away from their wedding. "It's a girl, right?"

She laughed. "I just told you she was." She shifted the weight of the baby to her hip, freeing up a hand which she laid on his arm. "How have you been? How's the brewery? Alec doesn't tell me anything."

"Uh, it's fine. Doing more of those elven blends now that berries are back in season. And we're running more and more with heavy hops. They might add another few men to the night shift to keep up with demand out of Empire City now that Foundation's caught on." But she wouldn't care about any of this stuff. This was the stuff Alec would bore her with at the end of each day, when they were sitting together in front of a cozy fire. Maybe sneaking in a sly comment here and there about how Van worked for him now and how he couldn't believe she used to date the lazy titan.

She might describe it as dating him. Van might use different words to describe their relationship, if anyone were ever able to drag them out of him. He might describe it as tearing his own heart out of his chest, handing it to the most beautiful person he knew, and having her turn away in embarrassment. Turn away in embarrassment and find relief in the arms of the biggest asshole in Headwaters. The boy who'd tormented Van endlessly, made him ashamed of himself for years, and had then somehow managed to land the foreman job, a position which enabled him to dole out more shame, this time to a full-grown titan. A titan who sulked home alone after every shift, while his awful boss got to go home to her, waiting. If there were any gods still slumming it in the Open Nations, they must have laughed their asses off when they figured this one out.

Thankfully, the murmurs of the crowd swelled to cheers as the announcer made his way to center ring. Van gave an apologetic shrug to Annie, as if to say how sad he was they wouldn't be able to continue the conversation. She looked frustrated and the baby began fussing at the noise. She murmured that he should come by for a visit sometime and, with a sad look, shushed the baby as she trotted away up the aisle.

Van didn't bother watching her go. He didn't want to see the delighted look on Alec's face as she neared the seat he'd no doubt set aside for her. His beautiful wife and newborn child. Van brought his mug to his lips and realized it was empty, swore a little too loudly, and decided he really needed to get proper drunk tonight. He set the empty mug down beside him, then turned his attention to the ring.

High-Flying Hank was already in the ring, dancing around in beige shorts when the announcer introduced him in a flat voice. The crowd booed. The titan roared once then pulled his face into a not particularly convincing snarl. Van wondered if Hank would get up in the air at all during the match. He seemed planted pretty firmly on the mat at the moment.

The announcer threw a lot more energy into Richard the Living Portrait's intro. At its climax, the titan ran down the aisle opposite Van and dove into the ring under the bottom rope. He stood and paced the ring, ignoring his opponent. Richard's dark hair was slicked back, and he kept fussing with it, tossing it to and fro and running his fingers through it, all while trying to catch the eyes of every woman in the crowd. He was shirtless beneath a sparkling jacket that matched his tight, silver shorts.

The crowd greeted him warmly, rising to their feet. Van personally thought he was a bit of a tool, and definitely a poor fit with the working class town, but he was at least a well-known name with an okay record around the Uplands. He'd probably be among the last few titans vying for the right to get crushed under Owen Grit's heel in the regional finals. Not the worst draw they'd seen for the beerfest.

As the announcer described the rivalry between the two titans, or at least created one for the benefit of the crowd, Van looked around. The brewery president and his head brewmaster were with the other VIPs in a raised viewing box. The mayor was there, chatting animatedly with a thin man that Van hadn't seen before in a finely cut suit. A beautiful woman with blonde hair just touching her shoulders stood next to him. The pair had probably made the short ride up from Rockton to see the match. As Van watched, the woman turned away from the conversation and scanned the crowd. Her eyes stopped when she saw Van. She stared at him in naked curiosity.

Van dropped his eyes, scowling into his empty mug. Outsiders to Headwaters always scrutinized him more than he was comfortable with, curious about the titan who hauled barrels around instead of fighting for glory. The titan in the back row instead of on stage. He counted to ten then looked back up. The woman was facing away. Maybe she hadn't been looking at him after all.

The introductions were wrapping up as the Living Portrait stamped around the ring, working the crowd. The announcer was good at his job, or at least Headwaters's open taps had properly lubricated the crowd. They were yelling and jeering as the bell rang. Van let out a loud cheer, matching the crowd before him, as the titans clinched, locking their mighty arms and pressing their heads together. The ring trembled as their heavy feet pounded out the rhythm of the contest. The crowd leaned forward in their seats.

Van, with a careful look around, smirked and stood up. He quietly slipped out of the seating area and melted back into the shadows beyond the brightly lit square.

Chapter 4

The night air along the well-worn track between the town center and the brewery was cool after the heat of the crowd. Leaves had begun falling and Van's heavy footfalls stamped them flat as he walked. He was quickly met by five men, and the group talked loudly over the wind as they walked the quiet path towards the brewery. They'd been heavy in their cups all day, but amongst the six of them, they managed to set a reasonably straight course.

"It's about time," Wyatt was saying. "I ran out of credit at both Tyler's and the Meritus by midday. And then Darren closed the taproom and chased everyone out before dusk."

"I thought they didn't even let you in the door at Tyler's no more," Cormac replied with a laugh.

"He got my whole damn paymarker last week. He'd better open his doors." Wyatt scratched at his head. "Don't know that I helped my cause today, though. I'm not exactly sure I made it all the way outside for my last piss."

The men laughed easily. All worked the brewery, Wyatt and Devin in the docks, Van, Regis, and Cormac in the warehouses.

"What are you gonna grab, Van?" Regis asked. Without waiting for an answer, he said, "You know my vote is for Dotted Steer."

Van scoffed. "You have zero imagination, Regis."

"Just don't get that awful porter with coffee beans Garret keeps pushing."

"In what world was I going to get the coffee porter?"

Cormac chimed in. "What about the Topper Pale? That batch from last season should be just about peaking." He knew his stuff.

Van grunted as he considered it. He grudgingly said, "That was on my short list. I'm probably getting a Kingsland too. That's just tradition."

Van couldn't resist a surge of pride as the brewery came into view ahead of them. He did love it. The brewery itself was a sprawling, two-story building. It backed up against the mountains, the better to divert clear stream water into the upper levels. Water came in the back, and beer came out the front. Some was bound for one of the many warehouses to condition in barrels. Others went straight to the loading docks. The finest the brewery produced, its most premium barrels, were in a warehouse connected to the brewmaster's office. Van had no doubt the man knew every barrel and had a plan for exactly how long each would condition and where they were bound. Which meant if any were missing, he would take one step in the room late tomorrow morning and immediately sniff them out.

The stuff that went straight to the docks or was stored in the warehouses near there was mostly swill. Certainly not worth Van's time and attention on the only night of the year that there was no third shift and everyone in the town was distracted by two big idiots throwing each other into ropes. He was headed to the back warehouses. They were a mess of aging barrels of every variety and strain the brewery took on. There were schemes upon schemes of tracking the aging processes and optimizing when they left and where they went. The daily grind invalidated all that, and men came grabbing them as their orders demanded, usually going with the closest or easiest to extract. Some barrels lay neglected far longer than they should have. Others came out far too soon. It was a hodge-podge, a magical beer limbo the likes of which could be found nowhere else in the world, and tonight Van would have his pick of the treasure hoard.

The gates of the brewery were brightly lit, but the wide, wooden doors were closed, an unusual sight. Van had no doubt they'd find them tightly locked. The wall surrounding the brewery, wrapping all the way to the back, was made of logs banded together. It stood about nine feet high, a head taller than Van. Old Man Johan would be charged with the security of the grounds inside, his graveyard hounds scaring off the superstitious and raising the alarm at anything unknown. The festival guaranteed tonight was a night no one would be working late repairing equipment or filling urgent orders. It was quiet, the only sound the slight wheezing of Van's friends as they gathered around him, the full day of drinking having ill-prepared them for the uphill walk. He led them around to the side.

Regis scowled. "Why are we going back here? I thought you wanted a Dotted Steer."

"Did you drunk assholes think you could be quiet waiting right in front of the gates?" Van stumbled on the uneven ground and quickly caught himself. "And I told you I hadn't decided yet."

"Just think about how good a Topper would be, sliding down your throat, Van." Cormac gave his last-minute plea as Van slowed at a spot well out of sight of the gates.

Van gave a noncommittal nod, squaring up to the wall. "Where's the old man gonna be sleeping off his cups?" he asked the group. He reached into his pocket and threw something over the wall, listening carefully.

"Probably front of the docks," Wyatt said. "Wants to be close enough to the gates he can wake up if someone comes."

"Yeah," Van said, his ear pressed to the wall. He heard the sound of cautious footsteps on the other side. "See you in a minute."

Van leapt, his strong legs launching him to where he caught the top of the wall under his arms. He perched there a moment, studying the quiet, dark yard. A pair of glowing red eyes looked up curiously from just below him, a wagging tail behind them. Van threw himself over the wall and landed with a quiet grace. He gave a smile to the hound, then fished out another piece of dried beef from his pocket. "Good to see you again," he whispered, then set off across the yard.

Van fought to keep the grin off his face as he moved quietly across the dark, leaf-strewn dirt between him and the warehouses. The night air felt vibrant. His heart was beating fast, and he liked it. Just as he'd liked it the year before and the year before that.

He'd almost reached the cover of the warehouses when the wind stirred. The hairs on the back of his neck prickled, and he suddenly felt certain he was being watched. The yard was silent. He looked around, not seeing anything, no sign of Old Man Johan or any of his dogs. His grin faltered. As unlikely as it was with a single, drunk guard in place, Van would be in serious trouble if he got caught. Best to get on with it. He wouldn't be able to talk his way out of this one whether he had a barrel under his arm or not.

The walkways between the warehouses were pitch black, but Van had strolled them enough to need no light. Likewise, as he entered the dark of warehouse four, his personal favorite, he needed no lantern to pick his way through the long rows of barrels.

With no one watching, Van strode confidently down the center aisle, a lightness to his step that others around the town might not recognize. He'd abandoned his customary slouch and sulky expression. His back was straight and his eyes bright as he studied the stacks. Each pallet held four barrels, resting vertically. The stacks ranged from two to six barrels high. It usually required a three-man crew of pickers to get a barrel, using a heavy rolling ladder and series of ramps. Van needed none of that, and nothing made the pickers happier than when Van helped them out. Seemed only fair he helped himself out from time to time.

He leapt up to the side, caught hold of one of the pallets lined with barrels, and clung there as he looked more closely over the stacks with professional scrutiny. The rows trembled under his weight, but Van knew exactly how much give he had to work with. From his high vantage point, Van could see how haphazard the barrel rotation and removal had been. There were gaps everywhere. What had been designed as an orderly process had fallen victim to the demands of industry. Which just made it easier for him.

He crawled across the row of stacked barrels, hand over hand, until he recognized the Topper by the splashes of purple and green paint along the base. He hauled himself up towards the top of the tall row. He pulled out a matchbook and struck a match. The flame gave him the light he needed to catch a prime target, second row in. And just his luck, it looked like there was a Kingsland barrel next to it. Surely a sign. He blew the match out and tucked it back into his pocket.

Van began a tricky extraction. He got his elbows atop the front row of barrels and was able to lift the Topper out. He should run the heavy barrel back down, but he was getting bored and thirsty. Instead he tucked it between his legs, pinning it against the rows. He didn't have much leverage to get the Kingsland out. He tugged hard, gripping its lip in his strong, right hand. He gave a slight grunt as he lifted it, bringing it out to the edge of the row. He worked it under his arm and was holding both barrels, readying himself for descent, when he heard a voice in the darkness.

"Boo."

Van turned toward the sound. He found himself staring down at a woman in the center of the warehouse aisle. She was staring right back. There was just enough light to recognize the woman from the fight. The one with the blonde hair that he'd assumed came from the capital. What the hell was she doing here?

Van was completely frozen. The pallet he clung to wavered for a moment under his weight. He carefully steadied it, certain his eyes were going to pop right out of his head. His heart pounded as he stared at the woman. She looked calmly back at him, something like a schoolteacher waiting for an answer from a particularly slow student. She was a real beauty. Perfect hair fell in waves across her clear forehead; piercing blue eyes stared at him. But it wasn't her beauty that struck him. It was the absolute lack of fear in her. Something Van rarely saw in the other women who even dared meet his eyes. She'd somehow managed to follow him into a dark warehouse, alone, in the midst of an admittedly juvenile crime, and she was unafraid. Less so than he was.

They stared at each other for what felt like an eternity before the moment was broken by the sound of a bird calling outside. Maybe a real bird, maybe the assholes out back getting impatient. Van could feel the sudden sheen of sweat on his forehead. The strain of holding the barrels in place made his whole body tremble. He broke the staring contest, turned slowly towards the stacks, and put the Kingsland back into place. When he looked down again, the woman was gone. He glanced up and down the row, but there was no sign she had ever been there. She'd vanished.

"What the fuck was that?" he asked the empty warehouse. It had no answer for him. Van shook his head, tucked the barrel of Kingsland back under his arm, and leapt down, careful not to crush the Topper between his legs as he landed. The smart thing to do would be to leave them both here and get out as quickly as he could. But she hadn't raised an alarm, whoever she was. Of course, maybe she was headed off to do that right now. Definitely time for him to get going.

Van made his way outside. The perfectly ordinary moonlight and the gentle breeze stirring the leaves beneath his feet added to a sense that the woman had been some sort of weird mirage. Maybe he'd just imagined her, a product of the seven or eight Foundations he'd gotten in before running out of money? As he neared the wall, he could hear the giggling of his idiot friends. His shoulders unclenched at the sound. Maybe if the ghost reported him to the watchman he could have these guys provide him with an alibi. After they all drank the evidence, of course.

He tiptoed quietly to the wall, listening for a moment to Wyatt telling the same story he told every festival about the match where Durmstrong the Coward fled the ring and used Wyatt as a human shield to slow down Giant Tequa.

Van briefly pondered just chucking one of the barrels over the wall, maybe softly calling out "catch" before he did. Instead he hoisted a barrel up onto each shoulder, collected his balance, and gave a huge jump to land on top of the wall, followed by a far less graceful tumble down on the other side as he lost his footing.

The men collected their titan friend and the barrels, not in that order, and Van resolved to put the woman out of his mind as they made their way back towards the town. There was beer to drink. The finest across the Nations.

. . .

Van and his friends parked the barrels beyond the lights of the main street, back in the trees on a rise. He recalled this was the same spot he'd started really drinking before stumbling down to Annie and Alec's wedding and making a fool of himself. He did his best to show that thought to the door. She had a baby now, a little talisman to the relationship she and Alec enjoyed, and would continue to enjoy for a lifetime that did not include him. He wished she hadn't looked as amazing as he'd remembered.

Cormac had tapped the barrels while Wyatt ran off to steal mugs. Once both tasks were accomplished, they dove in. The sounds of the crowd's post-fight celebration washed over the group as they were joined by another friend, Mattson, who'd stayed to see the fight.

"Portrait handled him pretty easy," Mattson said. "Tense for a moment there, but once he got High-Flying Hank off the ground and into the air it was over. Never seen anyone more scared of heights. Portrait held him over his head, like he was gonna throw him out into the crowd. You would have thought they were atop a cliff. Hank was begging for his life. Guess that means the Portrait's the best hope for the tournament now that news came in Owen's down."

Cormac grunted. "Not much hope there. How many times has Owen kicked the Living Portrait's ass when he rose to the top of the local trash heap?"

"How many beers left in that barrel?" Mattson replied as an answer.

"Not too many actually. Van's been working that one pretty hard." Cormac grinned and drank his own beer down.

Van imitated Richard the Living Portrait's signature hair toss and glared at Cormac, then spoiled the effect by laughing and spilling beer on his pants. "Yep," he said.

He took a wrestling stance and turned to face the second barrel. "And for my next opponent…"

The men laughed and rushed to insert themselves between Van and the second barrel. Van was laughing as well as he began pushing his way through them. So he was caught off guard when the others abruptly fell silent, looking past him back in the direction of the town. Van turned to see his ghost walking into the light, the woman from the warehouse. She was staring at him, not quite as intently as before, as she approached.

"Boo," she said again to Van, this time more quietly, a secret between them.

There was a long silence. The other men stared open-mouthed at the bold outsider. Van wondered whether it had been short-sighted to immediately forget this woman had caught him red-handed stealing from the brewery. And the evidence of his crime stood right in front of him. The moment drew out. An owl hooted in the woods as they stared at each other. Finally, she raised her empty mug and gave a pointed glance at the tapped barrel.

Van took the mug and stepped over to the barrel. He carefully filled it to the brim, feeling her eyes on him the whole time. As he handed it back, she gave him a considering smile, then slowly turned and walked back in the direction of the celebration.

"And who, exactly, was *that*?" Wyatt asked when she had passed out of sight.

Mattson jumped in. "She's out from the capital. Part of the group what came to watch the Portrait for the regionals. You didn't think to invite her to stay, Van? Smooth moves." The men laughed hysterically.

Van glanced back, incredulous. "You could have said something to her. At least *I* poured her a beer."

"The sad extent of Van the ten-man's talent with women," Cormac said. "We all just witnessed it."

"Shut up, dick," Van said. His friends quickly went back to discussing the match, perhaps eager to move attention away from the fact that they too had clammed up at the presence of a pretty woman in their midst. Van continued to stare through the gap in the trees where she'd gone, long into the second barrel.

Finally, Cormac, sensing something amiss, wandered over to Van. "Think she'll turn up again?" he asked in a low voice so the others wouldn't hear.

"At this point," Van replied, "I'd be more surprised if she didn't."

Chapter 5

The next day's morning shift started after the lunch hour. Management had learned their lesson about expecting workers to turn up bright and early after the festival. Everyone would be nursing a violent hangover and tempers would flair. But half a shift, even one staffed by surly and disgruntled men, was better than nothing to the brewery's management. They'd invested good coin with the weather sorcerers for this year's crops and the cooling of the warehouses. They were in peak production, partly to satisfy the spike in demand that would accompany next week's Headlock of Destiny Tournament in Empire City.

It took Van a lot of work to get a hangover. But after the weirdness of seeing Annie plus that ghostwoman, he'd set out to get drunk and he'd gotten the job done. Today's pounding headache was the price. He hid it, though, making a point of smiling and whistling as he walked the yard, sometimes loudly greeting men with his booming voice, enjoying their flinches and mutters as he passed. The sun was bright; he'd only just arrived and was already halfway through his shift. Thoughts of strange women from the capital and other, more painful things, like seeing Annie with her new baby, felt like the distant past.

Van was hiding out between the back warehouses when Regis tracked him down and told him he was needed in the main office. Van was expecting to find someone waiting at the door with a list of barrels for him to fetch, but it was quiet outside the building. He stood there waiting until, finally, Alec appeared in the doorway and impatiently waved him in. Van was nearly inside when it hit him that this may have to do with last night. His stomach soured. Would they bring him into the office to fire him?

As he ducked in under the door, he saw that the office was full. It looked as though a meeting in the president's office had swelled to spill out into the visitors' area. A dozen-or-so men stood around, ignoring the wooden chairs along the walls. Van gulped hard as everyone's eyes turned to him. He nervously rubbed his hands together and stood close to the door.

"This him?" asked a man with an impressive mustache and a gut to rival Van's own. He looked Van up and down. "Foolish question, I suppose." He said to Van, "You're Van? The titan?"

It was one of the men who'd come in from Rockton. Another two stood beside him. No sign of the woman. The brewery president, a stern man named Peters, was glaring at Van through his spectacles. Surrounding him was the chief of operations, the warehouses manager, and Alec. There was another man Van thought was named Silas who worked for Mayor Holmes.

"Yes?" He couldn't keep the uncertainty out of his voice. The room felt far too crowded, especially since he needed to keep his head tilted to avoid the ceiling.

"You're not a wrestler?"

Van looked at his bosses for permission to answer, or maybe just a clue about what was going on, but they stared back at him blankly. "No, I'm not."

"You've never wrestled?"

"Not really. Not since I was a lot younger."

The fat man looked intently at Van. "Well," he said with a shrug, "you're competing in the regional finals tomorrow night."

Van leaned back in surprise and butted his head into the top jamb of the doorway. "What? I just said I'm not a wrestler." He rubbed at his head. His hangover was surging back.

"I don't particularly care," the man said, his mustache bristling. "We need a titan to face off against Richard the Living Portrait. It's got to be someone local to the Uplands. We'll see you in Rockton tomorrow night." He turned to the president and man from the mayor's office. "I want him at check-in tonight. The Loving Arms Inn. We'll have a room for him."

They both nodded and the man from the capital turned to leave. "Pleasure," he muttered as he passed Van. His entourage followed him out of the office.

Van stared dumbly after them, then turned back to the room. He was met with nothing but flat, unsympathetic stares from the remaining men, all brewery management. "Who was that?" he asked.

Peters, the brewery president, sighed and rubbed at his temples. He dropped into one of the chairs lining the walls of the visitor's area. Following his cue, the others found perches around the room. Peters shared a glance with the mayor's assistant. "That was Roland Something-or-other, an assistant for the Uplands Wrestling Coalition. I gather they're in rather desperate straits since Owen Grit got hurt." He looked around the room. "I think some whiskeys are in order. Alec, why don't you fetch the bottle from my office?" After a glance at Van, he added, "And pour our titan friend here a double."

A long silence ensued, broken only by the clinking of glasses as Alec poured for the men. At last Van said quietly, "I don't wrestle."

"Apparently you do tomorrow night, Van," the president replied.

"This is crazy. Why?"

"Because they don't have anyone else. You heard him. Owen had the Uplands Tournament of Destiny slot locked up long before he busted his knee. Most of the other talent has already fled. And what's left has been beaten so many times, no one has any faith in them. There's no one to turn to among the other locals. You saw High-Flying Hank pissing himself last night."

Van nodded, though he'd seen nothing of the sort. "Of course, of course." After a pause, "What about Giant Tequa?"

"Retired to some island to chase mermaids around. No time to get word to him, even if anyone knew where he was."

"Golem Jones?"

"That's what I would have thought, but they told us before you got here they think he took a bribe from the Vantages. Maybe Owen's injury wasn't just a freak accident. They don't want to take the chance."

Van rubbed at his forehead nervously. "I can't go to the tournament."

The men broke out into laughter. "Van, you're sure as hell not going to the tournament. Mercy on us all. You're just going to Rockton to put in a reasonably good show against the Living Portrait. Then he'll go to the tournament."

"A reasonably good show?" Van fought the urge to vomit. "Why have me at all? Why not just forfeit?"

Silas, the mayor's assistant, spoke up. "Why didn't we forfeit last night's match when we realized High-Flying Hank was scared to get into the ring because it was four feet off the ground instead of three? Because the event was planned and there was a lot of money tied to it." He sniffed at the whiskey glass in his hand. "I have no idea why they think you are a better option than someone who has actually demonstrated that they know how to not completely embarrass themselves." He took a long pull of the whiskey, eyes watering as he lowered the glass. "But we're not in a position to say no."

"Why not?"

"Van, that's just not how these things work. The tournament is a big deal. Governor Crowell watches it closely. No one wants even the slightest whisper they didn't do whatever the Coalition asked of them."

"So we lose Van for a couple days?" Peters was looking at his chief of operations, who shrugged and looked at the warehouses manager.

"Nothing we can't handle," the warehouses manager said. "Set us back a bit but we can add a few extra onto the night shift. Men'll jump at the overtime." The warehouses manager was looking at Van with an expression that was part pity and part laughter. "That is, assuming he comes back in the same shape."

The men laughed at that. "Don't look so worried, Van," Peters said, not unkindly. "The Living Portrait isn't all that. Just rumble around a little bit and pretend to get knocked out."

"Rumble around a little bit?" The words were foreign in Van's mouth. "I haven't been in a ring for ten years."

"And I'll remind you that was a loss at my hands," Alec broke in.

"Fuck you, Alec. We were like ten years old." Van glowered down at the prick. "You want to be the hero here, you could volunteer."

"No, Van, I can't. I'm well aware the Living Portrait could turn me into a pretzel. I'm not a titan. You are." He took a drink of whiskey. "That said, I wonder what shape he'll turn *you* into."

Van snorted angrily as the other men laughed harder.

"Mitch," Peters said to the chief of operations, "is there any good publicity here? Headwaters Brewery has its own titan in the regional finals. Maybe Van wears a brewery shirt in the ring?"

"Well, there could be, but—uh, no offense, Van—not if he gets his clock cleaned. Maybe better to, uh, not take the chance on promoting during the match. See how it goes and if Van does well, as, uh, I'm sure he will, then we tell the tireless tale of sacrifice and all that."

The president looked at Van. "Tell you what, Van. Do this thing. Do a good job and don't embarrass us. You got the name of the inn, right? Take a barrel of Kingsland with you and find some excuses to talk it up. Give some free pours to any Coalition people who seem pleased with you. And then, maybe, when you get back, we'll do a limited run with your name on it. Call it Titan Hero. Or Van's Stand. Something like that. Mitch, get Garret's team thinking on it."

"What about," the mayor's assistant was fighting a smile, "Titan Pretzel Ale?"

"Or Cracked Skull Stout?"

"Van the Titan Memorial Ale?"

"Living Portrait Footprint Permanently Embedded on Van the Titan's Face...Porter?"

"Van Has Head Forcibly Shoved Up Own—"

"Fuck you all," Van said. He shambled, hunched over and knees bent, across the room towards the president's office. If Alec wasn't pouring him more whiskey, he'd get it himself.

...

Van was outside less than an hour later. The men in the office seemed to be settling into a solid day of heavy drinking. Van lacked the privileges of an executive and his complaining about his sudden change in fortune was killing their collective buzz, so he was reminded of his task and shown the door.

The sunlight falling on the brewery yard was still at midday intensity, and it triggered the return of Van's headache. The whiskey fumes on his breath were making him nauseated, and he wondered at the wisdom of having hit it so hard before a long walk with a titan-sized ass-whipping at the end of it.

Wrestling? How was it that the thing he hated more than anything else was the thing everyone else seemed to think he had to do? Tiny shorts and flexed muscles. Outsized personas. Elaborate moves and styles when a simple fist to the face settled most fights. Flexible rules and bought refs. Why couldn't titans be...something else?

Van looked around, suddenly feeling very lonely in the midst of the bustling brewery yard. His mind went back to Annie. The short time they'd been together, he'd never felt lonely. She'd made him feel special. She had held him close and any bad feelings didn't stand a chance.

Of course, things had been so perfect in his mind for the six months they'd dated he'd been completely oblivious to her slow drift away. First he didn't see her for long and longer stretches of time. Then she found new friends who didn't welcome his giant presence at new kinds of parties which weren't all standing around a barrel in the woods. Finally came the slow creep of Alec into the picture. And then it was done.

Annie had cried as she ended it. He'd worked so hard to comfort her, assure her he'd be okay and that she shouldn't feel bad. It was only after she was gone that he realized he'd never fought for himself. Certainly no one else had. And she was gone. Hearing about the rapid progression of her relationship with Alec had just been more skunk in an already rancid beer. Van had swallowed his anger, packed it down until he'd vomited it up all over their wedding. Real titan-sized vomit. A table decoration no bride anywhere requests for her special day.

Van snarled at the men moving around him across the brewery yard. He'd better get going if he was to make

Rockton by sundown. He walked back to the warehouses to grab a barrel of Kingsland.

Not a single woman from Headwaters had spoken to him since the night of Annie's wedding. And that was over a year ago. Annie herself had been the first to break the silence last night. And that ghostwoman, but she was from Rockton and had said almost nothing. By wrecking Annie's wedding, by refusing to quietly take his seat at the back of the town and out of her life, Van had proven what the town had suspected all along. He was dangerous, embarrassing, and to be avoided. Just as they'd advised Annie all along. And as Van had always kind of known about himself. A big, dumb animal, good for hauling barrels around and not much more.

As Van made his way back towards the loading docks with the Kingsland tucked under one arm, he saw only a single team of horses hitched up. Rawly was out by the team, overseeing the loading of the last barrels. He glanced at Van's barrel. "Can't fit no more."

"Headed for the capital?" Van asked.

"Nope," Rawly replied. "South."

"Are there any headed to the capital today?"

"Not a chance. Went out as soon as we could get them on the road. If any make it back today, they won't set out again so late."

"I've got to get there by tonight."

Rawly gave him a long, considering look, then spat a chunk of tobacco on the dry dirt of the yard. "Sounds like you better get to walking then. I don't see more wagons. Guessing you can't afford no dragon, so unless you feel like killing a horse..."

"Walk all the way? It's like twelve miles. And I've got to bring them this." Van gestured to the barrel under his arm.

"Day ain't getting any younger, ten-man. I'm no genius, but I saw whose office you got called into. I'd get your ass to Rockton and try not to fuck yourself any worse than you've managed to already."

Van let out a sigh he felt all the way down to his bare feet, then turned and began down the dusty road.

Chapter 6

Van looked around the common room of The Loving Arms Inn. It was far nicer than anything in Headwaters, tastefully lit by candles on hanging chandeliers. He'd been to Rockton before, but only to deliver beer barrels. That was usually through the backdoors of places like this. He glanced down at his sweat-stained shirt, his feet still dirty from the long walk.

He'd arrived in the capital just before nightfall. After he'd tracked down the inn, been shown to his room, and stashed his barrel, he'd come down to find the Uplands Wrestling Coalition rep. The woman was packing up a bag with some papers, getting ready to leave.

"So do I need to check in or something?" Van asked.

She smiled softly and set her bag down. "No, I saw you come in. You're good."

"So, I just, what, show up tomorrow night? Where?"

"Sure, right. The fight tomorrow will be at Scott Hall. You can find your way down there or, if you want, I can send someone by here around dusk to help you find your way. You'll fight the Living Portrait a couple hours after sundown. You'll start in the ring, he gets the walk-in. That's about it."

"If that's all this is, why do they have a check-in?"

"To make sure you get into town okay. You titans are not always the most reliable, so it's pretty typical to require check-in the night before. What's your ring name, anyway?"

"I'm Van."

She laughed, and tried to cover it with her hand. "I mean, what name do you fight under?"

"I don't know. Can I just be Van?"

"Sure, whatever." Her eyes were on the door. "Work it out with the announcer. They're good at that stuff. Maybe Van the Strong or something simple. Anyway," she picked up her bag again and slung it over her shoulder, "not my job. See you tomorrow, honey. Try to stay out of trouble tonight."

Van gave her a soft wave, but she'd already turned her back. He was left alone in the common room. As silence fell, he turned a slow circle, staring at the portraits of important women and men lining the walls as he did so. It seemed no one else was going to show up and tell him what to do. He should probably get some sleep, maybe rest up for what was bound to be a long and horrible day tomorrow. Instead he decided to find the hotel bar. It didn't take much looking. Van pushed open a wide door off the lobby, letting in the sounds of laughter and the unmistakable smells of booze and beer.

The tavern was semi-dark, lit only by a few hanging lanterns, one of which Van knocked his forehead against as he entered the room. It sparked a fresh outburst of laughter from the dozens of city folk gathered in the bar. As Van scanned the room, he took in the unwelcome view of Richard the Living Portrait hulking over other drinkers around a crowded table. He should have seen this was coming. Richard would have been the other half of the woman's check-in duties. He fought a deep sigh. It looked as though the pressures of tomorrow night wouldn't have the courtesy to wait for tomorrow night.

Van could feel the eyes on him as he crossed the wooden floor, carefully ducking the low-hanging lamps. For the moment, he could ignore the presence of the other titan, but he knew that wouldn't last forever. The barkeep, cleaning a glass mug with a rag, as they always seemed to be doing, met him at the center of the bar.

Van perked up a bit at the sight of a long row of clean taps. "What are you pouring?" Van asked.

"If I'm speaking to an Uplands local," the bartender replied in a crisp, businesslike tone, "you'll be familiar with the Foundation and Topper, both quite popular here. If you're after something new, I'd recommend Derry out of Empire City or Ocean Pale from the Lone Coast." He smoothly dispensed two sample portions.

Van tasted each and nodded, pleased. Just what he needed after the long, hot walk. "I'll take a Derry."

"First one's on the house for our titan guests," the bartender said as he filled an enormous glass mug. Van nodded his appreciation and eagerly drained the first half. He wanted to pull up a stool. He wanted to put his elbows on the bar and waste the evening talking craft with the bartender. But he didn't think that was in the cards. He could already hear an expectant hush in the room. He slowly turned.

The Living Portrait was staring at him. His admirers had fled, and he sat alone at a massive circular table with a thick central leg. Everyone else in the tavern watched as Richard pushed a titan-sized chair forward with one large boot, inviting Van to sit. The scrape of the chair across the floorboards lingered in the air. Van picked up his mug and ambled over toward it.

The Living Portrait didn't just dress the part in the ring. He was wearing a bright, sparkling jacket, with a thin, V-neck shirt under it that showed off his chest muscles. He wore tinted glasses even though the tavern was dimly lit. His hair was still slicked back, and he ran his fingers through it, just like he did in the ring. He smelled of something strong, like alcohol and flowers, which stung Van's eyes. Van placed his mug on the table as he sat then leaned back, stretching his legs out with a sigh.

"You're Van?" the Living Portrait asked in a gruff voice. When Van nodded, he said, "I was just up in Headwaters. I didn't see you there."

"Yeah," Van said awkwardly. He used to be good about greeting other titans when they came to Headwaters. They were always surprised to find him there, living out his quiet life. After a few beers, they were happy to talk. Mostly about themselves. In fact, entirely about themselves. When Van had been a fawning youngster, his own dreams of entering the squared circle not yet properly laughed away, he'd enjoyed it. That faded quickly though. They weren't really talking to him. They were just reciting the same, tired story about how the world revolved around them. Then as Van had grown bigger, the titans began to see him less as an audience and more as a threat. He was as big as they were, so it was all sizing up and finding ways to assert dominance. Just as predictable, but more dangerous. Nothing worth his time, not when there was beer to drink.

"I never heard about a titan wrestling out of Headwaters," the Portrait said.

"I don't really. Wrestle. I mean, I haven't, really."

"That changes tomorrow, though, right?" A tone of irritation crept into the titan's voice.

"Yeah." Van sipped his beer, glanced around the room to find everyone else staring at them.

"You saw the fight the other night." The Portrait paused dramatically. "And you still are willing to take this on? You must have some kind of death wish." He took a long drink, peering at Van over the rim of his mug.

Van bit back a comment about how perhaps High-Flying Hank hadn't been a challenge worth bragging up, and just shrugged instead. That type of talk could cause him a lot of trouble here.

"Tournament's coming up," the Portrait said, continuing to feel Van out. "Could be a big year for the Uplands." He leaned back in his chair. "You don't talk much, do you?" When Van didn't respond beyond shrugging again, the Portrait grunted. "You know why they call me the Living Portrait?"

Van had spoken to enough titans to recognize the start of their boring, canned origin story. He waved his empty mug at the bartender, who gave him a professional nod and began drawing another.

The Portrait was annoyed by Van's lack of interest. "Well, do you?"

Van shifted in his seat and stared at the Portrait. "I'm guessing because you tell them to."

Richard the Living Portrait snorted, furrowed his smooth brow. Now that Van had met his eyes, he seemed to grow, his huge shoulders threatening to burst out of the tight jacket. Van felt a dryness in his throat despite the Derry. It was easy to mock this guy from a distance, with his slicked back hair and pompous fashion, but when he was right next to you, piercing you with a sharp gaze the tinted glasses only partially hid, it was different. He was enormous, muscles spilling out everywhere he hadn't strapped them down into tight fabric.

"No," the Portrait growled, leaning forwards across the table. His hand was folded tightly around his own mug, his knuckles white. "Not because I tell them to. Because that's what I am. A living portrait. A thing of beauty." He brushed his hair back with his hands and looked off into the distance. "The first time I crushed the Mighty Antis, and stood over his broken body, Corliss the Clever, who's a very famous bard by the way, told me someone should paint me. Said I looked like a portrait. I said, I am. Every time I move, it's another piece of beauty you could hang on your wall and gaze at during long, cold winter nights."

"Doesn't sound like my type of decorating."

"And," the Portrait pressed on, ignoring the interruption, "the ladies ate it up. They line up for miles, just to see me strike a majestic pose at the center of the ring. But that ain't the part that interests you."

"None of this interests me."

"No, what you should be interested in is the other part of that picture. 'Cause at the bottom of every portrait is a busted, broken titan who stepped in the ring when he shouldn't have." Richard burst into laughter and sat back in his chair. "Van. Van the Titan. Van from Headwaters. I've asked around all day. Not a single person here knows who the fuck you are. Well, just one guy, he said you're the big guy, sometimes delivers the beer. Van the Beer Man." There was a long pause as Van accepted a fresh mug from the bartender. The Portrait glared at the man's back as he left.

"You been to Empire City, Van the Beer Man? I'd bet not. Bit far even for a world traveler such as yourself. There's some strange titans in Empire City. Know why?" He didn't wait for an answer. "'Cause titans like to fuck a lot, and some of them like to fuck strange things. I've seen them. They'll fuck anything that moves, and some things that don't. So we get freaks like Golem Jones, the Minotaur, Lizardman, the Ram. Rumor is the Landshaker was born when Laslo the Giant fucked a cave. These are the titans that walk Empire City. And I've fought them and more. And *won*. But my point is, blood comes from blood, and every little bitty titan has a titan daddy. Only wild card is who or what the mommy is. I don't know who your daddy is, Van the Beer Man, but I've got a good idea where you came from. I think your daddy was in a show up in Headwaters, saw how ugly all the local women are, and then he fucked a beer barrel, and out came Van the Beer Man."

The forced smirk Van had plastered to his face slid off. His breath was coming fast. Waves of hot anger traveled up his body. He stared at the titan.

"So, Van the Beer Man, you sure you want to save all the fun for tomorrow night?" The Portrait moved suddenly, smashed his mug onto Van's. Broken glass and spilled beer cascaded across the table.

Van shook his hand clear of the jagged glass. "What the fuck, man?!" There was blood smeared across his hand where the Portrait's mug had crashed into it.

"You mean *ten-man*. Now, stand up, you little bitch." The Portrait rose to his feet, his chair crashing to the floor behind him. "You're an embarrassment to all of us, and you don't belong in that ring. Let's take care of this right now."

The Portrait loomed over Van, tension in his glare. Van was still in his seat. He couldn't seem to stop his eyes from looking everywhere but up at Richard. His breath came faster. Finally he shook his head.

"Ha!" the Portrait laughed. "No surprise there. All right, listen up, Van the Beer Man." His voice was loudly projecting through the room now, and the entire drunken throng looked on expectantly. "I'm going to hurt you. Tomorrow night, I'm going to hurt you bad. And I'm going to look *good* while I do it. Take my time too. Give 'em a show. You'll hear the cheers, two-man. You'll be broken on the mat, listening to the crowd whistling and cheering. Because I'm their champion and I'll be carrying the standard of the Uplands into the Headlock of Destiny. I'm just sticking round here long enough to stomp on the trash that rolls down from the mountain. Some dusty trash that needs to be reminded that it shouldn't poke its head out when real titans are around." He straightened, ran his fingers through his hair and adjusted his tinted glasses. "I'll be seeing you tomorrow."

The crowd let out a few whoops as Richard the Living Portrait left the tavern. Several scurried after him, including a squad of giggling ladies. A table of what looked like half-orcs were smirking at Van and chortling into foul-smelling mugs.

Van sat at the table for a moment, while the bartender wiped up the beer and broken glass. The hot anger bubbled up inside him. Finally he let out a huge roar, a roar so loud the shutters in the tavern windows rattled. Fueled by rage, fueled by shame, fueled by anger, he raised his fists and brought them both down on the table, breaking it in half over its center leg, its splinters ripping into Van's legs as the broken boards raked across them. The bartender fled back toward the bar. Van sat there, miserable, for a long moment. The wave of energy slowly drained from his body and a self-loathing and regretful calm seeped in to take its place.

The bartender came back with a fresh mug of Derry, nervously held before him like a peace offering. Van looked at the man's face as he accepted the glass. "Sorry," Van muttered, glancing at the splintered boards around his legs.

"Wouldn't be a proper check-in if something didn't get broken," the bartender replied kindly. "Shall I keep them coming?"

Van nodded miserably, staring at the door the Portrait had left through. He could walk through that same door, keep walking all the way back to Headwaters. Back where he came from. Back where he belonged. Let everyone laugh at him for being too big of a coward to even step into the ring with a real titan. He already was a joke.

Chapter 7

Darkness had fallen over Rockton, and the Uplands Wrestling Coalition still hadn't sent anyone to help Van find the venue. He was left hustling through the streets, met with peals of drunken laughter whenever he asked for directions to Scott Hall. He'd spent the day in his room, sleeping off the lateness of the past couple nights, totally uninterested in taking advantage of his rare chance to explore the capital. His rest had been broken and jagged, and he felt terrible. He couldn't wait to get the fight over with.

"Ugh," Van moaned as he joined the crowd flowing down a broad avenue, hopefully headed towards the arena. The buildings framing the street were taller than any in Headwaters. They pressed in close, funneling Van towards his doom. He was already covered in sweat despite the temperate air. The crowd seemed to have no urgency, treating the match as little more than an excuse to start their evening off with drinks in hand. The slow pace of movement made him worried he'd be late.

How the hell had he ended up in a fight against Richard the Living Portrait, a proper titan? Van wasn't even sure he knew the rules. He could have spent the day training, or at least finding someone to tell him what the fuck to do in the ring, and he'd done nothing.

"Titan, titan," some revelers in the crowd called after him as he passed. More than one handed him a beer, which he quickly downed with a nod of appreciation. He had the barrel of Kingsland wedged under his arm, but hadn't tapped it. He wasn't quite sure what to do with it while he fought.

Van neared Scott Hall, defined at the edges by the tall backs of wooden bleachers and a ring of security and ticket takers. Van broke away from the crowd to approach what looked to be a quiet entrance. Two security guards looked at him and quickly stepped aside. He walked up an aisle towards the brightly lit ring. The noise rained down on him as he drew deeper into the arena. Van had thought the prefight chatter in Headwaters had been loud. There were easily ten times as many people packed in here already, and more clamoring to get inside. Enormous lamps hung all around, especially atop the bleachers, where mirrored cones channeled the light onto the ring. Everyone would have a great view of Van getting his face ripped off by The Living Portrait. He made his way toward the ring, barrel of Kingsland still under one arm.

Ringside, three men in suits and a woman wearing a glamorous dress sat at a long table and eyed Van curiously. Van gave them an awkward nod, then looked at the ring. Nothing seemed to be happening there. Van hesitated, then turned to the table. "Is this…should I go up there?"

"All you, buddy," said one of the men.

Van rolled the barrel under the ropes and stood it on the mat. Then he climbed into the ring, his heart rising to his throat as he pulled himself by the top rope. He felt a brief sense of vertigo and a sudden sympathy for High-Flying Hank. The lights were bright and the crowd raised a half-hearted cheer. Van wasn't sure whether he should wave or not.

An announcer and referee stood in the center of the ring. The announcer was tall and wore a tight-fitting grey suit. The referee was a smallish man, thin with large eyes. He wore a striped white and black shirt and black pants. Together they looked at Van. "Can't bring that barrel in here," the ref said after a long stare.

"Oh, sorry," Van replied. He looked at the side of the ring for a minute, then parked the barrel on the apron just outside the turnbuckles. The ref glanced at it, then shrugged. The pair resumed their conversation.

Feeling the eyes of the crowd on him, Van looked down at his uniform. He had given zero thought to what he should wear for the fight. He settled for taking off his dark blue shirt, leaving him in belted, dark blue shorts, cuffs so worn they looked more like cutoff pants. His feet were bare. He fussed his hair down for a moment and smoothed his beard, then turned to the announcer and ref.

"Can I, uh, talk to you guys for a minute?" Van asked.

They looked at each other, then up at Van. "Sure," the announcer said slowly. "What's up?"

"Are there, like…well, what are the rules?"

"The rules?"

"Yeah. Like, what do I do? What can't I do?"

"Honest answer, guy, I don't think the rules are gonna matter much tonight." He straightened his suitcoat, brushing off imaginary flecks of dust. When Van's only response was a blank stare, the announcer nudged the ref. "Sounds like a job for you, Brady."

"Sure." Brady looked at Van as he nodded slowly. "Listen. Mel will do his thing and announce you. Then he'll announce The Living Portrait. The Portrait will come running in. He'll get the crowd worked up. Fight starts when he decides it does. You'll hear a bell, but just be ready. He might not wait for it. But if they," he nodded towards the four people at the table, "think the crowd's getting bored, they'll ring it. Then you fight. Last one standing wins. Pins don't really matter, boring way to end a fight, so don't waste my time. You're not supposed leave the ring. If you're out there too long, I'll start counting. Don't do too much of that stuff. Crowd gets bored if you keep running away. Just the two of you, no interference. No weapons. Other than that, anything goes. Punches, kicks, gouges, eyepokes, hooks, slams, throws, smashes, chokes, breaks, snaps, locks. All good. Make a good show. Try not to die."

"What if I, like…how do I tap out?"

Brady chortled, seeming to think that was funny, and the announcer broke into a broad grin. "You can pound on the mat. I'll try to get him to stop, but that's really up to him."

"What are we calling you?" the announcer asked impatiently.

"I don't know," Van said, turning back to the referee. "What do you mean, *it's up to him*?"

"Look, this ain't one of those *exactly-fair*-type situations, friend. Rules and all that. The two of you get in here, we ring the bell, and I raise the hand of the last titan standing. I could tell you all the finer details, but it's not gonna matter, and you look like you've got enough on your mind right now."

. . .

"Ladies and gentlemen, have we got a treat for you." The announcer had only a small cone-shaped horn to amplify his voice, but he seemed to make it carry to the farthest reaches of the gathered crowd. When the cheering settled down again, he continued. "The winner of tonight's match will have no rest. He will go on to represent the Uplands in the annual Headlock of Destiny Tournament." The announcer lowered his cone for another surge of cheering, then lifted it to his mouth again. "Carrying the honor of the Uplands forward to Empire City." The crowd booed loudly at the mention of the Open Nations' capital. "On one side, from nearby Headwaters, in the blue trunks, Van the…uh…," the announcer looked momentarily lost, but then his eyes settled on Van's barrel parked on the apron outside the ring. "Van the Beer Man!" A few in the crowd jeered. Most were silent, saving their energy for what came next.

"And now," those simple words flipped a switch, and the crowd rose to their feet, yelling and screaming, "a ten-man who can only be described, by himself, as the most beautiful titan to ever grace the ring, a titan whose elegance and style are surpassed only by his incredible strength and power, ladies and gentlemen, I give you Richard the Living Portrait!"

The Portrait strutted slowly down the aisle as the crowd pressed in around him, shouting encouragement and reaching out to touch his jacket, sparkling pink under the spotlights. Every visible inch of him gleamed with oil. He adjusted his dark glasses, ran his fingers through his slick hair, and waved to his fans.

Van waited, wondering if anyone would notice if he threw up. No one seemed to be looking his direction. Maybe he could sneak off right now, and they wouldn't notice he was gone. Back to Headwaters, to tell everyone he might be chickenshit, but at least he was alive.

It was too late. The Portrait was mounting the ropes. He climbed to the top rope and stood on the turnbuckles, huge, tossed off his jacket, flexed his pecs and biceps, and swung his arms to get loose. The crowd burst into a frenzied roar. Then he jumped down and stared at Van.

Van stood there dumbly. He was caught off guard when the Portrait suddenly ran at him. Van recoiled, his stomach jumping to his throat, but the Portrait stopped just before reaching him and laughed at Van's reaction. He turned back to the crowd, walked the corners, summoned cheers with his raised arms, and blew kisses to the women in the front rows.

Van wasn't sure if he wanted to hear the bell or not. On one hand, he certainly wouldn't mind delaying the beating headed in his direction. On the other, being a prop in this asshole's show was annoying. If he could just land a punch or two, maybe he'd surprise the pompous goon. Force him to make it quick, despite his barroom threats, so he wouldn't want to risk getting hurt before the Headlock.

Van scanned the crowd, taking his eyes off the Portrait for a moment. In an elevated box behind the bleachers, he caught a glimpse of his ghostwoman, her blonde hair billowing next to the brimmed white hat of a glowering dark-skinned man. It was hard to tell at this distance, and through the bright lights, but Van thought she might have nodded at him. Why did he have the feeling she had something to do with why he was here? If so, he'd have to find her and offer his sincere thanks after the Portrait wiped the mat with his broken corpse.

The bell rang, jerking Van's attention back to the ring. The Portrait glowered at the bell, annoyed that they'd chosen to cut his moment short. Van had a sinking feeling his opponent was serious about making this into a big show. With a quick stomp and a shrug of his shoulder, Richard the Living Portrait closed in on Van.

He came with both arms outstretched and locked Van into a clinch. Van at least knew this move and he held his ground, meeting the Portrait muscle for muscle. Van could feel him pressing forward, testing his strength. Van was strong, but the Portrait had a practiced, confident feel to what he was doing, an easy balance. Van had never felt more ungainly in his life, and he was sure every twitch of his muscles, every slide of his foot was conveying that weakness to this bombastic bully whose fingertips were crushing Van's shoulders.

Van took a deep breath and pushed with all his might, shoving Richard back a half step, and giving himself a small boost of confidence. But the Portrait tossed Van's arms aside and slapped him hard across the face. It happened so fast, Van wasn't even sure how he'd done it. Dazed, Van got his arms up just in time to absorb the next clinch. The Portrait tossed him aside again and slapped him across the same cheek. Van's face burned as he reeled back to catch his balance. The Portrait came at him again, and Van raised his arms. The crowd roared with laughter when he caught nothing but air.

Van shook his head to clear away the stars that seemed to be circling him. The Portrait, nowhere near Van, stepped away and smoothed his hair with both hands, preening for the crowd, as Van stood like an idiot with his arms outstretched. The Portrait leaned back against the ropes, hands on hips, and roared with laughter.

Van wasn't even sure what happened next, but the Portrait leapt across the ring and seized him, and suddenly Van found his arm twisted behind his back. When he stumbled away forward, trying to whirl out of the arm twist, the Portrait stuck a rigid arm out and caught him with a clothesline under his chin and drove him down on the mat.

Van felt the heat of the mat hard below him for only a moment before the Portrait lifted him up by his hair. The stinging pain on his scalp and the embarrassment of being manhandled made Van's adrenaline surge and he threw a wild punch. It came closer to hitting the ref than the Portrait, who shoved Van into the turnbuckles, where he fell again awkwardly. The Portrait crashed down, slamming his elbow into the side of Van's head. Van lay sprawled on the mat.

The shouts of the crowd came to Van in waves as he lay on the mat. The match had barely started and he'd never felt pain like this before. He'd never felt exhaustion like this before, either; his lungs burned as though he'd run a hundred miles.

The Portrait stood on the other side of the ring, talking with the ref. As Van looked up him, he smiled and stomped back toward Van. He knelt down and again picked Van up by the hair. Van didn't want to grasp at the hand pulling him upwards and show how much it hurt, but he couldn't help it. He clutched at the Portrait's wrist. Van closed his eyes, wincing, scalp burning, tears leaking out. The Portrait leaned in close. "Did you ask about the *rules*?" he whispered. "I'll teach you about the rules."

The Portrait delivered a brutal headbutt to the corner of Van's scalp, then looked over at the amused referee. "Headbutts aren't against the rules, are they?"

He threw his arm around Van's neck and pulled him down again, then he grabbed the belt of Van's shorts. Van tried to stumble away, but the Portrait anticipated his every move. Suddenly Van found himself up in the air, looking at the screaming upside-down audience. Then he came crashing down on his back. He rolled away in agony. "Bodyslams are okay, right?"

"What about," the Portrait stood up on one leg like a crane over Van, "knee drops?" and brought his massive weight down on one knee against Van's ribs. Then he did it again.

Van felt his eyes tearing. Through the blur and the lights he saw the Portrait spreading his hands in the air, egging on the howling crowd. Then Richard bent down, pulled Van up off the mat a third time, and hoisted him over his head. He spun around once…twice, and then threw their combined weight backwards, slamming Van into the mat again.

"What about that?" the Portrait hollered, more at the adoring crowd than at Van.

At this point, some part of Van was certain he was dead and in some sort of hell, condemned to a life of pain and humiliation.

"How about chokeholds?" the Portrait asked, looking at the grinning ref. He plopped down on the mat behind Van and locked his arms around Van's neck. Van was already sucking wind, and, as his air was cut off, he clawed at Richard's hard forearms. The Portrait brought his face in close again. "This about how you thought it would go, you—"

Whatever Richard had been ready to say was interrupted as Van, desperate for air, managed to get his feet under him and push back with all his strength, almost toppling the Portrait, who flung him aside and jumped to his feet.

The Portrait still had the same smile in place, ready to continue his taunt. Van clambered to his feet panting, stepped forward, and surprised Richard with a solid left jab to the nose. The Portrait surrendered no ground, but his face tightened in anger. His eyes blazed. He reached forward and clinched Van's shoulders again. The crowd seemed to fade away, the only sounds Van heard were the harsh breathing between himself and the Portrait and the tread of their feet on the mat.

"Maybe nobody here knows you, little two-man barrel bitch, but sure as shit someone will take the story of this beatdown back to Headwaters. I know how it works in towns like yours. When they hear about this, you're gonna be more of a joke than you already are."

Van was still trying to catch his breath, trying not to think about Richard's words, but he couldn't help himself. What *would* they think? What would Annie think? Alec would hear first, probably race home from the brewery to bring her the news. *A laughingstock. An embarrassment. Not even a real man, certainly no ten-man.* Van dug his fingertips deep into the Portrait's, felt him giving ground a little as he drove forward. The Portrait tried to toss off his arms again but Van held him tight. What else would Alec tell her? *He thought you loved him, what a joke. Made an ass of himself at our wedding. Embarrassed me. Embarrassed you. Now he's the joke of all of Headwaters.* Van felt a burn in his stomach. He ground his teeth, felt sweat drip from his temples.

A murmur rose from the crowd as Van forced the Portrait to his knees. The Portrait twisted out of Van's grip, crawled to his corner to collect himself, used the ropes to get back on his feet. He stepped forward and they circled the ring. The buzzing of the crowd rose again as they sensed the fight nearing its climax, but that wasn't what Van heard alongside the blood pounding in his head. Van heard Annie wearing down under Alec's pressure. *You were right. I don't know what I was thinking. I didn't ask him to come to our wedding. I thought I'd gotten him out of my life. I was just as embarrassed as you.* The Portrait lunged at Van, but Van ducked and punched him hard in the gut. *It was you, Alec. It was always you I loved. I never loved him. Don't believe him if he tells you otherwise.*

The Portrait charged again, but this time hesitantly. Van coldly assessed the move, slipped left, and clotheslined Richard onto the mat. Van hadn't trained? *This* pompous fool hadn't trained. This overgrown dandy was born into his size, born into his muscles. He hadn't hauled hundreds of pounds of malt sacks on his shoulders as sweat poured down his brow. Stacked barrels until his hands bled, trying to forget the shit hand he'd been dealt. Trying to forget *her.*

When the Portrait rose, chin bloody, Van shoved him into the ropes. As he bounced back, an instinct from deep inside Van, one he'd never tapped before, flared through him like fire. He jumped up and planted his bare heels hard into the Portrait's chest. Richard the Living Portrait stumbled back in pain, staggered around the ring, spitting blood. Van smelled fear beneath the sickly sweet scent of the Portrait's cloying cologne. Van rained punches on the Portrait, smashing through his face as though there was something he needed on the other side. In the corner of his eye, Van saw the ref take a step forward, but Van stopped him with a menacing stare. Van grabbed the staggering Portrait, oblivious to his own angry roar, and hoisted him in the air as easily as he'd flip a barrel.

Van remembered breaking the table at the hotel bar, driving his fists down on both sides, the calming feeling as the wood splintered over the post with a loud snap. He remembered the Portrait's threats. A cold rage washed over him. He raised the struggling titan higher over his head. He heard Annie's voice in the far reaches of his skull—*I never loved him. I told you I never loved him.*

The crowd fell silent as Van the Beer Man flipped Richard the Living Portrait up in the air, knelt one knee down on the mat, and drove Richard's falling body down onto his other, extended knee with all his strength and all his rage. A loud crack, like the sound of a tree trunk splitting, echoed through the arena.

Van turned coldly toward the ref, standing next to him, mouth agape. "That against the rules?" Van asked as his broken, defeated opponent rolled off his knee and thudded onto the canvas.

Chapter 8

Van's lather of sweat hadn't even dried before he was dragged to an office of shouting, unsympathetic people raging over his fate. It was an upscale space close to the arena, walls lined with bookshelves, a large desk to one side. Van sulked in the doorway as a group of well-dressed men and women stood at the front of the room being yelled at by a screaming man with dark skin wearing a smartly fitted white suit. Van's ghostwoman sat on a stool in the corner, unreadable as always. A titan Van guessed to be Owen Grit sat on a sofa in the back looking bored.

"Are you fucking kidding me?! Are you fucking kidding me?!" The screaming man was so animated, he was literally leaving the carpet as he yelled.

A woman wearing a glittering red dress tried interrupting. "Larvell, listen—"

"Listen! Listen to what? Listen to the sounds of the worst disaster in Uplands wrestling history?" He gestured towards the open windows, through which the sounds of the leaving crowd could be heard.

One of the men by the desk at the front chimed in, amusement in his voice. "I thought it was a good match. The new guy really came back."

Larvell zeroed in on the man. "You're an idiot!" He glared around the room daring someone else to speak up. As he took in the handful of others, he finally noticed Van in the doorway. "You!" He pointed at Van and shouted, "Whose pocket are you in?"

"Pocket?" Van asked, bewildered. He'd left one fight and somehow walked right into another. His face ached. His ribs throbbed. Even his hair hurt. And this weird little man was yelling at him.

"Who paid you to hurt the Portrait?"

"What?" Van asked. He felt everyone's eyes on him. "Nobody." Because more seemed needed, Van added, "He was trying to hurt *me*."

"Of course he was, you giant imbecile! You had no business being in that ring." Larvell turned to Van's ghost, who was seated against the wall. "This is your fault!"

"What's my fault?" she asked, immediately exceeding the sum of all the previous words Van had ever heard her say. Her voice held a quiet menace, no sign of intimidation in the face of Larvell's anger. "Owen's injury?" She gestured lazily at the titan seated next to her.

Larvell turned to the group in front of the desk, pulling his hat off his head and flexing it in his hands. "I want the Portrait."

The eldest of the men, it seemed to Van, with a frost of white hair slowly shook his head. "He looked hurt pretty bad, Larvell. Anyway he lost, and rules are rules."

"Fuck that. Fuck you. I'm not taking that *thing* to the tournament." He scowled at Van, his gaze sliding down to the barrel Van still held under his arm. "Oh, great, he brought fucking beer with him. What a celebration." His head was shaking. "Man, I have seen some truly out of place assholes in my time, but that performance was something else…"

Van wasn't sure if he should be defending himself. He sure as hell didn't want to go to the Headlock, hadn't even thought about why he might not actually want to win the fight. It had all been a blur.

"Let me fight." Owen's voice thundered from the back of the room.

"You can barely walk, you dumb shit," Larvell replied, slamming his white, brimmed hat back on and vigorously rubbing his face.

"I can fight."

"No, you can't. Or believe me, you would be." He looked at the old man again. "I want the Portrait."

"Those aren't the rules. Like it or not, we held a match for the regionals and the winner is standing right there." He flashed a soft smile, almost embarrassed, as he looked at Van. "I suppose introductions are in order."

Larvell jumped in. "No! No, they are not. I want the Portrait!"

"The rules state—"

"Then change the rules!"

"Larvell." The old man rolled his eyes impatiently. "You're being ridiculous. Maybe we could work around the rules—and *maybe* is a strong word to put in front of such a dumb idea—if the match had been closer. Maybe we could do something then. But the whole of Rockton just saw the Portrait get destroyed by a...a...beer delivery boy! You saw what happened. Richard will probably be in the hospital for weeks if not months. Do you have that long to wait?"

"But that's exactly my point." Larvell pointed at Van. "Nobody knows him. How do we know he's not a ringer from the Vantages?"

"He's not." The voice of Van's ghostwoman cut across the office.

"Well then, how do we know he won't take the first bribe he's offered? Spend it all on..." He gestured towards the barrel under Van's arm. "I can't even say it, it is so dumb."

"He won't." She stood from her stool and walked towards Larvell.

"And how do you know this, Kyle?"

She stepped forward and looked him square in the face. "I know plenty, Larvell, plenty more than you do. But that's not the point. You're acting like you were thrilled to have the Living Portrait. The guy you described as *more hairstyle than titan* just yesterday. We needed a contender, and we have a contender." She waved a hand at Van. "He's raw as hell and didn't seem to know what the hell he was doing out there, but quit pretending things just went from bad to worse. They went from fucked one way to fucked another way." She paused and leveled a long look at Van. "He won't take a bribe, though. And Owen can help get him ready."

"No," Owen said flatly from the back.

"Yes," Kyle shot back, a flash of anger in her eyes.

Larvell tried staring her down. "You knew this was going to happen. That's why you made me put him in the fight."

"I put him in the fight because I saw something in him out in Headwaters. I saw it again tonight. I'm not going to pretend anything beautiful, or even borderline competent, happened out there tonight, but I'm okay with the outcome. I'm at least reasonably confident Van will put up an honest effort in a tournament match and that's a lot more than I would say about the Living Portrait. That ten-man's vanity made him a clear mark for every nation with money for a bribe, and he's stupid enough to believe whatever promises they would have made him. Also, I would have had to spend the entire tournament babysitting him and smelling that putrid cologne."

Larvell stared up at Van. "Vanity shouldn't be a problem here. He brought a fucking barrel of beer with him to the ring. Just look at his gut!" He pointed at Van's ample midsection.

Van was torn between agreeing and taking offense. He was no wrestler. And a tournament match? Was his gut really that bad?

"Who is this guy?" Larvell asked, sounding genuinely mystified. The anger seemed to be draining out of him.

Kyle locked eyes with Van. The same look she'd given him in the warehouse. Totally unafraid. Expectant, a teacher waiting for an answer. "Van, tell him who you are."

Van squirmed under her scrutiny. "I'm Van." What did everyone want from him?

"No, Van, not your name. Tell him *who* you are. You can't stay in the shadows forever."

Her eyes held him fixed. He could feel an energy radiating from them, surging through him and reminding him of the strength he'd found in the ring, however fleeting. Finally he turned to Larvell. "I'm Van the Beer Man." He dropped the barrel to the ground with a heavy thud and leaned in over Larvell as it rolled to a standstill. "I'm the titan who broke your precious Living Portrait into pieces. Seems like I'm all you got left." The room fell quiet. Van glanced over at Kyle. From the smile on her face, Van thought maybe he'd done okay.

Larvell just shook his head. "This is going to be a disaster." He stormed out of the office. After a murmured apology, the old man and his followers ran after him.

Kyle looked to the door, then back to Van. "Looks like you're headed to the tournament, Van the Beer Man." Then, with no more explanation, she too left, leaving Van alone in the office with Owen Grit.

Van stood in the center of the suddenly quiet room. His head was reeling. He was headed to the Headlock of Destiny Tournament. To face the likes of Judge Cage, the Landshaker, even King Thad himself. They were saying Scott Flawless hadn't lost since the last tournament. What could Van do against someone like Billy Blades, Duke Roller, or Facestomping James? Would he dare get in the ring with Elephant the Titan, Grim Tidings, or the Ram? And those were only the ones he knew off hand. There would be many, many more, all better prepared than the likes of Van from Headwaters. They'd spent their whole lives getting ready for this. He'd just started thinking about it yesterday, and that thinking had been entirely dedicated to imagining a way out. Van let out a deep sigh and stood quietly, his shoulders sagging, in the middle of the office.

Finally, the rumbling voice of the ten-man at the back of the room broke the silence. "Is that barrel just a prop or what?"

Van turned towards Owen Grit. The titan was seated with his back against the wall, his left knee heavily bandaged. He stared expectantly at Van. "No," Van said finally. He could feel every bruise, every ache in his body. He wanted to go home. Instead, he began to look around for mugs and a tap. "Damn. I hate wrestling."

Chapter 9

The blue sofa in Annie and Alec's living room sat tastefully parked below the window, tan curtains partially blocking the view of the quiet dirt street outside, the bookshelf displaying bound volumes alongside mementos and wooden baby toys, the bassinet in the corner. Everything in perfect proportion to their tidy life. Van's own home was bare aside from assorted beer memorabilia he'd accrued and then been too lazy to get rid of. That and a giant mattress, strewn across his floor, where he slept alone.

Van felt huge and out of place as he loomed in the doorway, knuckles hanging by his sides. He wore his dusty brewery uniform even though it was an off day for him. He could never seem to keep his clothes clean and at least it wasn't torn too badly.

He hadn't known what to bring, and didn't have anyone to ask. None of the few people he called friends would have had any idea. He could have pulled up flowers from one of the many window beds he'd passed on the way here. But would that look like he was romancing a married woman? Surely more than one of the neighbors was noting his arrival while Alec was at work, where Van would normally be on a day like this. Maybe he should have brought a bottle of wine, but she said she wasn't drinking. Some sort of housewarming gift?

"I didn't know what to bring," he said with a shrug. Not the smoothest greeting, certainly.

Annie smiled warmly. "You didn't need to bring anything, Van. Come in. It's good to see you." They exchanged an awkward hug. She again held the baby and couldn't quite turn into him. He was trying not to hit his head on the archway between the foyer and living room. "Have a seat," she said, gesturing to the sofa.

Van carefully lowered himself down, feeling the wooden frame strain under his weight. He glanced out the window, wishing she'd open the curtains more so he could be seen from the street. He wondered how many of the neighbors were watching right now, ready to start the gossip mill churning. Best if they could see he stayed in the living room during the entirety of his short visit.

He glanced at Annie, who was placing the baby in the bassinet, making small cooing noises to keep her calm as she was separated from her mother. The sun fell on Annie's clean dress, a pretty print of blue roses. She'd always liked roses. It probably hadn't even occurred to her that tongues would wag. She was the wife of a foreman now, a prominent position in Headwaters, and that pinned a target to her. She'd always been a touch naïve about the cruelties of people, which might have been the only reason she'd seen fit to spend time with Van at all, not bothering to listen to the mud slung by the rest of the small town. Maybe he shouldn't have come. He didn't want to get her in trouble.

Why had he come? Her invitation at the beerfest to stop by had seemed a mere formality, yet when he'd run into her this morning at the market, she'd offered again. With nothing else to do today, he'd agreed. It had been three days since the fight. Van didn't need to start the trip to Empire City until tomorrow and the brewery had given him the day off without Van asking. He suspected someone with the Uplands Wrestling Coalition had sent a message to make that happen. Certainly not Larvell, who remained less than a fan.

Annie went to the kitchen and came back with tea. She placed the platter on the small table between them and took a seat across from Van. Her actions were stiff and precise, miles from the carefree way they'd interacted during their brief romance. Would Alec be upset when he learned Van had been by? Van didn't give a fuck about that asshole's feelings, but maybe he'd be mean to Annie over it. Van carefully reached out to take the small teacup. Why did everything have to be so delicate?

"How have you been, Van?"

She used his name a lot, and he always liked hearing it come out of her mouth. "Okay, I guess. Been kind of a wild few days."

"And more ahead, I imagine."

Van grunted as he drained his teacup. "What about you? How's motherhood?"

"Same as before," she said, smiling again. "Great. Exhausting. For a while I felt like a little queen with everyone stopping by. Now that those visits have slowed down and I have to get myself all put together to go anywhere, it's a bit of a challenge. But Carrie Peters has been a great help, and Margot Lester has a little one about the same age. They've both been a huge help." She leaned in closer to offer a conspiratorial whisper, "And they've got nannies, so when I really need a break I can visit them and hand off Lizzy."

Peters and Lester. Wives of the brewery owner and warehouses boss. Annie had climbed the ladder several rungs with her marriage to Alec. The brewery bosses played a big role in the community, their wives as well. Annie had always wanted to make Headwaters better. She'd have a lot more chances with people like that in her corner. Van didn't know what to do with his empty teacup. He'd drunk it faster than was polite. He settled for transferring it from hand to hand.

"How was the fight, Van? I know you don't like that stuff."

"Everyone thought I'd get my ass kicked, you mean."

"Everyone but you?" she asked gently.

"No," he smiled, feeling his cheeks redden. "I was pretty sure I'd get my ass kicked too. Guess the Portrait wasn't all he thought he was."

"That or you've got something we all were overlooking."

"Well, we'll find out, won't we?" After a long moment looking into his empty teacup, he continued. "I don't know how to feel about it. I hated being there, up in front of everyone. And it hurt. A lot. And when I was hurting him, that didn't feel right, either." Van struggled to gather his thoughts. Annie waited patiently, another thing he'd loved about her. She gave him time. Everyone else just jumped in. "But, there were moments when I felt strong and unafraid. Like, I don't know, proud."

"You should be proud, Van."

"Yeah, of what?" He looked around the room, not bothering to hide his envy, then immediately regretted it. "Sorry. It's just...the last few days have kind of worn on me."

"Well, I'm glad you're proud of yourself. We're proud of you."

Van nodded in appreciation, though he hadn't seen much sign of that. It seemed as though the whole town was shocked that he would be in the Headlock, like he'd suddenly grown wings and flown in formation with the dragons that passed over the mountains. Headwaters had become used to the titan in their midst, so long as he was hauling barrels rather than hurling other giants through the air. Now they didn't know how to treat him. Beyond a token congratulations and some quickly satiated curiosity from his friends, no one was doing anything differently.

A piercing whine erupted from the corner of the room, and Annie set down her teacup and walked to the bassinet. "She likes to be held." She looked at Van. "Do you want to give it a try?"

"I don't—"

But Annie was already picking up the tiny bundle and walking towards Van. With her free hand, she took the teacup from him and laid it on the table, tugged his arms into a better position, and then nestled the child in them. She stepped away with a strange smile on her face.

Van looked down at the tiny child. A blanket covered most of her face. Thin wisps of pale hair snuck out of the folds. She opened and closed her eyes, deep brown like her mother's, as she tried to get comfortable in Van's massive arms. "I've never held a baby before." He looked up with a nervous laugh. "I've never even seen one this close. Most people don't like titans near—"

"Van, stop."

"Sorry." He'd forgotten how much she hated his bouts of self-pity. He looked down again. The baby had settled against his forearm. Her breath gently stirred the hairs on his wrist. "So little," he said. He felt brutish and impossibly out of place with the tiny, perfect child in his arms. In another life she could have been his. A tear ran down his cheek. Van froze, irrationally hoping Annie wouldn't see it if he didn't move.

"Oh, Van," she said quietly, taking a seat beside him on the sofa. "What are we going to do with you?"

He sniffled, hating the weak sound, his eyes still locked on the child, and answered in a low voice. "Ship me off to the Headlock, I guess. I told the bosses I don't want to go. They said there wouldn't be a job for me at the brewery anymore if I didn't. So I'm going." He could feel the distance looming before him. He'd never been farther than Rockton, never out of the Uplands. And he didn't want to go. It was far away from here, this room, with her, the only place he could ever be something close to happy. A room in a house that belonged to someone else. With a woman who'd pledged her heart to someone else.

"Oh, Van, I'm so sorry." Annie put her hand on his knee and leaned in close, eyes wide with concern. "You won't let them hurt you, will you?"

"I'll try not to." But he would disappoint her, wouldn't he? Just like he had before, when he'd let her leave and again when he'd ruined her wedding. Van was caught up in something he had no control over. They were most certainly going to hurt him. That was what titans did.

Chapter 10

"Oh, good, the titan brought beer again." Larvell's voice dripped with sarcasm as he looked Van up and down. The morning sun hung bright in the sky behind him. The small group had gathered in a quiet dirt yard, loading a large carriage. Van's ghostwoman was floating around, he'd need to remember she actually had a name. Kyle.

Van carefully set down the two barrels he'd been given by the brewery for the trip. Management had wanted him to bring more. Of course they hadn't offered him a lift back to Rockton where the Uplands delegation to the tournament assembled before heading onwards to Empire City. Not much sympathy, either, once they realized how long they'd be without their resident titan at the docks, moving their largest barrels and supplies from place to place. No one at the brewery had rehashed the earlier threat of Van losing his job, but it hung in the air. Van needed to show up and do his part, take his lumps, or he was fired.

Van said nothing to Larvell. He still didn't know quite how much shit he was supposed to tolerate from the weird little man. Kyle gave him the bare minimum of a greeting, a slight nod, to his dissatisfaction. She looked to be in the midst of checking gear. Owen Grit was there as well, sitting on a tree stump, knee still tightly wrapped in bandages. Grit didn't even bother with a nod.

A short, wiry man in black livery approached Van with an air of urgency. He was followed by a cloud of stale tobacco smoke. "The new titan, then?" he asked. "Van, is it?"

"Hi," Van said in his rumbling voice and offered him a hand as large as the man's head.

"I'm Trent," the man replied. After a brisk shake of Van's hand, he continued, "I'll be your driver for the trip. This what you got?" He gestured at the two barrels.

Van nodded. At Trent's curious look, Van tugged on the small bag slung over his shoulder as if to provide evidence that he had packed more than beer. No one had given him any guidance as to what to wear in the ring, so he figured he'd just continue with his blue Headwaters Brewery uniform. He could at least keep the road dust off of it, he supposed, so he'd crammed it in a bag. The one change of clothes was all he'd packed.

"Governor's only springing for a single carriage to Empire, so it might get a little tight. Hope you don't mind riding up top next to me? Guessing Owen will claim the titan seat inside. I suppose you guys could always fight over it. That sometimes happens. Just don't do it by the horses."

"Top's fine."

"Good." Trent's narrow face twisted into a friendly smile. He leaned in a little closer as though telling Van a secret. "Heard the Living Portrait still isn't quite sure which side of the canvas he's looking at. Hell of a match, Beer Man."

Van returned the smile. He watched Trent expertly sizing up the barrels and studying the carriage to figure out how to best balance the load. Most of the ride would be downhill and smooth, but there was always a chance that rains or a pack of drunken orcs would force them off the beaten path. Both were common on the roads between Rockton and Empire City.

Van wasn't used to being around so many strangers. Who could he talk to during the long trip? He already missed the comfort of his routine and the four walls of his house, even if they did let in the cold mountain winds. He'd locked it up, first time using the bolt on the door since he'd moved in.

Van heard hooves pounding down the dirt road, and they all turned to look. An ornate carriage crested the hill behind the yard at breakneck speeds and began charging down towards them. It pulled alongside their smaller carriage, kicking up a cloud of dust that washed over Van's legs. Larvell gave an irritated cough as the driver of the carriage, in an elegant uniform of Uplands blues and yellows, swept gracefully off the driver's perch and opened the door to the enclosed seating area.

The woman who emerged, blinking her eyes at the bright sun and peering disdainfully at the dust as though she hadn't been its cause, wore a gown of white and silver. She was perhaps in her fifties, hair tightly pinned up, face creased with disapproval. She seized her servant's hand to descend the single stair of the cart. When she had lowered herself onto the dirt of the yard, she released the driver's hand, and then slapped him in the face.

The sharp crack hung in the air. Van realized his jaw had dropped at the sound, and his mouth hung open like a village idiot's. No one else reacted. From the servant's weary expression, it was no rare occurrence. She looked around the group, her face lighting up as she saw Kyle.

"Miss Kyle Vair! Darling!" she called out with delight. She opened her arms for a hug.

Kyle walked towards the lady, muttering to Van as she passed, "Close your mouth."

"Darling, you look as lovely as ever." The lady folded her into a matronly hug, then reached up to touch the blonde strands of hair which fell across her shoulders. "This is horribly out of fashion, darling. Too long in the sticks for you. We'll have to see someone when we arrive. I know a good man with some elven blood. I have" —she pulled Kyle across from her, gripping both her hands tightly— "so many suitors to introduce you to. One of the Uplands most capable and beautiful treasures still a single woman! A tragedy well past its third act and ready for remedy."

"Lady Dorothy, you know I'm always happy to meet them. No guarantees I'll bring them home."

"This will be the trip! This will be the trip!" Lady Dorothy gave a girlish squeal of delight, then quickly transitioned to a concerned look. "Now, what is this about there being no space for my servants? You know how chaotic Empire City can be, and during the tournament! We simply must squeeze at least Johannas in." She gestured towards her footman.

"Governor Crowell wanted to keep it small this year."

"What nonsense! She knows the demands of travel. We certainly would never see her undertaking a diplomatic trip, to the tournament no less, without ample support. Imagine what the delegation from the Vantages will look like. Am I to show up to the parties and galas in road worn clothes? Carry my own bag? Must I announce *myself* and pass out my own calling cards? The utter humiliation, darling."

"Lady Dorothy, I'll help you where I can, and we're staying at one of the finest hotels in Empire City. They'll have ample staff to support you."

"Somehow I doubt that, darling. I have no time to train a new staff and shop you about the town. You ask too much!" She coughed and waved dust away from her face. "I'll tell you what. Johannas has my carriage all loaded. He will simply follow us to Empire City. He'll be along to help, and if perchance you and I find that my carriage is a more comfortable ride, maybe we pass the afternoon catching up without bumping elbows with the titans."

"I'm sorry, Lady Dorothy," Kyle replied, pouting sympathetically. "The governor was very clear in her direction. This is a year to keep our heads down. If we're showing off wealth, it only will encourage the movement towards larger tariffs on the Uplands."

"But Johannas finds it devastating to be parted from me. He worries about me so!"

Van snuck a look at Johannas, his cheek still bright red from the slap he'd received. He did not appear at all devastated at the prospect of a little time apart from his mistress.

Kyle gave a firm, final shake of her head and Lady Dorothy sighed. Then she turned to regard the rest of the group who had been quietly watching the exchange. Her gaze breezed past Trent as though he were invisible. She gave Van a considering look with a sour twist to her mouth. He was annoyed she didn't deign to greet him, but was slightly mollified when she gave the exact same treatment to Larvell. Her eyes lit up again when she saw Owen. "Owen, darling, I was simply devastated to hear of your injury!"

Owen slowly rose from his perch on the tree trunk and loomed over Lady Dorothy. She showed no restraint as she gave him a hug around his midsection, which he met with an awkward pat on the lady's back.

"Would that we could once again ride your strength into the tournament, you mighty ten-man. But it will free you up to join me at the parties, at least." Her eyes sparkled at the thought of having a tournament-seasoned titan at her beck and call, holding her purse as she glad-handed her way across Empire City.

Kyle chimed in. "Owen will have his hands full helping Van in the tournament." They exchanged a loaded look. Owen didn't appear thrilled by either prospect.

"Yes," Lady Dorothy said. "Van *the Beer Man*." The words were laced with distaste. "Exactly the image the Uplands should be cultivating." She turned to Van and stared at him a long moment. "Larvell," she said flatly in greeting without taking her eyes off Van.

"A pleasure to see you again, Lady," Larvell replied, ignoring or oblivious to the slight. "We've arranged for every comfort—"

"Come, Kyle," she cut in, "if we must ride in this monstrosity, let's find what comfort we can before this dust ruins our clothes." She took Kyle's arm and led her to the carriage, then waited impatiently for Johannas to offer his hand so she could ascend the stair leading into the enclosed seating area. As he closed the door behind the women, she called out through the window. "Don't forget my things."

Trent's look was one of horror as he saw how many trunks and suitcases were strapped to Lady Dorothy's carriage. It looked as though she intended to move to Empire City. Van, having loaded his share of carriages, helped the driver as Larvell and Owen quickly found other, less strenuous tasks to do.

Any hopes that Johannas would be an ally to Trent and Van in their quest to transfer the seemingly endless loads of luggage were quickly dashed. He lorded over the two of them, insisting that every parcel was treated with care and respect, all while managing to carry next to nothing himself. Van shed any sympathy he had for the man by his third load. By his fifth, he'd have liked to slap the man's other cheek and maybe add an elbow drop in for good measure. When they were finally ready, the sun was high and Van was sweating. He loaded the beer barrels last and might have crushed one or two of the Lady Dorothy's suitcases under them. Surely she couldn't keep track of every little thing.

Van climbed up onto the driver's perch, leaving as much space for Trent as possible given the relative narrowness of the carriage. Trent finished prepping the team of six horses, Owen and Larvell climbed into the seating area, and they rolled out onto the road towards Empire City. Van pretended not to notice when Trent turned back to give Johannas the finger as they headed down the hill towards the horizon.

...

It would take them two days to reach Empire City. The Uplands weren't far outside the hub of the Open Nations, though they were far less dense than some of the other lands. The one main road, the same Van had walked to get from Headwaters to Rockton, ran onwards to Empire City through lightly forested hills. It was well worn and cared for. No bandits would entertain the notion of attacking a caravan with a titan perched atop. Harassment from young wyverns and drunk orcs was always a possibility but Trent carried long poles to keep the former at bay and a bucket of fish heads to bribe the latter.

Van had clearly scored with the driver by helping him load the carriage. Trent repaid the favor by chattering incessantly the entire morning, loudly filling the air with stories of titan matches he'd seen. Van's interest waxed and waned. He'd been a huge fan of some titans like the Hellhound and the Savage when he was younger, but had stopped following the matches in the past few years. He wasn't sure Trent's stories, which seemed oddly focused on the footwear of the titans, were going to reignite his interest. As valuable as it was to know who fought barefoot and who wore boots, and what those various feet and boots looked like in vivid detail, Van was thinking his time might be better spent talking to Owen or Larvell about whom he was facing and how to not make an ass of himself.

The carriage jounced over every dip in the road. Van lacked Trent's seasoned sense of balance and bounced around, growing steadily more sore as the morning passed. When they stopped for a break and Owen asked Van if they could switch places, he jumped at the chance to get inside the seating area, which presumably had cushions.

It was a trap Van should have anticipated. Being stuck inside the carriage with Lady Dorothy was far worse than having a sore rear end. As soon as Van entered, she wrinkled her nose and asked them to open the windows, complaining of a sudden assault by the smell of beer. He sat self-consciously in the single titan-sized chair, facing Larvell, Kyle, and Lady Dorothy, his bulk eating up much of the available space in the cramped quarters.

Lady Dorothy orchestrated the conversation inside the moving carriage with the same ease and firmness Trent used to guide the horses. Much of it centered around her diplomatic capabilities and the many relationships she and she alone maintained on behalf of the Uplands. She showcased a deep knowledge of the history of the region, occasionally making snide comments and references that sailed right over Van's head, though he was pretty sure she was landing some shots on him.

Van at least had the sense to surrender. He smiled and nodded when appropriate, letting her soft blows glance off him with minimal injury. Larvell refused to give up his attempts at joining the conversation, which was really more of a lecture, and Lady Dorothy skewered him expertly at every turn. Eventually she quieted, insisting the dust was making her throat dry. Before falling silent and staring out the window, she left

Kyle with instructions to consider which suitors she'd like to meet first upon their arrival to Empire City.

They rode in silence for a short time before Larvell leaned forward and peered into Van's eyes. "I got word this morning the brackets are close to set."

"And?" Van had given little thought to how things would actually work at the tournament. They'd put him in a ring with someone. It would be bad. He would lose. Then he would come home.

"And they're doing what we expected. You're an unknown, which makes you a risk, but they don't figure you as much of a threat given that you only beat the Living Portrait to get into the tournament. There's probably a little worry that you're a sleeper, that we planned all this, so they probably won't just hand you to the Landshaker. That's good for us. They must be worried you were faking those dismal first few minutes against the Portrait." He gave a mocking smile. "Remember those? When you made a total ass of yourself?"

"What do you mean, 'hand me to the Landshaker'?"

"Single-elimination brackets of thirty-two. They're set by the Open Nations Wrestling Coalition. The ONWC is run by a handful of powerful nations. The Vantages, Valley of Sevens, Leatherrow, Dunham North and South. They'll listen to any nation if it shows up with cash. They give the easy matches to the richest nations so they make it past the first round. You should be atop the list of easy matches but, like I said, you make them nervous. You might still get an ONWC favorite, a good one, but not an impossible first-round match like the Landshaker or King Thad. Venerate Holland is in charge of the ONWC, and he'll set it up so their own guys don't face much of a real threat until late in the tournament. Even then, the outcomes can be bought and sold. Just ask King Thad how he won the last Headlock."

Van rubbed sweat from his face, ignoring the look of disgust from Lady Dorothy. "So…"

"So I don't know yet. Not that it will make much difference. I'd hope that you land someone from one of the fringe nations like Kassim Island or Barreli or Kisket. But those guys will be fed to the ONWC machine just like you will. Best we can hope for is you get someone like Elephant the Titan or Duke Roller on an off day. So far off they completely forget how to wrestle." He took off his hat and wrung it between his hands. "Once we know who you're facing, maybe Owen can give you some pointers. You showed a smidge of strength out there, certainly some endurance, but these guys have all been training. And they're motivated."

Lady Dorothy had turned back from the window. She fixed Van with a flat look. "They didn't just wander into a ring where they weren't invited."

"Wander in?" Van said. "I didn't wander in, I was forced—" He cut himself off when he saw the dark expression Kyle was flashing him, as though she were telling him to be quiet about her role in this. But screw her. She'd gotten him into this and had given him nothing in the way of help since. "Forced in the ring by her." He thrust his chin towards Kyle.

"Darling?" Lady Dorothy asked, surprised. "You had something to do with…this?" She rolled her eyes toward Van.

"Van's overstating things. We needed another titan to wrestle the Living Portrait. No one anticipated he'd win, let alone win with such…decisiveness…that there would be no other competition."

"And we are all left with an unexperienced titan at the helm? I would expect you more than anyone know how important our showing in the Headlock of Destiny is for our reputation."

Kyle shrugged. "As I said to Larvell, we shouldn't pretend the alternative was any better. We know the Living Portrait would have been the weakest titan in the tournament *and* prone to bribery. We don't know that about Van. Maybe he'll prove the doubters wrong."

Lady Dorothy snorted, indicating exactly what she thought of that idea—not exactly a ringing endorsement. No one raised a voice to defend Van. And he didn't quite feel up to defending himself. He'd save that for when he was back in the squared circle with another enraged titan looking to hurt him. He wouldn't have to wait long.

The carriage fell quiet aside from the clop of the horses' hooves and the rattle of the wheels as they kicked up clouds of dirt and dust that blew through the open windows. Van settled back in the seat. It would be a long and boring trip. Plenty of time to think about all the mistakes he'd made to land him here, rolling towards this titan-sized disaster.

Chapter 11

On the second evening of the seemingly endless journey, signs of Empire City's fringes began to appear. The woods gave way to farmland, which gave way to country manors. Then towns, the most diminutive of which dwarfed Headwaters. Traffic picked up even as the roads widened and eventually the carriage carrying the group sat in a line, waiting for a turn at every precious inch of clear right-of-way. Local folks peered out of windows at the travelers, perhaps hoping to see a favorite titan roll into town for the tournament. They probably wouldn't have recognized Van if he'd been standing on top of the carriage shouting his name.

Owen had surrendered the perch next to Trent the driver, so Van sat above the endless train of carts, carriages, and wagons. Despite his vantage point, Van smelled Empire City before he saw it, a breeze laden with exotic spices and perfumes, raw sewage, and caged animals nearly made him gag. The clean and clear mountain winds suddenly felt a lifetime away.

The sun had all but set, leaving only a pink glow on the horizon, when they topped a ridge and the city lay spread out before them. Van's breath caught as he took in its enormity. Empire City was a sea of lights, sparked in advance of the coming night. Van's eyes were immediately drawn, as all visitors' eyes must be, to the coliseum in the center of the sprawl. Even the tallest buildings couldn't compete with the scale of it. A huge open bowl, overflowing with light that poured out and up, chasing away the dark. The entire city seemed to bend to its gravity.

Once he was able to pull his eyes away, Van saw the other, smaller arenas. Three more in his line of sight, all aggressively fighting for attention. Lights shone, flags waved, anything to draw eyes and people to witness the coming spectacle. Titans squaring off, the best the Open Nations had to offer. Along with a single, deeply-out-of-his-depths moron from the Uplands.

The delegation had hardly spoken for the last day and night. They held true to form as the carriage rolled down the ridge. The only acknowledgement that their destination was in sight was a weary sigh from Trent. Even his endless parade of stories of famous titans' feet had dwindled. Lady Dorothy had kept her energy up for a while, but clearly didn't appreciate the close quarters and lack of comfort the carriage offered. Kyle had gamely engaged her for a time, but too had tired of it. Van knew little about Kyle and understood less, but even he could see the act she fed the Lady was not a perfect fit, at least not for long stretches of time. Owen had been a relentless grouch. Larvell had matched Owen for grumpiness, the only difference being while Owen glared out the window, mad at the world, Larvell glared at Van, somehow blaming him for his bum hand.

Van ignored the rest of the group, a skill he'd been employing for a day and a half. He had a creeping enthusiasm no one else seemed to share as they began the slow descent into the city limits. He was here, so he might as well keep his eyes open and come back to Headwaters with some interesting things to talk about. He didn't think anyone back there had ever been to Empire City. Maybe the brewery owner or the mayor. A dragon flew overhead, hinting at the wonders to come. Van let a private smile crack his face.

The city didn't disappoint. Its gates were wide open, no guards visible on its towering walls. A banner reading *Welcome to the Headlock of Destiny Tournament* hung low across the entry arch. Once inside, the carriage rolled through a sea of people, and Van gazed down at them in wonder. The tournament began tomorrow, and Empire City was ready for it. Within the first block, Van saw goblins rolling dice on the street corners and eyeing drunk tourists. Street performers summoned jinns from ornate ceramic vases and ordered displays of light and fire to draw coin from gathered crowds. A pair of orcs fought over a garbage can at the edge of an alley, and a crowd quickly formed around them and began placing bets with a fat man in a purple robe. Van saw elves, dwarves, fairies, and a pack of walking skeletons that everyone pointedly ignored. Another dragon streamed overhead, delivering wealthy passengers to their hotels and scheduled party appearances. And everywhere were titans.

Van had never seen so many ten-men in one place. It seemed at least one towered over the crowds on every street. Some were glammed out in tightly-fitted, sparkling clothes, gold chains, and tinted glasses rendered ornamental by the falling darkness. Some wore foreign garb that looked like exotic pajamas. Still others wore simpler clothes not unlike those of the people around them. Van saw one ten-man walking down the crowded street completely naked. Apparently no one had the guts to enforce any sort of decorum when the violator was a descendant of giants.

Some manner of beer, wine, or liquor was in nearly every hand. Clouds of smoke, tobacco and more potent weed blends, filled the air. Vendors had claimed every space between the buildings, hawking their clothing, jewelry, souvenirs, drinks, smoke, strange-looking twisted meat on a stick that Van hoped was not lizard.

Some vendors loudly proclaimed to possess magical items—glass balls, rings, hats, ceramic and wooden idols—that were tagged with prices higher than a barrel of Kingsland. A thousand other things, many of which mystified Van. He had a sinking feeling that a smarter titan would have brought some money with him. All he had were two barrels of beer and some debatably clean clothes.

Luckily, Trent and the horses knew the way to their hotel. The crowds were reluctant to part, but Trent kept a smooth, professional pace that set the appropriate tone: fast enough that everyone recognized they weren't stopping for anyone yet slow enough to allow even the most arrogant and drunk of the partiers to stumble out of the way. Van did notice Trent didn't push too close to a couple titans that took their time stepping aside, their eyes pressing Van in an unspoken challenge, which he ignored.

After nearly an hour navigating the city, the carriage pulled up to a hotel on a quiet, well-lit street. A four-story structure of white walls and arched doorways, it would have served as a palace in Headwaters. Here in Empire City it seemed of middling opulence. Judging by Lady Dorothy's sniff as she looked at it, she would have preferred to stay closer to the higher end of excessive splendor.

A small army of footmen materialized to help with the bags, several quietly greeting Trent by name. Van took a deep breath and jumped lightly to the ground. He turned back immediately to collect his barrels from the top of the carriage. They were his only currency right now. He wasn't letting any footman get a hold of them. The rest of the Uplands party was already headed in the front entryway.

Van followed Owen as the ten-man limped up a wide set of stairs at the back of the hotel lobby. They turned down a hall lined with doors. Van tried not to gawk. He'd never seen a building this large. How would he remember which door led to his room? Would they have a room for him here? Was he supposed to find his own? At least the halls and doors were tall and wide, sufficient for a titan to navigate without ducking. Nothing in Headwaters was this size.

Lady Dorothy was led through a door off the hallway, her disapproving gaze lingering on the light fixtures. The others followed, and Van trailed in behind them, trying to be as quiet as possible. He had to turn sideways to make it through the doorway with a barrel under each arm. They clustered in a large suite around the head doorman as he explained the accommodations. He finished quickly and everyone promptly scattered among murmurs about the late hour. Van was left looking at the common room of the suite, packed with furniture that seemed design to fit both titans and people. There were a pair of overstuffed sofas, a few fancy wooden chairs that seemed to have reinforced legs, and a small writing desk. He looked up bewildered at the doorman, who smiled and carefully directed his hand over his left shoulder.

Van could see there were several bedchambers radiating off the common room. Two had larger doors than the others, presumably titan-sized. Owen entered one and closed the door. Van assumed he got the other.

"Any bags, sir?" the doorman asked.

Van set a barrel down and raised his small satchel as evidence. "Just this."

The doorman nodded. "Enjoy your stay." Then he vanished.

Van picked up the barrels and sidled into his room. It was fairly unremarkable, though it was nice to see a bed that would fit him instead of a mattress on the floor. Van lay down, his thoughts swirling. How was he going to handle his fight tomorrow? What should he do tonight? He shouldn't open one of the barrels yet, though he was dying for a beer. Maybe there was a hotel bar. Of course there was the whole problem of him not having any money.

He just lay there for twenty minutes or so, enjoying the stillness after the relentless motion of the carriage. Finally, when the boredom became oppressive, he stood and walked out into the common room. He was just in time to see the Lady Dorothy leaving, Larvell behind her. Van walked over to the window and looked down on the quiet street.

Trent was riding away with the carriage. Kyle and Owen were outside, standing under a streetlight, having what looked to be a heated discussion. The window glass muffled their voices. After a moment, Owen turned and walked away, an expression of disgust visible on his face even from the second-story hotel window. Kyle stared after him a moment, then whirled and stomped the other way down the street.

And just like that, Van was alone with no idea what he was doing. As he looked out on the street, suddenly lonely in its empty pools of light, Van felt a surge of homesickness. The match with Richard the Living Portrait had felt like a cruel joke, like the world having a laugh at Van's expense. His winning the fight had at first seemed only to prolong the jest. But now, looking out at the smallest part of a city made of thousands upon thousands of lights, a city gathered to see the violent clash of titans, anything funny about the situation withered and disappeared. Somehow, when he wasn't paying attention, destiny, or something far stupider but just as strong, had placed Van into a headlock and dragged him into a fight he was wildly unprepared for.

Van folded his trembling hands together to still them, then he reached out and pulled the curtain closed. He'd never been so afraid in his life.

Chapter 12

Larvell was the only one waiting for Van in their suite's main room when Van awoke late the next morning. His attempts to forget where he was and why he was here had led to a poor night's rest. He'd kept waking to the sound of a phantom bell followed by closing footsteps. He'd chased the tail end of a real sleep across the long morning, watching the sun stretch across his blankets and thinking about Annie.

Larvell greeted Van with his usual surly gaze. He said nothing as Van picked up a barrel and tucked it under his arm. Van already wore his uniform, wrinkled from being stuffed in a bag for the journey here. He'd decided before going to bed that he'd walk straight into the ring, lose, then try to hitch a ride back home so he didn't have to wait for the rest of these assholes to wrap up their business in Empire City.

Together he and Larvell left the hotel, Van glaring down at Larvell's hat as the Uplands Wrestling Coalition's only representative at the tournament led their out-of-place entrant towards his slaughter. No sign of Kyle, Owen, or the Lady Dorothy. The street outside the hotel was even quieter than it'd been the night before. Between Van's long strides and Larvell's hurried steps, the sun-kissed cobblestones flew by. The few people out and about were exotically dressed. Smells came and went like an assault. For a moment, the odor of excrement overpowered the street. Van looked down an alley to see a giant pile of dragonshit, the offender strutting proudly away.

"There are five rings in Empire City," Larvell was explaining. "For the first round, it's two days with one match at each of the four outer ones and then afternoon and evening doubleheaders at the coliseum, more or less. You're facing the Ram at Palace West. Don't let the name fool you. It's the shittiest of them all. Try to ignore the sound of the walls cracking and raining stone down on the crowds while the Ram is pounding you into the mat."

Van wasn't shocked by anything the man said anymore. "You're the worst fucking manager ever," he said.

"That's because I'm not your manager, Van. And you're not a wrestler. You're an ass, who's about to be shown the door the Living Portrait should have shown you, and I'm an idiot who didn't leave himself an escape plan and got stuck with you."

Larvell took his hat off to wring it in his hands. Van stared at the sun gleaming from his bald spot and resisted the urge to smash his barrel right on top of it. Which of course would be an incredible waste of Kingsland.

"What can you tell me about the Ram?" Van asked. He needed to get some value from this jerk.

For several steps Larvell ignored the question. Then he spoke reluctantly, as though he had better things to do. "He's not quite as big as you but he's fast as dragonfire. Rumor is he's the offspring of the titan Sandar Lynn and an actual ram. You'll see what I mean right away. A ram's head. Huge horns. Hoofed feet. And the horns are his game. He just charges, knocks people on their ass, drives them into the mat. If you don't get low, he'll toss you up in the air with his horns. Then you're screwed. If you stay low, he'll just batter you into a bloody mess and smear you all over the mat." Larvell looked at Van. "He's certainly not the best wrestler in the tournament, not by a long shot, but he's plenty good enough. Coresite Mount has a lot of scratch to throw around and they bring a huge contingent of fans. Probably bought the bracket slot opposite you after they heard about Owen's injury. They're hungry for wins. Hell, maybe they're hiring."

"So, how do I stop him?"

"I don't know. Owen never faced him."

The crowd grew thicker as they passed onto the main thoroughfare of the city. Van could smell meat cooking and hear the shouting vendors competing for coin.

"Well, what would you tell Owen if he was?"

"Owen didn't need me to tell him what to do. He did his own scouting, his own planning, and earned every match he won." Larvell took a few more steps, hopped over a passed out drunk lying in the street, sighed and continued. "I did see him get beat once, the Ram. Elephant the Titan kept him off balance by staying close to him. Don't give him space to build up speed. And don't let him square up to you. He's a hard nut to crack, because every inch of him is built to muscle those horns into you, but if you can disrupt his base you can do more to dictate the fight." He gestured ahead. "We're almost there. Put your game face on."

Van wasn't sure he had a game face, and settled for the standard I-wish-I-was-anyplace-but-here look he'd been perfecting since he'd first been called into the brewery office a short week ago.

Larvell and Van pushed through the thickening crowds as they moved down the open street towards the huge structure ahead. High walls rose above neighboring buildings. Even from this distance, Van could see cracks in the façade of Palace West spidering across its yellowing stones. The noise was growing, a crowd of thousands ready to see Van eat the canvas.

The crowd streaming past showed a heavy bias towards bright red clothing. Van realized many wore red scarves, signifying their loyalty to Coresite Mount. He groaned nervously. More than a few of the fans had painted their faces white and several had twisted paper horns on their heads. Many wore cowbells that rattled around their necks as they staggered by, smirking at Van. He saw none of the dark blue and yellow Uplands colors amidst the throng. Looked like this would be a hostile crowd, not that it mattered.

When Van had entered Scott Hall back in Rockton, he'd been met with indifference. Entering the Palace West was a different sort of experience. The second he passed through the stadium gates, the crowd greeted him with a chorus of boos. Thousands upon thousands of drunken, red-scarved hooligans showered him with anger. If Larvell hadn't kept walking forward, Van might have turned on his heels. Chalked it up as a loss without suffering the pain. Instead he kept following his jerk of a manager, eyes low. Luckily no one had quite enough courage to spit or throw anything. That would probably change soon though.

At least Van had someone to show him where he was going this time, and Larvell led him straight to the center of the stadium. As Van drew close to the ring and looked around, his feelings of unease grew more intense. His only public wrestling match had been in Scott Hall, a structure of well-fitted fresh wood. Palace West was all finely ground graying limestone and mortar. Long steps radiated outwards from the ring in every direction, packed with fans in red howling at Van. In the center of the stadium floor, four thick pillars rose up, holding an elevated slab of grey stone that had been fitted with a wooden mat, the only thing that seemed new in the whole place. The corner turnbuckles were affixed to the aged stone pillars. There were cracks everywhere. Dark moss that looked like blood covered the base of the pillars and the ground around them. It was like something from an old story, a place where primitives would have dragged enemies for sacrifice to their gods, spilling their lives across the stone as the watching masses cheered. If that were the case, the place hadn't changed much.

Van put that dark thought aside and planted his barrel on the apron just outside the turnbuckles. He climbed up onto the stone slab. The angry roar of the crowd grew as he entered the ring and nodded to the referee. He tried to shake off the noise but it was like a storm in his head. He looked around, trying to calm himself, as he swung his arms awkwardly, an imitation of the warm-ups he'd seen the Living Portrait do before their match. The ring was just a few paces across. The space seemed far too small for two titans. He supposed that was the point.

As Van scanned the crowd, he saw a massive, hooded figure in the front row across from where he'd entered the ring. The figure had his head down, and a black cloak covered every inch of him aside from a white...was that a muzzle? It was the Ram, waiting patiently to destroy Van. Steam rose from beneath his hood as the titan exhaled. He was surrounded by a team of handlers, all in red, all glaring at Van with malicious grins.

Meanwhile, Larvell had made himself scarce. Van wasn't even sure which direction he'd gone. Where was Owen? Or Kyle? He certainly hadn't expected Lady Dorothy to show up at his fight, but not even those two? His corner stood empty aside from his lonely beer barrel. The Uplands had neatly and collectively separated themselves from the embarrassment that was Van. The crowd was almost universally in red, hollering at Van, blood up and well drunk by the smell.

Was there not a single fan from the Uplands here? Van was getting pissed. They were asking him to go it alone. He'd been brought here as the butt of some joke he didn't even get. He could hear the words of the Ram's fans over the boos of the masses. The most vocal were those sitting behind and above the Ram himself.

"You're dead, Beer Man. You just don't know it yet."

"They're gonna roll you out of here in that barrel."

"No one stands against the Ram." This last evolved into a chant that some of the crowd picked up on.

A tanned, snappily dressed announcer stepped to the center of the ring. He raised a hand and quieted the crowd with practiced ease. "Welcome to the Headlock of Destiny Tournament!" The crowd roared and he waited for them to settle before continuing. "The premier sporting event of the Open Nations. A contest of strength and determination. The battles of our champions, who will determine which of the Nations are worthy of pride" —here the crowd cheered again— "and which are worthy of disdain."

"Fuck the Uplands!" someone shouted.

The announcer let it play out a bit, then drew the crowd back in. "In the corner with the beer barrel, new titan blood for the tournament, the ten-man who came out of nowhere to defeat Richard the Living Portrait, hailing from the Uplands, Van the Beer Man!" The crowd roared with anger and drunkenness.

"And in the other corner, a mighty titan of unmatched strength, son of the tournament champion Sandar Lynn, with victories over the Hill Giant, Stone Wilhelm, Svennet the Skull Skraper, the Armbreaker, and Evan the Crusher. This titan reached the round of sixteen at the last Headlock of Destiny, and today he begins this year's campaign. Ladies and Gentlemen, the hard-charging, never-stopping, relentless champion of Coresite Mount, the Ram!"

The crowd exploded, stamping their feet and shouting at the top of their lungs. The cowbells Van had seen among the crowd earlier rang out. The sound washed over Van like a tide. Several of the more fervent fans violently butted heads with each other, spilling shocking amounts of blood across their painted faces. Van was suddenly sure the entire place would collapse, burying him in thousands of tons of stone with an army of men and women who hated him.

The Ram threw aside the black cloak and rose to his feet. Or, Van corrected himself, hooves. The black hooves rose to strong, bony legs covered in white fur. His torso was the most manlike thing about him, massive and musclebound, though coated in thin, short fur. His head was where any resemblance to a man ended. His long face culminated in a thick, wet black snout. Two enormous horns curved backward and down from the top of his head and looped forward near his armpits. Steam shot out of his massive nostrils as he stared at Van with black eyes. The Ram had painted red stripes across the white fur under his eyes and his brown, bone-colored horns had red striping along their lengths.

The Ram bent his knees, his leg muscles bulging, and leapt from the stone floor up over the top rope and into the ring. His hooves clattered noisily on the mat as he landed. Van stared at the titan dumbly. This *had* to be his first and only tournament opponent? He couldn't start with something normal?

Van took a deep breath, waiting for his fear to subside. As the referee crawled gracelessly into the ring, Van heard a sudden renewed burst of enthusiasm from the crowd and saw a flurry of activity out of the corner of his eye. A group of Ram fans, five or so men with white-painted faces, were stealing his barrel of beer. The crowd cheered them on. "Hey," Van said, his voice squeaking out weakly. "Hey, don't touch that!"

They ignored him beyond a few furtive glances in his direction. Van stepped towards them, but they managed to get enough hands under the heavy barrel to pull it off the platform and clumsily careen back towards their seats behind the Ram. The crowd whooped with delight.

"Give that back!" Van called after them. They laughed, basking in their successful heist and other Ram fans slapped them on the back as they went by.

Van felt his anger swelling, crowding out the fear that had gripped him moments ago. He looked at the announcer and the referee. The announcer shrugged. The referee didn't even bother to do that. Van shifted his gaze over to the Ram again, only this time the blood pounding in his head banged a more primal drum. He was furious. He clenched his hands into fists and the bell sounded.

Chapter 13

The Ram charged straight away, just as Van expected. Van met him with a left jab right between the eyes. The impact of his knuckles on the Ram's skull coursed through his body. It stopped the Ram dead in his tracks. Van slid to the right, grabbed one of the Ram's long horns, and slammed the Ram into the mat, bending his knees as he put every ounce of strength he had into the move.

The Ram bounced off the mat, quickly rolled away, and found his feet again.

Van smirked as the crowd quieted. *Steal my fucking beer?*

The Ram charged again. This time, he turned his head, using a massive horn to knock away another jab from Van, and Van was left exposed. The Ram squared and drove his head into Van, knocking him backwards. The horns were as hard as steel, and Van's shoulder throbbed from the impact. He managed to push the Ram off to the side and whirl away.

Again the Ram charged but Van was able to catch his horns, one in each hand. The Ram had leaned so far forward in his charge that his arms were out of reach. Van's arms trembled as he clung to the horns and both titans set their feet, driving into each other, seeking dominance. Van gritted his teeth tightly, let out a low growl. The Ram's dark eyes locked on Van's; his snout twisted into something Van had to assume was a sneer. The steam from the Ram's nostrils floated into the air between them. In some distant place at the back of Van's mind, the crowd was roaring.

Van tried to hurl the Ram to the side, but the Ram was ready. He tried the other way, but he couldn't shake the relentless press of the horns. They were locked together, straining with all their might in the center of the ring, when their combined force tore the plywood and canvas mat into pieces below them. Jagged edges of wood and nails littered the suddenly treacherous floor. Van had no time to figure out what the hell had happened before the Ram jumped up and drove at Van.

Van caught the Ram's left horn with his left hand, pulled the Ram across his body, and punched him in the side of the head with a hard right hook. He followed it with a shove and the Ram stumbled on the splintered wood beneath his hooves and fell on his side. Van used the moment to catch his breath.

The Ram gave his head a hard shake and stood up among the ruins of the platform. He kicked away a broken board and slowly approached Van. Van backed up slightly to set his feet among the shattered remnants of the ring's floor, and the Ram caught him with a quick whirl of his horns. Van fell back on his ass. He looked up and saw the horns descending. He rolled, barely avoiding the crash as the Ram hit the mat, sending up a spray of splinters.

As Van stumbled to his feet, the Ram backed up to the corner against a pillar, steam billowing from his nostrils. Van could have sworn his black eyes were turning red. The Ram clicked his hoofs against the mat and the crowd immediately responded, clapping out the beat. Van got a bad feeling as he realized he was on the opposite side of the ring, a full twenty feet away. *Don't give him the space to build up speed. And don't let him square up to you.* Van had been given the tiniest crumb of advice, and he couldn't even follow it.

The Ram charged, building up incredible speed over the short space. Van dove into the scattered remains of the mat, rolled forward, clipped the charging Ram's legs. The Ram's hooves caught Van hard in the side as he went past, but the Ram lost his footing, flew into the air, and crashed his horns into the stone pillar at the far corner of the ring.

The pillar split with an enormous cracking sound, tumbled over, and pulled the turnbuckles and ropes down into the debris, raising a cloud of dust and leaving long tendrils of ropes across the ruins of the platform. The referee was on his back, fighting to disentangle himself from the mess, but the Ram found his feet and snorted hot and loud at the destruction.

The Ram's legions of fans howled as the Ram turned back to glare at Van. They'd come to see a tournament victory, and they smelled blood in the water. Who could stand against their titan, who was tearing the ring to pieces, literally bringing down the house? Somewhere out there, they were drinking Van's beer. Passing it out to their friends. One big happy family, united in their desire to see Van's ass kicked and this monster across from him showered in…oats, or whatever the fuck it viewed as a delicacy. Van's shoulder still ached from the Ram's horns, his hands were beyond weary from holding off his charges. His side radiated pain from the hooves.

The Ram charged again, hooves clomping on the broken boards. Van feinted left, then ducked right. He managed to get just outside the range of the horns and grip one as the Ram passed. Van turned, pulling hard as he did, using the Ram's speed against him. He spun, once, twice, then Van heaved the Ram like a barrel, throwing him up and out of the ring. The Ram crashed to the stone steps far up in the stands.

The crowd screamed, scrambled to get away from the angry titan. The Ram sat crumpled a moment, his eyes locked on Van. As he rose in a furious cloud of steamy breath, his fans cleared him a path back to the ring.

The Ram let out an enormous bleat, an eerie sound that was somehow as powerful as it was ridiculous. He charged down the steps, chips of stone flying under his clattering hooves. He ran as if the broken stone steps were a perfectly smooth surface, the slope helping him reach an incredible speed as he raced back toward the ring.

Van was out of ideas. He set his feet and hoped something would come to him. Something other than a massive, unstoppable force and an emergency run to a hospital.

But as the Ram reached the floor of the stadium, he swerved unexpectedly and drove his horns directly into a corner pillar, this time striking it below the elevated platform. It shattered under the force of his charge, and the entire ring collapsed to the side, sending Van tumbling towards the Ram. The noise of the crowd was deafening. Van saw the ref careen past him and tumble out onto the floor. Great plumes of dust rose all around them. Another pillar collapsed outwards. Van scrambled to find his feet where the tilted surface met the ground, then swore as he realized he'd lost the Ram in the chaos.

The sound of hoofbeats gave Van only a second to brace himself before he was nailed in the back by the full force of the Ram's horns. Robbed of even the breath to cry out in agony, Van crumbled to the ground, and lost sight of the Ram again.

Van squeezed his eyes shut, dying for breath. Every inch of him wanted to quit. And he would. But he had a little more work to do first. If the Ram was coming, let him come. Van was sick of playing everyone else's game. He'd landed exactly one real blow in this fight, and that was right between the Ram's eyes, the only time Van dictated what happened. Other than that, he'd just endured a relentless assault. An assault on his dignity, his freedom, his life. He was sick of it. This was going to end right now, one way or another. He opened his eyes and stood.

Van couldn't see through the billowing dust around him, but he collected himself and leapt up into the air anyway. He raised both hands high above his head in a hammer position. The world seemed to slow as he hung in the air. Just as he'd anticipated, the Ram appeared in the cloud in front of him, horns lowered, barreling forward. Van came down with both fists, driving them down into the Ram's skull, even as the Ram's horns slammed into him, sending him flying backwards to smash into the lowest step. The thunderous crash of the collision echoed through Palace West.

The crowd fell quiet. An enormous dust cloud washed over the center of the stadium, covering the broken remnants of the ring. The single standing pillar jutted upwards from the cloud. Men and women who had wisely covered their beers to keep the dust out slowly removed their hands and stole sips as they waited for resolution. Nothing moved on the stadium floor.

The first object to become visible was the referee, covered in dust except for his bulging wide eyes. He looked every which way as he hunted through the wreckage for the titans. There was a collective groan as the dust began to settle, revealing a sprawled-out Ram, face down in the rubble. Next was Van the Beer Man, slumped against a stone step, eyes closed.

There was a murmur in the crowd. What if both titans were down for the count? The referee looked back and forth, from one to the other, the same questions burning in his mind.

The Ram moved his head sideways and a burst of steam erupted from his nostrils. He staggered, first to his knees, and then to his hooves. The crowd let out a massive cheer, but it quickly evaporated when the titan toppled back to the ground. The referee clambered over the wreckage toward the center of where the ring used to be.

Van could see the Ram's tumble from the corner of his eye. Would the Ram's last stagger count as a win? No. Van wouldn't let that happen. He used a forearm to push his weight off the stone steps. Pulled one foot underneath his bruised and battered body, then the other. With a massive howl even he didn't know he had in him, he lurched to his feet and stood. He spat blood out onto the ground. The ref hurried over to Van, seized his sweaty arm, and raised it in victory. The stadium was utterly silent.

Van pulled his arm from the ref's grip. He stumbled over the broken boards and crumbled stone of the ring, dust falling off of him as he strode, and mounted the stone steps of the stadium. The bewildered crowd scattered before his approach.

Van closed in on one particular circle of fans. A few of them ran screaming but several others stood dumfounded as Van approached and loomed over them, sweat and dust dark in his furrowed brow. He pointed a massive dirty finger at the center of their circle.

"That's *my* barrel," he said.

The terrified Ram fans nodded. Van saw the front of one's red trousers darken with piss as his fear got the best of him. They were not so brave now that their titan champion no longer stood between them and this ten-man from the hills of nowhere. Van gave a single sharp nod, and the men split the circle in front of him. He stepped forward and grabbed the barrel, tucked it under his arm, and made his way through the shuffling, dumbstruck crowd and out of the stadium.

Chapter 14

Holy shit, did Van's back hurt. As he made his way down the street, he alternated between keeping it straight and slouching to see if either way relieved the ache. It didn't seem to matter. The damage the Ram had done followed him around as he wandered aimlessly through the streets around Palace West.

Van was having trouble finding stable ground. The whole experience had been insane. The crowds, the fight, the pain, the victory. And suddenly he was still here in Empire City, alone amongst the masses. He'd actually won. Won a match in the Headlock of Destiny Tournament. That was insane.

Van had no interest in seeing Larvell again so he could get an earful about how he cheated his way into another match where he didn't belong or how any success Van managed in the tournament was fleeting. He was annoyed with Kyle and Owen, too, for leaving him high and dry before the match.

Other things also fought for space in his crowded head as he felt the stones below his heavy bare feet, his massive shoulders rolling as he walked, the heavy barrel held loosely and easily under one arm, cradled against his giant hip. There was the way he'd felt in the ring. He'd felt alive, truly present in a way he'd never felt before. That feeling was fading as he put distance between himself and the whole experience, and he wasn't sure if that temporary high was something worth chasing or not. He didn't know what he wanted...beyond a beer. He definitely wanted a beer.

But somehow setting his barrel down in the middle of the street and drinking it by himself didn't seem the right move.

Van watched as an untethered goat strolled past and into an alley. He fought a sudden temptation to call after it and tell it that he had just laid out its bigger brother. As he looked back to the street, he saw a halfling stood boldly in his path. Van stared a moment. He'd rarely seen the race. They were similar to humans, only about two-thirds the size, which meant the little guy barely reached Van's waist. They were creatures of large appetites known for traveling and trouble. This one wore some sort of foreign garb of a sandy color, many folds of cloth wrapped tightly about his body. He had several pouches slung over his shoulders. His bronze, unshaven face was youthful and sunny, and he had wild, wiry hair not unlike Van's.

The halfling grinned. "Hey, titan. You won me money." He bowed at the waist. "I am Rakesh," he said proudly, "the best gambler in Empire City."

Van gave him a long look, then replied, "So buy me a beer."

Rakesh's smile grew. "I will happily buy you many beers, Van the Beer Man. It is but a short walk to a welcoming place." He looked around. "This part of Empire City is not the best, I think. The goblins watch us from the alleys." He glanced up at Van. "Or at least they watch me. I'm guessing they'd leave you alone."

Van nodded and fell into step with Rakesh, who lit a thin cigarette as they walked, leaving a trial of fragrant smoke behind them. "You hail from Headwaters, Van the Beer Man?" the halfling asked. "I have been to nearly all of the Open Nations, but not yet there."

"You've been to Coresite Mount?" Van asked, chuckling as he watched a group of distraught Ram fans arguing in the streets.

Rakesh chuckled. "I have. It is a place of great pride. They have very high opinions of themselves and very low opinions of others. It makes them terrible gamblers. When the line on you, who were to me as to everyone else an unknown before today, moved into the ridiculous category, I cheerfully laid down my marker. Many will be returning to Coresite Mount with the double sting of a first-round tournament loss and a lighter purse."

"So you follow the tournament closely?" Van asked.

"I endeavor to follow it as closely as possible. By virtue of the holy bracket, I will make more money this week than in the rest of the year, proving my luck holds. Every serious gambler of the Open Nations is here, and many from beyond."

Van grunted as he ducked under a wooden sign jutting out from a doorway. He knew others in Headwaters gambled on titan matches, but he'd never really taken to it. He hadn't given any thought to the idea that it might be at a whole different scale out here. "So who do I fight next?"

"Well, firstly, be aware that the ONWC is known to change the bracket mid-tournament, so nothing is certain. That in itself is the topic of many bets. They are supposed to set the seeding for the thirty-two competing titans based on the schedule up to the regionals, but they have their favorites and they shift the brackets to protect them. They pretend they lost paperwork or forgot to tally victories. They have so many excuses ready to go, no one even bothers to hold them to any degree of honesty anymore." He took a long drag off the cigarette. "But, to answer your question, you are scheduled to face the winner of the fight between Panam Manley and Slingshot Kohn. They fight even now at the Stomping Grounds and I, along with the rest of Empire City, eagerly await the result."

"When?"

"Any minute."

"No," Van said, "when's *my* fight?"

The halfling stopped and looked up at him. Van stopped, too, and the crowds of fight fans flowed around them. "You are a curiosity, Van the Beer Man. Most titans are carefully guided and coached through the tournament. They do not walk the streets, seeking the guidance of degenerate gamblers. But, again to answer your question, whomever you fight, it will almost definitely be within a day or two at most. They can tinker only so much with the schedules. They must keep the matches going to keep the crowds entertained. The finals will be on the seventh day."

"Who's going to win? Between Panam What's-it and Slingshot guy?"

"Panam Manley is heavily favored," Rakesh said, turning and continuing down the crowded street. "I did not like the lines much either way so I did not lay on it. But he will win."

"So what's his deal? I've never heard of him."

"The people of Palos Soros would be upset to hear that. He is a rising star in the west. Some have placed on him to win the tournament, though it is certainly a long shot versus the Landshaker or King Thad or Billy Blades. I do not know him very well. There will be others who can describe him better where we are headed."

"Which is?"

"Only the finest gambling establishment in Empire City." Rakesh made a sweeping gesture with his hand as they rounded a corner. Their destination was not marked by any sign or grand entryway, but rather a large crowd of men smoking cigarettes and arguing in the street near a doorway. As Van watched, young boys and girls raced in and out with small pieces of paper clutched in their hands, darting through the bottleneck with practiced ease.

The crowd parted before the diminutive Rakesh with nods and smiles as though he was well known amongst them. Van received considering looks but they likewise made room for him to duck through a dark doorway.

The interior of the gambling hall was huge, extending farther back than Van could see. There were several bars, clusters of tables, vendor stalls with clothing, crafts, and food, and more than one large chalkboard covered in marks in front of which lively debates were taking place. High windows along the walls let in pockets of sunlight, adding to the impression that this was many different places together under one roof. A diverse crowd packed the large space. There were a good number of halflings, several dwarves, who were shorter and stouter than the halflings, and a few willowy elves with their customary aloof expressions, all studying the boards and waving their purses about. Van saw more than one titan looming over the rest, weaving their way through the crowd.

Rakesh led Van to the nearest bar, a beautiful wooden structure that looked out of place on the dingy floor. It had an impressive line of barrels stacked around it, however, with a few nameplates that Van recognized. A dwarven bartender stood atop a box behind the bar, a gleam in his eyes as he watched Van approach. He had a thick beard, typical of dwarves, though his was tightly trimmed. Probably kept it from steeping in the beer he served.

"Who's your friend, Rakesh?" the dwarf asked.

"Van the Beer Man," Rakesh called out loudly, "fresh off a tournament victory."

The bartender offered Van a smile as he handed a frothing glass of dark beer to an elf who, by the uneven way he raised it to his lips, looked like he'd had a few already. "Been hearing your name an awful lot these last twenty minutes or so, Beer Man. I'm Rockhammer." He gestured across his line-up of barrels. "What can I pour for you? First one on the house, of course."

Van scrutinized the barrels with a professional eye as he slid his own barrel to the ground and sat on it with the practiced ease of a brewery man. He sighed as the pain in his back faded slightly with his weight off his feet. In the ring, he was a novice. At the bar, he was a pro. "Give me an Ocean Pale while I think about it."

"Sure," Rockhammer replied. He poured out a titan-size mug of golden ale topped with a rocky head. As he handed it over, his eyes strayed towards the barrel parked under Van. "What you got there?"

Van took a huge drink of the beer. No one could beat Headwaters for taste, but the Lone Coast certainly had a touch. Everything they brewed tasted fresh and sunny. For the first time today, Van felt good. He gave the barrel between his legs a soft slap and shrugged. "I'm not sure you'd be interested."

The bartender laughed. "Beer is my living, and I *am* interested."

"This is a fresh barrel of Kingsland Ale, pulled right off the line about three days ago."

His eyes widened. "It is not."

Van finished his beer with a long pull and handed the glass to the dwarf to refill. "It is indeed."

The dwarf stared at the barrel, then back at Van. He shook his head. "So what do you want for it?" He wiped his hands clean with a towel, then leaned forward on the bar across from Van. "I could pay money, of course, but a prize like this is best exchanged in *barter*."

Van smiled. "I couldn't agree more."

The bartering commenced. Rockhammer tried to pawn off some local Derry barrels to Van first, trying to overwhelm him with quantity like Van was a rookie.

Van laughed him off and pressed for more info on his premium stock. He was holding some amazing barrels. In addition to a fresh Crater Ale with their brewmaster's seal on it, he had three barrels of Ocean Stout, an impossible-to-find brew south of Lone Coast.

Rakesh, who had pulled up a stool to watch, chose to weigh in on Van's side. "Let's not pretend this barrel is created equal to all others of Kingsland. This specific barrel is the one and only to be carried into the ring by the mighty titan Van the Beer Man. Who not only completely annihilated the heavily favored Ram but also climbed into the stands to retrieve this barrel from a pack of thieving Coresite Mounters, killing several men in the process."

Van looked sidewise at him. "I didn't kill anyone."

"With all due respect, Van, our dwarven friend here can choose to take your word for that, or he can tell whatever tale he would like that increases the prestige of this particular barrel. I imagine this is the kind of barrel one keeps long after it is empty, perhaps for a table or a stool built for titans—certainly the kind of piece that sparks the interest and invites customers into any upstanding establishment."

Van grunted. "I like the way you think, Rakesh."

Rockhammer peered at Rakesh under a furrowed, furry brow. "I'll confess I do, too, though you are driving up the price for me right now."

Van eyed the dwarf. "How about a straight exchange—the Kingsland for the Crater Ale, plus you open another Ocean Pale right now and pour for the three of us the rest of the afternoon?" Van looked around the spacious hall, wondering at the strange allure of the capital city. "And for anyone else who wants some and isn't a jerk about it."

When Rockhammer nodded, Van reached out to shake his hand. The dwarf ignored Van's hand and grabbed Van's beard, giving it a formal tug. After a moment's hesitation, Van carefully did the same to the dwarf, which apparently sealed the deal. Van moved the Kingsland behind the bar and helped himself to the Crater barrel. A fresh pour of Ocean Pale waited for him when he bellied back up to the bar.

Rakesh was looking across the room at one of the clusters of animated discussion around a chalkboard. "With that done, Van, perhaps our friend would watch your barrel while we take a short recess to check the latest tournament results."

Van nodded, picked up his mug, and followed the halfling across the gambling hall.

Chapter 15

Van was on the receiving end of smiles and backslaps as he walked through the crowd of gamblers. They liked having him there. He felt a twinge of regret that the feeling had been such a rarity in his life so far. Maybe there was something to this world of wrestling. He had a sudden flashback to the Ram pounding down the stadium's stone steps towards him. Maybe not quite worth the price, but at least the average person here was treating him better than the Uplands contingent.

"So that's the bracket?" Van asked as they approached the chalkboard. The board was dominated by a single elimination tournament bracket with thirty-two slots. Van could see where they'd crossed out the Ram and advanced Van's name to the next bracket. It seemed Van the Beer Man had stuck as his official tournament name. He wasn't sure he liked it, but no one had exactly asked him what he thought anyway.

Sure enough, Rakesh had been right: Panam Manley had beaten Slingshot Kohn. And a titan by the name of the Wave Rider had defeated Marvell Sugarman. A list of the first-round matches were below the bracket, with odds on every possible bet Van could imagine for each match. Surrounding the tidy bracket was a mess of dashed lines and numbers, half-erased odds and initials. A woman who looked perfectly ordinary aside from her blue skin was tallying a complicated series of bets. Van looked closely at the four remaining matches for the day.

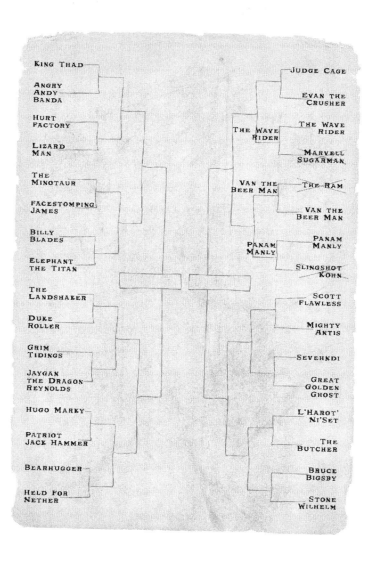

King Thad was headlining the main event against Angry Andy Banda tonight. Scott Flawless would fight the Mighty Antis on the undercard. The afternoon doubleheader, which looked to be going on right now, was Judge Cage versus Evan the Crusher and the Patriot Jack Hammer against Hugo Marky.

"What's going to happen there?" Van asked Rakesh, pointing to Judge Cage's match.

"Judge Cage." The halfling had another lit cigarette in the hand with his beer mug and a coin in the other, which he kept dancing across his knuckles. He studied the board with bright eyes. "Won't be interesting at all. Evan the Crusher is from Dunham North, and he's a big one, but he's got nothing on Empire City's own. You've heard of Judge Cage?"

"Just the name."

"He's not just a titan—he's the head of the Empire City Guard, which is one of many law and order forces within Empire City. He has two-hundred-or-so men reporting to him and busting heads at his direction. The Empire City Guard has a poor reputation, truly a group you do not want to run across. And Judge Cage is big, he's mean, and he fights dirty when he needs to. See this?" Rakesh pointed to one of the prop bets listed under the fight. "Decent odds that his opponent doesn't even show. You won't find that anywhere else across the bracket. Titans who find themselves pitted against Judge Cage have a tendency to miss their fights. Either handcuffed to the bars in some Empire City jail cell or at the bottom of a lake." Rakesh looked at the board again. "Not that he'd need to cheat against the Crusher. But when the ranks get tighter, titans will be on their guard. He's one of the favorites."

"Who else is favored?" Van sipped his Ocean Pale. He needed to learn as much as he could from the little gambler.

"King Thad. The Landshaker. Scott Flawless. Bearhugger. It's a packed field. Billy Blades. Judge Cage. And a bunch more contenders. Anything can happen at the Headlock of Destiny. It is far less predictable than..." Rakesh watched intently as the woman running the board spoke with a group of runners waving slips of paper. "She's thinking about your match. The crowd will start to get antsy if she doesn't set a preliminary line on it. Experienced betters will find others who aren't dragging their feet." He swayed back and forth as he watched her. "If you don't want to hear the odds they place on you versus Panam Manley," he said without looking at Van, "now would be a good time to vacate this area."

"I can take it." Van looked more closely at the bracket. There was one slot with no name. It simply said *Held for Nether*. Van had stayed in a foster home with a grandmother who was fond of stories about the Nether. Usually it was called the land of storms and nightmares, or simply the land of dead souls. In the stories, a storm would come and when it fled, people would be missing, having been lured into the Nether while the wind howled. Or a child in the grips of a nightmare would awaken to see their screams had summoned a representative from the Nether, and they would be carried away. Then the grandmother warned everyone to stay close during storms and to be quiet in the night. Looking back, it seemed pretty obvious what her goal was in telling the stories. She had a houseful of rowdy kids to keep in line, and she valued her sleep. Van hadn't thought of the stories since his childhood and was surprised to see the name on something as important as the Headlock of Destiny bracket.

"Why's that there?" Van asked, finishing off his beer and glancing back over his shoulder towards the bar. His back was beginning to hurt again. He wanted to get off his feet, maybe just watch the sun stream through the windows and slide across the floor from a seat at the bar.

"Slots are held by nation, not titan. The tournament carries forward the tradition of holding a spot for the Nether, though they have never sent a titan to represent them."

"Is that place even real?"

"Real or not, it has a slot in the tournament. And given there are twenty-nine nations and two cities represented, it helps make the math work."

"So," Van squinted at the name just above the Nether's slot, "Bearhugger basically gets a bye?"

"That's right. No doubt the Southwoods made a significant investment in the future of the ONWC to earn such an honor."

Finally the blue-skinned woman slid forward across the board and, right where Van's and Panam Manley's names converged, she wrote a series of numbers he couldn't decipher. The crowd began chatting vigorously.

"What's that mean?" Van asked Rakesh.

Rakesh gave him a forced smile. "Nineteen to one."

"I don't do much gambling. What exactly does that mean?"

"It means, they think that if you fought Panam Manley one hundred times, that he would win ninety-five of them." He hesitated. "I think perhaps few people will place bets on your match."

Van felt a sinking feeling in his gut. "That bad? I did just send the Ram home."

Rakesh shook his head sadly and reached out and patted Van somewhere near his knee. "Panam Manley is not the Ram. And he sent his own titan home. Slingshot Kohn, I am sad to tell you, would have also been heavily favored against the Ram. And rumor puts Slingshot Kohn currently in the Empire City Hospital, courtesy of Panam Manley. A wonderful facility which will no doubt grow more crowded as the Headlock carries forward."

"Sounds like a place I may get to know soon." Van turned away from the board. Did he really value his job so much he wasn't going to skip out of this whole thing? Maybe they'd let him slide since he pulled a miracle out of his ass and got the Uplands one victory. He grunted. Unlikely. Now he'd just shame himself worse if he ran from the fight. He looked down at his empty mug. "You've never been to Headwaters?"

"Regrettably no."

"Well, let's get back to the bar and I'll tell you about it. Then you can tell me everything you know about Panam Manley."

Chapter 16

Van's concerns about his next fight proved to be no match for the seventeen-or-so beers he swallowed to chase them away. He and Rakesh passed the afternoon drinking and talking about wrestlers of old. Rakesh did most of the talking and Van listened. The halfling had seemingly traveled the entirety of the Open Nations, gambling on every wrestling match he found.

He told Van about Lem the Looter managing to throw a match despite his opponent being firmly deceased before Lem even dragged him into the ring. Rakesh recited to Van an endearing saga of the Halfling Prince, a diminutive wrestler who won matches using his wits, which Van was sure was about ninety-nine percent bullshit. He spoke of Kurt Mullet the Victorious, who had an unbroken streak of being beaten unconscious and immediately wetting himself. It had become an enduring prop bet, with inevitable accusations of fixing. Rakesh's greatest single day winnings came from a ladder match in Dunham North in which the Soldier Bleak defeated Breaker Jarles by paying a pair of fairies to carry Soldier up to the belt when the ref was distracted.

Rakesh had a knack for finding trouble, and somehow kept up with Van beer for beer despite being less than a quarter his size. As the sunlight falling through the windows faded, torches inside the gambling hall were sparked, making the vast space look even more like a cave. When their barrel of Ocean Pale had tapped out, Rakesh slyly mentioned that the parties would be getting going soon. They left together in search of one, the unopened barrel of Crater Ale under Van's arm.

Rakesh led him a couple streets over, into a raging celebration. The courtyard of a hotel had been converted into a fighting showcase, and exotic creatures of all sorts were trotted out to violently face off for the amusement of the partygoers. A one-armed ogre crushed a pack of screeching goblins. A pair of dragons bred to be the size of dogs fought, spraying bloody scales into the crowd as they gnashed and clawed each other. Rakesh lit up when a halfling took center stage with a coil of rope, and he hurried off to place a bet. Soon after, a scorpion as big as a man was released into the ring. To the disappointment of the crowd, the halfling dodged the scorpion's claws and poison-tipped tail with practiced ease and tied the creature up in a tight bundle. Rakesh wandered back with a thick purse, bragging up his inside knowledge of the halfling scorpion hunters on the northern fringes of Corliss. Apparently one of his many cousins made a good living that way.

Rakesh suggested another party so they left. The second party was even more lively than the first. It was in the basement of a large mansion. Bright, multicolored flames flashed around the space and loud drummers boomed out a thunderous beat. A troop of fairies were finishing up a mesmerizing aerial dance routine when Van and Rakesh arrived. The follow-up show was a surprisingly complex competition in which two goblins tried to trick each other into drinking the glass of poison on a table between them. Rakesh shook his head firmly when Van asked him if he would bet on the outcome, muttering something disparaging about goblins and their trustworthiness. Eventually one of the goblins quaffed the poison with such suspiciously perfect comedic timing that Van suspected the whole thing had been prearranged. Next, a pair of robed wizards stepped to the center of the basement for a duel.

Rakesh tugged at Van's uniform. "Van," Rakesh said, "the opportunity is now, Van." Rakesh gestured towards the large arched entryway of the basement. "You wished to know more of Panam Manley. The titan himself is here."

Van tore his gaze off the readying wizards to see a titan ducking under the archway. He was huge, towering over the crowd closely gathered around him. He wore tightly fitted animal print pants with tears across the thighs, a mesh tank top that showed his muscles, and a bandanna knotted below his chin. His hair was long and wild, though he was clean shaven. He held a beer mug in his hand. He looked around the party and smiled approvingly. When his gaze fixed on Van above the sea of revelers, he tilted his head down and eyed him over his tinted glasses. He gave Van a nod and then made a casual gesture, inviting Van over to speak with him.

"The opportunity is now," Van muttered to himself as he approached the titan he would face in the tournament the day after tomorrow. He could hear the crowd buzzing with excitement at Panam's arrival.

"Well met, fellow ten-man," Panam said as Van drew close. He slid past his entourage, gripped Van's hand tightly, and pulled him in for a one-armed hug. Van tensed at the familiar gesture but the other titan released quickly and stepped back. "You carry the party with you," Panam said, nodding to the barrel tucked under Van's arm. "Not a bad way to travel." His voice was gravely but he had a light, playful tone. "Is that one from Headwaters?"

"No," Van replied. "Brewer-stamped Crater Ale."

Panam tilted his head, eyebrows raised. "That is some excellent brew. Only had the Rosalyn Brew's

Moonbeam myself. If you start pouring from it, let me know." He took a drink from his own mug.

Van nodded. In the back, the crowd cheered as the wizards' contest began to get heated. It looked as though the goal of the duel was to use magic to force the other wizard into a dress. Several partygoers had been caught in the crossfire and struggled against attacks from magically animated articles of clothing.

As they watched, Panam slid next to Van, subtly turning him in the process, so they were both facing the same direction, the wall at their back, effectively giving them a measure of privacy which his entourage seemed instinctively to understand. They were left alone in the midst of the packed party. At least that was the feeling Van got.

"I heard, Van the Beer Man," Panam said, "that you laid down one hell of a fight this afternoon. Heard they have to reschedule all the Palace West fights after you and the Ram totaled the place. That, my friend, is fucking cool."

Van tried not to smile. "I heard you didn't do too bad yourself."

Panam nodded gravely. "Slingshot Kohn is a great fighter. He came strong, he stayed strong. It was a match I was proud to win, and I'll be proud to see Kohn keep racking up victories. He's from the Land of Eighton, and he sure did the Land of Eighton proud. Tough ten-man, great fighter."

Van glanced sideways at Panam Manley. It was surprising to encounter a titan so friendly, and seemingly genuinely nice.

"What they got going on here?" Panam said, peering across the dark basement at the dueling wizards. "Looks crazy, man. Got to love Empire City. They think of everything."

Van didn't answer. This was so unlike the conversation he'd had with the Living Portrait. He was waiting for Panam to start shoving him around. But Panam simply watched the contest a moment, then turned back to Van. "Wild. Party I was at last night had a water demon fighting a dragon. "

"A full-sized dragon?" Van asked.

"Yeah. Actually a pretty shitty idea. No one could see anything through all the steam. I tried to make friends with the dragon afterwards. Fucker nearly took my arm. Everybody had a good laugh at that one." Panam nudged a mohawked man, part of his entourage, who stood in front of him. The man turned back and grinned at the memory.

A silver-haired gentleman materialized before them as if by magic. He was impeccably dressed with youthful eyes. "Panam, so glad to have you here." He stepped forward to shake Panam's hand, quite comfortable with the hug and complicated handshake he got in return.

"Glad to be here, Danforth. Your hospitality is the best hospitality." A slight pause. "Hey, Danforth, I hope you don't mind, but me and Van here were just having a quick chat. Can I come find you in a minute? We'll hit up more of that whiskey you like, smoke some green. Cool?"

"Most definitely." The man, who presumably owned the mansion they were currently in, nodded as though pleased with the dismissal. "And I've got a couple ladies looking forward to meeting you."

"Very cool," Panam said. When the man had gone, the titan turned back to Van. "Van, I'm not trying to steal too much of your time. I know you got some serious partying to do and I don't want to get in the way of that. Just want to say I'm looking forward to the match. We're gonna have some fun, and we're gonna give them a hell of a show. I got a good feeling about your future career, ten-man, and I dig your style." He stood there nodding for a moment, as though waiting for Van to add something. But before Van could think of anything to fill the momentary lull, Panam gave a sort of embarrassed shrug.

"To Danforth's office!" he called loudly, mobilizing his entourage. He grabbed the shoulders of the man with the mohawk in front of him and began steering him through the crowd. "You remember where it is, Slade? You threw up on his rug last time we were in Empire City." With a backwards smile at Van, Panam Manley and his crew filed out the archway.

Van was staring after the titan when Rakesh appeared at his side. "And how did that go?"

Van had no idea. "Either he was fucking with me, which is entirely possible, or he's the nicest titan I've ever met. And pretty damn cool to boot." He tugged at his beard in consternation, then glared at his empty mug. "Every time I think I have the smallest piece of this city figured out…"

Rakesh shook his head. "In constant bewilderment is the very best place to dwell. Come, Van. The next fight will be costumed dwarves recreating the first-round tournament battles, I hear. And soon you will turn that barrel from a decoration into a contributing member of our gathering, lest everyone begin to speak of your stinginess, prompted and encouraged by me."

"Can't have that," Van replied, making an effort to push Panam Manley out of his mind as he set the barrel down to start the search for a tap.

Chapter 17

"You're a hard ten-man to find."

The words floated at the edge of Van's consciousness, but that place seemed to be uncomfortably bright and demanding, so Van retreated back into sleep. The words were easily dismissed, coming from a voice he'd never heard before. The splash of stale beer in his face that came next was far harder to sleep off.

"Ugh," he said, opening his bleary eyes and raising a hand to mop the stinking liquid off his face. There were three indistinct shapes before him in what looked to be a hallway. Sunlight from a few small windows at one end stung his eyes. His back pressed against a wall. He must have slept slumped against it. The blows the Ram had dealt him had stiffened across his body overnight. Van groaned loudly, closing his eyes again as the beer dripped off his beard.

"Wow, is there any fight left in you?"

The speaker wasn't leaving. Van slowly opened his eyes a second time. A tall man, standing between two far taller titans, was staring at him expectantly, waiting for a response. He wore a tailored suit with pinstripes that looked wildly out of place amongst the trash-strewn remnants of whatever party Van had ended his evening at. The man had slicked-back hair over a long, stern face. The two large titans on either side of him were covered in tattoos. Both wore armored plates on their shoulders, fitted with nasty-looking spikes. Their grizzled faces spoke of violence. Nothing about this conversation seemed inviting to Van.

He sat up and opened his mouth to ask the man his name, but then made the sudden decision that he should instead vomit, which he promptly did all over the floor between his legs.

"This is just marvelous," the man said lurching back a step. He turned to the titans behind him. "Get him up and drag him over there. Someplace we can talk away from that smell." He pulled a handkerchief from his pocket and pressed it to his face as he moved down the hall.

As he watched the man go, Van might have smiled if he wasn't afraid it would cause him to puke again. Then the thick, unforgiving hands of the titans were digging into his armpits and pulling him to his feet. "You throw up on me, you die," one said. He had a tattoo of an eagle with its wings spread across his face.

The other, this one with a tattoo of some strange sort of monster on his face, leaned down to pick up a dirty rag off the floor and used it to wipe Van's mouth like a child. "Get your shit together, ten-man," he said.

Get your shit together. Sounded like a pretty good idea right now. Van had easily drained the Crater Ale he'd brought to the party and the beer hadn't stopped there. The acrid smoke of a wide variety of the Open Nations' most popular drugs had filled the basement at some point, and Van had found it difficult to breathe. He'd sought the open air and been led straight into the arms of another gathering. He currently had no idea where he was or what he'd done since. He'd certainly done himself no favors if he wound up alone in a dirty hallway with two goons pinning him to a wall next to a pile of vomit.

"Who's that?" Van asked in a gruff voice once he was sure his insides were going to stay put.

One of the pair looked back over his spiked armor plates. "That, ten-man, is Venerate Holland, head of the ONWC. You know what the fucking ONWC is, right? So put your head on straight and speak respectfully." One of the huge hands which held Van to the wall tightened painfully. "He don't like disrespect. We don't like disrespect."

Van was too weary to even nod, but as he straightened the pair backed away. "And you?" he asked.

"I'm Eagle," said the titan with an eagle tattooed on his face.

"I'm Creature," said the titan with some sort of creature tattooed on his face.

"Right," Van said, "very clever." He pushed between them and began lumbering down the hall toward Venerate Holland. He ignored the wreckage of the party around him, broken mugs, discarded clothes, cigarette butts, as he went. His escort fell in line behind him.

Holland was waiting in a sitting area at the edge of a great room, just as littered as the rest of the place. He looked immaculate next to the filthy surroundings. He held a clean glass of water, which he drank from as he watched Van with cold eyes. He said nothing as Van approached.

"Sorry about that," Van said as he took a seat across from Holland. His unease deepened as Eagle and Creature took up positions just behind Holland, each crossing their massive arms.

"I'm disappointed in you, Van the Beer Man. This has been a horrible way to start a friendship. We need to talk about how to salvage it." Holland set the water on a glass side table with a loud ringing sound. "First off, you didn't think it was important to come and see me the minute you arrived?"

"This is kind of new to me, if I've done something wrong…"

Holland gave a humorless laugh. "Van, I don't even know where to start. The ONWC runs the Headlock of Destiny. And I run the ONWC. I can forgive a little fumbling around from some hick who wandered into Empire City trying to make a name for himself, but you have seriously fucked up the tournament, and the tournament is my business. So we got a problem." He was clenching and unclenching his fists as though holding back a surge of anger. "Look, we're all big boys, so we're gonna talk about this like big boys and I'll get to the point. Coresite Mount paid good money for that slot. That investment did not pay off and someone's got to pay for it."

Now that he was upright, Van was settling in to a truly spectacular hangover. His head pounded as he tried to follow what Holland was saying. He wiped at his forehead but he wasn't sweating. Not yet. "Uplands told me to fight, do my best. It's a problem that I won?"

Holland stood, grabbed the water glass, and hurled it past Van's head to shatter against the wall. "It is a *huge* fucking problem that you won, moron! That win damaged my reputation, and, I assure you, my reputation is something I care about very much."

"They buy a slot they must know there's still risk."

"Not in my tournament. And definitely not in the first round." Holland sat back down, patting his hair back into place. "Listen closely, Van the Beer Man, because you smell like puke, and I don't want to be in this shithole a minute longer. You're going to lose your next fight. Panam Manley is a bigger draw, better for the tournament. You don't do shit for the tournament, aside from fuck up the brackets. I shouldn't even have to say this, because Panam is going to kick your green ass, but I'm not taking a chance on another debacle like the Ram fight. Put up whatever kind of fight you want, make for a good show, if you can, and save some of that dignity you hold so tightly." He scoffed with a gesture at Van's messy hair and beard, which, in fairness, did have some chunks of vomit in it. "But you *lose*. And you already cost me money, so if you even *ask* for compensation something very bad is going to happen. Throw the fight, go home with your limbs intact. Stay out of Empire City at least a year. Then if you want to crawl back we can talk about how you pay off your debt to me. But if I hear about you setting foot in a ring anywhere in the Open Nations, well, we're back to that something bad happening." Holland stood and smoothed the wrinkles from his suit. "Understood?"

Maybe it was the hangover, but something about this guy repulsed Van. He was probably a wine drinker. Van couldn't stand the idea of this creep thinking Van was working on his behalf. "No," he said firmly.

Holland froze. He glanced at Eagle and Creature, the pair of evil-looking hedgehogs behind him. "You told him who I am?" He turned back to Van. "I'm not a man you get to say *no* to. So you're gonna have to clarify yourself. I assume you know what that means? That means you tell me what part of your clearly laid-out instructions you don't understand. And before you do that, I'll even put it in simpler terms. Lose the fight. Then get the fuck out of my city. Understand?"

Van would probably lose the fight and leave Empire City anyway, so the right move would be to keep his mouth shut or even agree to Holland's terms. "Fuck you," he said.

Holland's eyes widened, then he laughed and shook his head. "Oh, ten-man, you are just *made* of mistakes this morning." He slowly looked Van over, and finally turned back to his goons. "Which knee did Grit lose?"

"His left," Eagle replied, his hungry eyes never leaving Van's face.

"It seems to me like you think you don't have to follow the rules, ten-man. It seems like you think you're special. I am sorry to disappoint you. You are not special. You aren't even gonna make your next fight. Eagle, Creature, help Mr. Van the Beer Man find an excuse to miss his fight. Start with the left knee, so he and Grit can have a matching pair as they limp back home."

Eagle and Creature were already moving forward, a tide of muscles and spikes, as Holland turned to the door. He'd almost reached it when he shouted back over his shoulder, "And if he gives you any trouble, kill him."

Chapter 18

The room fell quiet aside from the footfalls of the approaching titans. Van could feel a rising tension, something like a storm brewing. There was violence on the horizon, a feeling he'd been getting to know better. As Venerate Holland's goons drew steadily closer it washed over him.

They moved slowly, posing as they approached, flexing their arms and pivoting so the light caught the spikes jutting cruelly up from their armored shoulders. Neither was as big as Van, but they were still huge, proper ten-men.

Van glanced around as he stood up from the chair. The long hall was behind him. Before him was a massive room with tall ceilings, a few pockets of furniture, fireplaces that had long since gone out. Litter from last night's party was everywhere illuminated by greasy daylight filtering through the high windows. Nothing to help him escape. Van had never fought a titan outside of the ring, let alone a pair of them. And this pair looked used to working together. His hangover came surging back. Van fought a fresh urge to vomit.

"Beer Man," Creature called out softly, "there's still a chance to do this the easy way. Just sit back down and close your eyes. Won't take long."

"No," Van said, barely managing to keep a tremor out of his voice.

"I was hoping you'd say that," Creature replied.

Eagle came in with his shoulder lowered, the long spikes headed right for Van's chin. Van turned away only to catch Creature's fist across his jaw. Van shook his head to wake himself from his stupor. Both titans pummeled his ribs, causing Van to stumble back and trip over a bunched-up area rug. He rolled to the side just before Eagle slammed into the ground, spiked armor ripping holes in the rug and scraping deep grooves into the stone floor below it.

Van reached out and yanked Creature's leg out from under him. He fell on top of Eagle, caught an assful of metal, and let out a howl. Van jumped to his feet and sprinted down the hall, knocking a vase from a pedestal as he careened off a doorframe.

Van heard the goons at his heels as he entered some sort of wine storage room. Racks of dusty bottles lined the walls. Despite the room's size, there were only a few chairs in the center. Van picked one up and threw it at Eagle.

He missed, sending it into a wall of wine racks. Shattered glass and burgundy liquid rained down on the floor as Eagle was at Van again. Van dodged Eagle's left jab, and shoved him backward into Creature, buying himself time to pick up another chair. This one he swung overhand like a cudgel with all his force. It shattered against Eagle's shoulder armor. Eagle gave a dark grin as Creature swung around him, poised to attack again together.

Creature landed a right hook on Van's cheekbone, and Eagle followed with a stunning left jab to Van's nose. Van was losing track of who was hitting him, a blur of fists and spikes. He tried to drop to his knees, but one of them got an arm around his midsection. Van winced and braced himself as the titan swung around and drove Van hard into the stone floor. He gasped for breath, pushing the spiked plates away from his face, only to see a descending boot thump his head hard into the floor again. Another boot found his side. He groaned and rolled over, his only thought for the moment was the pain.

The goons stepped away, giving Van a moment to fight for breath. He coughed hard into the stone floor, surprised to see no blood in his spit. He lifted his head to see the two titans stepping towards him again, smiles plastered to their tattooed faces. "Beer Man, how about some wine?" Eagle asked. Each held a bottle of wine, tiny in their enormous hands. "We thought of a special way to serve it to you. Bottle and all."

Van stumbled to his feet. He thought for a second he would come up with some sort of witty comeback. Instead he turned and ran. One of the bottles exploded over his shoulder as he ducked through an archway. As he passed out of the room, he reached back and grabbed the wine rack mounted on the wall near the archway. With one powerful tug, he tore the whole thing, floor to ceiling, loose from the wall. He heard the titans swear as the structure teetered for a moment, then rained wine bottles down on them like missiles. Van didn't risk a look back as he ran out of the room.

The next room in the seemingly endless mansion had a wrestling ring in the center and chairs all around. It looked like a personal audience chamber for fights. No place to hide. He saw another archway on the opposite side of the ring, this one covered with a white cloth. He ducked through.

It was another large room. This one seemed to be under renovation. There was scaffolding all around the walls, rickety wooden poles tied together with haphazard streamers of rope. Bright red and black paint was on the walls in bright splotches and in cans stacked all around the high scaffolding. Van turned to face Eagle and Creature as they pulled aside the white cloth behind him.

Eagle walked ahead of Creature, shaking his ugly mug back and forth so it almost looked as though the tattoo of the bird on his face was flapping its wings. "Shouldn't have given us trouble, Beer Man. This isn't gonna go well for you." His earlier playful look was replaced with a furrowed brow and gritted teeth.

Van gasped for breath. The stitch in his side burned like fire. He had probably broken his nose on the bottom of Eagle's boot. Win or lose, Van was pretty sure he was going to puke again.

"You're not looking so hot, Beer Man." Creature gave a knowing nod to his partner. Eagle let a smile crack his scowl and began climbing up the scaffolding on a side wall. It shook under his weight, boards and paint brushes falling down as he ascended. Van backed away, trying to keep an eye on both titans as he considered options.

"Here," Creature said, "let's make this more fair." He tugged on one of the metal armor plates on his shoulders and pulled the whole rig over his head and off. He let it clatter to the floor. "Makes it easier" —he began running at Van—"to do this!"

He dove at Van, wrapped around Van's legs, and tackled him to the floor. Van punched at his shoulders and back to no effect. Then Creature got his legs under him, straightened up, and hoisted Van over his head. Van punched at the titan below him again, then suddenly realized what the real threat was. Van was straddled atop Creature's shoulders, exposed. He saw Eagle leap off the scaffolding, flying right toward him.

Eagle still had his spikes on, and Van figured he had about a half second before he was skewered in midair. He let out an embarrassing squeal but managed to catch a massive spike in his hand and turn Eagle's momentum just enough that all three titans fell to the floor in a heap.

Van tried to jump up before the others, but fell to one knee as Creature gave his entangled leg a painful twist. Van felt like his knee might pop. He punched at

Creature's tight grip. Creature laughed but eventually let go, and Van pulled away from the pair to catch his breath. Van's knee throbbed in pain, warning him of how close Creature had come to seriously injuring him. And that's what Holland had told them to do. Hurt him. If Van let these two goons win, it wasn't just an embarrassing trip home. It wasn't back to a life he suddenly realized he didn't miss very much. If he lost this fight he might never walk again. He might not live to see the sun rise again. He might never drink another beer.

He watched the goons clamber to their feet, all laughter and sheepish grins. "Almost got you, fucker," Eagle said. "We call that move the Hand of the Apocalypse." He turned to Creature, who was collecting the armor he'd shed. "This is such a waste. I wish there was a crowd here to see the rest of this ass-whipping."

Van watched the titans approach, growing angrier by the second. He'd done nothing to invite this. He didn't deserve this. His breathing slowed, and a calm confidence found a footing inside him. "You wouldn't want anyone to see what's going to happen next. Playtime is over." He dropped into a fighting crouch.

Creature laughed as he tightened the straps holding his armor in place. "Good. We're done playing too, Van the Beer Man. Hope you've made peace with your shitty life."

"Not yet," Van said.

They came at him together again. This time Van jumped between them, swinging both arms high in a double clothesline that knocked them off their feet. He drove his heel into Eagle's eye socket, then turned and seized Creature where his armor met his chest. With a strength born of anger, Van hoisted Creature into the air and hurled him into the scaffolding. The titan crashed to the floor under a clatter of boards and poles. Van picked him up again, ignoring Eagle's fist as it drove into Van's side, and smashed Creature's head up into the scaffolding above them. The spikes on his shoulders drove into the wood, trapping him there, legs dangling.

He turned to catch Eagle's fist in his hand as the titan fired another shot at Van's midsection. "Your turn." Eagle swung the other fist, but Van bent out of the way, still clutching his captured fist. He turned Eagle and spun him, just as he had the Ram, and launched Eagle. Eagle went crashing right through the wall, leaving a messy silhouette in broken plaster and boards. Van turned back to Creature. The titan was out cold, pinned to the scaffolding. Van gave a humorless laugh and strode through the impromptu doorway Eagle had created.

Eagle was scrambling to his feet, blood running from his nose. He stumbled and ripped a tapestry off the wall in his attempt to stay upright. Van saw fear in his eyes. "Not so tough without your buddy, are you?" Van asked.

"We can talk," Eagle said, eyes darting around the room.

"No, we've already talked." Van realized, as he looked around, that they were back in the room where they'd had their pleasant conversation with Venerate Holland, where Holland told this goon to kill him. Same room, same furniture, same empty fireplaces. They had done a circuit of the ground floor of the mansion. Van looked at the closest fireplace, ashy stone with nothing in it beyond a few old and charred logs, then turned back to Eagle. "Get over here."

Eagle tried to run, but Van caught him easily by the armor straps on his back. Van swept his legs and slammed him face-first to the floor. The titan was easier to handle after that. Van carried him over to the fireplace. There was no way a ten-man would fit in there. It was perfect.

Van gripped Eagle's shoulder-plates between the sharp spikes and pushed him backward toward the fireplace. Eagle thrashed and fought, but Van drove him down into the fireplace. Old logs snapped and soot rose as the titan's legs skidded back, fighting for purchase. Van kept driving forward, then punched him in the gut, forcing Eagle to bend at the waist and hunch inwards. Finally, with one last push, Van wedged the ten-man's armor into place, trapping him in the fireplace as his bulk forced the sharp points into the stones and up the flue.

Van stepped back with a satisfied smirk, dusted off his hands theatrically. "I changed my mind," he said. "We can talk. Or, at least, you can listen." Eagle gave one last struggle, fighting to get out of the fireplace, before he grew still, and glared at Van. "Yeah, you're listening," Van continued. "You tell Holland I'm fighting Panam Manley tomorrow with everything I've got. I'll probably lose and leave Empire City anyway. But I want your asshole boss to know I'm not working for him."

His message delivered, Van turned to leave and nearly jumped out of his skin to see a man standing next to him. He wore a butler's uniform and had a horrified grimace on his face. As Van watched, the butler's eyes slowly scanned the room, taking in the destruction all around them. Broken furniture, shattered plaster, smashed wood. A creeping river of burgundy wine and broken glass streaming in from the neighboring room. A hole in the wall which revealed collapsed scaffolding and the dangling feet of a defeated titan. The butler ended his survey by looking at the glaring, angry titan wedged in his fireplace. Then he stared back up at Van, eyes wide and mouth agape.

"Good party," Van said with a nod. He headed for the exit as quickly as possible.

Chapter 19

Van had to ask directions three times before he got back to anything resembling familiar streets. The sun shone from well overhead by the time he had a bearing on the hotel. The bout of morning violence seemed to have helped his hangover, leaving Van with a lightness to his step. He couldn't help wishing he had some friends to explore the city with before facing the reality of his next match.

He moved slowly through the streets, in no hurry to return to Larvell's criticism and Owen's surly gaze, Kyle's frustrating indifference or, worse than all of those combined, the sharp tongue of Lady Dorothy. He might enjoy running into Rakesh the gambler again, but the halfling seemed to attract trouble, and Van could do with some quiet before the next shitshow on his horizon.

Van was watching a pack of Urdesta fans, easy to pick out by their bright green hats and matching wristbands, when a plan for the afternoon came to him. He caught up with them. A quick conversation verified that they were headed to watch Billy Blades's first round match against Elephant the Titan at the Stomping Grounds. They laughed when Van asked if he could join them or if he would need a ticket. "We heard about you, Van the Beer Man. I'm guessing you won't have any problems getting in."

Van didn't, and some minutes later he settled into a seat a few rows back from the ring at the center of the slowly filling Stomping Grounds stadium. It was vastly more modern than Palace West, with enormous, comfortable bleachers around a wide, flat ring area. The sun shone on Van's face. He was early enough that the crowds weren't yet pressing into his space and he was excited at the prospect of being a spectator rather than the main event. He might catch some heat from any other titans in attendance, seemed like that was inevitable wherever he went, but he could handle that if it meant getting to see two real titans in tournament-level action, close up, with neither of them focused on killing him after the bell rang. He leaned back and closed his eyes.

. . .

Kyle watched as Van took his seat near the ring. This surprising titan, who had actually won his first match. He looked the worse for wear in his tattered clothes with what appeared to be vomit clinging to his matted beard. What had she gotten herself into by making this play? What had she gotten all of them into? She tightened her black coat around her and weaved silently through the stadium crowd to find a spot on the bleachers just behind Van.

She walked slowly, enjoying the feel of the hot sun. The tournament was only a day old, and it had already been an exhausting series of twists and turns. The Uplands had been in a poor position even before Owen Grit went down. A series of alliances had formed well before the regionals and the ONWC had been ready to take steps against the small nation. Van's victory had given them pause, and they would focus on extracting what they could from Coresite Mount, at least for the next day or so. They'd turn their attention to the Uplands soon enough. But maybe this titan could buy them some more time.

She leaned in close behind Van. "Boo," she whispered into his ear.

Van cracked an eye open at the sound of her voice. He shot her a look of annoyance, then closed his eyes again.

"What's got you so sensitive?" she asked.

When he didn't respond, she jabbed him on the shoulder with a small finger.

He sat up, a surly expression on his face, and turned to her. "You know, getting into that ring isn't the easiest thing in the world. And I had to do it all alone. You got me into this. And you weren't even watching."

She smiled softly. "Oh, I was watching, Van. I was pulling for you."

"Well, you have a funny way of showing it. All these other titans have fans. I just have a pack of people who hate me for no reason." He studied her a moment. "Why are you here? Why are you in Empire City? Husband-hunting with Lady Dorothy?"

She gave him a flat look. "If need be."

"What's that mean? Do you ever give a straight answer?"

"When it benefits me, I can be very straightforward. I'm here on behalf of the governor, no secret there. My job is to have the talks that help the Uplands and stop the talks that don't. But I don't have the luxury of a nice clear path like you do."

"A clear path?" Van asked as a titan lumbered by, pausing to glare at him. He was enormous, muscles on his muscles, and every inch of him covered in scars. Van stared at his feet as the titan passed. "A clear path with guys like that blocking it."

"Sure, but at least you know the objective."

"What's that mean? You're here having talks and stopping others and you don't know why?"

"I know the *why*, Van. It's because the nations funding the ONWC are banding together to force everyone else into what amounts to slavery. I just don't know the *how* part of my objective."

And she really didn't. The ONWC held all the cards, as they had for years. She could do nothing but play defense. And that wasn't the only thing troubling her. No one had shown up at the Rain of Spears meeting. Her order was dwindling. What had once been a coalition of strength, pledged to the highest of callings, had diminished to first an obligation and then even less than that. Kyle had waited at their scheduled gathering alone.

Van surprised her by saying, "I met Venerate Holland this morning." He delivered the words casually, then leaned back again and closed his eyes.

"And?" she asked, the tiniest strain of urgency in her voice.

"And he's a prick."

"That's news to no one, Van. What did he have to say?"

"He said," Van's eyes were still closed, "that I fucked up his tournament by beating the Ram, and I should throw my match with Panam Manley. And when I said no, he set a pair of goons on me."

"You seem to be looking remarkably hale for someone who said no to Venerate Holland. Are you going to stand by that?"

"I told him, I'll probably lose anyway, but I'm not gonna lose for someone like him." He sniffed. "Looks like a wine drinker."

"You are full of surprises, Van the Beer Man." She let some warmth creep into her words.

"Not that anybody cares," he said.

She sighed and shifted on the uncomfortable wooden bench. "And here we go again. I didn't come over here to massage your bruised feelings. In fact, it would be better if I wasn't seen talking to you at all, but seeing how you seem determined to march around the Empire

City streets getting into trouble rather than staying at the hotel, this is the only chance I've got." She took a deep breath and rubbed her temples. "I just wanted to say thank you. That win meant a lot. I know you didn't do it for me or for the Uplands, or for any other reason than to save your own neck, but it means more than you know. And if you already said no to Holland, well, that's another victory."

There was a long pause before she asked, "Think you can do it again?" She let a hopeful smile crack her serious expression.

Van sighed dramatically. "That's gonna be up to Panam Manly, I suppose. But I'll give him hell."

"That's my boy." She patted his neck then rose from her seat. Her mind was already rolling through her next moves as she edged down the row. Whether the titan won or lost, she had things she needed to get done. The governor had told her this would be Kyle's last tournament under the table. By next year she would be promoted as a legitimate representative of the Uplands. Then Kyle could step out of the shadows. Less stalking dark alleys, sniffing out assassination attempts, stifling plots, occasionally orchestrating her own. Kyle would be openly playing politics, using the weapon of paper instead of knives. She had no idea if that was what she wanted. More importantly, she had no idea if that was what was needed. It somehow didn't feel as though it was. Something deeper, more core to her was calling out for attention.

As she reached the end of the row, she turned back. Van already had closed his eyes again and lay back, ignoring the curious looks of everyone around him. She fought a smile. There was a certain charm to the titan. Or maybe he just made a favorable contrast to Richard the Living Portrait. And who wouldn't?

Kyle pulled her coat tight and began shouldering through the thick crowd.

...

After Kyle left, Van flagged down a beer vendor and talked him into a free mug for the tournament titan. At least some things he was good at. He took a long drink and stared after the departed Kyle. Kyle Vair, who worked for the Uplands and appeared mysteriously from nowhere at will. Damn, she was pretty. Van hadn't wanted it to feel good when she'd thanked him, but he couldn't deny it. It made the sun seem a little brighter. He wondered how affection-starved he must be, what lengths he'd go to just for some simple gratitude. He wondered how well she knew that.

The crowd had filled in and the stadium grew louder as the match approached. Elephant the Titan took his place in the ring to little fanfare. Since arriving at Empire City, Van had been learning more and more about the tournament titans, seeing as that was all anyone was talking about. Van had heard Elephant the Titan had an earned reputation as a tough, cagy, and consistent fighter. Van sipped his beer as he studied the titan. Elephant had a golden skin tone and a chiseled, hairless chest. He lacked some of the flash and gimmick of the other tournament titans, but he'd notched a lot of victories over the years. As he waited in the ring, stretching and generally killing time, he oozed confidence.

Billy Blades, one of the highest ranked titans in the tournament, didn't just ooze confident. He produced waves of it that flowed out over the crowd, which went wild as he swaggered down the aisle towards the ring. The Urdesta fans immediately broke into chants of "*Be afraid the Blade*," which struck Van as a pretty awkward turn of phrase.

Blades was huge, taller than Van and significantly leaner. The combination of his tiny, spangled green shorts and his hairy chest made him look almost naked. His hair was oiled back and he wore thick gold chains around his neck. A giant toothpick jutted out of his mouth, surrounded by a self-assured smile. He raised his hands in the air and circled outside the ring as though he'd already won the fight. At last he vaulted up over the ropes, ignoring his opponent, stomped to his corner and removed his titan-sized gold chains. He summoned a ringside attendant and handed him the gold. As the worker staggered under the weight, Blades pointed at him fiercely, promising an ass-kicking if they weren't kept safe. Ritual complete, Billy Blades turned to his opponent and spat out his toothpick.

Billy Blades then proceeded to kick Elephant the Titan's ass. Elephant the Titan fought gamely, but was simply no match for Blades's size, strength, and technique. He attacked from all angles, always pressing. He won the grapples. He won the ground battles. He won in the air. Van's beer sat forgotten by his side as he watched it happen, trying not to imagine himself playing the role of Elephant the Titan in this lopsided tragedy.

Finally, Blades hoisted Elephant up into the air and tossed him into the stands. Van was forced to dive out the way along with most of his section as the enormous titan crashed into the seats. Elephant lay in a pile of broken limbs. Van stared at the mangled titan, then looked up at the ring to see Billy Blades laughing. He strutted around the ring for a while, arms raised in victory, then collected his gold chains. As he left the ring, he passed by Van and shot him a challenging look. Van quickly found something interesting by his feet to stare at.

The crowds filtered out, the Urdesta fans still chanting and singing over their victory. When Van stood to head back to the hotel, the sun was just as bright as it had been while he waited for the match to start. It didn't feel that way though. It felt like the shadow of something massive had fallen over him and he had no opportunity to get out from under it.

Chapter 20

Van moved slowly down the street, delaying his return to the hotel. He pondered the wild ride the last few days had been. He'd seen Empire City, he'd fought in the Headlock of Destiny and won, he'd partied with some of the wildest crews he'd ever imagined. What was preventing him from just taking off? Did he really value his shitty job so much? And couldn't he argue that he'd done enough? A lot of people here wanted to hurt him. Sticking around seemed like the worst possible thing to do.

Van liked Panam Manley, at least the little he'd seen of the popular titan, but he had no illusions about how their fight tomorrow night would go. Van would be Elephant the Titan to Panam's Billy Blades. Van was garbage. He'd edged out the Ram and given hell to a couple goons, which was better than nothing, but Panam Manley was a rising star for a reason. As nice as the guy seemed, it wasn't going to stop him from kicking Van's ass.

If Van was staying because of Kyle, because of her rare moments of kindness and her random bouts of faith in him, that seemed like a sad state of affairs. Was he so desperate that even the slimmest gaze from a beautiful woman pinned him down in a city that hungered to see him publicly beaten and broken? Sometimes Van hated being a fucking titan.

The sun was setting as Van realized the streets around him were empty, a rare lull in the Empire City crowds. His feet dragged on a quiet dirt road as the denizens of the buildings on each side began lighting oil lamps and sweeping the day's dust off porches and wooden sidewalks. There was a scraping sound in the distance, one Van associated with plows tilling the fields of grain back in Headwaters. His head was down when an unpleasant smell hit him.

It was something deep and musty. Something rotten. Van wiped his nose and looked around for the source of the stench. Even the porches had been abandoned now. The sunlight was fading, the sky fast growing dimmer with the promise of a black night. The few lit lanterns on the street were impossibly tiny and weak in the strengthening dark. The smell was everywhere, sending Van's mind tumbling into places it didn't want to go. He remembered the smell of chalk as he labored through lessons at school, bored and lonely. The smell of hay when he was forced to sleep in barns after he grew too large for the homes of his foster families. The smell of the wagon that carried him from home to home, every year or so, to be greeted with looks of annoyance and despair as another family reluctantly took him in. The smell of a bad batch of beer, of Van being blamed for the sour stink and sent out to work the warehouses, laughter behind him. The smell of Annie leaving him. The smell of violence, of death. A storm on the horizon. The scratching sound was growing louder.

Van took a breath in through his mouth, suddenly deeply afraid. He was far away from home, far away from safety. The smell grew stronger. The scratching seemed closer. Something was coming. He had nowhere to hide. He was too big.

Down the street, against the red of the setting sun, Van saw a titan. He hauled the darkness along with him.

He wore a farmer's clothes, but maybe the kind a farmer would wear to a funeral. Clothes that spoke of toil and death, toil and death. A worn, black suit, dignified but horrible. He labored under a heavy burden, pulling something behind him that Van couldn't quite see. The titan stared at Van as he approached. He had long, fiery red hair and a thick beard. His eyes were bright white, seeming almost to glow out of the gloom he carried with him. He was a head taller than Van with enormously broad shoulders, one of the largest titans Van had ever seen.

When the titans were separated by only a few feet, Van found the strength to step aside, but he could do no more. He lacked the will to run, though that was all he wanted to do. Run all the way back to Headwaters and never leave again. Never get a better look at what approached. But he was paralyzed.

The titan dragged a coffin of black pine behind him that scraped a deep furrow in the dirt road. As he pinned Van in place with his white eyes, he carried forward, stoically hauling his heavy load. The coffin was massive, large enough to fit a titan of Van's size. For a moment he was sure that's what would happen. The titan would stop, force him in the coffin, and drag him off someplace horrible. But, as Van saw the depth of the furrow behind the heavy coffin, he was sure there was already someone or *something* in there.

"Follow me," the titan commanded in a gravelly voice, eyes piercing to the core of Van.

There was power behind the words, and for a moment it made sense to Van. Why resist?

"No," Van replied. His voice quavered with uncertainty, as though it had been a reasonable request he wasn't quite sure he wanted to comply with just yet.

The titan eyed Van as he continued down the dirt road, rumbling by him at an arm's length. "The harvest has begun. The wars return. You will follow me one way or another, titan. Choose the easy path and follow me now."

Van could feel the pull of his words, but any desire to agree was overwhelmed by the relief he felt as the titan walked past him, still dragging the coffin. He didn't stop.

"No," Van said again with a token of greater assurance.

The titan glared back at Van, like a farmer might look at a stubborn patch of weeds to be pulled, or rot to be culled from the crops. A look not of violence, but of death. Of a promise to return and finish his harvest on the morrow.

Van looked down at the deep furrow behind the titan. It ran all the way down the street and out of sight. Van had no desire to see where it began. And even less to see where it ended.

As the smell slowly faded and the scraping receded, the strange hold placed on Van loosened. He turned and ran. He wanted the hotel, wanted to be back with other people, wanted the safety of Headwaters, where he'd never have to see something like that again. The words *you will follow me one way or the other, titan,* trailed him through the darkening streets.

Chapter 21

Van had lost his key, probably during the fight with Holland's goons, so he had to knock at the door of the hotel suite. Owen Grit eventually opened the door, his face unreadable, then limped back towards the living room and threw himself on a large sofa. Larvell was seated on the smaller sofa, watching Van curiously as he entered the room.

"Van the Beer Man," Larvell said finally. "Where ya been?"

"Around," Van said with a shrug. "Where's everybody else?"

"Your guess is as good as mine. Impossible to keep track of Kyle. Lady Dorothy is at some party the likes of you and me could never get into. Grit never goes anywhere, so he's right there."

Owen said, "I'm headed out tonight."

"That so, ten-man? Well, so am I, so don't think you're special." Larvell flashed a smile at Van. "Can't let this guy get a big head, right?"

Van glared at Larvell. He didn't like this sudden, friendly turn. Maybe didn't *trust* was a better word. "Whatever, Larvell."

"Lot's been happening in the tournament," Larvell said. "Word is Jaygan the Dragon Reynolds is on the outs with the ONWC, that's why they gave him Grim Tidings in the first. Minotaur is looking good but not as good as Billy Blades." He took a breath. "You know you're facing Panam, right?"

"Yeah, and I already know the odds, so you can spare me the lecture on my chances."

"Okay, Van my ten-man, but did you hear about the OverLord?"

"Who's the OverLord?"

"That is the question on everybody's lips. A titan showed up at the Nether's scheduled fight. Bearhugger was keeping the crowd amused by smashing boards on his forehead, expecting a forfeit. Titan said his name was the OverLord. He crushed Bearhugger, made him look like a child. Then he sealed him into a coffin and dragged him off into the streets."

"I saw him," Van said, memories of the ominous scraping and the horrible stench of death rising like bile in his throat. "He was...scary."

"You are not the only one who feels that way, Van the ten-man. Empire City is scrambling to figure out how to deal with this development. Everyone's hoping it was a one-time thing. But what do we always say?" He looked at Owen, who ignored him. "Got to be ready for anything. So I looked at the bracket again and you'll be glad to know he's on the opposite side of it. The lucky next titan scheduled to face whatever the hell that thing is—"

"The Patriot Jack Hammer, I know," Van said.

Larvell nodded, stared at Van. "You want to talk about Panam?"

"Do I want to hear you tell me all about how little chance I have against a real titan? No thanks, Larvell."

"Who said that? I didn't say that. Not after you handled the Ram. I think there's a real cha—"

"Larvell," Owen cut in with his deep voice, surprising them both. "Where you headed tonight?"

"Party down at Station's Landing. A couple off-the-books titan matches. You want to come, Van?"

Before Van could say no, Owen said, "How 'bout you get going, Larvell? I need to talk to Van for a minute."

Van looked curiously at the titan, who wasn't meeting his eyes.

"That cool with you, Van?" Larvell asked.

"Yeah," Van said. Any chance to get away from Larvell, even if it came from an unlikely source.

"All right, I'll roll. You want to hang later, you find me at Station's Landing."

"Sure."

Larvell took his time gathering his coat and hat, then, with a wink at Van, he was out the door. In the quiet room, Van checked that his other barrel of Kingsland, parked near the window, was still undisturbed. Then he took a seat on the sofa across from Owen.

Van waited to see if Owen really had something to say or just wanted to get rid of Larvell. He seemed in no hurry, and they listened to the dim sounds of traffic from the street below. Finally, Van couldn't stand the quiet any longer.

"So what's with Larvell being nice?" he asked.

Owen grunted before he answered. "He's stuck, Van. He knows he fucked up the tournament bid. Now that you notched a win, he's realizing he spent the last few days antagonizing his only salvation. Larvell's stubborn and self-serving, but you can always count on him to be checking all angles. He doesn't lose anything by being nice to you. So that's the game he'll play."

"Lucky me."

"Yeah, lucky you."

There was another long silence, long enough that Van began to wonder what to do with his evening. He didn't want to sit across from this morose titan all night, but he didn't know if it was a good idea to go back out into Empire City with no idea of a destination. Not with the likes of Eagle and Creature about, and the OverLord who knows where. But Van knew he didn't want to be alone, not like that first night.

"I've been a dick," Owen said finally. He nodded as if that explained everything.

Van waited for more, but that appeared to be all the titan had to say. Owen struggled to his feet and started walking towards the door. "You coming?"

Van stared at him, then shrugged, guessing he'd just witnessed about the full extent of Owen Grit opening up. He also rose to his feet.

Owen gestured towards the corner. "Then don't forget that barrel."

. . .

"It is Owen Grit and new friend Van the Beer Man! Good fortune smiles upon me." The titan who had opened the large door at Owen's knock had skin several shades darker than Van's. Bright white teeth flashed from his wide smile. He was short for a titan, not really all that much taller than a man, but with thick arms and legs. He wore a simple, cleanly tailored outfit of uniform grey, his feet bare. After a brief nod to each of his visitors, he led them back into the apartment with a muscly walk that spoke of coiled strength.

"That's Sevendhi," Owen said to Van as they ducked through the doorways and entered a thick haze of smoke. "Wrestles for Kisket."

"Wrestles makes it sound like I simply show up!" Sevendhi called back over his shoulder. "I bring great victories to the great land of Kisket, you mean to say!"

Sevendhi reached a dimly lit seating area and vaulted over the back of a titan-sized couch to settle in. As Van followed Owen in, he saw there were two other titans in the room. They passed a pipe that gave off a thick, acrid smoke. Despite the tight hallway and doors, the apartment was furnished to accommodate titans. One wall held a large Kisket flag. The other a chalk bracket with the names of the tournament competitors written on it, similar to the one Van had seen at the gambling hall yesterday.

One of the other titans stood and walked over. He was pale-skinned, tall and slender. His hair was pulled back in a tight ponytail of brown and grey. He wore monkish robes that reached the floor. "Owen," he said warmly, embracing the titan. He leaned back to examine Owen's leg. "I was deeply saddened to hear of your injury."

Owen simply grunted. "This is Van," he said, tipping his head in Van's direction. "Van, this is L'Harot'Ni'Set. Brings great victories to the great land of Kassim Island."

Van nodded and shifted the barrel to his other arm to shake the titan's hand. He hoped no one would test him on the name later, but the tall titan made his life easier by opening with "Call me Harot." Harot looked at the barrel and smiled. "I see the Beer Man comes as advertised. A welcome addition."

"Yeah," Owen said, as he shifted past to greet the third titan. "Help him get it pouring."

The third titan turned out to be yet another tournament fighter, this one for the Lone Coast. He was the Wave Rider. Van recalled he'd notched a victory against Marvell Sugarman yesterday around the same time Van had faced the Ram. He had long blonde hair that fell over his deeply tanned face. He wore an open shirt that exposed his smoothly muscled chest, shorts that showed long, hairy legs, and sandals.

In short order, all the titans were seated, beers in hands, and the glass pipe began another journey around. They all seemed to be on good terms with each other, friends even, which struck Van as unusual. He'd hardly ever seen a titan view another as anything beyond an obstacle to be thrown out of their way or choked out on the mat.

Sevendhi was looking at Van. "So, Van of the Uplands, the world is gracious to bring to me the titan who sent the Ram and his annoying legion of followers back home early." He had a clipped and precise way of speaking that made him difficult to follow.

"Uh, yeah," Van replied.

Sevendhi nodded "So many victories fill the room! I have a joyful heart. Van sent the Ram home, Marvell Sugarman falls before the mighty Wave Rider, Harot put an end to the dark dreams of the Butcher. And I have vanquished Great Golden Ghost in my long quest to tournament victory. And, of course, our friend Owen rests comfortably, knowing he has accrued more Headlock of Destiny victories than any titan in this room."

Owen, who was leaning over to take the pipe from the Wave Rider, looked at Van. "Sevendhi talks a lot. It's part of his charm."

"Sevendhi has no charm," Harot said in a solemn tone.

"Amazing how your wisdom turns on and off like a faucet," Sevendhi replied, his smile undampened. "I believe it is stuck in the off position right now."

Owen exhaled a thick cloud of smoke. "Van's got Panam next. I don't know if that's better or worse than Scott Flawless."

"Indeed," Sevendhi said, glancing up at the bracket across from him. "Flawless will be a great challenge. But if I must best all to win the tournament, why not bring the best early and often?" He took the pipe from Owen. "Mind, my legendary confidence did take a small hit when I saw that draw. Of course, the brackets may change. And it could be worse. Wave Rider has Judge

Cage." He shot the other titan a teasing glance. "Odd that our group of misfits has drawn so poorly..."

"What will the ONWC do about the OverLord?" Owen asked.

"A topic we discussed at great length before the unexpected pleasure of your arrival, friend Owen. We are of one mind that they will leave the Patriot Jack Hammer where he is and see what happens before they shift everything around to protect their precious Landshaker. King Thad, Scott Flawless, and Judge Cage are all already clear by virtue of the holy bracket."

Van took the pipe from Sevendhi. He was trying to figure it out as he said softly, "I saw him today. The OverLord."

"I saw him as well," L'Harot'Ni'Set said. "A very one-sided affair, which is ominous given how talented the Bearhugger is."

"No," Van replied. "I saw him in the streets after the match." The room fell quiet. "He walked past me dragging a coffin."

"He placed Bearhugger in there," Wave Rider said, voice solemn. "Stuffed him in like a child and latched the lid shut. That much I saw. I didn't see where he went, but the rumor is he dragged it to the center of the Parkland Cemetery."

"Yes," Sevendhi said, "and then threw it into a giant hole, which he then himself jumped into. Given he's no longer down there and the pit appears bottomless, people are quite reasonably presuming it is some sort of gateway to the Nether. And it remains open, even now."

"He talked to me." Van was still studying the pipe as he spoke softly. He had smoked plenty of weed before, just never through something so complicated. He drew deeply, watching as the smoke flowed from chamber to chamber before charging down his throat. He coughed loudly and chased it with some beer. When he looked up, they were all staring at him.

"And what did our visitor from the Nether say?" Sevendhi finally asked.

"He said the harvest has begun and the wars return. Then he told me to follow him." The words fell short of delivering that feeling of dread that had accompanied the titan, as heavy and solid as the coffin dragging behind him. Just thinking about it again, the idea that the land of storms and nightmares might be real, as real as the horrible thing Van had crossed paths with, made him feel small and afraid.

"Holy shit." Sevendhi's smile had faltered. "Troubling words from a troubling presence." He gestured to Van to pass the pipe across to Harot. "Do you know Kisket, Van? It is a beautiful land of flowing fields. While some do not believe in the Nether, in Kisket we very much do. In part because our land is so much like paradise—the opposite must also have station on this world."

"You all fuck sheep," Wave Rider said. Everyone laughed.

"Our sheep are so beautiful we simply cannot help ourselves," Sevendhi said in mock seriousness. "Never have you seen such beautiful sheep. The presence of sheep so beautiful we offer as proof there must be some sort of hellish sheep in other parts of the world."

"I think Van already fought your hell sheep," Wave Rider replied. "And destroyed Palace West while he was at it. They had to move my match."

"Indeed. A far more thrilling fight than that dished out by the OverLord. And friendlier grounds for discussion amongst us." Sevendhi had the pipe again, Van was losing track. "Have I told you, friend Van, that I had a tournament victory last year? I defeated the Minotaur. It requires a similar strategy, or really a corollary one, to that which you employed against the Ram."

"Huh?" Van said. The smoke was getting right under him. He leveled off by finishing his beer and rose to draw another.

"The Ram is all straight lines. He must be countered with circles. Change his direction, move his force. As you did." Sevendhi used his hands to describe the strategy, miming circles and lines. "Until the time came to break the rules. You met him in strength at the beginning and the end of a worthy match. Well strategized. I saw the hand of master wrestler Owen Grit in it." He leveled a look at Owen. "While we weep for your injury, friend Owen, none of us would have looked forward to a date in the ring with a healthy Grit brother. But so the Minotaur, he fights in circles. Turns and grapples. Always twisting you from your center to toss you to the ground and fall upon you with those nasty fucking horns. Him I countered in straight lines, dictated the fight." Sevendhi looked up, then blew a perfect smoke ring. He pierced it with a straight arrow of smoke in his next breath.

"If only you fought half as good as you bullshit, Sevendhi," the Wave Rider said.

"I must bullshit," Sevendhi answered. "I am but a slip of a ten-man compared to you tournament titans. Plus I faced a bull."

"You've been talking about that fight for a year."

"Bear with me. I will soon perfect the story of my more recent victory against the Great Golden Ghost and you can listen to that numerous times. That and my subsequent victories over Scott Flawless and whoever else the ONWC foolishly places in my path."

Owen took another slow pull on the pipe. He expelled a lungful of smoke into the center of the room, then spoke casually. "That fight against the Ram was all Van. I didn't help him prep."

Harot and the Wave Rider seemed to have universally placid demeanors, but Sevendhi looked shocked at the comment. "Why not?" he asked. When Owen simply shrugged, Sevendhi leaned forward. "He is your countryman. He is here to bring honor to the Uplands. You don't view your support of the Uplands as a duty?"

Owen shrugged. "Guess I didn't. I'm starting to change my mind though." He didn't look at Van.

"Well, take your time," Sevendhi said, a touch of irritation in his voice. "Surely the tournament will pause as you find a stable mind on the matter. Perhaps Harot has some books on the subject. We could form a weekly study group to help you on your journey."

"Fuck off, Sevendhi."

"I will never understand this lack of pride in one's homeland. You don't wish to see the Uplands earn respect? Even if it is not you in the ring?" He shook his head, then picked up the pipe and began repacking it with dense green herb. "If you were from Kisket there would be no doubts in your mind."

"Please don't start talking about how attractive the sheep are again," the Wave Rider said. "I ate before coming by."

Sevendhi smiled again, glancing up at the titan. "Are we to pretend you don't go on and on about the beauties of the Lone Coast?"

"I don't have to. Anyone who comes never wants to leave."

"Let it go, Sevendhi," Owen said with a growl. "I'm gonna help Van now. We're not all such flag-waving patriots. Doesn't mean I want to see the Uplands lose."

Harot jumped in with mock sincerity. "Yes, Owen, why can't you be more like the Patriot Jack Hammer?

Charging around the ring waving that flag, getting all the little Peakfall fans on their feet?"

"We'll see who's charged up if the OverLord comes back," Owen replied. He pointed to the bracket showing the Patriot facing the champion of the Nether.

Sevendhi was ignoring them. He stared intently at Van. "Friend Van, we are new to our acquaintanceship, but allow me to give you some advice. Representing your nation at the Headlock of Destiny is the highest of honors. Too many titans believe that they themselves are the focus of the crowds, that the goal is personal glory. It is far greater. It is a chance to be the champion for your people. All of your people, from the highest to the lowest, richest to poorest. When you truly embrace that feeling, you are not alone in the squared circle. You are the voice of thousands, the strength of thousands. Van, do you love your homeland?"

Van didn't answer the rhetorical question, though images flew through his mind. All the bad things he'd thought about when the OverLord drew ever nearer on the quiet street. Van's loneliness, the way he was carted from one house to another as a child, starved for love and encouragement. The way everyone treated him like an afterthought and a failure now. But there was another side to it. There were things he loved about Headwaters. The beauty of the mountains in the distance. The brewery. The way everyone came together at festival time and even the lowliest shift worker could exchange words with the owners. Of course, he'd never been anyone's champion. They'd have laughed their asses off if he offered.

Sevendhi spoke through the cloud of smoke surrounding Van. "Van, we are raised to greatness, not by virtue of our size and strength, but by virtue of the faith and trust placed in us by our people. Kisket has named me their champion. I am humbled and invigorated beyond words. And when another replaces me, I will stand beside him, for now he is my champion as well. And we will bring great victories to Kisket."

Van, who had followed maybe one word in three of that speech, looked around the room. He leaned forward, bringing the pipe Sevendhi handed him to his lips. "Ain't that fucking right."

Chapter 22

The beer flowed and the pipe continued to pass. The titans moved about the room with comfortable ease, such that it seemed to grow larger and smaller as the flow of the gathering dictated. Or maybe Van was just getting too high for his own good.

He looked over as the Wave Rider slid onto the sofa beside him. The Rider gave a friendly nod and swept his hair back out of his eyes. "So you've got Panam Manley next?" he asked. "Have you met him?"

Van nodded.

"Super cool ten-man," the Wave Rider said, "He brought his crew out to Lone Coast for a month last summer. We had some fantastic times." He shook his head and let his fingers tap out a beat on the arm of the sofa. "Absolute bitch of a draw for you though. He's one hell of a wrestler. Guessing that's not news to you, though."

"No. But if I listened to the odds, I'd already be back home."

The Wave Rider chuckled. "That's the spirit."

"You've got Judge Cage?" Van tried to make the words casual, like he was used to these kinds of conversations.

"Yeah. Nightmare, that one. Likes to handcuff his beaten opponents, kick them around the ring for sport." There was a hardness to the Wave Rider's eyes that belied his casual tone. "And it's not just titans he picks on. He's a real force of evil in Empire City. No way he'll be a pushover, he's one of the ONWC glory boys for a reason, but it sure would add a sweetener to a tournament victory to have it be against that fucking fascist."

There was a pause before Van asked, "They call you the Wave Rider because you surf?"

"You know, I actually don't. The Lone Coast is all about it, but I'd rather just chill on the beach. I didn't come with a name so they gave me the easiest one they could come up with. I tried telling the tournament people I don't surf once or twice. They don't care."

Van glanced over at the barrel of beer parked in the corner. "I know how that goes."

"But after a while I kind of grew to dig it," the Wave Rider said. "Back home they hardly believe me about what a big deal this all is."

"Are there a lot of Lone Coast fans around?"

"Probably none would be my guess."

Van grunted and took a drink from his beer. "They'll be a match for the Uplands crowd then. Normally they love the tournament. Not this time around, for some odd reason." His laugh was loaded with self-pity.

"Don't sweat that stuff, ten-man. They'll come around. Jump on that bandwagon after you send Panam packing." He offered an easy smile with a certainty Van could never match. "The Lone Coast, though, the tournament isn't really our thing. The politicians sweat it and no one else does. My friends think it's a little weird that I travel here every year. They'll listen to the stories, long as they're interesting, but not their thing."

"So is it national pride that gets you to step into a ring with the likes of Judge Cage?"

"No. My pride isn't tied up into the Headlock. Everyone's got their own take on it, and that's all good, man. Sevendhi's got his national pride thing. Harot's all about titans' rights and the history and all that. Owen loves the sport. Me, I like the concept."

"The concept?"

"Yeah. It's kind of beautiful. You see that bracket over there?" He pointed to the large chalk bracket Sevendhi had marked out on one wall. "What does it look like to you?"

"What do you mean?"

"To me, it is a thing of beauty. I mean, look at it. The ugliness of the mechanism offset by the passion of the names. Thirty-two titans, each one fueled by hopes and dreams. And all ONWC does is put a schedule to the conflict inherent in those dreams. All they do is lay out a series of places and times. And we do the rest. ONWC has done everything they can to monetize it and create order for the benefit of the crowds. But they can't challenge the core of it. The core is me and Judge Cage stepping into the ring. Who is strongest at that exact moment in time, in that exact space in the world? Only one winner in the squared circle. And then repeat again and again until there's only one standing. It's beautiful music, almost like the waves crashing against the sand. I love it."

The Wave Rider seemed someplace far away for a moment, as though looking out on a far horizon. Then he gestured around the room. "These guys don't all talk about it the same way, but when they win, they know what I mean. When they lose, too." He leaned back into the sofa, smiling a satisfied smile.

As the pipe came around again, Van stood to refill his beer. He might not be able to handle getting much higher. L'Harot'Ni'Set stood by the barrel, and gave Van a welcoming nod. The titan had a relaxed manner like the Wave Rider. But where the Rider seemed fully at peace with his surroundings, possessing a sort of contagious ease, Harot held an intimidating intelligence in his gaze, as though the world were a puzzle to solve. He reminded Van of the brewmasters in Headwaters, when their talk of hops strains and the qualities of a new yeast grew in complexity and nuance far past what Van could hang with. He had a feeling Harot could talk with them for hours.

"Do you know your parentage, Van?" the titan asked.

"No," Van said, shifting uncomfortably. "Well, I know who my mom was but she died in childbirth."

"A not uncommon phenomenon. There are large bodies of research available to prevent such occurrences, but the Open Nations is wildly negligent in distributing it. The current system suits them quite fine."

"Huh?"

"If more women die in childbirth with titan babies, then women will be reluctant to get pregnant with titan babies in the first place. Thus the titan population is kept manageable." Harot took a drink, peering at Van over the rim of his glass. "That your father chose to have no role in your life, well, that is another piece of the current system that suits the Open Nations just fine."

"I never heard anything about a system to manage titans."

"It is all around you, Van. In fact, you stand in the very heart of it. You were educated in your local school? And raised by local families, probably different ones over the years? Did you ever think to ask why?"

"Why what?"

"Why the Headwaters took it upon themselves to raise you as a community?"

"I don't know."

"But what were you told, either directly or through custom? Why did the community raise you?"

Van was getting confused, wondering if he'd smoked too much. "Because then they get a local wrestler, one with ties to the region. One who helps them compete in regionals, maybe even the tournament. Up until a few days ago I just worked in the brewery but even if I wasn't a wrestler, I guess I was a pretty good worker. I gave something back to the community…most of the time." He couldn't keep the defensiveness out of his tone.

Harot was nodding. "Yes, you were raised to be a champion, as Sevendhi would describe it. Or at least a candidate for a champion. But that is not why they did it, Van. Or, I should say, while some may believe that, whether they do or not, it is *against the law* for them to do otherwise. To do anything other than raise you in the community where you were born. It has been since the Titan Wars."

"We learned about the Titan Wars in school."

"But I have a feeling, Van, the lesson you learned was colored by the Open Nations, tailored to serve their ends." Harot set down his beer and folded his hands behind his back. Van sensed he was gearing up for an epic lecture. "The truth about the Titan Wars is—"

"Yes," Sevendhi broke in from the seating area, "tell us the truth, Harot! Let the lies no longer cloud poor Van's mind!" He held up the pipe, fully loaded with green herb again. "But first smoke this." He somehow shot Van a wink without breaking eye contact with Harot.

Harot gave an insulted sniff, then waved a hand at the pipe. It began floating across the room towards him. Van stared in disbelief as it hovered past his face. "What the hell?" he asked.

Harot plucked the pipe from the air. He inhaled deeply then sent a lungful of smoke out into the room. He shot Van an amused look. "You've fought a giant ram, seen dragons fly the skies above, and you question this?"

"Uh…" Van stammered. He'd seen magic, but never so closely or delivered so casually. Most sorcerers got good at one or two tasks, like controlling the weather or making fountains, and then made a good living doing it over and over again for rich people. They were supposedly quite dull.

"Titans have far more to offer than many understand," Harot said in his lecturing tone. "We are born closer to magic than humans. If more titans bothered, they would see there is much untapped potential." He looked at the pipe. "I can move things with my mind. Not incredibly heavy things, and not incredibly fast. It helps me distract opponents. And keep students awake." He looked over to the group on the sofa, which sagged under the weight of multiple titans. With a gesture, he made a bottle of whiskey on the table levitate a few inches, then loudly slam back to its surface. "Now where was I?"

Owen cut in from the sofa's lowest point. "Did I say Sevendhi talked a lot? I meant Harot. Will you at least give him the brief version? You already wowed him with your little trick. Incidentally, Van, if you ever face Harot in the ring, expect to be hit by some random objects right when you're trying to focus on—"

"The brief version?" Harot was indignant. "Of the Titan Wars? Literally the defining event of the Open Nations?"

"Yes, please," Owen answered.

"And try not to use the word...um...*neutral*," Sevendhi added with a smirk. "I've always hated that word."

"How's this for brief?" He sent the pipe levitating back across the room and turned to Van. "Titans assembled to face a great terror, an army of the undead which threatened all living things. They successfully defended our world. When their purpose was fulfilled, they turned to look for a homeland. All the lands were taken and their peoples feared the titan army. War ensued. A coalition of men, formed of what is now the

Open Nations, stopped the advance of the titans, drawing on vastly superior numbers. The titans were forced to disperse across their lands."

"Pretty good," Owen said. "Maybe the best description of the Titan Wars I've ever heard. Cut right through that boring debate over whether it was one war or two."

"It was two. Thus the plural." Harot turned to Van. "The important foundational understanding, Van, is whether one believes titans were descended from giants or ascended from man."

Owen shook his head. "You're slipping back into lecture mode, Harot."

"It's an important point. A foundational understanding."

"You said that already," Owen quipped.

Harot gave Van a pained look. "It's like this. The Open Nations would have you believe we are descended from giants. Our creation myth, and I assure you it is a myth, is that at the dawn of the world, giants lived in the skies above. But the giants Jugor, Ergoth Sintan, and Malachisin turned to stone and fell to the earth below. The titans are their shattered pieces, all that remains. It is an important myth, because it paints titans as being of another race. A threat to be contained. It also paints us as fallen from greatness. We could just as easily tell a legend of titans growing from men. But they wouldn't like that. That we should be respected rather than feared. No one knows the truth and so we all choose to believe the stories that suit our purposes.

"Say you are the Open Nations, a fragile coalition in its early days, what can you do to manage the threat of this titan army? Much as you'd like to kill them all and wipe your hands of the troublesome titan race, you lack the balls and the means to slaughter its remnants, knowing that the start of a genocide would trigger yet another war. They call us ten-men, but in war we are more like thousand-men. The numbers and cost associated with the first struggle against the titan army were immeasurable. Yet no one wants to surrender their lands to the remaining titans. Ideally you want to divide them, so that they cannot again form an army around a singular cause. So you take the following steps. Firstly, you give them some lands and station, but divided across the Open Nations. Secondly, you insist each titan of following generations is raised where he is born, giving every titan ties to a different homeland. Finally, you salt the soil of their culture and comradery by introducing and promoting combat as the exclusive means by which titans interact. An aggressive, winner-take-all format, which has the byproduct of paying for itself and entertaining the masses. What we now call wrestling. Over time, you find the destructive energies of the titans pointed towards each other rather than the Open Nations. It's almost genius. Van, you were raised by your community not because they wanted a champion, but because it is the law. And now you are representing them in combat against the very people they fear you uniting with. If every titan has ties to his home and hates every other titan, we will never come together again." He gestured at the listening titans. "Look at us here, gathered solely to crush each other. There may be peace in this room, but if you place two of us in a ring, we will strive to destroy one another in a vain pursuit of glory. But the ring is not a stage, it is a prison." He picked up his beer, slugged it down, then set it on the barrel with a clunk. "And that's the fastest I've ever made that point."

There was mocking applause from the three other titans as Van stared at Harot. His head hurt. It had started hurting when Harot used his mind to float the pipe over. The subsequent lecture had only made it worse. "Why do you fight then? If it's all a sham."

"Because when I win, I gain power and esteem. And then others will listen. As it is now, you can see how I barely hold the attention of my closest titan friends."

Sevendhi laughed. "We all have different reasons, Van. I fight because I love my home, I love my people, and that is all I know. If it is a cage, I have grown to love my cage. Besides, who wants to live in a land of all titans? Can you imagine the smell?"

Van refilled his beer and the titans all settled back down onto the sofas as the pipe made its way around again. Van was so lightheaded he felt like he might float. "Can I ask a stupid question?" he managed. When Harot nodded, he asked, "What about women? Why are there no female titans? How does that fit in the stories, the…uh…creation myth?"

Harot nodded sagely. "Far from a stupid question, Van from Headwaters. Many have asked but no one truly knows. There may be a female equivalent to our race. But it operates under a feminine guise rather than a masculine. Meaning it does not content itself to smash heads for the entertainment of others. I believe the female titans have a different form. And not only have they chosen a different path, they have also chosen to conceal it at this time. Could be they are having far greater success than we are, but I do not know how.

"Some believe the female guise or equivalent of the titans is the valkyrie. From that same creation myth I just gave you the ridiculously abridged version of, they are descended from the giants of the skies, those who did not turn to stone and fall to the earth." Harot began flicking his fingers, and the smoke above the titans formed birdlike shapes. "They guarded the borders of the skylands, keeping the stone giants from doing greater harm." He let the smoke dissipate. "How that ties to reality is anyone's guess. No one has seen valkyrie since the Titan Wars. It is rumored that they were part of the effort to stop the titan army but that chapter in history has always been prone to manipulation."

Van looked around at the others, then back at Harot. "What are valkyrie?"

"Winged women soldiers of great strength, the type that would match a titan."

Sevendhi leaned across towards Van, the sofa creaking under his weight. "For the record, Van, you should be aware that Harot knows absolutely nothing about women."

Van thought of Kyle, Annie. And all the other women he'd chased after only to have them run a little faster or swerve into someone else's arms. "That makes two of us."

The titans all laughed and continued drinking late into the night.

Chapter 23

Van woke in his bed, head spinning from a hangover laden with heavy thoughts. It was a match day. His time was up. Panam Manley would correct the balance sheet tonight and remind everyone that Van didn't belong here. The weighty talk of last night had just reminded him of how large the world was, and how small he was by comparison. He felt more than ever like he was caught up in vast currents that he could do nothing to shift or escape.

The rest of the Uplands group was nowhere to be found, so Van hit the streets by himself. Sevendhi had asked him last night, several times in fact, if Van would be at his fight against Scott Flawless this afternoon. Van set out for the Coliseum, the center of Empire City. It was impossible to miss, looming over the other buildings like a palace.

They let him in without a ticket, and he passed long rows of wooden bleachers to take a seat near the ring. Creature and Eagle sat across the way. There was no sign of Venerate Holland, ONWC's ranking asshole. Van cheerfully gave the finger to the bodyguards, then leaned back and closed his eyes while he waited for the fight to start. Kyle failed to materialize and whisper in his ear, to his chagrin. He hadn't seen her since yesterday.

He'd like to watch the Wave Rider face Judge Cage, but they were scheduled to overlap with his own fight against Panam Manley. If Panam Manley somehow managed to knock himself out of the fight, maybe break his legs during his walk-in, Van would face the winner of those two.

The crowd filled in around Van. This didn't appear to be one of the hottest tickets, though there were plenty of enthusiastic Scott Flawless fans. Van gazed around the Coliseum while he waited for the bell. The bleachers seemed to climb up to the clouds, but they were secondary in scale to the hundreds of raised boxes that formed high walls around the structure. They were densely packed with thousands of well-dressed socialites, gossiping amidst clouds of smoke, armed with a variety of drinks in hand.

Sevendhi strode down the stone steps. He rolled under the ropes and stood to a smattering of applause. He waved cheerfully to Van, then bowed deeply to one of the high boxes. A woman with dark skin and an ornate headdress leaned over the box railing and returned the gesture.

The crowd didn't really get excited until Scott Flawless was announced. The massive titan strode down the aisle, his black curls bouncing gently in the sunlight. He wore a tight pink one-piece, and walked to the ring slowly, giving everyone time to look at his chiseled face and carefully clenched muscles. Instead of simply stepping into the ring, he climbed to the top rope and balanced there with his arms outstretched as the crowd cheered. "Flawless," he said loudly, gazing down at his impressive pecs, then he leapt onto the mat. Van thought it was one of the dumber things he'd ever seen.

The bell rang and the titans got down to business. There was no doubt Van was pulling for Sevendhi. He had been friendly and charming and seemed like a genuinely good titan, something Van hadn't known existed before meeting Owen's friends last night. Scott Flawless was clearly a prick. He also represented the

Valley of Sevens, which was firmly on the ONWC side of things.

But there was a reason Flawless was recognized as one of the best technical wrestlers in the business, and it became apparent early. He seemed to laze about the ring, hands hanging by his sides, but Van noticed he never wasted any motion. Each step brought him closer to Sevendhi. He seemed to always be in the right place, and when he suddenly surged into an attack, he had lightning speed to match his precision. Van could tell why he was one of the favored titans in the tournament.

Sevendhi matched his speed, attacking low and high, trying to prevent the larger titan from trapping him in the corners. He smiled widely as he worked the angles, seeking a crack in Flawless's careful defense. But Van watched the smile slowly fade as Scott Flawless continued to handle him with ease.

Flawless was brutally efficient, taking advantage of every mistake Sevendhi made. Sevendhi slowed as the punishment of endless slaps, backfists, and throws began to pile up. Flawless dealt harder and harder blows as Sevendhi's ability to escape faded.

Finally, Flawless got Sevendhi off the ground and hoisted him overhead. He slammed Sevendhi brutally into the mat. Sevendhi cried out as he rolled over, cradling an injured arm. Flawless smiled, then kicked the arm. Sevendhi screamed as the heavy boot struck him. Flawless laughed and reached down to pull the injured limb away from Sevendhi's torso. He twisted, forcing Sevendhi to roll over. Then he lined up and dropped a knee carrying his entire weight on Sevendhi's arm. A loud snap echoed through the stadium. Even the most bloodthirsty of fans winced at the sound.

Van thought he might be sick. Sevendhi's face was ashen, his eyes closed, as Flawless preened around the ring. As cheers rose again, Flawless stood basking in the attention, and dusted off his shoulders. Then he slowly raised his arms in the air, turning to face all four sides of the ring. For a grand finale, he climbed the ropes, flexed his biceps, and loudly proclaimed, "Flawless."

. . .

After the match, Van headed through the quiet back halls under the Coliseum towards Sevendhi's locker room. He could smell the sweat that slickened the stones beneath his bare feet. Thousands of titans had walked these halls, always preceding or following violence. A doctor scurried past Van, shaking her head and hastily shoving bloodied bandages in a black bag.

Van was nearing the open doorway which led to Sevendhi's locker room when the sound of crying stopped him in his tracks.

"I let you down. I let everyone down."

Van peeked around the doorframe. Sevendhi leaned over a dressing table, one hand to his forehead. His other arm was tightly bandaged to his side. He forced his stilted words through tears.

A woman in an elegant robe that reached the floor and a jeweled crown atop her head that sparkled in the light of the torches had her arms wrapped around him. Her voice was maternally patient. "You did no such thing, Sevendhi. We are proud of you."

"I'm so ashamed," he said with a fresh spate of sobs.

"There, there. My mighty titan. You carry on so. We are all proud of you. Kisket is proud of you." The woman began humming softly, something like a lullaby, as Sevendhi cried. Then she continued, "Dear Sevendhi, must we go over this every time? We know what you are up against. What we all are up against. You cannot blame yourself."

"I'm the one in the ring," he said, wiping tears from his dark cheeks. "And I've failed you again."

"Hush, Sevendhi. It will be okay. It will be okay."

"Will it?" he asked, eyes rising to meet hers. Van ducked back out of sight.

The woman sighed. "It will be as it always is. The Valley of Sevens and the Vantages and Moggy Flats will continue to squeeze everything they can from our land. They will threaten, coerce, and bully at every turn. You defeating that...that fucking peacock wouldn't change that."

"It would have helped. You know it would have helped. It would have shown them our heads are not bowed."

"Dear Sevendhi. You have shown them that." She sighed, taking his hand in hers. "Yours is the heart of an elephant, but we cannot ask one man, even one ten-man, to do the impossible. You have given us every bit of yourself. You are our champion. You are my champion. Perhaps even more so on the days when I must pick you up rather than the days you lift me." She kissed him on the forehead. Sevendhi's eyes were closed, tears streaming down. "My champion," she said again softly.

As Sevendhi settled into another spate of quiet crying, Van looked up, startled to see Owen Grit standing next to him. Owen gave a nod towards the door. "I think he needs us."

Van looked back with wide eyes. "I don't know if I should..." He trailed off.

"Come on," Owen said, giving Van a gentle shove on the shoulder. "He needs to know he's not alone. We all suffer sometimes. Even fucking titans."

Van slowly nodded. As Owen limped past him into the locker room, he summoned his courage and followed.

Chapter 24

The sun set and the crowds gathered for the evening matches. Under the bright lights of the Empire City Coliseum, the Wave Rider would battle Judge Cage. A substantial crowd waited at the Stomping Grounds to see if the OverLord would appear again, this time to square off with the Patriot Jack Hammer. And, finally, in the largest draw of the evening, Van the Beer Man was up against the wildly popular Panam Manley in Dunham Arena, which everyone just called the Cylinder.

The Cylinder was a vertical structure, designed to bring the crowd as close to the fights as possible. The ring was a regulation five-and-half titan paces across. Multiple levels of creaking bleachers swayed around it under the weight of the crowd. Chain-link fence was stapled to the enormous beams that formed a cylinder around and above the ring, often the only thing preventing drunk and overzealous fans from toppling over into the action. With tonight's fight just moments away, the crowd was pressed up against the fencing, howling for blood and entertainment. Beer and broken glass rained down from the highest levels, seeming to spur on the crowd below, which grew louder and wilder as the whole structure shook and trembled.

Van stood in the center of the ring, waiting, fighting the urge to piss his blue brewery uniform. Owen leaned casually against the ropes in Van's corner, a barrel of a local Derry, mediocre at best, inches from his bandaged knee. Larvell, who had talked nonstop all the way here about his faith in Van's ability to pull this off despite the towering odds against him, had a reassuring smile plastered on his sweaty face. The terror in his eyes told the true story.

"I'm so fucked," Van said quietly to himself, wondering if there had ever been another tournament titan less suited to be standing here, patiently waiting for his total humiliation and physical destruction. He'd seen no sign of Holland and his goons, Eagle and Creature. Holland had probably figured out how little chance Van had to win this fight. He'd get what he wanted if he was patient. "At least it can't get much worse than this," Van muttered.

Then Panam Manley entered the Cylinder.

There was no long walk, no rising murmur as the crowd recognized his approach. He wasn't there, and then suddenly he was ringside, standing tall in outrageous red-and-gold zebra-striped pants and a pink tank top, mirror shades parked atop his head. Tanned and handsome, muscled for days, a damn god, come to take the glory that was his by right. Van was ready to surrender before the match even began.

Thousands of rowdies in the crowd wore the green and gold of Palos Soros and thousands more wore brightly colored and ridiculously patterned getups that looked like an attempt to pay tribute to Panam's uniquely insane style. They were all here for Panam Manley and they jumped to their feet, stomping and cheering. The noise fell onto Van like a waterfall, pressing him down into the mat, pushing him from all directions at once so that it felt he was being squeezed down to a smaller size. Maybe if he got smaller he could just slip away. Van looked over at his corner and received an awkward thumbs-up from Larvell, whose smile was so wide Van thought he might have broken something internally. Owen simply shrugged. What a team.

Panam Manley vaulted into the ring, clearing the top rope with a single leap from the Cylinder's stone floor. He landed amidst the broken glass, the shreds of chain link, and other assorted garbage that had been littered into the sacred squared circle. Panam gave it a slow and curious sweep with a gold boot, then smiled up and around at the crowd. Which they fucking loved. Everywhere his gaze fell, a new frenzy exploded. They shook the fence until Van was certain the whole thing would collapse. It would be Palace West all over again.

Then Panam turned his deep, ice-blue stare to Van. Van felt the full force of the titan's charisma, amplified by the howling maniacs all around. His body couldn't make up its mind how to surrender to its fear. Panam, with the slightest tilt of his eyes, left Van standing in the center of the ring and sauntered over to Van's corner. He greeted Owen Grit with a hug, then broke away with a conciliatory gesture towards Owen's injured knee. Van felt slighted, as though Panam had already landed the first blow. Then he felt guilty for feeling that way. One of Panam's friends from the basement party, the mohawked Slade, took a spot in Panam's corner. He leaned over the ropes, glass of brown liquor in one hand, lit cigarette in the other, and offered Van a friendly nod. Should Van go hug *him*? He hated this shit.

Panam finally strolled back to the center of the ring to meet Van and the ref, yet another indistinct, small man with carefully combed hair. The ref murmured some words about fighting fair, while he stared up at Panam in naked awe. Van was surprised he didn't ask for an autograph. When he finished, Panam did the thing he'd done so well at the party, shifted his body and closed in on Van, slow and nonthreatening, indicating that he and Van would be stepping into a private conversation for a moment before he separated Van from his limbs. Van swallowed as Panam gently placed his giant hands on Van's shoulders. Would he throw him to the mat? Embarrass him like the Living Portrait had? But Panam simply leaned in close to Van's ear.

"It's just us here, right now, Van," Panam said softly. "And I want you to know that I consider every titan I fight to be a brother for life." He paused a moment, glancing around them with a smile as though there were no place he'd rather be. "Such a beautiful world. I gotta tell you, I fucking love the Cylinder." He looked Van in the eyes. "In a second, we're gonna start bashing each other good, and one of us will be left standing over the other at the end. But after that end, we'll be brothers for life. I hope you feel the same, Van. Just something I say before every match, but not everyone hears it. I got a feeling you do, brother."

Van met Panam's eyes, deep and blue as the ocean, and nodded. Panam smiled and stepped away, not afraid to show Van his back. Van looked over to his corner. Larvell had moved over to chat with Slade and was shaking his head. Owen nudged Van's barrel with his good leg, probably wondering how long it would be before they could open it...and whether or not Van would have an unbroken arm left to lift a mug with.

Panam Manley started hyping up the crowd. He struck pose after pose, slowly building up energy, using his eyes and body to assure everyone in the Cylinder, from the ground level to the fifth balcony, that they were about to get a show. He ended by dropping into a split, arms extended, and rose with a self-deprecating smile. Van thought the crowd was loud before; they were practically deafening now.

All traces of Panam's friendliness disappeared as he turned once again to face Van. Suddenly those eyes, so warm and inviting, were steel, a hunter's eyes. The giant hands that had caressed Van's shoulders were coiled like venomous snakes, ready to tear him to pieces. Panam became a predator. An alpha who had been challenged and aimed to correct that mistake with the ferocity of an angered dragon. He dropped into a fighting stance. The ref took his cue and waved for the fight to begin. The bell followed, startling Van, who had been as enraptured by Panam's theatrics as everyone else.

Van met Panam's initial charge and they locked in a grapple. As when he'd grappled with the Living Portrait, Van could feel Panam's superior balance, his more experienced grip. But Van could match him for strength, and he leaned into Panam. They circled, entwined, until Panam suddenly dropped into a split again. Van stumbled forward and Panam punched him in the nuts. Then Panam whirled around, slipped an arm behind Van's legs, and tossed him, still cradling his testicles, backwards onto the mat.

Panam jumped to his feet. Rather than press his advantage, he worked the crowd, waving his arms to keep them standing and cheering, as Van tried to recover. They howled and shook the fence, raining more beer and glass onto the ring. Van stood, broken glass crumbling beneath the toughened soles of his bare feet. One hand clutched his smarting balls. He tried to wipe the sad-dog expression off his face.

Panam came at him again. Van threw a straight right. Panam ducked it and smoothly wrapped Van into a full nelson. Van struggled in the titan's hold, and threw his head back. Panam craned his neck and dodged it. Panam cruelly tightened his grip, crushing Van's head down onto his chest. Van felt the bones in his neck separating. He threw everything he had backwards, but Panam sprung the hold. Van overbalanced, staggered backwards. Panam landed two punches in quick succession to Van's kidneys, then slid an arm between Van's legs and hoisted him up sideways. He charged the ropes and threw Van out of the ring.

Van crashed to the floor of the Cylinder and rolled into the chain-link fence outside the ring. It took him a moment to find the strength to even groan and roll over. The fans, thrilled to have the latest victim of their favorite titan at their feet, screamed in his ears and poured beer on him. Van clambered to his feet again, staggering, as his hip, which had led the charge to the hard floor, pulsed with sharp pain. Panam was still in the ring chatting with Owen. The ref stood next to them like an awkward hanger-on at a party, desperate to join the conversation.

Van climbed painfully back under the ropes and into the ring. Panam ignored him, acted like he didn't know Van had reentered the ring until the crowd let him know with their delirious screaming that Van had taken a fighting stance. He turned to Van, grinning.

The two titans squared off again. Van sensed a difference in Panam's approach. He moved more slowly, seeming to analyze Van's reactions to the shifts of his boots on the mat. Van tried to figure out what Manley was doing. *I'm not what he expected*, Van realized as he felt the titan's eyes on him. *He thought this would be a real fight. He wanted a real fight.* The question then was how Panam would make a good show of it for his raving fans.

He would destroy Van.

Panam stepped slowly toward Van, clenched his shoulders again, and again flipped Van around and locked him into full nelson. He bent Van forward and drove him headfirst down into the mat. Then he dragged Van off the mat—all Van saw was the string of drool winding from his mouth—and bodyslammed him down on his back. Panam waited just long enough for Van to struggle back to his feet, then he hit him with a running clothesline. The crowd's cheering felt like an earthquake in Van's ears. He lay sprawled on the mat, not sure if he was awake or dreaming.

Panam kept piling on the abuse, and Van's mind stubbornly clung to consciousness well past an advisable point. If he just let go, it could be over. He looked forward to slinking off back to Headwaters where he belonged as soon as this nightmare was over. Every part of his body begged for relief. He felt the imprint of a thousand punches on his face and ribs, a thousand knees and shoulders on his back and chest. He was done, all kinds of done, no longer even bothering to watch Panam set up the next torture. As Van lay on his back in the center of the ring, he heard the rising roar of the crowd. It sounded like something big and horrible was coming his way. He was amazed they had the energy left. He realized his eyes were closed, so he opened them slowly.

Panam was a speck in the distance above. He clung by one hand to the fence wrapping the Cylinder, nearly up to the third balcony, the big toe on each foot nestled into the spaces between the links. Van watched with growing horror as Panam raised his arm, orchestrating the crowd into a frenzy that shook the arena. Then he leapt, somersaulting in midair as he plummeted toward Van.

Panam Manley had an almost mesmerizing grace and poise as he fell. The air blew through his long hair like a summer breeze. Time seemed to slow as Van watched him gain speed. The sight was so impressive it took Van a moment to recall exactly where he was and to understand that the steadily growing titan shape, falling like a meteor, was headed directly at him. When the understanding came to him, Van screamed like a girl and rolled hard to the right.

Van's foot flailed out wildly as he rolled and, by pure chance, caught Panam Manley on the descending chin. Panam lost control and his head rocked back as he slammed into the mat where Van had been daydreaming moments before. The mat trembled, buckling so hard Van's heavy body was briefly airborne.

Then everything fell quiet.

Van climbed to one knee and painfully craned his neck to look at Panam Manley. The titan was stretched out on the mat, all signs of life gone. "Holy shit, is he dead?" Van asked, unsure if anyone was listening. The ref looked at Van, eyes wide. Van pointed towards the still titan. "Fucking check his pulse, man."

The ref initially shook his head, but after a moment's hesitation, he moved towards Panam. The silence of the crowd was deafening. He reached out tentatively and snuck a hand under the titan's chin. Finally he spoke, relief in his voice. "He's alive."

Suddenly Owen was by Van's side, whispering in his ear. "Get him to raise your hand and then we gotta get the hell out of here."

"What?"

Owen didn't wait. He limped forward and grabbed the ref, then dragged him protesting over to Van. "Last ten-man standing! Raise his fucking hand!"

The ref looked back and forth between Van and Owen. Then he looked over at Manley stretched out on the mat. Somewhere in the distance, Slade was coughing, the only sound in the otherwise still arena. Van thought he might have swallowed his cigarette. Finally the ref shrugged, reached out, and seized Van's arm. He raised it with a decided lack of enthusiasm and turned to walk away.

A trickle of boos started up, then picked up intensity as more of the ludicrously attired Palos Soros fans slowly realized what had happened—that the limpdick titan who'd spent the last fifteen minutes getting his head ground into the mat while clutching his balls had just stolen a Headlock victory from their champion.

Beer and glass, along with some of the foulest profanity Van had ever heard, rained down from the Cylinder. Owen shoved Van. "Grab that fucking barrel and run."

And so Van the Beer Man's second tournament match ended and he and his corner fled for the exit, steps ahead of a bloodthirsty mob, robbed of the tantalizing victory that had been seconds away. The frenzied crowd protested as they were left behind, but once they no longer had a focus for their anger, they likewise went for the exits, carrying with them the story of how Panam Manley had reached for the skies but instead crashed to the hard and unforgiving ground.

Chapter 25

Empire City was up late partying, the night warm, the streets packed. Musicians played at nearly every corner, half of them partnered with sorcerers who orchestrated flashes of light and color in time to the beat. In the blocks between them, storytellers fought to be heard over the din, dredging up tales of wrestling matches old and new. Beer poured freely and spontaneous fights broke out, some good-natured, some not.

The crowds were happy to include a tournament titan in the mix. And once he'd left the arena, no one seemed to care exactly how Van's victory had come. They handed him beer after beer as he made his way through the busy streets.

Owen and Larvell trailed behind Van. Owen was uninterested in the scene. He provided a surly escort for a few blocks, but after the third beer stop in as many blocks, he left, murmuring something about wanting a more quiet environment. Not Van, though. Tonight he wanted the crowds.

Van shook Larvell by pretending he needed a piss and ducking out the backdoor of a tavern. Then he was on his own in Empire City, free to follow his dirty bare feet where they took him, second tournament victory under his belt.

Much to his delight, Van found that his reputation as a beer man had spread like wildfire. All the local brewers followed him through the city and implored him to taste their brews and explain what made them unique. They were conversations Van could have enjoyed for hours even if their topics would be more suited for a master brewer rather than the guy who loaded barrels onto wagons.

In addition to the brewers clamoring for Van's ear, he found that several, more shapely and better smelling personages had joined his entourage. Women, never Van's strong suit, approached him with abandon, practically throwing themselves in his arms. Van blushed and stammered his way through awkward conversations, ignoring the sharp peals of laughter that broke out whenever he threatened to say anything approaching clever or funny. They didn't seem to mind that he was a titan, even seemed to like it. Van was slightly overwhelmed, but, though he was no Living Portrait, he managed to corral the most forward of the orbiting women onto his arm and inelegantly suggest they go back to his hotel room. She seemed to think it was a great idea, laughing in a way that made her curls bounce on her shoulders, then clung to his side like a burr for the remainder of the walk.

A small crowd had gathered outside Van's hotel. Larvell had beaten them there, and even after being ditched by his titan, he wasn't prepared to surrender center stage. He stubbornly refused to shed his usual dapper suit and hat despite the evening's warmth, and he flung his hands about as he regaled the crowd with what sounded like a story showcasing his long, successful career as a wrestling manager. He lit up even more when he saw Van approach. "*There* you are! Folks, it is hard to keep track of this remarkable ten-man. Come here, Van. You did good, son."

Van stared down at Larvell as the man reached up to fold his arms around Van's waist, in the process forcing Van's female companion to unglue her arm from Van's sweaty back. Van took a drink of his beer as he stared flatly out over the crowd, waiting for Larvell to let go.

When Larvell finally released him, Van watched as the manager, his manager he guessed for better or worse, turned to address the crowd again. Van calmly reached down with his large hands, plucked Larvell's hat off his head, and ripped it in half. Then he gently placed the pieces back on Larvell's bald spot, trying not to grin as they slid off and tumbled to the ground. The crowd hooted with laughter. As Van regathered his newly acquired lady friend and pushed his way toward the hotel entrance, he could hear Larvell making excuses and shaking it off as a joke between old friends.

Van passed through the hotel lobby and up to the suite without further delay. He expected to see Owen moping on the sofa in the living room, but the seating area was empty. Van wasted no time in leading his lady to his bedroom. He threw the door open with what he hoped was not an overly eager flair, and pulled her laughing in behind him.

"Boo." Van nearly jumped out of his uniform. Kyle was seated on the edge of his bed in her tight, dark suit. She had a strange smile on her face, her eyes sparkling in the light of a single lit lamp.

Kyle sitting on his bed was a sight that normally would have thrilled Van to the moon, but there was the complicating factor of the no longer giggling woman on his arm. A deep frown flashed across the young lady's face that was immediately replaced with arched eyebrows and wide eyes. "Kyle," she said. "Why am I not surprised?"

"Hilda," Kyle replied coldly.

The two women simply stared at each other for a long moment as Van looked back and forth between them. Finally he broke the silence. "Uh, Kyle, this is Hilda."

Kyle shot him a quick smile. "I know that, Van. Or should I say, I know her? The Hilda name is new. She works for Moggy Flats. Or is it Urdesta? I can never keep track. Her real name is Helen Graf and she's from the cutest little town on the outskirts of Dunham South."

"Oh, Kyle." Hilda sighed dramatically. "I should have smelled your self-righteousness from the hallway. Shouldn't you be out watching your precious Uplands getting sold piece by piece to the Vantages? I hear they're hiring. Which is good because I'm sure you'll be looking for a job soon."

Van's head spun. He had enough trouble keeping up with some of the brewing conversations earlier. Now he had to follow politics?

Kyle gave her a sharp look. "Vantages are pushing hard, no doubt. Urdesta's been quiet this year though. Will they make a late play?"

Hilda, or Helen, or whatever her name was, sniffed. "I wouldn't hold my breath. They've had a good trading season. My bet is they stand pat and hope everyone forgets how awful they were last tournament."

Van stood fidgeting with his beer mug, forgotten in the center of the room. He wasn't sure exactly where his emotional state should be. Somehow, having two good-looking women in his bedroom seemed like a downgrade from just a few moments ago.

Hilda toyed with her curls as she stared at Kyle. "What will the Uplands do with its unexpected capital? Spend it all on hops?"

Kyle stood up from the bed. "Bye, Hilda. Time for you to run along."

Hilda sniffed again. Then without so much as a backwards glance at Van, she turned and left the room, leaving the door open behind her.

Van stared after her the same way he might look at an empty barrel. Or maybe a barrel someone had just poured out on the dirt for no reason. He turned back and glared at Kyle as she walked past him to shut the door.

"Thanks, Kyle," he said with an exaggerated eye roll. "Always nice to see you."

After a long moment in which Kyle seemed to confirm Hilda-Helen had left, she turned to Van. "*You, Van*," she said, looking him up and down with a furrowed brow and pursed lips. "You need to be more careful with the company you keep."

"She seemed fine," he replied. He sipped his beer, not quite able to hide his head behind the glass.

"Of course she did. That's her job. Seeming fine and ferreting secrets out of you for the benefit of whatever nation she's working for at this tournament. I'm pretty sure it's Urdesta. It usually is. She's not very creative."

"What kind of secrets is she gonna get from me?"

"Well, not just secrets. Access." She broke into a smile and met his eyes for the first time. "By the way, nice win tonight."

"Huh?" he asked as she walked past him to the window. The noise from the street below filtered into the room. "Wait, don't change the subject. Why'd you have to scare her off? I can take care of myself just fine." Had Hilda really been some sort of spy? Was that why it was so easy? Were *all* those women spies?

"Seriously, Van? You have no idea what she's like. She wouldn't be above slipping you something before your next fight. How'd you like to take on Judge Cage with a dose of troll urine in your system? Or a prick of raventhorn?"

"Troll urine?" Van sat down heavily on the bed. His mood was definitely falling. After staring suspiciously at the beer in his hand, he shrugged, tossed it back, and placed the glass on the night table. Then he swung his legs up onto the sheets and laid his head back, looked up at the white-speckled ceiling. "I hate Empire City."

Kyle was still at the window, looking out as the city lights painted her face in flickering orange. "I can understand that." She let out a deep sigh. "I hate coming here, too."

"Really?" Van hid a smirk behind his hand. "I thought you were having a wild time hunting eligible suitors with Lady Dorothy."

She pierced him with a glare. "That was bullshit, Van. I'm pretty sure you're familiar with it."

He grunted, miffed, then sat up and toyed with his empty beer mug. "So, you…just like…tell her what she wants to hear?"

"That's kind of my job."

"You don't seem to do that with me. Seems like I catch the sharp end of your tongue more often than anyone else…when you even bother talking to me."

She shook her head. "It's things like that about you I don't get. You're just…different, Van. This weird mix of strong and gentle drowning in a massive well of self-pity."

Van kept quiet. *Massive well of self-pity*? She *did* pick on him.

"The truth is, Van, I have to interact with a lot of people, doing what I do. And, I don't tell everyone this, but generally my approach is to mirror them. For the strong and self-righteous, I give them strong and self-righteous. For the conniving, conniving. For Lady Dorothy I am a strong woman with good prospects in the political game, and I am relentlessly on the hunt for opportunities to advance those prospects. And one easy way to do so is to marry outside the Uplands. That's what she wants to see. That's what she gets." She paused to look at Van for a long time, doubled by her reflection in the window. "Then there's you. Do you know why you're here, Van from Headwaters?"

"Because Owen Grit got hurt."

"If it had just been that, the Living Portrait would be here."

"You said he sucked."

"Well, he does, but that's beside the point. You're here because I told Governor Crowell you were our best shot. That's what got you into the ring with the Living Portrait, despite having zero record and zero experience. And do you know why I did that?"

The streets outside seemed to have quieted. Van tried to feign disinterest as he waited impatiently for her to finish her thought.

"I did it because of what I saw in that warehouse at your brewery, when you thought no one was watching."

"When I was stealing beer?" Van didn't like where this was going.

"It wasn't *what* you were doing, Van. It was *how* you were doing it. When I arrived in Headwaters, checking out the rumors of a sleeping titan was a small item at the bottom of a lengthy to-do list."

"I'm a *sleeping titan*?"

"Yes, Van, that's what we call a titan living a quiet, normal life." She stepped away from the window to stand at the foot of the bed. "You're not the only one. When I arrived, I saw you sitting at the back of the fight. You're big, and obviously strong. But you carried yourself like a sheep among lions instead of the opposite. And then you ducked off for some hidden agenda as soon as everyone was distracted. At least everyone but me. I was intrigued and I followed you. And in the warehouse, the moment you thought no one was looking, you straightened your back. You walked like a giant down the row of barrels, like you owned the place rather than had snuck in while the guards were distracted. You jumped up to the top row in a single bound and started moving 250-pound beer barrels around like they were full of air. The whole time your eyes gleamed in a way I'd bet no one in Headwaters would even recognize."

Now Van didn't know where to park his eyes. Continuing to stare up at the white ceiling seemed safest.

"You probably haven't spent much time around titans, Van. Not a lot of titans spend much time with their peers. There's a long story about how and why titans have been separ—"

"I know it," Van said, surprised Harot's history would ever be useful.

"Well, I spend a lot of time with them, whether I like it or not. And I can tell you that it is incredibly rare to see a titan perk up when he is alone." She gave him a sly smile. "Or at least think they are. Most titans absolutely deflate when they are alone, when the crowds leave. They get angry, depressed, and lonely. They diminish." She took a seat at the edge of the bed. "I've seen it time and time again. So they do everything they can to chase that crowd, that approval. They fight in the center of it. They sacrifice body, health, and pride. When the fights are over, they choose company that will indulge them in endless regurgitations of the moments they were the center of attention. Maybe they get that rush from seeing other titans fight. Or they find other highs to chase, drink themselves to death. It's like they have this weakness inside of them and the ring drives it away for a time. They certainly don't *hide* things, Van. They don't hide strength, confidence. You are different, somehow more yourself away from the crowds than in front of them."

Van felt Kyle staring at him as he stared at the ceiling. He wanted to say something, but he didn't know what. At last she continued. "So I saw you and I thought, if there's any way to flip this, a way to turn this natural strength and grace on...maybe you'd find you had something special." She laughed softly. "But you sure do screw up my mirror approach. I never quite know what you want to see. I never know which part of you to reflect back—the titan who owns the shadows or the one who fades in the light." She laughed again, and Van decided he liked the sound of it. "So you get this, my titan friend, a confusing mirror for a confusing titan."

Van lay silent, listening to his own breathing. He was still hung up on her earlier words. And afraid of the answer to the question he wanted to ask. "What about that something special? Do you still think that?"

She shrugged her shoulders. "Well, you certainly exceeded everyone else's expectations. You already justified my endorsement. You've helped me out a ton, Van. And I'm extremely grateful for that. Not satisfied, but grateful. I think you can take it further."

"In the tournament?"

She sighed as though that were the wrong answer, and stood to move back to the window and look out on the city lights. "Yes. And maybe even beyond that. Titans can do more than fight. They can do better. We all can."

Kyle pulled her jacket tight around her waist. She was readying to leave, her body language closing the conversation. Van didn't want it to be over. He didn't want to be alone with nothing better to do than think about what she'd said. "Why do you care?" he asked. "Why does the tournament mean so much to you? You don't strike me as a…I don't even know if this is the right word…*fan*."

She smiled. "You can't see me cheerleading a titan on, then latching onto his smelly arm after a big, sweaty victory? Heading back to his hotel room, laughing at his awkward jokes?"

Van didn't appreciate the image, too close to reality. He brushed it aside. "No, you seem more serious, like what you do has consequences. The rest of this is…ridiculous."

"I was a wrestling fan, once. I used to love it. It was so unlike me. And so refreshing in its simplicity. But that was a long time ago. I left that behind. I gather my strength at the edge of the crowd and need to plan carefully before using it. Not you guys. You get to lean right into it. Roll the dice. Now I see all the problems it creates. And how it's become a weapon. I'm in politics now, in case you haven't figured that out, and like it or not, politics moves in lock step with the tournament. It shouldn't, but it does."

Van thought that *in politics* seemed like a pretty vague way to describe being a spy. But that's what she was. That's what Hilda was, too. There was a network of spies, working along and inside the Headlock of Destiny. He shouldn't be surprised. Any time you got all of the Open Nations together in the same city, there'd be spies. He was just surprised he'd ever managed to cross paths with someone so...*interesting*. Someone who cared about the world beyond their next beer.

"In lock step how?" he asked. He was hovering somewhere between actually being interested and just wanting to keep her from leaving.

She stopped in the middle of buttoning her coat. "Our peace is a lie," she said. "Every one of the Open Nations has a standing army. They just don't fight in the sunlight. No more fields of corpses. The war now is asset seizure, commerce rights, political independence. Look what happened to Dunham South. They had been self-governed until about ten years ago. Now they are completely ruled by Dunham North. Moggy Flats has squeezed Barreli and grown to twice its size. The Valley of Sevens basically owns the capital of Titan's Shoulders. None of this should be so closely tied with the tournament, but it is. Early exits are a sign of weakness, and as the powerful laugh at the backs of the departing weak, they plot."

"Is someone coming after the Uplands?"

"Everyone is coming after the Uplands, Van. Everyone. Because we look weak. Owen helped us fight that reputation, but it is persistent. The biggest threat is the Vantages. King Thad himself. He's swallowed smaller nations before. Sometimes they keep their name, sometimes not. But you can bet your ass everything they earn flows to him. He sucks them dry, the whole time praising the peace the Open Nations has brought to our world, even as his troops come around collecting taxes and taking anything of value for themselves. He'll get rid of the governor, replace her with a puppet, just like he did with Western Springs and Rising Water. Venerate Holland helps him make it all look legitimate, and together they get stronger."

"And somehow Headlock wins can prevent that?"

"Not all of it, but they help." For once she looked tired. "Every tournament, I have a set of threats on my list, bombs to defuse. This time is the same as last time. Locking the Uplands into a tariff structure that drains off what little surplus we can gather."

"A tariff?"

"The Uplands has a fairly independent economy. We produce one, single commodity that other nations find really hard to imitate. Beer. I know you're close enough to it to understand the kind of volume we move. In addition to all the other goods we trade, every service that makes our economy hum, we have a cornerstone that is the envy of many other nations. We're not alone, of course. Moggy Flats has a lock on weaponry, the Valley of Sevens on clothes, Palos Soros on fruit. But we have beer.

"There are two ways to drain the Uplands of value, Van. The first is to seize it by force. But that's hard. The terrain would create a protracted fight and give everyone else a chance to see what's happening. Other nations might decide to take a chunk out of the Vantages's ass while they dealt with us. The most valuable asset in the Uplands, believe it or not, is your brewery, and it's fairly high up in the foothills. Not an easy place to take and hold. At least not without destroying it. So the second option is to find a way to get a cut. And that means tariffs. But it needs to be a coalition, not just be one nation."

"Why not?"

"What happens if the Vantages taxes our product? We just work around them. We shift trade routes and send beer elsewhere. Change our markets. But if it is taxed at every border, we can't do that. My job is to prevent that kind of alliance from forming. Worst case would have been you losing that first match like everyone expected. I guarantee the Uplands would have been one of the first topics on the agenda when King Thad and the others met, before you even cleared the city walls."

Van tried to imagine King Thad, whom he had never even seen, sitting down at a giant, marble table to discuss a takeover of the Uplands. "Who would have been on the guest list at that meeting?"

"Good question. Representatives from Moggy Flats, the Valley of Sevens, and Coresite Mount. His puppets from Western Springs and Rising Water, maybe. If they form up against the Uplands, that's the start of some serious trouble."

"So how do you prevent that from happening?"

"That's the tricky part, Van, and the answer is never the same." She stood and finished buttoning her coat. "But the Headlock of Destiny is the one event that brings all nations together. Wars happen in its wake. Alliances. Betrayals. All schemed up in Empire City and sealed in smoky back rooms. And tournament losers suffer, Van. It sounds ridiculous but it's true. That's why I'm grateful for your help. But now I need to go."

If she had to leave, he wanted to go with her. "Can I come with you?" Van asked. "I…uh…could help."

"Van, I've got a night of sneaking through the shadows ahead of me. I don't think bringing a giant along would help." She reached out and tugged on his beard, which Van only pretended to dislike. "But I appreciate your asking." She stepped towards the door, and grasped the handle, but paused before opening it to say, "Good night, Van. I'm glad to be here with *you* instead of the Living Portrait."

Van struggled to think of a way to keep her longer, but he came up blank as usual. "High praise," he muttered sadly. He watched the sway of her hips, visible even under the coat, as she walked out of his room. "Good night," he called lamely after her.

With a frustrated grunt, Van kicked his feet up on the bed and stared at the ceiling again. The lights from the street seemed dimmer now and the crowd outside had quieted, leaving an uncomfortable stillness to the evening. Somewhere in the distance a dog barked. Van was sore and tired and his thoughts were a jumble of commerce and clotheslines. Still, his next course of action seemed clear enough.

Van counted to ten then rose from the bed to follow Kyle wherever she was headed.

Chapter 26

Van guessed Kyle would head out of the hotel via the back exit behind the bar. If she was on some sort of mission, the spy wouldn't want to run into Larvell out front as he tried to hold on to the remnants of his crowd. So Van stepped out into the alley.

It was dark, the light and noise from the nearby streets at a minimum. Van carefully scanned the terrain of fences, the ugly, squat backends of buildings, trash piles, and stray dogs. He was rewarded with a glimpse of blonde hair trailing out in the slow wind, attached to a shadow that melted around a corner. He hurried after her, his bare feet whispering on the cobblestones.

He kept to the darkness at the edge of the buildings as best he could. A man who seemed to be fighting demonic possession of some kind ran toward Van, filling the night with screams that broke the delicate quiet. Van stopped and pressed against a wall, and the man passed by without noticing him.

Kyle was far down the next alley by the time Van turned the corner. He caught a flash of motion under a light, and then she was gone again. He kept his eyes locked on the place she'd vanished from, and jogged lightly down the dirty alley.

Now that he was outside and alone in the darkness, he couldn't help but question his actions. He didn't have a disguise or anything, or even some sort of cloak to hide his face. Nothing but his dark skin and deep blue uniform to blend into the night. He was going to be worthless out here, and she'd said she didn't need his help anyway.

He rounded the next corner. No sign of her. He made it halfway down the alley and then paused, feeling eyes on him. He anticipated the word a moment before it came.

"Boo," she whispered from just behind him. Shit. It hadn't taken her five minutes to catch him. He turned slowly. She had her hands on her hips. "Van, you've *got* to be kidding me. What are you doing out here?" When he just shrugged, she sighed and said, "Shouldn't you be resting? You took a pretty bad beating earlier tonight."

"Nope," he said, trying to display the confidence she thought he should have. "Don't need to. Thought I could help." He glanced up and down the alley. "Where are we headed?"

"You're going back to the hotel. Where I'm going isn't important."

"I don't know," he said. "I'll bet it *is* important. And I'll bet it's dangerous. Maybe you could use a titan bodyguard. In case you didn't notice," he puffed out his chest, "I defeated the mighty Panam Manley earlier tonight."

"He defeated himself, Van." She sighed again, but then she almost smiled. "Fine. But you do what I say, when I say it. And try to look a little less like a giant trying to pass as a halfling."

Van felt his chest expand for real this time. He nodded, not exactly sure what he was getting into but glad he was getting into it.

. . .

He fell in line behind Kyle, and they moved together through the dark backsides of Empire City. Most stretches of their journey were quiet—the city slept—but other times, late night revelers laughed and shouted just behind a fence, or around a corner, and the smells of beer and liquor, smoke and blood hung heavy in the air. Kyle ignored these rambunctious pockets as if they didn't exist, and led Van across the city.

She practically glided, silent as she went, no trace of her passing. Van struggled to keep up. At one point he accidentally kicked a can that clattered across an alley, but no one seemed to notice. Watching her back, he was reminded of Harot's musings about female titans, or female titan-equivalents. This was her true element. She seemed built for stealth in a way that male titans, the ones who were making a routine of kicking Van's ass, were built for the squared circle. Was she unique in this, or was there a silent army of string-pullers behind the scenes, making the Open Nations dance to these females' bidding? He only knew he was glad to be on her side...he hoped.

At last she halted, drawing up to the dark corner of a four-story brick tenement and motioning for Van to do the same. "Take a look around. We're headed to the back of that building."

"Which one?" Van asked, but his question trailed off as he caught a glimpse of a party, the likes of which put every other party in Empire City to shame, raging in front of a brightly lit office building. Strings of lanterns projected out from the building to its neighbors, spanning the streets in all directions and throwing vibrant color on an enormous crowd of partygoers. Van saw people in all manner of dress and undress. Titans roamed among them, bellowing loudly and carrying enormous mugs of beer. Dwarves scrambled aside to avoid being stepped on. Elves drank from long flutes of wine. What appeared to be a pair of fairies openly procreated on the cobblestones. Sorcerers and street performers worked the edges of the crowd, and roaming musicians created a cacophony of notes that echoed through the streets.

The front doors to the building were open, and party guests streamed in and out. A titan bouncer stood at each side of the door, glancing up and down at each guest who braved the path between them. Just above the entryway hung a sign. *Open Nations Wrestling Coalition.*

"Is this Holland's party?" Van asked.

Kyle nodded. "He throws one like it every night of the tournament. I've been to a couple of them these past few days but I'm a little too well known in that crowd. And *you* would definitely attract the wrong sort of attention. So, like I said, the back." She gazed around at the nearby buildings. "Venerate has a private office at the rear of the building. There's a balcony off of it. I climbed up there last night. He likes to bring people out there, has some interesting conversations. I've probably already missed several tonight, but I had to hang back and keep you from letting Helen Graf rifle through my room."

He hoped she could see the long look he gave her despite the surrounding darkness. "And congratulate your titan on his tournament win, of course."

"That too, I suppose," she said. She looked around some more, seemed to be plotting her course toward the back of the building.

"So what do I do?"

"You wait below the balcony and stay in the shadows. Whistle if someone comes. And if something goes wrong and I fall"—she patted Van on the arm— "try to catch me."

. . .

He and Kyle made short work of a tall, wooden fence that surrounded the back courtyard. They landed in the carefully cultivated space amidst fountains and trimmed hedges. The quiet space struck Van as surprisingly delicate for the ONWC, but it was clearly designed for the dual purposes of solitude and ostentation. Van imagined Venerate sitting there in the sunlight politely offering visiting kings and queens their choice of teas and accepting compliments on his rose bushes. At night, though, it was small and dark, a world away from the raging party out front. Van found a spot in the shadows.

Kyle studied the side of the building for a moment before she began her climb. She ascended the smooth, brick façade with ease, making the second-floor balcony before Van even realized she wasn't standing beside him. He watched her shapely rear end as she scrambled up a drainage pipe, and he felt a surge of desire, followed by an ache of sadness. Here he was, again chasing something that wasn't his and never would be. She reached the third-floor balcony in no time.

The balcony was a rectangular slab of stone, held to the building by thick steel cables and surrounded by ornate wrought iron railing. The windows in front of it were brightly lit. Kyle clung just below the stone, somehow wedging herself into a sitting position between the drain pipe and the brick wall. She was visible to anyone who looked up carefully from the ground behind the building. Or if someone came out on one of the other balconies below her. Van hoped she knew what she was doing.

Party sounds from the interior and the front of the buildings drifted to Van in waves of laughter and intermingled shouts of glee and violence. A path curled around the corner of the building to the front. If someone came back, Van was positioned to intercept them, but he'd have to be careful. Wouldn't do to attack someone bringing trash back to the alley or something like that. Someone who wouldn't think to look up at the third-floor balcony's underside for spies.

And what if she fell? She'd joked about him catching her, but he'd sure as hell try. No idea if he'd be able to.

He'd caught plenty of falling beer barrels in his time, even kept some of them from exploding against the ground, but never a falling person. One whose bones break if you squeeze too tight or if you miss. He hoped this little exercise didn't last long.

Van fretted in the shadows, rubbing his hands together nervously and pacing in a small circle. Finally, he heard voices from above, faint from this distance. The balcony doors swung open, and out stepped Venerate Holland and a titan Van recognized instantly as King Thad. Van grinned. This was exactly the kind of payout Kyle had been looking for, assuming they talked about anything of import.

Van could see the heads of the chatting pair as they took a practiced and easy position at the railing of the balcony to look out over Empire City. King Thad dwarfed Holland. It was always strange for Van to realize he was as big as some of these legends, but it was true. King Thad was maybe half a head taller than Van. Probably comparable in weight as well, though the King had more sculpted muscle and less gut. The similarities ended there, though. King Thad had pale skin, a long, serious face with a hawkish nose. He wore a crown outfitted with rubies and emeralds the size of his eyes. Around the crown, his hair was swept back in careful waves of blondish brown. His beard was darker, tightly trimmed to hug his jawline. The King wore an enormous purple robe with white fur fringes. As he leaned over the railing, he folded thick hands, decked out in countless rings of gold, together. Even from the ground far below, Van could sense the coiled strength of the titan, the only one in the Open Nations who represented his country in the tournament and ruled it as a king.

Behind King Thad, another titan stood like a bodyguard. From this far away, Van could only pick out his cleanly shaved head and thick neck. The titan waited patiently as King Thad spoke with Venerate in long, even exchanges. Van could make out nothing of the words. Neither seemed particularly excited, almost bored, passing time together as the evening's party kept raging.

Judging by the noise level drifting around from the front, the party was not slowing down anytime soon. Kyle was still exposed to whoever came back here, and Van was sure it was just a matter of time. Whenever he heard voices from around the corner, he was certain they were coming this way. Each time he was wrong. Then, as the party noise seemed to hit a momentary lull, he heard something there was no mistaking. The sounds of heavy footsteps on the path, coming around from the front.

Van pressed himself against the cool brick of the building as two enormous shapes moved past him, one following the other. He sighed as he recognized the silhouettes of giant shoulders and jutting spikes. He knew these jerks, and they were headed to a place where they could easily look up and see Kyle.

Van's mind flashed back momentarily to Kyle's talk of playing the role of a mirror. When you showed people a reflection of themselves, they were easier to disarm. They expected it, thought it was natural. Van stepped out of the shadows. Eagle and Creature whirled at the sudden sound.

"Hey, assholes," Van called out, shattering the quiet. "I've been looking everywhere for you two."

The pair looked dumbstruck only for a moment. Then their faces cracked into toothy grins.

Chapter 27

"That's funny," Eagle said. "We were looking for you, too. Mr. Holland isn't very happy."

"I don't give a fuck about Holland," Van replied. "I just heard you assholes were here and I started wracking my brain. I'm not the smartest ten-man in the world, but I just can't remember giving you permission to get out of that fireplace I crammed you and your pretty little spikes into. Seems to me our score isn't quite settled." He cracked his knuckles loudly. It was kind of fun to talk like other titans.

He had Eagle's and Creature's attention, but his heart jumped in his chest as both glanced up at the balcony above. They were looking for Venerate. Van hadn't thought of them checking with their boss for approval before squaring off with him. Actually, he hadn't really thought this through at all. For all his bluster, he'd barely survived his first fight with these two. And he was still sore from having his ass kicked earlier in the night. At least they weren't yet raising an alarm. Van could only hope he'd given Kyle enough warning to find a hiding place up there.

Van made an exaggerated turn to look up at the balcony. A tight knot inside of him loosened as he saw Kyle was out of sight. Venerate and King Thad were looking coolly down on the scene below them.

Van had borne Venerate Holland's gaze before. A chance to lock eyes with the mighty King Thad was more interesting. His eyes were cold, dispassionate. The eyes of a man used to pricing and purchasing his enemies. He slowly looked Van up and down as though he were a new species. There was a patience to his stare, a slow-burning confidence.

Van shifted his eyes to Venerate. "Well, look up there," Van said. "The man himself. I do hope he gives his little pets permission to play." In a louder voice, "What do you say, Venerate? I didn't listen to your request that I throw the fight against Panam. You can't be happy about that. So can the hedgehog twins come out to play?"

Without waiting for an answer, Van turned from the head of the ONWC and marched around towards the front of the building. Moments later he heard the heavy footfalls of Eagle and Creature following him.

The street in front of Venerate Holland's building remained a riot of activity. The crowd parted as Van marched boldly into their midst. With Eagle and Creature on his heels, there was little question about what was happening. Titans moving with such purpose usually preceded violence of the most entertaining kind. The crowd pushed back to create space, the more experienced connoisseurs of the wrestling game quickly maneuvered to the front row of the rapidly forming circle, hands clapped protectively over the top of their drinks.

The excited voices of the crowd and charge to the air brought back to mind Van's childhood, when he'd often found himself inside circles like these. He'd always been a target for the older boys who wanted to scrap out a few victories against a two-man before he grew too large. Their eyes gleamed as they pinned him to the ground, twisting his limbs and pushing his face into the dirt. Alec had been the worst. When Van had finally grown large and strong enough to take on his chief bully, he broke Alec's arm in two places and earned himself an early exit from his foster home, which had no interest in harboring a *violent* titan, especially one who'd hurt a member of the prominent Durheed family. Another trip across town to another family who didn't want him. Alec strutting around like his immobilized arm was a symbol of pride, getting all the pouting girls to pamper him. None of the girls in Headwaters spoke to Van for nearly a year after that, cautioned by their mothers to avoid that monster who had injured the brave Durheed boy.

Eagle and Creature had that same eager look Van knew so well. The real bullies were never afraid in the circle. The fight was where they shined. If you wanted to see them afraid, look for it in class when they have to read aloud in front of the others, or when they ask a girl to dance, anyplace other than the fight. Van thought about running. He wasn't helping Kyle anymore—he'd gotten the two goons away from the back of the building. But a part of him knew that calling them out had been about more than a distraction. It was about revenge. Because they'd scared him last time. Now it was his turn.

Van took a fighting stance and readied himself. Eagle and Creature separated to flank him, and the three titans slowly circled the makeshift ring, not quite ready to engage. A small tussle broke out at one edge of the circle and a visibly drunk magician burst through the throng and staggered into the open space. He wore brightly colored robes and waved a glowing wand back towards a cluster of men that tried to restrain him. Van and Holland's two goons stopped to stare.

"Unacceptable, unacceptable," the wizard shouted, driving his pursuers back with the swinging wand. "Bad form to ask a wizard to leave. Bad form to ask a wizard to do anything other than exactly what a wizard wants to do."

"Just stop trying to come back inside," a large man following him pleaded. "You've already started like eight fires."

"Starting fires," the wizard slurred, "is a gross generalization. I'm not some dick running around with matches. I used *fire magic*. And if I did it must have been with good purpose. Makes for a lively party." He looked around at the circle he'd stumbled into. "Am I right?!" As he yelled to the crowd, he waved his wand and flames leapt up to catch a string of paper lanterns. Their flaming husks rained down as he took a bow. The crowd roared their approval even as the wizard's handlers, who Van presumed worked for Venerate based on their ONWC-branded shirts, hustled off to contain the spreading fire. "Anyway," the wizard continued, glancing suspiciously around him, "what the fuck are you all looking at?"

The wizard squinted around the ring, and finally noticed Van and Venerate's thugs staring at him. "Ah-ha! A fight! Excellent! Let's get this rolling." He touched the wand to his throat, and when he spoke next, his voice carried over the crowd. "In one corner," he pointed the wand at Eagle and Creature, "two assholes covered in spikes!" Then he looked at Van with a furrowed brow. "And in the other corner, a guy who looks like he has no idea what the fuck is going on! What a match-up! Boom!" He whipped his wand around above his head. Flames leapt up, setting the flags hanging in front of the building aflame. More of Venerate's staff surged forward, freshly motivated to get this guy away from their property. They still seemed scared to touch him, though.

Van was distracted by the drunk wizard, but Eagle wasted no time. He charged Van from the side. Van absorbed the rush, spikes catching on his clothes, and tossed the titan away, sending him tumbling onto the cobblestones. Creature lunged from the other side, and Van sent him keeling in the other direction. Both found their feet quickly and stood glaring at Van. The crowd roared for more.

He'd need to keep the two brutes from working together, but his space was limited, and the circle seemed to be closing in. Eagle charged again, he seemed to like that move. Van stepped aside, seized the straps that held Eagle's shoulder armor in place, and spun him. He had the idea that he'd send Eagle flying into Creature, but Creature attacked from the other side, so Van settled for launching Eagle into the crowd, which frantically parted. Van turned toward Creature, and the goon punched him in the face. Van grabbed his arm as Creature drew back his fist to repeat the effort, but a deafening howl froze them in place. Their heads turned as one.

Eagle's spikes were stuck to the ass of the largest titan Van had ever seen. The titan, who wore a tight singlet of green and blue over his bulging body, was several feet taller than Van and twice as wide. His eyes were fiery as he looked back over his shoulder, trying to discern what exactly had pierced his hindquarters. Eagle was hunched forward, head lowered, as he struggled to free himself from the titan's flesh. He twisted and plucked the titan's torn singlet from a spike, then took a step back. The enormous titan seized Eagle by the throat, raised him off the ground with one hand, and brought the struggling ten-man's face level to his own.

Van knew the Landshaker only from description, and this giant, with biceps bigger than a man's waist, fit the description. He was the champion of Moggy Flats and one of ONWC's most dangerous wrestlers, an early favorite to win it all, who'd sailed into the round of eight with victories over Duke Roller and Grim Tidings. Looking at the Landshaker, Van could believe the story that titans had once been giants who roamed the land, leveling mountains. Of the many peoples in the Open Nations, nothing was as big as a titan, and this was the biggest titan Van had ever seen.

The Landshaker's cheeks and forehead were flushed a deep, ugly red. He was bald on top. Long, stringy hair hung down from the sides of his head, tangled into a reddish-brown beard. He bellowed with rage into Eagle's face. His open mouth looked like it would fit over Eagle's entire head. The Landshaker's gaze swung over to Van and Creature, still locked together in the center of the circle.

Van glanced at Creature, who still clutched Van's shirt in one hand. The other hand, the one that had been poised to punch him, was now pointing at Van, indicating he was to blame. Van looked back at the Landshaker, and shook his head, pointed back at Creature. The Landshaker's eyes flicked back and forth between the two for a moment, then he let out another roar and threw Eagle back over his head to crash into the crowd somewhere disturbingly far away. Before Eagle even hit the ground, the Landshaker was in motion, rumbling through the crowd towards them at a frightening pace. The ground shook as he stomped into the circle. Creature and Van disentangled just in time to each receive half of a brutal, two-armed clothesline.

Van's world turned upside down as he flipped over and crashed to the stones. For a moment he had no idea where he was. His childhood fights had never involved anything quite like a Landshaker clothesline. When he opened his eyes, the drunken fire wizard was standing over him.

"Dumb move, dude," the wizard said, laughing and shaking his head.

Van pushed the wizard aside and scrambled to his feet, soliciting a string of curses, but luckily no flames, from the wizard. He looked around desperately for the Landshaker, who wasn't hard to find. The giant had Creature up in the air by the neck, just as he had with Eagle. Maybe Van could bolt while he was busy.

As if sensing the thought, the Landshaker turned to Van and yelled, "Stay there!" spit flying into his beard. "I'll deal with you in a second."

The force of the ten-man's voice was such that Van nearly complied. But rational thinking reasserted itself, and Van took off running. He made it about two steps before crashing into a solid wall of people. The circle had tried to shift to encompass the evolving fight and found itself too drunk to accomplish the task. It collapsed around the battling titans. Van heard the Landshaker roar again and turned to see that Eagle had rammed into his side, leading with his spikes. The Landshaker dropped Creature and gripped Eagle by his shoulder straps. He began ripping his armor off with his bare hands. From Eagle's screams, it was not a pleasant sensation.

Van tried to leave, but his way was firmly blocked by the crowd, who were enthralled by the latest attempts of Holland's staff to keep the wizard from burning the entire square down. He looked back and saw the Landshaker closing in on him.

Van turned to face him. He took a fighting stance, readying himself for the punishment of his life, when he heard an impossibly calm, friendly voice near his right hip. "Van the Beer Man! I'm so excited to meet you."

"Huh?" Van looked down to see a fat little man standing next to a beer barrel. He felt, by the trembling of the ground, the Landshaker still approaching.

The man gestured to the barrel with a flourish. "I was hoping you'd try my special—"

Van reached down and picked up the barrel, hoisted it over his head. Then he turned and heaved it into the

Landshaker's face. It shattered, raining broken staves and golden ale onto the crowd in a foaming mess. The Landshaker stumbled to a knee, shaking the beer from his scraggly locks like a wet dog.

"I like it," Van yelped, and he took off running.

The small seam Van found in the crowd let him get only a few feet before he met a waiting Creature. The titan swung a punch at Van's midsection, but Van yanked a drunk from the crowd and dragged him between his gut and Creature's fist, and the punch landed squarely in the man's stomach. The poor sap doubled over and crumbled to the cobbles. Creature raised his head in surprise, and Van landed a straight right to his jaw that knocked him over backwards.

The world turned upside down again as the Landshaker, or perhaps one of the nearby buildings, crashed into Van's back, sending him sprawling over Creature and into a group of musicians, judging by the sounds of jangling strings and clattering bells. Stumbling forward, Van swore as he tripped over something lying on the ground—the passed out wizard, perfect—and sprawled out on the stones.

"Would you be interested in a promotional opportunity for my special brew?" The beer guy leaned over Van's prone body. "Stunner Ale. All you can drink while you're in Empire City."

Van clambered to his feet. He glanced over his shoulder as Eagle, stripped of his spikes, had again attacked the Landshaker. Now another titan was with him, or at least against the Landshaker. Van had an idea it was Evan the Crusher based on the size of his hands. Creature was getting up, which put at least two titans in the line between Van and the Landshaker. Time to get back to running away. After he caught his breath. Van spared a look at the beer guy. "What kind of special brew?"

Before the beer guy could answer, Van felt a titanic hand on his shoulder. This was not a grip of violence, but neither was it a grip of friendship. Van smelled something like flowers doused with paint thinner. He spun around to see Richard the Living Portrait.

"You son of a bitch." The Portrait's words were slurred with drink. He looked awful, his pristine hair mussed, his clothes wrinkled and torn, and worst of all, that cologne. Van wanted to retch. He must have fallen into hard times after the loss to Van. Richard's mouth moved as if searching for more words. "Son of a bitch." He swayed stiffly and Van saw he wore a large back brace of leather and metal.

Van wasn't quite sure what to do. He looked around. For some reason, Eagle and Creature were now fighting each other. The Landshaker had the newly arrived Evan the Crusher upside-down, set up for a piledriver. The drunken wizard had gotten up and stumbled next to Van, looking green, apparently unaware that the hem of his robe was on fire. The beer guy waited expectantly for Van's answer as if this were a standard negotiating circumstance.

Van was frozen in the midst of the chaos. Then the wizard hitched his breath, preparing to heave. Van quickly grabbed him and pointed him away. As a result the wizard vomited all over Richard the Living Portrait's tight, sparkly pants. The Portrait looked down in horror. Van let out a single, sharp laugh. The earth shook below them as the Landshaker delivered Evan the Crusher to the cobblestones.

"I love Venerate's parties," Van overheard a nearby musician say to a tambourine-rattling friend. A fairy nursing a crushed wing shot the pair a piercing glare.

The wizard decided to lie down on the ground again at Van's feet. Eagle and Creature were entangled to Van's right. The Living Portrait stood in shock to his left, pulling at his hair and moaning as he stared down at his vomit-covered clothes. The Landshaker was standing at the edge the circle, one foot on Evan the Crusher's chest. Van leaned over to the beer guy. "A barrel now and I give you my answer after I taste it…assuming said barrel is in *that* direction." He pointed through the crowd, the only way not blocked by furious titans or drunk musicians. The beer guy winked and made no protest as Van scooped him up under one arm and began to run.

…

Van's eye was swelling up from his impact with the ground and he was pretty sure his side had a few punctures from Eagle's spikes, but he smiled as he walked down the dark street with a newly-acquired barrel of Stunner Ale tucked under an arm. He noted how the clear night sky allowed for a mesmerizing view of the stars. He rounded the corner of a squat boarding house and found Kyle waiting, leaning against a building angrily tapping her foot on the cobblestones.

Van looked her up and down, ignoring her disapproval, then raised his barrel. "Not a total loss. Look, fresh beer."

She gave him a disgruntled look, but Van thought he saw a smile hiding somewhere in her deep blue eyes. "You get anything from Venerate or King Thad before those idiots messed up our fun?" he asked.

She started walking back towards the hotel and Van fell in next to her. "A deal with Moggy Flats," she said, all businesslike. "They didn't get into specifics, but they did give me an idea of what they think of you after you showed your face."

"Are they interested in joining my fan club? Titans have fan clubs, right?"

"Venerate called you a wild card." She picked up the pace, trying to outspeed Van's long strides. "He hates wild cards."

"Who doesn't?" Van asked.

"King Thad wants to know your price. I get the impression—and, mind you, this is based on a very short exchange—I get the impression he's wondering if you're a piece he could use on the playing board. You've already pissed off Venerate too much. He just wants you broken. You need to keep an eye on your back."

"I always do," Van said. Then, realizing he hadn't once checked if they were being followed, he glanced behind them.

"Relax, troublemaker. They let you walk from this one. Otherwise I wouldn't have waited for you."

"So where to next?"

"The hotel. I need a break, Van, and you need some sleep." She slowed her pace and looked at him, head to toe, considering. Van tried not to show the tingle it gave him. "Tomorrow night, you've got a date for a party at the Regal Ballroom."

"Great! When do we leave?"

"Oh, not with me," she said, stepping back into her quick pace toward the hotel. "Or, at least, not *only* me. Lady Dorothy is finally ready for your social debut. Prepare for some serious purse-holding."

Van scoffed. "No way. I'll pass."

"Not that simple, Van. You thought those two titans were tough. Wait until you get between Lady Dorothy and what she wants. Unfortunately, right now, that's you."

Because he'd won, suddenly she was aware of his existence. "I knew there was a price."

"There's always a price, Van. Win *or* lose."

They walked together in silence for a nearly a block. At last, Van said, "You'll never guess who's in Empire

City!" Kyle said nothing, so Van continued. "Richard the Living Portrait. And boy, was he excited to see me." He chuckled at his own joke.

He nearly whistled as they continued down the street. He'd won the fight, sort of, and impressed the girl, maybe. He'd made the right call following her out. And he got a fresh barrel out of it. The pressure of a party with nobles was for tomorrow. Tonight was for relaxing, maybe seeing if Kyle would join him for the first pour of the barrel of Stunner. He couldn't wait to get back to the hotel. And something on this street smelled like a dead rat Van had once found in a corner of warehouse seven.

A voice gurgled out of the shadows. "Van."

Van and Kyle jumped at the sound. A massive figure stepped forward from the dark alley they'd just passed. The smell of death accompanied it in a surging wave, and Van was certain for a moment the OverLord had come to take him down to the Nether. There would be a coffin just behind him. A tight fit for a titan as large as Van, but he'd make it work.

The titan who stepped into the light wasn't the OverLord or any titan Van recognized. He was taller and wider than Van, and his skin was a sallow gray. His eyes were completely white and he reeked of dead animals. He was dressed for the ring, tight shorts under ragged, half-open overalls. "Van," he said again.

"Who the hell—" Van tried to keep the fear from his voice. All the good feelings of a moment ago vanished as this new monster stepped closer, somehow more real and terrifying than all of the titans Van had just faced combined.

"Van," the titan pressed on, its white eyes glued to his. "He's listening for your screams. He's asked for you, Van. He *wants* you."

Van gave a start as Kyle spoke, as casual as ever. "That's the Bearhugger." In his terror, he'd forgotten she was there. He wracked his brain. The Bearhugger had lost to the OverLord. He'd been placed in the titan's coffin and dragged through the streets, thrown into the Nether. How was he here now?

"Come with me," Bearhugger said, taking another step forward. Van heard another voice, too, a deathly rumble he had heard before overlaid the steely, northern accent of the Bearhugger. *You will follow me one way or another, titan.* The OverLord.

Van's knees trembled. The OverLord had somehow possessed Bearhugger, and would probably do the same to Van. Van would be a mindless extension of the Nether's deathly harvest. Maybe the OverLord would just whisper into Van's ear until his will floated away like ash. Van's freshly won barrel fell from his nerveless hands.

Kyle suffered from no such debilitation. She sprinted at the Bearhugger, ducked his clutching hands with ease, and in a blur of black suit she scaled the titan and perched on his shoulder, legs wrapped under his armpits. She laid a wicked knife against the Bearhugger's throat. The titan's face was devoid of any surprise, of any emotion at all.

"Van's not going anywhere," Kyle said in the titan's ear, voice as calm as if she'd asked him the price of a beer.

"He is to follow me," the Bearhugger said, rolling his head and eyes back to try and look at her.

She shifted the knife to point into a white eye. "I'll take these eyes, Son of Malachisin. I'll render the vessel useless."

The deep voice spat out, "An old enemy. A little bird." The Bearhugger's dull eyes stared straight ahead for a long moment. "There will be no place to hide," he gurgled, then he started back down the dark alley. Kyle jumped off his back. She tensed as she hit the ground, knife raised, but the titan simply lumbered back into the shadows as if it had forgotten they existed.

Van breathed heavily as he stared down the alley. "Why didn't you just kill him?" he asked once he was certain the monster was gone.

"Because I didn't actually know if it would work. And if it didn't we'd be in a world of trouble."

"Why did he call you a little bird? Does he know you?" Van licked his dry lips, his eyes flickering all around them.

"Signs of an old evil. But no, he doesn't know me."

"That was...uh...I didn't like that," Van said.

"What's to like?" She looked around the dark, empty streets. "Had enough for tonight? I'd like to get some sleep."

"More than enough," Van replied, looking at the openings of all the other dark alleys lined up like mouths on the street ahead. He had an idea there was little sleep in his future. Not after hearing that thing call his name from the shadows.

Chapter 28

Van perched nervously at the edge of a sofa in the common room of the hotel suite. He could hear Kyle and Lady Dorothy comparing earrings in their bedchambers at the far end. The voices drifting towards him were light and easy, nothing like how he felt. Van's sleep had been fitful after the previous night's encounter with the Bearhugger, full of dark dreams and unanswered questions. The concerns of the daylight should be small by comparison, but he was rattled to his core, and even the mundane seemed overwhelming. He wondered what a party with nobles would be like. Hopefully they drank beer.

He tugged at his starched collar. Lady Dorothy had commissioned a new set of clothes for him. Surprisingly, it was not dissimilar from his old brewery uniform, though a better cut and lacking the ragged edges. It had the same basic look—dark blue one-piece with short pants and short sleeves, complete with pockets. He actually liked it, though the feel of new fabric took some getting used to. It looked fairly sharp and came with a pair of shiny black boots. It had been years since his last pair of boots. Anything titan-sized was hard to come by in the Uplands and once his old boots had fallen apart they were too expensive to replace.

Though Van was pleased with Lady Dorothy's selection of clothes, he was less pleased by her approach to his hair. The self-proclaimed *stylist to the stars* that Lady Dorothy had hired to fix up Van's wild hair and unruly beard had burst in on Van in his room as he was admiring his new boots, one foot up in the air to see the reflection in a tilted mirror. The man had been flanked by a pair of tittering fairies who laughed constantly for no apparent reason. The stylist announced his intention to make Van the centerpiece of the party. His own hair was an intricate rainbow-dyed structure of elevated slopes and walkways that Van studied in horror. By the time the stylist had laid out a series of instruments, scissors being the only elements Van even remotely recognized, Van had hardened his resolve. He politely but firmly rebuffed the man's efforts, fighting shrieking protests and blasts of different colored spray bottles directed at his head. Van was saved by his height advantage; the stylist was unable to massacre what he couldn't reach. Still, the agile and persistent beautician had put Van's wrestling skills to the test, and before the brief struggle ended, he had somehow managed to frost the bottom edge of Van's beard carnation pink.

After Van drove the man and his tittering accomplices out and locked the door of his room, he tried and failed to fix his beard with his fingers. At last, he decided to ignore the damage and look at his boots in the mirror some more. Eventually he'd heard the visitors make a squealing exit from the suite and guessed it was safe to come out of his bedroom.

An hour after Van tired of looking at his boots, the ladies finally emerged from their wing of the suite. The Lady Dorothy looked as immaculate as she always did. Kyle looked, well, amazing. She wore some sort of make-up that darkened and deepened her eyes, which Van couldn't stop staring at.

"Uh, hi," he stammered. "Are you ready to go?" After a moment of awkward silence he added, "You look lovely." He stood up from the sofa and swiveled his head to address the comment to the both of them.

Kyle merely raised her eyes, but Lady Dorothy clapped her hands together, clearly delighted. "Such a gentleman," she cried in a tone that made Van feel about five years old. She fluttered her lashes at him. "Isn't he something?" she crowed to Kyle.

"He's something," Kyle muttered in reply, winking a shadowy eye at him.

Van had no idea if he'd just won or lost points, but he knew he had about as much chance of winning this game as he did of winning the Headlock.

"Hold this for a moment, will you?" Lady Dorothy handed him a small pink leather purse with a large gold clasp. Van held it awkwardly as she swung a fur stole around her shoulders and parked a hat with a bright peacock feather carefully on her head. Then she went for the door without reclaiming the purse.

"Your purse," he called to her back, but she was already heading down the stairs, the first time he'd seen her leading the way rather than following a wave of servants. First time he'd seen her open a door herself too, actually. He looked down at the purse, tiny in his massive hands. Hadn't he been warned about this?

Kyle shot him a look as they followed her out the door. "Rough start, Van."

He stared after the women, then exhaled a deep sigh and followed them out.

. . .

They squeezed into a carriage, and Van tossed the purse onto Lady Dorothy's lap. She furrowed a painted brow at him, then turned to Kyle and began itemizing the various bachelors who were expected to be in attendance, their social standing, future prospects, and family fortunes.

Van paid attention for the first few sentences, thinking he should learn something of who would be at the party so he didn't accidentally insult a king or snub a governor. Then he lost interest and spent the ride staring out the window at the passing lights.

The bruises from last night's beating, more from Panam Manley than the streetfight, had faded overnight, though his neck was still slightly sore from two extended stays in Panam's full nelsons. And a long day with nothing pressing to do had helped him catch up on sleep. So Van felt okay physically. His head was a different matter. He was totally disoriented. Not only had Panam Manley reinforced the idea that Van belonged nowhere near a ring, but hearing his name gurgling from the tongue of the Bearhugger made Van deeply uneasy. He had the feeling he should be getting out of Empire City. Instead, it seemed he was sinking in even deeper.

It was too late to change anything tonight. Just as the previous night had been, tonight was about survival...and avoiding being a walking purse-rack for Lady Dorothy. She tried to dump the little pink thing on him again as he held the carriage door for her but he pretended not to see it. Van followed Lady Dorothy and Kyle into the Regal Ballroom.

The Regal Ballroom was the ugliest thing he'd ever seen, and he'd been threatened by an undead titan on a dark street just last night. Pink and gold velvet drapes hung around a massive, gilded ballroom. Garish potted plants crept everywhere from plinths that seemed only there to support the draping of more heinous pink velvet. Gaudily attired men and women chatted animatedly below a massive crystal chandelier that would certainly annihilate at least half the partygoers should its thin gold chains fail. Peacock feathers seemed to be a popular accessory, often decorating jackets of weird voluminous ruffles. On the dancefloor an ancient couple swayed slowly to the music of a black-tied orchestra. Worst of all, everyone was drinking wine.

Van tugged at his collar again, realizing with alarm that Lady Dorothy and Kyle were already engaged in lively chats with people in the entry and were on their way to leaving him behind. As he walked closer, careful to step lightly with his new boots on what looked to be an expensive carpet, he scanned the party for other titans. There were several, though none he recognized. Most were better dressed than him, closer to a noble level of decadence. They conversed and caroused, apparently at ease in their surroundings. Van, not so much. There were no barrels in sight, and he was beginning to panic. He felt a tap on his shoulder.

Owen Grit handed him a large mug of beer. Van heaved a sigh of relief. "Thanks."

"Thought you'd need that," Owen said. He'd found a tasteful balance between his usual wrestling gear and the finery of the gathering. Pretty much just his usual outfit plus a tailored jacket pulled over his massive shoulders. He took a lopsided stand— his knee clearly pained him—next to Van, and observed the party.

"How's the knee?" Van asked, glancing down.

Owen ignored the question and grinned at Van. "I like the pink beard look. Did I hear you picked a fight with the Landshaker last night?"

"Wasn't my fault." Van tried to keep his hand from reaching up for his beard.

Owen snickered. "I'd hope not."

Van tugged at his damn collar again—it was stiffer than his new boots—and sought to change the subject. "How's your crew faring?"

"My crew?"

"I never found out how Wave Rider did against Judge Cage. And didn't Harot face Bruce Bigsby this morning?" He cursed himself inwardly for not going to that one.

"Both lost," Owen said quietly, his grin fading. "So we get Flawless versus Bigsby, OverLord versus Landshaker, which will be interesting to say the least, Blades and Thad, which everyone's saying is already the finals, and you against Judge Cage. Round of eight is packed with assholes. Not unusual."

Van shot him a sideways glance, not sure if Owen was putting him in that category too, and a silence hung in the air between them. Van looked out over the party, saw Kyle flirting with a young nobleman, a bright smile plastered on her face, and his mood soured. Her so-called mirror was shining in every direction. Every direction but his. Probably because she knew he was already in her pocket. He gulped his beer, glanced at Owen.

"What?" the titan asked.

"Why are you here, Owen?"

"Our mutual friend thought you'd need some support." He nodded his head in Kyle's direction.

"And you listen to her?"

"She's pretty convincing, Van. And she made it quite clear that if I don't step it up in helping you she'd drop a few choice words to Governor Crowell."

"She's got the governor's ear?"

"And then some, ten-man." Owen drank, his eyes never leaving Kyle. "But if I'm honest, Van, I'm here to help because I'm starting to think I've misjudged you. These past couple weeks have been hard ones for me. This was meant to be my tournament. I've had to deal with everyone's disappointment, everyone talking like I'm invisible, like I'm worthless, just because I'll need a couple months to get back into the ring. And now they're all excited about you. I'll admit, I'm glad to see you win. I'm not one of those titans who wants to tear everyone else down." He sipped his beer and smirked. "I mean, don't get me wrong, when I'm healthy you're gonna be reminded of your place in the pecking order of Uplands titans. Until then, though, I can be a ten-man about it and do my part. You did your part by being there for Sevendhi yesterday. That's important. Being a titan isn't just about being stronger than everyone else. Because it isn't just the weak who sometimes need a champion. ONWC works together. Those of us outside their sacred circle need to do the same. So take people who offer you friendship seriously. You never know when you'll need them." He nodded at his mug and then finished it.

Lady Dorothy chose that moment to approach them. Another woman, who could have been her twin in dress and style, stood at her side. "My two favorite titans!" the Lady crowed. She hugged Owen with the same lack of restraint she'd shown when they'd gathered for the journey to Empire City and playfully slapped Van with her purse. He saw it more as a warning than a sign of affection.

"As I said, Edith," the Lady chittered, "you simply must meet our Van the Beer Man. An unconventional style and an unconventional look, but he defeated the formidable Panam Manley to make the round of eight! Long is the list of mighty nations falling before our lowly Uplands." Dorothy looked Van up and down like she might purchase him to decorate an alcove. Finally she snapped out of it. "Van, this is Governor Edith of Peakfall."

On hearing the title, Van nervously straightened a bit. He nearly tugged his collar again, but Edith shot him a disarming smile and said, "Relax, Van. Not my first time meeting a titan." She reached out a delicate hand, which he engulfed in his and pumped up and down, only spilling a small amount of her wine. She laughed. "Lady Dorothy has been bragging up your successes all around Empire City. I *do* hope you're enjoying yourself."

Was he enjoying himself? He spoke softly when he addressed her. Did you have to use formal titles with governors? "Peakfall brought the Patriot Jack Hammer, right?"

She nodded grimly. "Yes. A´ victory over Hugo Marky and those clods from Rising Waters, but then that horrible OverLord showed up and dragged him off."

Van tried not to think about the encounter with the Bearhugger last night. Had the Patriot been similarly...corrupted? "Has anyone seen him?"

"No, and it certainly has us worried. We're keeping a watch on that pit in the graveyard. And you can be sure we're not the only ones. If he shows up for his match with the Landshaker, we'll be on hand to ask him some *very* pointed questions." She produced a fan from her sleeve, snapped it open, and waved it in front of her face, seemingly more out of habit than an actual need to cool off. "Frankly, I'm not too worried. I'm sure the ONWC is on the case." She shared a knowing look with Lady Dorothy. "No money to be made if the Nether wins the tournament, is there?"

Lady Dorothy returned the devious smile, then abruptly sneezed. The peacock feather jutting out of her hat flopped down over her face. "Oh, bother," she said, quickly handing her purse to Van so she could fix it. "Anyway, Jordanese over there is flapping her eyelashes at that miserable Urdesta delegate, Edith. Let's say hello." She looped her arm under the governor's and was quickly gone.

Van was left staring at the purse in his hands. "What is it with her?" He wondered if the damn thing would fit in his pocket but realized he'd have to crumple it to do so, which just might cause a scene, so he tried to cover as much of it as possible with his hand and held it against his stomach.

Owen started pointing out various people at the party, showcasing a surprisingly deep store of anecdotes. Van listened and laughed while trying to not track Kyle with his eyes. They passed the time this way for a good half hour. Then a deep cough behind them drew their attention.

Van turned to find a large titan standing just behind them, staring directly at him. He had a yellowish tint to his skin—orc blood probably—and jagged teeth jutting upwards from his lower lip. Small eyes darted under a heavy brow. His face was a brawler's, scarred and battle worn. His head was shaved and free of even a hint of stubble. He wore a dashing, tailored black suit with a glittering pink-and-gold ascot.

"Name's Donovan," he said in a voice like a landslide. He glanced down at the purse in Van's hands and his eyes showed the tiniest sparkle of amusement. "King Thad wants a word."

From the shape of his head and the thick neck, Van suspected Donovan had been the titan Van had seen on the balcony behind King Thad. He took a long drink of beer to buy himself time to think. "He's here?" Van asked.

Donovan snorted and shook his head. "No, he's got a private gathering just down the street. Wants you to come by. Won't take long."

Owen's face was concerned. "I'm coming too," he said.

"Nah, ten-man," Donovan said to Owen. "You're not. He said he wanted to see Van. If he wanted to see you too, he would have said so."

Owen glowered at Van. He shifted his eyes back to Donovan, looked him up and down. "Why do you work for him, Donovan? I saw you coming up through the ranks. Never pegged you for the life of a servant."

Donovan offered a cold smile. "Oh boy. Owen Grit is out of wrestling for a couple weeks and is already focusing on his mental grappling skills. Don't know you're gonna find your footing quite as easily on this new ground, ten-man. But to answer your question, I work for King Thad because he pays me, and pays me well. We weren't all born to a fancy family of famous titans like you. Show me a titan who's managed to hang onto any possessions beyond his muscles when the wins aren't coming, then we can talk about who's a servant and who ain't. We all got to work." He shifted his glare toward Van. "And we aren't all from an Open Nation that doesn't have twenty titans lined up to vie for the tournament, should it fall vacant due to..." He looked down at Owen's bandaged knee and smirked. "...bad luck."

"No," Grit replied, "you're from a Nation where nobody has to line up because the spot has been bought. Nobody is standing in line. Nobody who knows shit about anything."

"Man, Grit, you really are a drag sometimes." Donovan shook his head and turned to Van. "That bullshit give you enough time to make up your mind, Van the Beer Man? I don't know if I can handle another round." When Van hesitated, he shook his head again. "Ask Grit, ten-man, he knows. The King gets what the King wants. You can walk to him on your feet or be dragged to him like a dog."

Another summoning. What would Kyle want him to do? He could guess at her answer. Go, but with open eyes and ears. And try not to do anything stupid. If they wanted to take him out of commission, they'd probably be a little less obvious. Then again, the ONWC didn't seem to operate with many restraints. And it sounded like it wasn't really a choice anyway.

"Thanks, Owen," Van said. "I got this." He looked awkwardly at Lady Dorothy's purse for a moment, threw it into a potted plant, and turned back to the King's messenger. "Let's go."

Chapter 29

Donovan led Van out of the party and down the street. Van watched the heavily muscled titan's back as the crowd parted before them. Not the most comforting guide to follow into the lair of Van's enemies. Donovan clearly had a healthy share of orc blood. Orcs were supposedly stubborn, hard to move. Impossibly dense. Given this one was firmly in King Thad's pocket, he'd be no friend to Van. Donovan looked like a real threat, radiating competence and intelligence that would put him higher up the chain than titans like Eagle and Creature. Of course, Donovan reported to King Thad and the idiot brothers reported to Venerate Holland. Van wasn't sure how much spitting distance was between those two units. Probably either camp would happily bury him.

They had walked about a block before Donovan turned to a building with a recessed entryway, dominated by gilded columns. It looked something like a castle that had been stretched vertically into the shape of a four-story apartment building. Eagle stood on one side of the entryway, Creature the other. They were wearing ties over their armor plates.

Donovan barely acknowledged the two thugs, simply shoving the doors between them open and walking in. "Hello, ladies," Van said as he passed.

A stone hallway lit by evenly-spaced torches in sconces led deeper into the building. Roaring laughter came from farther down the hall, presumably their destination. They entered an enormous chamber set up as a dining hall, filled with titans packed into three long tables set in a U-shape.

The titans inside were variously arguing, arm wrestling, and spilling food and drink all over the tables and stone floor. Two in the corner were fighting. Van followed Donovan straight to the center of the room, scoping out the titans even as they took notice of him. Three titans Van didn't recognize sat to his left alongside the Landshaker, who was too busy counting a pile of gold on a plate in front of him to raise his head at Van's entrance. Van presumed one of the titans next to him was Jaygan the Dragon Reynolds, judging by the ten-man's pet baby dragon. The fierce creature perched on the table in front of him attacking what had once been a fried chicken. A titan to the left of Landshaker was probably the Butcher based on his truly spectacular mullet. Van didn't recognize the third.

At the head table, King Thad sat at a huge wooden chair with a high, ornately carved and decorated back. Scott Flawless sat to one side of him, Venerate Holland, the only human in the room, on the other. From what Van had learned from Rakesh, Owen, and Larvell, he was looking at an assembly of most of the wrestlers who were closely affiliated with the ONWC. Lair of his enemies indeed. The only one missing by his count was Judge Cage, Van's next opponent in the Headlock.

Donovan stepped aside and nodded at Van to come forward. The titans around the tables all continued laughing and joking. When King Thad saw Van approach, his laughter trailed off. There was a long pause Van wasn't sure if he was supposed to break.

"The Beer Man!" King Thad called out suddenly, raising his glass in the air. The other ten-men repeated the titan's words and laughed. King Thad took a long drink, then waved a hand at Donovan. "Get him a beer,

Donovan, he's not just gonna stand there and watch us drink. Not the *Beer Man* himself."

Thad set down his mug on the table and studied Van. Then he pointed a massive finger around the room. "That's Hugo Marky, the Butcher, and Jaygan the Dragon. You met the Landshaker last night, I hear." The Landshaker growled as he looked at Van. "Oh, play nice, Anthony," King Thad said before turning to the other table. He fired off the introductions like a necessary evil. "Great Golden Ghost. Dim Hurgen. William the Defeater. James Scraps is around here somewhere, maybe under the table. A couple young dickheads from the Valley of Sevens whose names I forget. Scott Flawless is over here on my right, and," he nudged the man next to him, "I hear you've also met Venerate. Venerate's boys on the door are Eagle and Creature. Donovan should have introduced himself if he's got any manners. I'm King Thad. You can call me Thad if you like." He nodded. "Did I miss anyone, Donovan?"

"Nah," Donovan replied casually from the corner as he drew a beer from a massive barrel.

"Good. That's done. Now, Van. How the fuck did you beat Panam Manley?" King Thad threw his head back and roared with laughter at his own joke.

The rest of the titans laughed along, but Van didn't sense any real malice in the question. He offered a small grin. "I'm learning that crazy things happen in the tournament."

"Damn straight," Thad replied, a smile in the center of his neatly trimmed beard. As Donovan appeared behind Van with a beer, King Thad raised his own for another toast. "To crazy things happening in the tournament." Van joined the others as they drank. The beer was good, very good in fact. An amber ale with a sweet, toasted malty note that wasn't usually Van's style, but it was rich and smooth. King Thad belched loudly, slumping back into his thronelike chair. "Anyway, Panam Manley never belonged in the round of eight." He shot a dark look at Venerate as he said it.

With King Thad busy giving Holland a glare, Van's eyes were drawn to Scott Flawless. The slender, muscle-bound titan sat almost primly at the table. His hair fell in perfect dark curls and he wore a tight, flashy jacket. The table in front of him was free of beer puddles and spilled food. A single wineglass stood there, filled with red. This was the titan who had broken Sevendhi's arm and ended his tournament hopes. Van wouldn't mind returning the favor. His thoughts must have been written on his face, because Scott Flawless stared right back at him, eyes fiery. The room grew quiet as they swapped glares.

King Thad watched the exchange with a grin on his long face. He rubbed his beard thoughtfully. "Trust the tournament to fan the flames of passion between us all." He stood and began moving around the table. "Let's take a turn, Beer Man."

Van backed out of the middle, meeting King Thad near the entryway. As Thad stepped out into the hall, Van puzzled briefly what to do. Was he walking voluntarily right into a trap, at the price of a tournament-ending injury? Owen was the only one who knew where Van was. If he ended up needing help, it would be slow coming. He swallowed hard and followed King Thad down the hall. Donovan fell into step behind him.

They strolled slowly down the carpeted, stone hallway past hackneyed oil portraits of old titans, maps, and landscape paintings of the Open Nations, alongside tapestries that were so faded Van couldn't tell what they were supposed to be. At one corner of the hallway, a full suit of titan-sized armor, complete with a visor and an enormous polearm, stood on a wooden dummy. Van had never seen the like before. It must have cost a fortune.

The King's slippers whispered on the carpets as the three titans delved further into the depths of the building. Finally, after a long silence, King Thad turned his head towards Van. "How's the beer?"

Van nodded. "Good," he said honestly. "Really good."

"I had Donovan bring it up from the cellar before I sent him to fetch you. And incidentally, sorry for dragging you from that other party, but I much prefer to host. At other people's parties, I get a lot of parasites asking me for money and favors. Everybody wants a piece." A laugh rumbled in Thad's chest but failed to escape his mouth. "But the beer. Can't serve the Beer Man just anything. It's a blend of grand cru from Dunham North brewery and an elvish tonic with a name I can't pronounce without spitting all over you." He smiled. "Mixed by my personal brewmaster, the lovely Lady Sheeha, whom I hired away from the governor of the Valley of Sevens. I wish I could tell you its price, but, frankly, it has no peer. I could send a barrel home with you, if you like."

Van's eyes shifted nervously. Any gift he accepted, no matter how casually offered, would hide a hook, and he didn't like King Thad's intense gaze. There was a painting on the wall behind Thad of an old woman seated at a chair, a shiny tiara atop her head and a cluster of jewelry around her neck. Van latched onto it for a distraction. "Who's that?" he asked.

"That, Beer Man, is my beloved mother. I keep her here in Empire City, close to the site of the tournament." Thad smiled at the painting as if the old woman might reach out of it and pat his cheek. "I have many homes, of course, and this is far from the most impressive. It would make more sense to keep this original at my palace in the Vantages or my lodge in the Valley of Sevens. I spend more time at both. But I like it here. I like to think she gives me a little extra motivation. Sometimes I can feel her watching over me. And I need all the help I can get, with the likes of you in the field. The Landshaker, Scott Flawless. What a gathering." He shook his head as though in awe. "Still, she was here when I bested all comers in the last two Headlocks. No doubt she brings me luck." He started walking again. Van sipped his beer and followed.

"Here's what I wanted to show you, Van," Thad said as they rounded another corner. Trophies and championship belts lined the walls, the gleam of gold reflecting the flickering light of the torches. It was a stunning display, and Van felt a surprising stir in his chest. There had never been belts like these in Headwaters, but every boy in town had dreamed of hoisting such treasures up in the air. Van had never even imagined the idea of a hall filled with them, each one a testament to wrestling glory.

King Thad had won practically every tournament he'd ever entered, what looked like hundreds. Some of the biggest trophies included eight matching Tournament of the Vantages belts. Three from the Northern Division of the ONWC. The Rumble of Giants. The centerpiece of the collection was a set of two Headlock of Destiny belts. A wooden rack stood between them, waiting for a third.

"Again," the King continued, "it would make more sense to keep these in the Vantages. But I like them here. I'm not a shy ten-man, Van, and I tell you honestly, I like to show them off."

Van could feel King Thad's eyes on him as he studied the many trophies. He was torn between admiration for the collection and skepticism, given the rumors King Thad had bought more matches than he'd won honestly.

"Van, wealth is not merely measured in gold. Don't get me wrong, I've got plenty of gold. But there's more to wealth than having more money than everybody else, which I do. And it's not all fame, either. I've got plenty of that too, as you know. But my favorite of all the different kinds of wealth I've earned is victories. Knowing I've raised my hands in victory on the greatest of battlefields, against the greatest of opponents. Your career is young, titan, but you may yet know these thrills. Of course, gold has its place too." He paused his speech and turned to Van. "I understand you haul barrels for the brewery in Headwaters."

Van nodded cautiously.

"Not a bad living, I'm sure. Not that I've ever done anything like that. Do you like hauling barrels, Van?" Van kept silent and King Thad reached out a hand to caress one of the golden belts. "I could make it so you never had to haul another barrel in your life, you know. I could make it so the owner of your brewery personally delivered a barrel of his finest ale to the front door of your mansion every day on his way home from a day of sweating labor. Or his wife could deliver it. Naked." He chuckled, then stopped abruptly. "It would be easy. As easy as snapping my fingers." He snapped his thick fingers. The loud crack hung in the air.

Van looked at Thad's hand, not sure whether he was being bribed or threatened, probably both, and met King Thad's eyes. All motion in the hallway ceased for a tense moment, except Donovan's heavy breathing behind him. Finally King Thad smirked and began moving again.

"The tournament separates the weak from the strong, Van from the Uplands. Of course I still think there are a couple weaklings who've snuck into the round of eight. Happens every year. They'll be eliminated shortly. You've got Judge Cage, I know. No pushover. So we get to find out whether Van the Beer Man is for real. If that's not the case, Van, you can come back for a barrel any time. A meal. A place to crash. I respect a tournament titan. If you do make it past Judge Cage, if you are for real, then we can have a whole different conversation. You can name a price, and I can pay it."

"A price for what?"

King Thad loomed closer, a half-head taller than Van and just as wide. "A price for whatever I want from you. And believe me when I tell you this. *Everyone* has a price. And everyone has something I want." He glowered and for a moment the lights in the dark hall seemed to dim. Then he burst into his big booming laugh. "Sometimes my hardest job is figuring out what it is I want though, isn't it, Donovan?" He winked at the orc-blooded titan. "Paying for it is easy. So easy it bores me." He laid a heavy hand on Van's shoulder. "Let's get back, shall we? I'm thirsty," and without waiting for an answer, he continued down the hallway.

Van followed behind King Thad, shooting a troubled glance towards Donovan, which was ignored. They rounded the corner back to the original hallway, having walked the halls which circled the main dining room. Now, however, as they approached from the opposite direction, there was a commotion near the large doors. One of which looked to be hanging by a single hinge.

King Thad grunted and gestured to Donovan, who sped smoothly past Van and King Thad and rushed towards the open door. A voice rose above the din. "You fucking cowards! You fucking cowards!"

Van followed King Thad back into the dining hall. A titan stood in the center. Billy Blades, the ten-man from Urdesta, who'd reached the round of eight by decimating Elephant the Titan and tearing the horns off the Minotaur. Blades's normally slicked-back hair dangled over his reddened face. His hands hung in fists by his sides. Either Eagle or Creature lay on the floor in front of him and one of the tables had been tipped over. But for the moment, Blades just stood there yelling loudly around the room, his gold chains rattling against his chest. "Cowards!"

"Easy, Billy, easy," King Thad said soothingly. "Calm down."

Billy looked at the King beneath heavy furrowed brows. Sweat trickled from the titan's temples. "Fuck your calm! You're all trying to set me up!"

"I said *easy*, Billy," Thad repeated in a more commanding tone. "Now, what's the problem, Billy? Why did you come in here and smash up my mahogany door?"

Billy pointed a colossal finger at Venerate. "He changed the bracket. Switched me with the Landshaker, set me up to face the fucking OverLord."

"Who, Venerate?" Thad asked. "You think Venerate did that on purpose?"

"Of course he did it on purpose." Blades shifted his hard gaze back to King Thad. "And he wouldn't have done it without your say-so. You scared to face me, money man?"

"This is news to me, Billy. I haven't heard anything about a bracket change. You're saying, instead of fighting you, I've got to fight that monster of a ten-man over there?" King Thad gestured at the Landshaker. "And you have to face the OverLord? And you think I had something to do with it?" His look of concern faded as laughter bubbled up. "Well, you'd be right, Billy Blades. Enjoy your date with the OverLord." He leaned back and roared laughter at the ceiling.

Billy Blades leapt at King Thad, but Donovan caught him and pushed him back. All the other titans were laughing at Billy. Someone, maybe the Butcher, threw a leg of mutton at him. "You sons of bitches!" Billy snarled, struggling against Donovan even as Hugo

Marky crashed into his back. "Cowards! Weaklings!" he yelled towards Venerate.

"Life isn't fair, Blades," Venerate replied. "When's the last time Urdesta did anything for anyone?" Eagle and Creature took positions before Venerate, cracking their knuckles and grinning those ugly, toothy grins. All the titans were on their feet, ready to rumble. "Now why don't you try something?"

King Thad broke from his fits of laughter long enough to throw a handful of gold coins down the hall towards the exit. "There you go, Blades. I just doubled Urdesta's take from the tournament. Gather 'em up and make them into more fancy necklaces."

Van just stood there, watching the drama unfold. Blades was strong, stronger than any of the others except maybe King Thad, the Landshaker, and Scott Flawless. But his courage faltered in the face of so many titans laughing at him. Deflated, he walked away from the throng and headed out through the doors, shooting Thad a furious look as he passed.

Rakesh had hinted that the bracket might change, had flat out asserted there'd be at least one change to the ONWC's advantage. It looked like King Thad wanted nothing to do with Billy Blades and the Landshaker wanted nothing to do with the OverLord. Van didn't think any of the titans wanted to face that reeking monster. So Venerate Holland had made the switch, putting the ONWC's biggest rival for the championship on a collision course with the scariest behemoth in the tournament. A titan even King Thad knew he couldn't buy. The OverLord.

Van shook his head in disgust. It was time to get out of here. With his host distracted, he scurried for the door. The laughter continued long past Billy Blades's exit. None louder than King Thad's, whose howling amusement chased Van down the hallway and out onto the busy street.

Chapter 30

Van left the hotel early in the morning, clean blue uniform and new boots on, a bounce in his step. He had Judge Cage tonight, a distant cloud on an otherwise sunny day. Judge Cage would be a handful, but no one had stomped Van out yet. And before his date at the Coliseum, he had the whole morning and afternoon to explore Empire City, assuming he could avoid Venerate's goons or another appearance by the Bearhugger.

The doorman flagged Van down before he'd gone more than a couple steps. Panting as though he'd run miles rather than the few feet from the front desk to the street, he held up a note for Van. The folded paper was scented with the strong smell of lilacs that washed over Van even before he took it from the doorman's gloved hand. Van opened it, ignoring the doorman's impatient eyes as he angled for a tip. It was from Hilda, the spy from Urdesta. Seemed she wasn't going to let Kyle scare her away from her prey. She wished him luck with his match and invited him to a different sort of wrestling afterwards. Van chuckled quietly, then turned away. The doorman huffed and stomped back into the lobby.

Van glanced down at the note again as he tread down the dusty street. Kyle would want to hear about it, might even appreciate Van bringing it to her attention. Ugh. Was he smitten? She was playing him, too, like she played everyone. He'd tell her, but maybe not right away. He thought about keeping the note. When was the last time a woman had written him a note? Had a woman ever written him a note? Instead he crumpled it into a ball and threw it to the side of the street. Fuck it. Much as he'd like to share his bed with someone, it didn't have to be with a spy for another nation. One with an annoying laugh.

Thinking about Kyle and telling her about the note was a pleasant distraction as he walked down the street past the bustling shops and the smell of freshly baked bread. It also might have been the reason why it took Van so long to realize he was being surrounded.

There were a lot of them, a couple dozen at least. Stiff-backed men in black, the uniforms of the Empire City Guard, Judge Cage's people. They spread out across the streets in front of him, allowed him to pass through them, and collected in a bunch behind him. They weren't titans, but they were many, and they didn't seem afraid of Van when they closed in on him. Maybe that cloud on the horizon was closer than Van had thought.

The people in the crowded street who were not dressed in stark black uniforms were quickly making themselves scarce. Van saw a frightened woman throw a backwards glance towards him as she hustled into a tailor shop and slammed the door behind her. Another pulled her child into an alley, held the girl still with white knuckles, ignoring the child's screeches. Two men lingering on a porch smoking sweet-smelling pipes chose to move their morning conversation inside. Quite quickly Van shared the streets with thirty-or-so Empire City Guards and no one else.

Van stopped and the guards circled around him. The tallest barely reached his armpit, but their titan boss would be somewhere close by. Van waited for Cage to appear, but it was a beady-eyed little guard in front of him who spoke first. "Are we doing this the hard way?"

"Doing what?" Van asked, looking around. Seemed Judge Cage was leaving this to his minions, whatever *this* was. His mind flashed back to Eagle and Creature trying to injure him to get him out of the tournament. Was Judge Cage so afraid of Van that he'd send his goons to soften him up?

"You're coming with us."

"No, I'm walking past you. Got a free morning all to myself, and I haven't even had a beer yet."

The guard was nondescript, like all his friends. It almost looked as though they were chosen to blend in with the scenery. All plain faces, clean shaven, short dark hair. He raised a pair of iron shackles, sized to fit a titan. "So the hard way then?"

"Looks like," Van answered.

The sound of thirty men all unsnapping thick cudgels from their belt holsters in unison was something Van could have done without. It was almost laughable that he'd been moping about people ignoring him back in Headwaters. He was getting plenty of attention in Empire City, none of it welcome.

They didn't rush him like Van expected, but sniped in from behind. The first blow caught him hard in the back of his calf. As he whirled to face that man, another blow slammed into his elbow. When he turned back around, two other men were already closing in.

Van needed a plan, a strategy. He ignored the next sneak attack, not that it didn't hurt, and leapt to his left, out of their circle. He wasn't going to let them herd him, control him. He seized one of the guards and lifted him off the ground. The rest circled behind him, and beat his legs and lower back with their cudgels as he hoisted the guard up and slammed him back down onto a cluster of club-swinging guards. A loud crack on the back of Van's head made him cry out. He grabbed another guard and hurled him backwards over his head to crash into the throng. One of the guards had the balls to circle around and attack Van from the front, but Van ended that with a straight punch to the face, same as he'd done to the Ram. The man fell on his back, staring bleary eyed up at the cloudless sky.

But the remaining guards continued relentlessly slamming their cudgels down on Van's head from both sides. One knelt down and slapped an iron cuff on Van's ankle. Van kicked and thrashed, jerking the other end of the attached cuffs from the guard's hands. More guards dove onto it and grabbed it. Van roared as he lurched his leg, bringing three clinging guards crashing into him. Then he whirled in a circle, swinging the guards into their cohorts who attacked his other side. He flung his leg in the other direction in a roundhouse kick that sent the guards flying up onto a nearby porch, one crashing through a large glass window.

But the time it took to free that leg was costly. Van found himself cuffed on the other ankle with five dug-in guards pulling him down. In the precious seconds he tried to wrestle them, the original chain was seized again. With Van's mobility severely curtailed, the others found the courage to attack him from the front and began walloping him on the forehead. Blood obscured Van's vision as it poured down from the brutal lacerations on his head. He roared again and leapt forward, having failed to notice that his ankles were completely bound. He fell on top of two guards, crushing and twisting what limbs he could get a hold of, half-mad from the pain of the wounds on his head and shoulders. The remaining guards piled on top of him all at once.

Van still struggled and thrashed, his massive hands ripping and twisting and punching. Then a tremendous blow right to his balls paralyzed him. He screamed in silence, the wave of pain so strong his entire body went rigid. The guards began working their way off of him as nausea roiled Van's gut. He sought to curl into a ball, to protect himself, but his every limb was tightly chained.

"Let's roll this big fucker over," a new voice said, deep with the timbre of a titan.

They turned Van over, the chains trussing his arms up tight. He looked up and saw Judge Cage standing over him.

He was huge, even for a titan, and especially from Van's view from the ground. His skin was pale, dotted with ugly freckles. He wore a wide-brimmed black hat that cast a shadow over his eyes. His black uniform had yellow stripes down the arms of his short-sleeve shirt and legs of his pants. He wore thick black boots that stunk of boot polish.

"Know what this is, son?" Judge Cage held up a balled-up piece of paper as he spoke down to Van. Even under the shadow of his hat, Van could see the amusement in his eyes.

"A love letter from your sister?" Van was fighting to hold still, ignore the pain radiating from his balls.

Judge Cage let out a short, barking laugh and shook the crumpled lilac-scented note. "No, son. This here is litter. And I won't have litter on my streets. You are under arrest."

"You don't want to settle this in the ring?"

"Son, we've got plenty of time for that. First we got to settle the matter of this…" He took the note, rolled his eyes at it, and threw it over his shoulder. "…violation of our laws."

Van stared at him for a long second, then he kicked out, aiming for Judge Cage's crotch, aiming to return the favor.

Judge Cage twisted his leg ever so slightly so that Van came nowhere near striking him. He laughed again as the guards tightened their already painfully tight hold on the chains. "You think this is my first rodeo, Beer Man?"

He continued as he stepped over Van. "Now, we're gonna have a little talk. But not in the dirty street, like hobos. You're coming for a little stay at the Warehouse." He suddenly dropped to one knee, driving the full force of his weight into Van's gut, and Van was left gasping as his breath fled his body. Judge Cage leaned in closely, sliding his hat back off his head to reveal a tight, military crewcut, small, piggish eyes, and yellow teeth. He leaned in, inches away from Van's face, gripped Van's collar with one hand. "You, son, are one ugly motherfucker."

Then he brought his other fist down in a punch so hard it knocked Van out cold.

Chapter 31

The world was black, the walls pressed in, and Van was being dragged someplace horrible. The scratching sound on the dirt must mean he was headed towards the cemetery pit, the path to the Nether. *You will follow me one way or another, titan.* Then the scratching sound faded and Van realized that, although he was awake and alone in the dark, at least he was not pressed in a coffin.

He was slumped in the corner of a jail cell, with an itchy crust on his face that he assumed was dried blood. The tiny cell had bars on one side and damp stone on the three others. He stood up, hunched to avoid hitting his head on the ceiling. The heavy manacles were still chained to his wrists and ankles, their rattle the only sound in the dark beyond Van's own labored breathing and the thumping of his heart. The cell was so narrow he could barely straighten both elbows at the same time.

There was no comfortable way for Van to stand in the small cell and no way to sit, especially wrapped in chains from his ankles to his wrists. After being some version of upright for a few minutes, he sat. Then he rolled on his side. Then he lay on his back, knees up. Then he stood again. Then he swore. Nothing brought any relief. He stared grimly through the bars, eyes unfocused in the dark. Time passed, or it didn't.

Van wasn't sure if his eyes were open or closed when he finally saw a light in the distance. A single, vertical line of fiery sky, like the sun rising on the horizon…turned on its side. Van walked towards it, the manacles gone from his limbs. He walked for days, growing no closer, before he finally stopped. "What is that?" he quietly asked no one.

But voices answered from the dark. First the OverLord. *The harvest has begun. The wars return.* Then the Bearhugger. *There will be no place to hide.* Finally another voice Van thought he recognized: *Titans are the shattered pieces, all that remains.*

"Harot, are you here? Can you help me?" he called to the dark.

No, just as you are not here. These lands are ephemeral and even the knowledge gained here is fleeting.

"Why then?" Van could hear the rasp of his own voice echoing off the stone walls. "Why am I here?"

All I can tell you is you'd best prepare yourself, ten-man. Your captors return. What comes next will be neither easy nor pleasant.

"Has anything been?" Van asked, then the arrival of torchlight, flickering in impossible realness, drove away the images that had intruded into his head.

"How's our little birdie doing?" came the husky voice of Judge Cage. The cell door swung open and Van fell out onto the floor.

. . .

"Welcome to the Warehouse. Nothing else like it in Empire City." Judge Cage was beaming as he raised a lantern to illuminate yet another row of cells. Blinking bloodshot eyes peered out from between thick bars.

Van saw every shape of eye, every shape of body in the dancing lantern light. Goblins and elves in the same cell. A lion. A troll. A sleeping titan who spoke softly in a language Van didn't understand. A sick and clearly dying centaur, all four hooves chained to the walls. But mostly he saw humans. Men, women, even children packed into cell after cell. Empire City's denizens of darkness. No explanation as to what they'd done. Never any argument or pleading. Just a hopeless despair that seemed somehow worse.

Judge Cage glowed proudly at each new hall. Van found them indistinguishable, all equally awful.

"What day is it?" Van asked finally, his throat hoarse from thirst.

Judge Cage laughed. "Same day, ten-man. Solitude does play tricks on you. Sun will be down in a few. Then we go for a ride."

"I'm guessing it isn't to the Coliseum."

"That remains to be seen, son." Judge Cage gave him an amused look, then turned back to the tour.

They kept walking, Van's chains rattling as he shuffled down the long hall behind Judge Cage. They were trailed by countless guards in their midnight black uniforms. Judge Cage kept pointing out captives he found particularly interesting. "All lawbreakers," he said. "All in need of a little Warehouse time. Remind them that freedom is earned, ain't theirs by right...Hey, what the hell are you looking at?"

Van had stopped and stood staring at a young woman, pretty features beneath the dirt and dark-ringed eyes. She held a small baby, which fussed quietly. As the light came back with Judge Cage, her eyes shifted down. "This one," Van said, feeling the weight of the manacles on his wrists. "What did she do?"

"Her?" Judge Cage scoffed, then reached out and caressed the bars of her cell. "That's Winona. She's behind in payments to her pimp, a fine chap called Tailor Jim."

Winona showed no reaction to hearing her name. There was something broken in her. Van despaired at seeing it. But that wasn't why he'd stopped. It was the child, the baby, that had stopped him. He remembered holding Annie's little Lizzy. Soft and fragile, unspeakably beautiful, belonging to a world with no place for Van.

"That's a baby." Van looked at Judge Cage, seeking some sign of anything beyond a monster in those piggy, little eyes. He was met with a flat stare.

"That's a *whore's* baby, son." Cage spat the words out with distaste.

"How long will they be in here?" Van wanted to tell her he'd be back, he'd find a way to free her, but he didn't want to lie.

"As long as I say they will. They sure as hell ain't repaying their debt, so we'll see how long Tailor Jim wants her in here. Give the right idea to the others. Whores, that is."

"Is everyone in here for debt?"

Judge Cage snorted again. "Most. We ain't the only police force in Empire City. We let the others lock up the drunks, bar brawlers, purse snatchers, pickpockets, snake oil salesmen, vandals, men who piss in public, litterers…sometimes." He leered as if he and Van were sharing a joke. "We specialize in the degenerates. Those who don't pay what they owe. It's our sweet spot and, son, let me tell you, it is *sweet*." He rubbed his fat fingers together like he could see the coin trickling between them. "I noticed you had no money on you, Van the Beer Man. I could lock you in here for vagrancy for that." He laughed again at his own joke.

Cage shoved Van to get him moving again and they trudged down the black hallway, away from the woman and her quiet child. Van thought of Annie, imagined her in the hands of this demon, felt his temples sweating and his stomach churn. When Judge Cage halted abruptly at the end of the hall, Van nearly stumbled into him. He was stopped by the guards behind him yanking hard on his chains.

Judge Cage stood before an open cell door. This one was enormous. It was also packed with more guards in black uniforms, staring out at Van with hate in their eyes. Judge Cage chuckled. "You're getting me all excited, Van. Today's gonna be a great day. Business booming at the Warehouse with all the foreigners in town. Another tournament win for me tonight. Sun'll go down soon, make for a beautiful night. But, before I can enjoy the blessing of evening, I have to rectify the sins of the day." He fitted his black-brimmed hat tightly onto his head. "See, Van, you hurt a lot of my men today. Good thing you didn't kill none, good for you, but I still owe them a chance to"—he leaned in close—"*make things right*."

With that he shoved Van into the cell and walked away as the first sticks and boots began raining down.

Chapter 32

Van's head smacked into something hard. He opened his bleary, swollen eyes to look around. He was in the back of a violently jouncing cart. It was not much larger than the cell he'd been in earlier. He was chained to the dark, wooden frame. Turning wheels dipped and rose as they clattered along a quiet road somewhere outside the city. Moonlight streamed in through a single, barred window at the back.

From the sound of it, it was just the one wagon, drawn by a four-horse team, no caravan, no crowds. As Van tried to raise his head, the bruises all over his back flared to life. The guards had worked him over to the point of unconsciousness, then kept working, apparently. His entire body felt like it had been stuffed with broken glass and then trampled by a team of titans riding stone dragons. His clothes were torn and he was thirsty and exhausted.

He'd been warned about Judge Cage. And still he'd wandered carelessly out onto the streets and into his trap. Now Van was headed to a shallow grave on the outskirts of Empire City. At least he wouldn't be locked forever in the Warehouse, rotting in the darkness until he forgot his name and lost his mind. At least the grave would be an end to this journey of pain and humiliation that had started up in Headwaters a lifetime ago.

The wagon clattered to a halt and Van braced himself for what came next. He was surprised to see Judge Cage himself throw open the door of the carriage cell. Shouldn't he be at the Coliseum, pretending he had no idea where his opponent was until they declared him winner by forfeit?

Judge Cage grinned as he reached in and grabbed hold of the chain linked to Van's ankles, dragged Van out of the back, and dropped him hard on the dirt below, kicking up a cloud of dust in Van's face. Every inch of Van's body throbbed as he lay on the ground, writhing in pain, coughing and choking. Judge Cage leaned back against the wagon, which creaked under his heavy weight, and waited for both Van and the dust to settle down.

Eventually the pain faded to a manageable misery and the dust cleared. Van looked around. They were indeed far outside of Empire City. Its lights were visible on the horizon. In the opposite direction, the moon shone over forested lands, where the road continued through the dark trees. Van looked back to the police wagon. It was of black painted wood, drawn by black horses. It seemed to soak in the moonlight, reflecting none back. Four of the guards sat on its roof, staring at him. Finally, he looked up at Judge Cage through bloodshot eyes.

"Okay, son. We got time for a quick chat, and that's about all. It's decision time." Judge Cage stood, hands on his hips, looking toward the forest, Empire City behind him, then he bent over Van and continued. "I call myself a judge, because I am the titan in charge and I make the decisions. But I ain't too prideful to fail to understand that I ain't the *only* judge, the only boss on the scene. You know who I'm talking about, don't you?" When Van didn't answer, Judge Cage's brow darkened and he drove a boot into Van's side. "Don't you?!"

"Venerate," Van said gasping. "You're talking about Venerate Holland."

"That's right, son, very good." There was a creak as Judge Cage settled back on the edge of the wagon. "And Mr. Venerate Holland says you got a choice. You walk, right now, down that road. Venerate knows the two of you got off on the wrong foot, but that ain't no reason to kill you, least not yet. So option one is you walk off. That way's west, take you back to Headwaters. Assuming you make it past the wolves and goblins, which shouldn't be hard for a titan, even one as soft as you. When you get back, you tell them whatever the fuck you want. Won't nobody believe you about what happened today. You're a coward, Van, and they smell it on you sure as I do. So you can run, coward. That's option one." He paused, waiting.

Van rolled over with a rattle of chains, pointed his face towards the trees. He knew he should be terrified, but all he found when he scoured the depths of his mind was calm. He was being given a choice, one that might actually be his to decide. It had been a while since he'd had a real choice. "What's the other option?" he asked.

"Well, that's where things get more interesting. Mr. Venerate Holland told me your other option is you die. I kill you right now. Snap that weak little neck of yours, leave a couple men to make sure the wolves find you before anything on two legs does. Won't be my first." He chuckled. "Sure as shit won't be my last. And then I ride back to the Coliseum, wide-eyed and baffled as to where my opponent got off to. Them's Venerate's options." Judge Cage pulled his hat off, worked it in his hands the same way Larvell always did.

"But I got an extra special option for you of my own. Mr. Holland thinks you're tough on account of what you did to his trained little doggies, Asshole and Creature. He doesn't want you in the ring with me, a loyal ONWC man. Me, I'm not so sure. I saw your fight against the Ram. Saw your clumsy luck. Heard all about how you got your ass kicked somethin' fierce by Panam Manley. Frankly, I'm a bit miffed to find Mr. Holland with so little faith in me. But the world ain't always what we want it to be."

"Tell me about it," Van said quietly, still staring off at the trees.

Judge Cage spat on the ground. "So the third option, my *own* option for you, is you come back and fight me. I'll be honest with you, Van, 'cause I don't bed down with lies. You're gonna lose, and when you do, that pretty little whiff of an escape from Empire City will be gone. Venerate will kill you or he'll give me just what I want, which is to lock you on the lowest level of the Warehouse, the one where it gets so dark even the rats can't see, and leave you there until time itself gets too old to care." Judge Cage's boots scuffed on the dirt and the wagon creaked as he stood again. "But at least it ain't the coward's way. So, what'll it be, son?"

If Van took the option to walk, assuming Cage didn't just kill him anyway, how long would it take him to get home? They'd told him he'd lose his job if he didn't see this through. But surely they'd bend if they knew what he was dealing with here. Was there a chance he could slip back into his old life? Leave all the danger and the fighting to someone else? There would be quiet afternoons where Van could be alone, drinking beer in the woods. For a moment Van wanted nothing more than to be home, where he knew himself and his place. Where people didn't throw him in cages and beat him. Where they just politely ignored him, ashamed of the titan who had settled for an ordinary life, a life like theirs. The sleeping titan. A tear splashed on the dirt inches from Van's face.

But he'd seen too much. Now he couldn't go back to sleep. If he took the chance to walk, when he closed his eyes back in Headwaters, he'd see those other eyes looking back at him out of the darkness, out from between the bars. If he took that walk, it wasn't just him that would suffer. This monster who wanted to lock up the world would keep winning, him and his bastard friends. Lock up and stomp down everyone without a champion to keep them safe.

Van drew a shuddering breath. "There's nothing for me back home," he said. "There never was." He rolled over, fighting sore and aching muscles as he raised his head to meet Judge Cage's eyes. "Let's fight, you giant sack of shit."

Judge Cage's chuckle rumbled like a wagon wheel. He slid his hat down over his eyes. "Pick him up, boys. The Beer Man appears to have found his spine." As he walked off towards the front of the wagon, he tossed back over his shoulder, "And that will just make it easier for me to rip it out of him."

Chapter 33

The wagon roared back through the streets of Empire City. Van, still chained in the back, was tossed with every jounce of the wheels on dirt and stone. Crowds parted before them, and Judge Cage never slowed even as they neared the Coliseum. An abrupt turn and the open sky vanished, the clip of the horses' hooves echoed off tunnel walls below the Coliseum. They rode along in near darkness, the light from Judge Cage's lantern hanging at the front flickering on the stone walls. Van could hear the din of an eager crowd even underground.

Judge Cage shouted back from the driver's perch, over the clatter of hooves, "Don't worry, Van! They know the way! They've hauled many a coward titan into the Coliseum ring!"

Another sharp turn and they resurfaced near the center of the Coliseum. The bright lights shone through the bars of Van's rolling cell as the wagon raced around the ring, and the crowd thundered its approval for the show. Van could hear a healthy mix of boos tossed in.

Judge Cage leapt off the top of the wagon into the ring, leaving it to rock to a slow halt. Van was stuck in the back, staring through the barred window at Cage waving his hands at the crowd. Van kicked the door but it was bolted shut. Cage circled the ring, out of Van's line of sight, but Van heard him a moment later.

"Friends!" Judge Cage yelled from the center of the ring, loud enough to echo from the Coliseum's distant walls and carry back to Van in the wagon. "Empire City! I have news! I have news!" As the audience quieted, he filled the void with his powerful voice. "You were very nearly cheated out of tonight's match. Cheated by cowardice. Cheated by Van the Beer Man." There were scattered boos. "Earlier today I got word he was running away. Fleeing Empire City, as fast as his big ol' gut would allow, rather than give you people the show you deserve. I said I won't let that happen in *my* city! So I went out and found him, ran him down at the gates. He was headed back to his little backwater in the foothills."

Van fumed. The coward. The liar. The hypocrite. He pulled at his chains, kicked the door again, shook the entire wagon on its rickety wooden wheels. More of the crowd seemed to notice the movement and turned to stare at the wagon.

"Oh, yeah, folks, don't worry. I got him. He's in there. Begged me to let him go. Said he wanted to throw the towel in, forfeit the match. Cried like a little girl. He even licked my boots."

The crowd began to boo and hiss wildly as Judge Cage fired them up with his tall tale.

"Believe me, folks, I listened to his sad story. I gave him his chance to spill his guts. I damn near shed a tear, and woulda if I ever did such girlish things. But I said, no, sir, I don't care how scared you are. You are coming back! And we are rumbling! We owe that much to all these good people. And when I hoist that trophy, no one's gonna say I didn't win it fair and square. No coward escapes judgement. No coward escapes Judge Cage!"

The crowd was loving it.

"Should we bring him out?"

The door opened and four of the guards pulled Van from the wagon. He stood and shook them off, but the chains running through his ankle and wrist manacles kept him from going anywhere. He looked up at Cage in the ring.

Judge Cage stood in the center staring down at him, bright lights on him. He was laughing. "I'm sorry, son," he yelled for the entertainment of the crowd, "no escaping the long arm of the law." He looked over at his men. "Haul his ass up here."

They pulled Van to the apron and Judge Cage leaned over and jerked Van under the ropes by his chains. Van's face slid across the canvas. He felt a heavy hand grip his collar, then Judge Cage dropped a knee on Van's back.

"Sorry, coward," Cage drawled. "Slipped on the mat."

Van tried to clamber to his knees, but Judge Cage put a boot on his ass and shoved him forward again. The crowd hooted and whistled. Judge Cage waved his men out of the ring, then reached down, wrapped a chain around Van's throat, and pulled it tight. Van struggled to breathe, felt his face flush red. "I could kill you right here, Beer Man," he whispered in Van's ear. "They'd love it. Big show." He tugged the chains, glared sideways at Van's bulging eyes. "What you got to say about that, son?"

Van thought for sure he was about to die for the entertainment of a few thousand wrestling hooligans when the referee finally crawled up under the ropes and took hold of Judge Cage's arms. Cage laughed and let go of Van's chains. Van staggered back, fighting for breath. Judge Cage walked over to his corner and shed his uniform shirt. Under it he wore a thin, white tank top soiled with yellow sweat stains. He carefully folded his uniform and placed it in his corner, then laid his hat atop it. He waved to the crowd, a smile plastered to his ugly mug.

Van stood there in chains, wondering if they'd even take them off before the bell. He'd been beaten unconscious twice by this monster. Van stared at him, thinking of all the people locked in the cells at the Warehouse—all the people at the mercy of this one giant piece of shit—and he got angry, real angry.

He grasped a few links of chain in his massive hands, took a deep breath, and pulled the iron links apart. The crowd burst into a thunderous uproar. Judge Cage looked at Van with a smile. Van tore apart the remaining chains until he was left with steel cuffs on his wrists and ankles and nothing else. He stretched his stiff back, felt power surging up through him.

Judge Cage was still grinning, readying to close in, but Van could sense a quiver in the Judge's bearing. Van glared at him. This shitstain of a titan who said he didn't *bed with lies*. His whole world was a lie. He'd never fought a fair fight in his life. And he was afraid, maybe just a little but it was there, in the blinking of his beady eyes, in the bobbing of his Adam's apple, the white knuckles of his clenched fists. The bell rang.

Van stood there, still as a mountain, as Judge Cage closed in and delivered a tremendous blow to Van's face. Van felt his nose crunch, heard the cartilage pop. Blood ran down his lips, over his chin, soaked into his uniform. And still he stood there. As he looked into the piggy eyes of Judge Cage, he saw the doubt growing stronger. Judge Cage threw another punch, this time at Van's eye. Van moved just an inch and took it on the cheek. And shrugged it off. The same way he'd shrugged off all the beatings since this journey had begun. He'd never asked himself how or why he could keep going, endure the pain and humiliation and keep coming back. But now he knew. He was a titan. Not a simpering shadow standing at the back, out of the way, waiting his turn. He was a titan, a champion titan, in a way Judge Cage could never be.

Van tasted the salty, metallic blood seeping from his wrecked nostrils. He locked eyes with Judge Cage and broke a smile.

Chapter 34

Rakesh leaned forward on the bar in the bustling gambling hall. A wonderful weariness coursed through his small bones, and he took a long drink from his mug of Kingsland. He waved for another. Rockhammer the dwarven bartender was on break, but he'd left another bearded steward in charge of slowly selling Van's barrel back to Rakesh, one delicious mug at a time.

To one side of Rakesh, a shaggy-haired man quietly cried into his own drink. Fortunes had been won and lost this evening. The man had lost, large. Judge Cage had been considered the closest thing to a safe bet in the round of eight, and the sobbing man was not alone in his great distress at the unprecedented upset. The pit bosses were no doubt watching the man closely to ensure he wouldn't bolt before settling up.

On the other side of Rakesh, an argument raged. One of the favorite debate topics amongst fans of titan wrestling was which match had the most epic beatdown in the long and storied history of the Headlock of Destiny. The local experts had no shortage of contenders. An oft-cited historical example took place in a match between Dunham North and Dunham South while the North was slowly carrying out its commercial takeover of its weaker southern sibling. For nearly twenty minutes, the South's last great titan, Johann the Giant, pulverized his northern opponent, Axeman Goreth, with jackknife splashes, facebusters, and foot stomps, and finally stripped off Axeman's singlet and wrapped him in the Dunham North flag like it was a diaper.

Another contender for the top spot was the beating dished out to Sandar Lynn by the Hellhound. The match took place after Sander was observed in all corners of Empire City mocking the Hellhound's blind stepbrother, staggering into people and falling over trash piles. He'd even secured a white cane to use as a prop. The Hellhound was extremely devoted to his brother and brought him everywhere, so the brother had a ringside seat for the beatdown the Hellhound dished out when the match finally arrived. He didn't seem particularly bothered by the large amounts of blood that splattered all over his clothes. Rumor had it Sandar Lynn still lived in a quiet town near the southern border of Billayou and turns pale as a ghost whenever he sees a white cane or dark glasses.

The debate next to Rakesh raged on, and would continue to rage on into the late night. Because there was a new contender for the title. The beating Van the Beer Man had handed Judge Cage needed to be given its proper place within history. Perhaps at the very top.

Just in front of Rakesh, in a large, neatly stacked pile on the bar, a fortune in gold coins rested. The halfling smiled as he took another drink. Few had bet on Van to beat Panam Manley. Even fewer had wagered on Van to beat Judge Cage. And only an insane person would have placed a sizable bet on Van to win the entire tournament after he'd limped out of the victory against the Ram. Rakesh had done all three. Whether Van continued his unlikely run or not, Rakesh had already won more at this tournament than he had in the past decade of his gambling career. And he was well positioned to win more.

For Van had not merely defeated Judge Cage. After he'd beaten him around the ring like a limp doll, he'd then walked straight from the ring to his opponent's home, the much-feared Warehouse, the headquarters of the Empire City Guard. Van had battered down the doors with a steel barricade and vanished into its depths for close to an hour. Eventually exhausted men, women, and creatures began pouring through the front door to quickly melt away like ghosts, freed from the Warehouse but terrified of the bright lights of the Empire City night outside. Van himself had emerged, accompanied by a stoic, foreign titan. Van carried an unconscious woman with a baby in his arms. He took her back to her home and made clear to her neighbors that she was to be cared for. He'd also made it clear he wanted words with the pimp who had placed her in Judge Cage's hands. Rakesh had no doubts the pimp was currently fleeing Empire City as quickly as he could.

The Warehouse burned. Whether the fire was set by Van the Beer Man or by one of the rival police forces which descended upon it was not much debated within the gambling hall. They didn't care. What they did care about was how the post-match activity affected the historical rankings of beatdowns. An old toothless sage next to Rakesh was currently saying, "If you really want to beat a titan, you don't just dominate him in the ring. You go to his house afterwards and burn it to the ground."

Rakesh had joined the other wide-eyed gamblers in watching the odds on Van change spectacularly. The Beer Man would face Scott Flawless next, who'd breezed to victory over Bruce Bigsby. Speculative bets had been permitted before the match with Judge Cage, and the odds of Van beating Scott Flawless had been set at one-to-forty. Following the manner in which he beat Judge Cage, the line shifted to one-to-three. It was the largest shift ever seen in the history of the tournament.

The field had narrowed to four, two of whom had been completely unexpected. The shocking rise of Van the Beer Man was matched by the seismic impact of the OverLord.

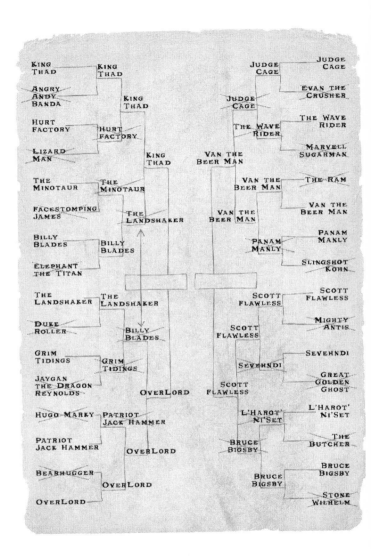

Earlier in the evening, word had filtered back that Billy Blades refused to fight, instead holing up in his hotel. The OverLord had waited for him in the ring until a forfeit was declared, then stalked off towards the hotel. He'd come out dragging his omnipresent coffin. It left deep ruts in the streets as he returned to the cemetery, heaved the coffin into the black pit at its center, then followed it down. No one had seen Billy Blades since.

King Thad remained the favorite. He had a powerful showing against the Landshaker to advance to the semifinals. The crowd had eaten up the match between two of the most dominant titans of the age. Only the closest of observers thought to question how easily the Landshaker went down. But amongst the gambling circles Rakesh rolled in, one learned to respect who had a price. And who could afford to pay it. Moggy Flats would leave the tournament richer than if the Landshaker had won, Rakesh was certain, and the nation will have appeased the Vantages and the ONWC. The only victim was the pride of the Landshaker, and anyone foolish enough to bet against King Thad when facing someone in the ONWC pocket. Rakesh had no sympathy for either.

The interesting wrinkle was that now the OverLord was on King Thad's side of the bracket. They could switch it again, but even the last change had stretched credibility. Two of the ONWC's favored sons, King Thad and Scott Flawless, remained. And two interlopers. Would the ONWC put Van in the path of the OverLord? Or figure out some other way to get King Thad into the finals? Only one could win the Headlock of Destiny Tournament and the field had narrowed dramatically, as it was wont to do.

Rakesh finished his beer and waved for another. When Rockhammer finally returned, Rakesh asked the friendly dwarven bartender for his finest barrel and a trio of stout men to cart it, and, with a smile on his lips, confidently set out looking for Van the Beer Man. The ten-man had never proven hard to find.

Chapter 35

Kyle made her way carefully up the dark stairwell. She'd gone high enough that the streetlights no longer leaked through the few small windows, leaving only the faint light of the moon to paint the steps before her. The building was abandoned from outside appearances, but she'd heard booming laughter from the rooftop, seen the shadows of titans atop it from the street below. Her boots made no noise on the cracked, wooden stairs, but still the movement ahead of her stopped momentarily as though reacting to her presence.

"I can't move any faster," came a lazy voice. "You'll have to wait." It had the deep timbre of a titan, with an accent Kyle struggled to place. As she reached the bend before her, she saw an enormous sofa wedged on the landing above. Long fingers tugged at its edges and the wooden frame creaked alarmingly as they freed it to continue its journey up the stairs.

A titan hoisted the sofa onto his head, gave a weary sigh, and continued upwards, giving Kyle a chance to study him. Long shorts, tanned legs, thin but powerful. This was the Wave Rider, a friend of Owen and the Lone Coast's representative in the tournament. He'd beaten Marvell Sugarman before falling to Judge Cage. Kyle had never met the ten-man personally but had been on the receiving end of enough stories from Owen to carry a fondness for him. At the next turn of stairs, the titan turned to observe her, placid eyes that nevertheless conveyed strength.

"I'm a friend of Van's," she said.

"Well, he's up there." The Wave Rider gestured with his eyes, then maneuvered the sofa again, a little more smoothly on this turn, and began plodding up the next set of stairs.

Kyle followed, taking time to sort through her thoughts. With his string of victories, Van had challenged the narrative of the Uplands as an easy target. Over the past several nights, Kyle had found and exploited cracks in the alliances formed against them. She'd have a strong report prepared for Governor Crowell, which was good, because she was coming. Three wagonloads of Uplands dignitaries approached, ready to bask in the glory of the unexpectedly deep tournament run.

The political threat may have been blunted, at least temporarily, but she had a feeling the present stability of the Open Nations was an illusion. She could feel a sort of shimmer, as though the curtain were about to fall. The tournament was just a setting for something larger. And she had a feeling she was getting the shape of the other side. The danger would come from beneath, spreading their darkness as the Open Nations squabbled for petty privileges.

The Rain of Spears order had shown no signs of life, even as the OverLord stalked Empire City. She could still hear the voice of the Bearhugger in her head, see the evil gaze of his white eyes. She'd taken every step she could to alert allies to the danger. The talk of the return of the Titan Wars. They didn't want to hear it. They were unprepared. She felt like the only one seeing the closeness of the threat. She needed a plan, and only the faintest edges of one were visible as she followed a titan with a sofa up the stairs.

The stairs soon ended at the rooftop door, which the Wave Rider shoved open with one end of the sofa. A pleased voice greeted the titan, "He returns! Our savior."

Kyle stepped out onto the roof after the Wave Rider and the sofa. The moon lit the gravel-strewn surface. A short parapet ran around its outer edge, over which the lights of Empire City could be seen in three directions. There was a large, black gap in the view off the back of the building, even with dawn approaching rapidly. The Parkland Cemetery was the only patch of Empire City without lights. Van sat in a chair looking out on the darkness. He didn't turn at their arrival. Another titan that Kyle recognized as Sevendhi of Kisket held a pair of scissors, apparently trimming Van's hair. A stoic titan lurked near Van, another stared off the other side of the building. Farther away were a halfling and a dwarf, chortling as they drank from foamy mugs. As was often the case, Kyle was the only female around the wrestling boy's club.

Sevendhi was the one who had greeted the Wave Rider so jubilantly. As his dancing eyes caught hold of Kyle, he smiled. "And he brings a beautiful woman with him." Sevendhi, whom Kyle had met before, shot her a wink before looking back to the Wave Rider in mock reverence. "What cannot this ten-man do?"

The Wave Rider groaned as he dropped the sofa and flopped down heavily on it. "Save it, Sevendhi. If I'd have known you had so much breath, I'd have asked you to come down and help."

"Bah! You need no help, mighty titan. I am no carrier of sofas. I am an artist." He gestured towards Van's hair with the scissors. His other arm, the one broken by Scott Flawless, hung in a sling. "Simply look upon my work and marvel." He glanced playfully at Kyle. "I apologize, pretty lady. My artistry has created a competition for your beauty."

Kyle returned the smile and walked towards Van. He did look much sharper. Sevendhi had narrowed and tightened Van's wild, black hair. Not quite a Mohawk, but the suggestion of one. His beard was similarly streamlined, eliminating its pink shading and adding sharp angles to his soft face. His nose looked to have been broken, but the swelling had already subsided. Van's uniform had not done well against Judge Cage and was torn in several places, though still an upgrade from the rags he'd worn when he first entered the ring. He had his black boots on and a somber expression as he gazed out over the dark grassy hills and stone monuments, sparing no glance for Kyle. There was a seriousness to him she hadn't seen before. Another layer to this puzzling ten-man she'd need to figure out.

She sidled up next to Van. Sevendhi made a few final clipping motions with his scissors, seemingly more for show than anything else, then brushed off Van's shoulders and wandered over to the Wave Rider.

Kyle stared out at the blackness of the cemetery. She'd seen the pit before, in the daylight, but never from above. There were no lights in the cemetery, just faint glimmers where the moon struck the palest of the headstones. But at the center was a blackness so deep it seemed to suck the rest of the light down into it. The pit sat open like an eye, watching Empire City from a place of death.

Van broke the silence. "You probably recognize Sevendhi. The Wave Rider carried the sofa." He gestured to a tall, silent titan who stared out over the cemetery. "That's Harot, short for L'Harot'Ni'Set, titan from Kassim Island." He waved a hand at the others. "My friends Rakesh the gambler and Rockhammer the bartender. And this," he said, eyes on the hulking titan standing behind him, "is Harlan." Van's brow furrowed. "At least I think that's his name. He doesn't talk much." With that, Van fell back into silent contemplation of the horizon.

"He's the one you freed from the Warehouse?"

"Yes."

"Any idea what he did to get inside?"

"Don't know, don't care. Given it was Judge Cage that put him in, I'd guess he just ran out of money."

Rumor put Judge Cage on the roads north of them, racing towards Dunham South. A rat that crafty always had a hole ready to crawl into, but his position in Empire City had been burned to the ground just as thoroughly as his beloved Warehouse. Fear had helped his reach grow long. It had only taken one loss to eradicate that fear. One titan. One unexpected, perplexing titan from the quietest part of the Open Nations. Kyle reached out a hand and caressed Van's neck, smooth from a fresh shave.

"Nice win tonight," she said softly. "You look good, Van." From the way he stiffened, she didn't know if he welcomed or disdained the touch. She looked at his face closely for a moment. The bruising from Judge Cage's fists had already faded to memory. "You heal so fast."

Smoke, and an accompanying sweet smell, drifted across the rooftop as those by the sofa huddled around a joint. Van showed no interest in joining them and Kyle was again struck by his seriousness. He didn't even have a beer in his hand.

"Van, I owe you an apology." He didn't reply, but tilted his head as though curious. "I should have done more to protect you. I never should have let Judge Cage get to you before the fight."

Van turned to look at her, then back to the black emptiness before him. "That's not your job. Not your fault. I'm the one who wandered into a trap."

"It's a big part of my job, Van, to make sure you get a fair chance at these fights. And that was far from fair."

He shrugged. "It worked out."

She'd been expecting more. More self-pity, more anger. But he seemed to have already moved past it. She continued, "Judge Cage sent guards to the hotel too. They got hold of me, Larvell, and Owen. We put up a fight, but there were too many."

"They hurt you?" The words were loaded with menace.

"No," she said quickly. "Just tied me up. It took me a few hours to slip away. I got to the Coliseum just in time to see the fight. Larvell and Owen took more of a beating trying to get loose."

"Judge Cage won't bother us again," Van said. "Scott Flawless is next. Tomorrow night. And King Thad gets *that*"— he pointed out towards the cemetery, the black hole at its center that seemed to swallow the light, the gaping abyss to the Nether—"tomorrow night. Unless he shifts the brackets again, like he did with Billy Blades. Then I get *that*."

Rakesh called out from the sofa, "He won't. He's got to deal with the OverLord sooner or later. It already strained credulity that he shifted the round of eight."

Van nodded without looking back. "So Scott Flawless then. But every step takes me closer to that chasm." His nose wrinkled as though he smelled something bad. "And I'm still not strong enough."

Kyle stood beside him in silence a moment before replying. "No one knows how strong you are, Van, least of all you."

"Maybe, but I've seen him, really seen him, and I don't think I'd stand a chance. Scott Flawless, on the other hand…against him there's a chance. Maybe not a great one, but a chance. I can take him."

"Sevendhi believed that too," Kyle said, quiet enough that the Kisket titan couldn't hear her. She smiled softly. "What happened to the *I don't belong here* version of Van the Beer Man who stumbled through his early rounds?"

"I was given a choice…by Judge Cage. Maybe the first time since this all began that I really felt it was up to me. I could have walked, dealt with losing my job and dealt with the scorn of Headwaters. But I didn't. I stayed. I've chosen. The sleeping titan is awake. And I'm not losing to Scott Flawless, not after what he did to Sevendhi. Not with what he represents. I'm not losing to King Thad and his money. And I'm not losing to *that*." He pointed a thick finger out into the black, but he gave an almost imperceptible shudder as he said the words. "I don't know if I'm ever going home again, which leaves me only one way out of this, one path forward, and that's to win this thing."

Kyle was no longer sure the tournament was the end of any of this. She laid a hand on Van's shoulder, feeling that what she was about to tell him would hurt far worse than any blow Judge Cage had landed. "I don't know how you'll take this, Van, but home is coming to you. A delegation from the Uplands is scheduled to arrive this morning. They'll be expecting to see you at the hotel."

Van scowled. His mouth opened, and for a moment Kyle thought the old Van would return, that he would begin complaining about anything and everything around him, but he swallowed his words. Instead he gestured out over the cemetery. "Have you seen it?"

"Seen what?"

"Harot says at dawn, for just a moment, there's a sort of horizon that appears over the hole. A bright, vertical stripe. That's why we're here." He leaned back in his chair. "He actually already showed it to me once, but he keeps arguing that was a hallucination." Van leaned over close to Kyle and spoke in a stage whisper, obviously meant to be overheard by L'Harot'Ni'Set. "*He's been kind of a dick about it.*"

Harot turned to them from the parapet and rolled his eyes. The tall titan managed to make even this childish gesture seem sophisticated. "Whatever you saw or didn't see had nothing to do with me. If you brought an amalgamation of me or some version of me that made an impression in your battered head earlier today, it had nothing to do with the actual me. When you were locked in the cells of the Warehouse, I was busily delivering a lecture over at Empire City College on the eastern front dynamics of the Battle of Flats Gateway. Much to the dismay of the students, no doubt, I was very much present in mind, body, and spirit."

Van nodded sagely, then leaned back towards Kyle. "*See? A dick.*"

"What do you think it is?" Kyle asked. She threw the question into the air between Harot and Van and wasn't surprised when Harot answered.

"A link, a vestigial connection. Some sign of whatever magic holds the gateway open. Perhaps it renews each morning at dawn. Perhaps that is merely when we can see it. In short, I have no idea."

"I want to see it," Van said.

"You should go back to the hotel," Kyle replied. "You'll be safer there."

"I'm safe enough here." He gestured back towards his friends, who remained clustered around the sofa laughing in a cloud of smoke. Harlan hung nearby, arms folded like a bodyguard.

"It's one thing to be confident about facing Scott Flawless in the ring, but with just four wrestlers left in the tournament we've got to keep an eye out for assassins, sabotage. The ONWC will do anything to win."

His eyes were still on the cemetery. "They might have their hands too full to bother with me."

"They will find a way to deal with that. And then turn their attention to you. As far as they are concerned, you and the OverLord are both threats and they have a long history of crushing anything that threatens their chokehold on the Open Nations."

Harot had wandered closer. "The Nether opens a gateway into the heart of Empire City. Its champion preaches that the Titan Wars return. We may all have our hands too full before long."

Van continued looking over at the entrance to the Nether. "I'm not going in that coffin."

Harot folded his hands together. "I've no doubt the others said the same thing."

Van's gaze snapped away from the cemetery and he stared long and hard at the titan beside him, a scowl on his face. Harot ignored him. Even to an untrained eye, Van's anger at the comment would be apparent. But to Kyle, who had spent her life learning to read faces, the fear was as plain as day. He looked as lost as he had back in Headwaters, stumbling to find a path that didn't end in loneliness and pain. Finally he looked back to the cemetery, let the moment pass without additional comment.

Kyle stood for a minute. No more words were exchanged, though quiet laughter and murmurs from the sofa carried over with the clouds of smoke. Finally she grew restless, made her excuses and left. As she went, she looked back to see Van's eyes still glued to the pit below them.

Sevendhi intercepted her at the door to the stairwell. He gave a short bow. "Always I am saddened to see the departure of such beauty. You have a safe passage home arranged?" As Kyle nodded, Sevendhi slid next to her and turned back towards Van. "He has had a tremendous victory tonight. And I am not speaking of the tournament."

"How's the woman he brought out of the Warehouse?"

"She is well, as is the child. And both will continue to be well. She will carry forward the memory of the titan who rescued her from the darkness. She will tell stories to her child as it grows. No one forgets their first champion, especially when it conquers a beast like Judge Cage and delivers you from so bleak a place." Sevendhi had passion in his quiet voice. "She will not forget. Neither will he."

He looked down at his injured arm, then returned his gaze to her and continued. "We failed him today. He walked into that ring alone. We let him down. It cannot happen a second time. We are surrounded by vanity, greed, and death. I only hope we are strong enough to give him the chance he has earned. And I hope he will be strong enough to take it." His uninjured hand flexed open and closed and his voice tightened. "I have spoken with my queen. She has no more doubts. The Titan Wars are coming and something rots the ground beneath us. We have grown soft. I pray not yet so soft we prove no match for what approaches. She would meet with you."

Kyle nodded. "I'll find her." She reached out and gripped the titan's large hand. "Sevendhi, champion of Kisket. Comfort is elusive in these hard times, but I draw comfort from knowing that, come what may, we will fight on the same side."

"Always," he replied softly, then turned back to the other titans.

Kyle was left alone at the door to the stairwell. She gave one last look back at the darkness of the cemetery pit, the gateway to the Nether. Van had followed her into the dark night once before. Would he follow her into a place she herself feared to go, if she had to? If this path led where she dreaded? For a moment she struggled to breathe, wrestling with her fear. As she pulled it back under control, she walked around the door, over to the far edge of the rooftop, a place quiet and blocked from the view of the gathered titans. She looked down on the empty streets below.

So Queen Aoleon of Kisket had opened her eyes. And others would as well. If Kyle could wake the Rain of Spears, she would have to move quickly. There were other things she had to do. And no time to waste.

She pulled her coat off her shoulders, letting it fall to the gravel at her feet. Beneath she wore a backless black shirt. Her skin shone in the moonlight. She drew a deep breath, looked up at the sky, then pitched forward off the rooftop. As she fell, the ground hurtling towards her, Kyle spread wings that had not been there a moment before. The wind filled the dark feathers as they beat the air. Moments later, Kyle was no longer falling. She flew off over the low rooftops of Empire City, dark and quiet, clinging to the night's shadows as easily in the air as she had in the streets. Soon the valkyrie was a dot on the horizon.

Chapter 36

"My ten-man got himself a haircut!" Larvell exclaimed as Van topped the stairs up from the hotel lobby. "And those threads are looking good." He made a show of walking around Van, examining him from all angles. "I would have gone with a different color for the uniform, maybe slap your name on the back, but that's just me. You look sharp!"

Their hotel rooms were just down the hall, and Van could hear a mix of voices from inside. The new Uplands contingent, which included several people from Headwaters, had arrived. Van wasn't quite ready to take the last few steps yet and face them. He peered down at Larvell. The manager had found a replacement hat somewhere, and from under its brim he smiled at Van through a busted lip. He was swollen around one eye.

"I heard the Empire City Guard got a hold of you," Van said.

Larvell's face tightened, but he quickly smiled it away. "These things happen, Van. Not my first time in Empire City."

"Kyle said you and Owen took a beating trying to get loose."

"Would have been nice to get you a warning. A few too many of them, though." He rubbed at his eye, smile undiminished. "And they were pretty upset when Kyle slipped away. I did enjoy the looks on their faces when the rival Empire City police forces showed up, though, looking brave since you put Judge Cage in a world of hurt. Our captors were dragged off and our freedom swiftly returned. I'll sleep better not knowing what happened to the Empire City Guard."

Van gestured to Larvell's bruised eye. "I appreciate that you didn't make it easy for them. I'm sorry I wasn't here to help."

"Not your worry, Van. You took care of your end. Big time."

"I did. But it's not going to get any easier." He extended a hand. "Maybe from here on we can work together."

Larvell shook the hand and sighed in relief. "I'd like that, ten-man."

Van nodded. "I need all the help I can get." He looked at the door to the hotel rooms, behind which a throng of Uplands bandwagoners waited, no doubt. "So why aren't you in there?"

"Honest answer?"

"I'd prefer that."

"Looks bad if I walk in there without you. They've already asked me where you were a dozen times and I got tired of saying I didn't know. Gives them an excuse to start blaming me for everything that's gone wrong."

"Seems like more has gone right than wrong. Isn't that why they're here?" Van stared at the doorway, brow furrowed.

"Well, Van, I don't disagree, but one of the first things you learn about important people is they love to fix things. Somehow find a way to twist what happened before they turned up into a mess, and what happens after they turned up into salvation. I've already been scolded up and down the chain this morning. I wouldn't be shocked if Kyle were getting it, too, right now. She's in there."

The idea seemed ridiculous to Van. He stared hard at the door. "Who else?"

"Bunch of people from your brewery. Your mayor. Governor Crowell and a couple key nobles. I can give you everybody's names if you like."

"Nah." Van took a deep breath. "Together, then?"

"Let's do it." Larvell led the way into the rooms.

Van was immediately struck by the number of people crammed into the small space. All the furniture had been rearranged, the titan-sized sofas pushed against the walls to make room for the large standing crowd. Everyone chatted amiably, drinks in hand. Van recognized the brewery president, Peters; his chief of operations, Mitch; and Garret, the head of sales. There were some other men Van had seen around the brewery but didn't know by name. Others he'd never seen before. One small group was seated in the corner, backs to the center of the room. Van saw a smartly dressed woman leaning in towards Kyle, the two speaking in quick, hushed tones. Van had a feeling he was looking at the governor of the Uplands.

As Van watched, another pair walked in from one of the opposite halls. The mayor of Headwaters turned back laughing as Alec Durheed followed her into the room. The prick had managed to weasel his way onto the trip and was using it as an opportunity to suck up to the mayor. Van felt a black rage creep beneath his skin. Would they stop him if he just grabbed Alec by the throat and smashed him through a wall? If he didn't even wait for the first snide comment? The intensity of the anger startled Van, and he abruptly realized how close he was hovering to that knife's edge, how close he was to letting something dark out of its cage. He shook his head to dispel the dark cloud around him. The overpowering anger disappeared as quickly as it came, though it left a bitter aftertaste like a beer in which the hops had been boiled too long.

Peters, the brewery president, was the first to notice Van hulking in the doorway with a confused and dark expression on his face. "Ten-man of the hour!" he called out, raising a nearly empty beer glass. A hodgepodge of cheers followed. The Headwaters group seemed well into their cups and Van noticed a few fresh barrels stacked against the walls. At least they always brought plenty to drink.

Within moments the brewery crew had gathered around Van, all except Peters, who appeared to be trying to work his way over to Governor Crowell. Van felt uncomfortable under their scrutiny as they looked him up and down. Larvell offered words of welcome and shook hands, buying Van some time to wrap his head around the strangeness of being back in this circle, and for once being at the center rather than the edges.

"All right, Van," Garret said, "got a lot further than expected, didn't you?" It was more words than the man had ever directed at Van before.

Van shrugged.

Mitch said, "We think it's great, Van. Really great." He nodded, looking wide-eyed around the group for backup. "Been hearing all sorts of buzz, haven't we, Garret?"

"Sure thing," Garret blurted mid-sip, dribbling beer onto his shirt. "Been real good for sales. Everybody's talking about the Uplands and the Headwaters Brewery."

"You been having a good time, Van?" Mitch asked, already gazing around the room as though he wasn't particularly interested in the answer.

Van stared at him. A good time? He'd been locked in a prison cell all day yesterday, beaten within an inch of his life multiple times, probably while these guys were tapping their third or fourth barrel on the road.

Peters arrived and the circle opened around him. He wore a scowl, maybe due to being rebuffed in his efforts to get to the governor. He snapped at Mitch. "You ask him yet?"

"No, not yet." Mitch met the president's eyes, then turned back to Van. "Van, we've got to ask, did you endorse Rosalyn Brew's Crater Ale? Cause we stopped at a few places on the way in, and they were all saying everyone knows Van the Beer Man drinks Crater Ale."

Van scoffed. "You kidding me? You know I almost never drink that stuff." The hard looks around him didn't soften, and he realized that wasn't true. They *didn't* know him. None of them knew him. Probably the one in this group who knew Van the best was Alec, and they hated each other.

There was a long silence. "Give me a break," Van said. "No, I never endorsed Crater Ale."

"But did you say this year's batch of Crater was better than our latest run of Foundation?"

Van had a drunken recollection of saying exactly that to Rakesh and a large group of dwarven brewers at a wild party near Station's Landing. Oops. Nevertheless, he shook his head no.

"Well," Peters cut in sharply, "whether you did or you didn't, the story's out there. And those two barrels of Kingsland we gave you never got to the Meadow Tap. We told you to get them to the Meadow Tap."

Van honestly couldn't remember if they had or hadn't told him where to bring the barrels. He'd thought he was free to use them as needed.

"So where'd they go?"

"I traded one for a couple brewmaster-stamped barrels and shared the other with...uh...an international gathering of...uh...important people." Would they think it was better or worse if they knew other titans had drunk it? He looked around defensively. "I've been carrying barrels to the ring. Everyone knows I'm Van the Beer Man."

"But you haven't been promoting the Kingsland and the Headwaters Brewery's other brands, Van. Everyone is running around claiming you drink this or that. We wanted you to be an ambassador for us, not for every swill in the Open Nations."

"I can't help what people say," Van said. This was unfair. He looked around the room for help. Governor Crowell was rising from her chair, ending her conversation with Kyle, who was making her way toward the exit. He thought Kyle looked upset. Maybe her own unhappy reunion. He understood how she felt. He wanted to get the hell out of here, too.

"Well, Van," Garret was saying in a soothing tone, as if he were placating a child, "we just need you to do a little better in helping *all* of us out."

Van thought he was keeping his expression blank, but Larvell must have seen something in it, because he slid smoothly in front of the titan. "Gentlemen," he interjected, "you know that my ten-man Van is a team player. If some people are saying things you don't like to hear, we're all ears about how to turn that around."

Garret nodded enthusiastically. He and Larvell spoke the same language. "Well said. Here's what we got." He gestured over to the barrels against the wall. "We've got a new beer. We're calling it Titan's Reach Red Ale."

Van could see several barrels were marked with a red logo, with what looked like a gorilla flexing its biceps in the center. "That looks nothing like me," he muttered softly.

Garret either ignored or didn't hear Van's comment. "We brought sixteen barrels. Enough to whet the appetite of Empire City and drive some additional orders with our preferred vendors. When we got word late last night about your victory over Judge Cage, we sent a note back to accelerate production. Congrats, by the way," he added as an afterthought.

Van looked at him skeptically. "How'd you get a new beer into production so quick?"

"It's just a relabel of the old Dotted Steer barrels," Alec said, a hint of mischief in his voice. He took a drink to hide his smirk. He, unlike the rest, knew how much Van hated the Dotted Steer.

Van fumed. But Garret was on a roll now and there was no stopping him. "Think about it, Van. Everyone watching. You'll have a crowd of thousands at the Coliseum tonight. You come in with a brand new barrel, one no one has ever seen before. We'll leak word to the media. You can hoist the barrel over your head before the fight. Maybe you could even offer Scott Flawless a beer before you guys get started."

Scott Flawless? Van would rather smash the barrel into that pompous asshole's face. He shook his head and said, "I'm pretty sure he's a wine drinker."

"Ah." They all fell quiet, sharing a moment of collective bafflement.

"Can we get the logo on his uniform?" Mitch asked Garret, staring at Van's chest. "He doesn't even have the brewery logo. Where'd you get that outfit, Van?"

Garret rubbed his chin. "Sure, sure. Brewery logo *or* the Titan's Reach label."

"I don't think that's such a good idea," Van said.

The group quieted, stealing glances towards the brewery president to see how he reacted. He rubbed his nose as though warding off a headache and shot a pointed look at Alec.

"What?" Van asked. "Why are you looking at him?" He was sick of this conversation.

Alec sighed like a distressed damsel in a stage play. "They're looking at me because I'm your boss, Van. It reflects on me when you're screwing up."

"Wait, how exactly am I screwing up?" Van glared at Alec. "I'm one of the last four titans standing. If you had any idea what I've been through—"

Mitch cut in. "No one is questioning your success, Van. Maybe you just need a little more…direction from here on. Some guidance on how you can do a little work for *all* of us while you're here. It can't all be fancy haircuts and new clothes."

Van tugged hard at his newly trimmed beard. He wanted to spit on the floor of the fancy hotel room. He'd taken one step away from the sad standards of his Headwaters life and they didn't like it. "It hasn't been. It's been nothing like that." He was startled to find tears welling in his eyes. Wouldn't that be great, the titan crying because he was feeling picked on by his bosses? He swallowed deeply, clenched his fists, summoned the anger he'd felt before. Better to lose it than let his weakness show in front of these jerks. His voice deepened as he let the words rumble out. "It's been hard. You have no idea how hard. And I've been winning. Alone, with none of your help and none of you watching my back. And if you don't understand that, or don't care about that, maybe you could all just *fuck off*." The circle was stunned into stillness. "None of you believed in me. And you still don't."

Van turned to the door, only to see Venerate Holland standing there, his eyebrows raised in mock surprise. "Bad time?" he asked with a laugh. He slipped smoothly into an oily smile and began shaking hands.

Van was pushed to the side as several sycophants in the room squeezed past him to greet the head of the ONWC. Venerate kept one amused eye on Van as he shook the hand of Governor Crowell, who had made her way over at blinding speed, then the mayor of Headwaters, then the brewery president. There was a line forming to greet the ONWC chief before Van found the will to move again. He turned back to the circle, now just Alec and Mitch with Larvell lurking behind them. "Why the hell is he here?"

"That's the head of the ONWC, Van," Mitch said helpfully.

"I know that," Van replied through gritted teeth. "Why is he *here*?"

"Well, we invited him, of course. You said it yourself, one of only four nations standing. Puts us in a great position."

Mitch excused himself and hustled over towards Venerate, who had the crowd around him roaring with laughter. "I said one of only four *titans* standing," Van muttered quietly.

"Friend of yours?" Alec asked. Now that his bosses had left, he was able to smirk openly.

"Why the hell are *you* here, Alec?"

"A chance to see you get your ass kicked in front of thousands? Who could pass that up? Plus, you know I'm a Scott Flawless fan and we've got wicked seats." He struck one of Flawless's famous poses, looking like an idiot. "Did you really just say you opened a barrel of Kingsland at *an international gathering of important people*? You are such a dick. Van, I couldn't be happier with the way this is working out for me."

Van turned away and headed for the door. He had to pass Venerate to get out, and the ONWC chief extended a hand to stop him. "Leaving so soon, Van? It's always a pleasure." Venerate gripped Van's shoulder, pulled him down close, and whispered into his ear, hot breath on Van's cheek. "Scott tells me he can't wait to kick your ass and send you and your loser friends home."

Van shook the hand off his shoulder and shoved Venerate back. The circle of glad-handers caught the stumbling ONWC head and murmured angrily towards Van. Van marched out the door. As he left he heard

Venerate say, "No, it's not a problem. After all, isn't that why we love titans so much? They get to act out like children, do the things we sometimes wish we could. And what could be more *amusing* than that?"

. . .

Van wanted his room and his bed, which meant leaving the hotel might be a bad idea right now. He'd just have to wait for the party to calm down and Venerate to head to his next gathering. He'd sent Larvell back into the suite to do damage control, make sure Venerate didn't get too close to the governor. In the meantime, Van found his way to the roof. He needed air.

He wasn't surprised to see Kyle standing fearlessly at the rooftop's very edge, looking over the city. The sun was high in the sky, but a cold wind had risen up and it tossed her shining blonde hair from side to side. She didn't turn as he approached, but something in her stance told him she knew he was there.

"Another day, another roof," he said. Neither of them pretended to be amused at the comment. "How'd it go?" he asked over the rush of the wind.

"It went," she sighed, "poorly." She pointed down to the street. "Your new friend Harlan is watching the door." As Van leaned out over the edge to glance at the titan below, standing stoic with his back to the hotel entrance, she asked, "You building an army, Van?"

He ignored the question. "Larvell said the important ones try to make everything that happened before they show up seem like a failure."

She nodded. "Larvell has a pretty good understanding of how people work. It's disappointing how often he's right." She pulled her coat tight around her. "It's disappointing when you think you're moving things in the right direction, and it turns out you're no closer than when you started."

"What did she say, the governor?" Van asked.

"The threat of a tariff is gone. We can thank you for that. I can't tell you more, Van." Van waited her out. In a lull between gusts of wind, she eventually continued. "The only thing I can say is, well, it wasn't the conversation I'd hoped it would be. Remember how I mentioned that the nations who exit early tend to get preyed on by those who last into the later rounds? And how that was a bad thing?"

"Let me guess. Suddenly someone wants their turn at being the bully. I saw Venerate come in."

She looked at him, a hint of surprise. "Exactly. And *someone* is so interested in taking her turn at the big table that she isn't paying attention to the real threat. Hardly anyone is. The threat that seems to be even more important than the tournament."

They'd already said it last night. After Kyle had left him, Van had seen the horizon over the cemetery as dawn's light rose. The path to the Nether opening, or resetting, or something. And when he'd taken his eyes off the hole in the center of the cemetery, and the light above it, he'd seen something far worse. The OverLord himself, standing at the cemetery fence, staring up at Van. The titan had said nothing, but Van had still heard his message clearly. *One way or another.* By the time Van had called the others over to ensure he wasn't hallucinating, the OverLord was gone. But the Nether champion would be back tonight to drag away King Thad, and then again the following night. After that who knew. The gateway could close or it could open wider, maybe wide enough to swallow Empire City.

Kyle spoke quietly. "I was listening outside the door down there, Van. I heard you."

"Heard what?"

"I heard you say no one believed in you. But that's not true. I believed in you. I was the first one." She gave a crooked, weary smile. "You know that, right?" She looked away, her eyes filling with tears.

"What's wrong?" he asked. The weariness on her face alarmed him.

"Nothing," she said. Then she shook her head. "I'm scared. And I feel alone."

"But you're not." He reached out and put a hand on her shoulder.

"I guess that's true. I just wish things were different." She turned to smile up at him. "Maybe after this is all over, maybe we could get dinner? This time without kicking off a riot. Would you like that?"

"Of course."

She looked out over the buildings again. "I see a hard road ahead. But you're right, Van, I'm not alone." She turned to him and took one of his giant hands in hers. The wind swept her hair across her forehead, and he wanted to use his free hand to brush it aside. "You're not going to disappoint me, are you, Van?"

"Never," he replied. Not if he could help it.

"Good, that's good," she said, as though something had been decided. A look of pain crossed her face. "We're going to need each other to find our way out of the darkness." She looked back out over the city, then turned and left the rooftop without saying goodbye.

Van didn't like seeing her leave so quickly. And not with such heavy words. He stared after her a long moment, his hand tingling where she'd held it. He slowly raised his eyes to look out over the neighboring rooftops. The wind was cool on the newly shaved parts of his scalp. He took a deep breath.

The unwelcome intrusion of his homeland had shaken him. He had finally felt like he was finding himself. Now he was surrounded by people intent on reminding him of his place. Helping him to remember that when this ended, there was a lonely cage back in

Headwaters waiting for him. They'd brought Van a fresh supply of fuel for his seemingly relentless desire to give up, to quit, to not even try in the first place, to find a corner to drink alone and nurse his self-pity.

Could he find enough of whatever it was he'd found in the ring when Judge Cage had backed him into a corner and robbed him of everything but his pride? Maybe that was all he needed. He was a tournament titan, a real one, and try as they might, even Alec and the others couldn't take that away from him. They could laugh and push and prod all they wanted. But it wasn't up to them.

Van stayed up there on the roof, letting the wind break against him, until his head was on straight. Soon they'd be readying the Coliseum for tonight's doubleheader. He should get some sleep. Flawless would be merciless, as he had been when he snapped Sevendhi's arm like a twig. He would be a flawless representative of the titan race, cruel and vain. Only Van could decide if he was going to be better than that. And for the first time, he was eager to get in the ring and find out. Just him and Scott Flawless. A fair fight, and a chance to prove himself in front of the very people who doubted him the most.

Chapter 37

Van the Beer Man walked the tunnels underneath the Coliseum, a barrel tucked under his arm. Larvell led the way. Owen Grit and Harlan stalked behind Van, forming a wedge of titan muscle. In a group effort, they'd managed to chase away the hangers-on from the Uplands crew. Garret in particular had proven stubborn, deeply wedded to his visions of standing in Van's corner throughout the fight. Finally Harlan had ended the debate by stepping in front of him and cracking his knuckles. The point was made.

The tunnels were sporadically lit by torchlight so Van walked in and out of darkness. It was a far different experience than the last time he'd been here, in the back of Judge Cage's wagon with chains on his wrists and ankles. Or when he'd been in Sevendhi's locker room, trying to comfort the titan after his brutal injury at the hands of Flawless.

"Just a little farther," Larvell said coolly. Now that he was on Van's side, Van found comfort in the manager's depth of experience as he navigated the labyrinthine passages. Larvell had tread this path before, had led titans into battle hundreds of times, occasionally even to victory.

As they rounded the corner, Larvell slowed. Van caught up to him and immediately saw why. King Thad was waiting for them in the center of the dark tunnel, arms folded across his massive chest. He was dressed for the ring, shirtless under the fur-lined cape draped over his shoulders. Van looked him up and down, considering. It wasn't out of bounds for the titan to be down here given he was scheduled to face the OverLord immediately after Van's match. But he still couldn't be trusted.

King Thad offered his smug smile. "Just seeking a quick word, Van." He looked around the empty tunnel to show he was alone.

"Make it quick," Owen said.

King Thad ignored Grit and stepped closer to Van. For a moment, Van got a whiff of something unpleasant. The smell of dead grass, of musty cobwebs. The smell of the old carts that hauled Van from unloving foster home to unloving foster home. Then it was gone, buried under the heavy cologne the King had apparently bathed in. Thad smiled again. "How will it go tonight, Beer Man?" he asked.

Van studied Thad a moment, then said, "It'll go how it goes. I'm not rolling over for Flawless, and he's not rolling over for me. It'll be a fair fight. You comfortable with that?"

Thad's smile widened as though there were a joke in there. "Of course. I just wanted to wish you luck. And I owed it to myself to follow-up on my offer...I assume you haven't reconsidered."

"And that offer was?"

"Whatever you want, Van."

Van found himself hating King Thad's voice, the oily sound to it. The titan tried to wield his charisma like a weapon, but it rang false. He was nothing like, for example, Panam Manley, whose friendliness made you want to be around him, to open yourself to him. When King Thad smiled, it made Van want to check his back to ensure no one was creeping up behind him.

"Anything I want?" Van asked. "And all I have to do is crawl into your pocket?" He looked at Owen, then Harlan. "Fuck that."

"I thought you'd say that. Frankly, I'm glad you did. I've been friends with Scott a long time, but even if a miracle happens and you win, I'm always happy to face some new blood in the ring." He rubbed his hands together eagerly.

"You sound pretty certain you'll be in the finals, rather than stuffed into a coffin and dragged screaming from the Coliseum." Van hadn't forgotten his own encounters with the OverLord, the power radiating from the monstrous titan.

"Do I?" The King's smile widened. "Nothing is certain, but I've always found a measure of faith in myself to be a sound investment."

Van wasn't sure how to respond. "That all?" he asked. "I've got to get to the ring."

"By all means." King Thad stepped aside. "Don't let me stop you. At least not yet."

Van passed him in the tight corridor, half expecting the titan to attack. He didn't. He stood aside, grinning his wide grin. Van realized it had been the first time he'd seen King Thad without Donovan lurking like a shadow at his side. It looked somehow unnatural, like an important piece of King Thad had been severed. He caught another whiff of the unpleasant odor before he got by Thad and began to hear the rising buzz of the crowd. The wind from the open doors ahead pushed away the thoughts of what was behind him.

Larvell stepped through the opening into the bright lights and a roar went up from the crowd when Van joined him. They howled as Van made his way toward the ring. The lights were blinding. He could almost feel their heat as his thoughts moved toward settling the score with Scott Flawless.

...

When Van had fought in the Coliseum before, he hadn't had a chance to appreciate the enormity of it.

He'd been carted ringside by Judge Cage, half-unconscious, and dragged into the ring in chains. Now he walked to the center ring on his own feet. The grandstands stretched toward the sky as far as Van could see. He marched forward, grateful this was the one fight he wasn't entering alone. The crowd was explosive, shouting his name, chanting "Beer Man, Beer Man." Others, mostly Flawless fans, yelled insults and threats at him, threw cups of beer.

Van climbed to his corner and set his barrel down on the apron. As he looked out over the crowd, he could see the Uplands contingent, just a few rows back. Garret was frantically waving for him to turn the barrel so the Titan's Reach logo was visible. Van ignored him. He saw Alec, Mitch, Peters, and a few others he didn't recognize. No sign of Kyle, but she had always favored the view from the shadows.

Owen didn't bother with any pre-match banter, that wasn't his style. And Harlan remained steadfastly silent. The only time Van had exchanged words with him, learning his name and that he was from beyond the northern borders of the Open Nations, he'd struggled to understand his thick accent. Still, Van trusted him and he valued his stoic company.

Larvell was making up for the pair of quiet titans, chattering away so fast Van could barely follow him. He seemed to be trying to calm Van, rather than himself, but it wasn't working. Van gave him a light shove towards his position in the corner. Van exchanged a nod with the referee and announcer, then puttered around a bit, still not fully comfortable with the whole warm-up thing. When the noise of the crowd had finally died down, the announcer addressed the crowd.

"Ladies and gentlemen, creatures of all races, have we got a match for you tonight! When the Headlock of Destiny Tournament comes to town, you know it comes large!" His voice was magically amplified, echoing across the endless sea of people. "We open with a mainstay of wrestling, a titan who many contend is the best technical wrestler in the world, versus an exciting underdog and relative unknown. And after that incredible matchup, King Thad, unchallenged as the most powerful ten-man in the Open Nations, winner of the last two Headlock of Destiny Tournaments, squares off against a force of evil the likes of which haven't been seen since the Titan Wars. Billy Blades tried to hide from the OverLord and was still dragged away. King Thad, and I heard this from the mighty ten-man himself, has made it clear we'll get no such cowardice from him. He is in the building, he will face the demon, face death itself, in front of *all* valid ticketholders. One thing is certain. Whatever happens tonight, it's sure to get *weird*.

"So let's get it rolling! For the first match of the evening, in one corner, in the blue uniform, our newcomer. A titan no one expected to remain standing past the first round, let alone into the semis. The ten-man who bested the Ram. Who outlasted Panam Manley. Who took Judge Cage to the woodshed in this very ring last night. This titan has defied all expectations, laughing in the face of his doubters. All while enjoying a cold Crater Ale. Straight from the Uplands, I give you Van the Beer Man!"

The crowd gave a half-hearted cheer and smattering of applause, which was more than Van had gotten at any previous match.

Van sensed the crowd's surging anticipation of the announcer's next words. "And squaring off against the newcomer, a titan whose record speaks volumes. A titan who bested the Mighty Antis, who sent Sevendhi the titan back to Kisket to lick his wounds, who dominated Bruce Bigsby in the round of eight. A titan unlike any other. He is…Flawless. Scott Flawless!"

The crowd erupted as Scott Flawless appeared in the wings, mirrored lights swiveling to illuminate him. He'd traded his pink one-piece for one of powder blue, still wrapped tightly around his carved muscles. He sauntered slowly towards the ring.

Really slowly. Painfully slowly. Flawless soaked in all the adulation, his face pinched in arrogance, as he made his way down the aisle. Van sighed, wondering how long it would take Flawless to actually reach the ring at his glacial pace. He glanced at Larvell, who shrugged. Nothing to be done. Maybe Van could sneak a beer in while he waited. He paced his corner some more, grabbed the ropes and pretended to stretch, ignored Larvell's attempts to call him over for last minute guidance.

The crowd kept its energy up during Flawless's long parade down his personal catwalk, but Van could sense the frustration of the announcer, who finally left the ring, and the referee, who yawned and rubbed his hands together. Van waited, pondering whether the run-up to the Judge Cage fight had actually been more pleasant than this. Certainly less boring.

When the titan finally reached the ring, Van was shocked anyone from the crowd was still interested or even awake. Flawless drew himself up in front of Van, and Van prepared for the customary stare-down, but his grandiose opponent's pre-fight rituals weren't done. Flawless went to his corner turnbuckles and climbed the ropes, and raised his hands in the air. The crowd seemed to come alive again, greeted him with a barrage of cheers and whistles, clapping hands and stomping feet. He repeated the action at each of the other corners, breaking the routine only when he reached Van's corner and faked a left hook at Larvell, making the little man duck out of the way and lose his new hat.

Then he repeated the trick he'd done in the match against Sevendhi, balancing on the ring's top rope with his arms outstretched, loudly proclaiming the stupid trick as "Flawless" as he jumped off and landed. The crowd had no shortage of people dumb enough to cheer the move on.

Finally, Flawless strode to the center of the ring, beckoning both Van and the referee to him like servants. Van couldn't help but notice the immense musculature rippling beneath his singlet, the incredible confidence in his stolid glare. Standing in the ring facing this ten-man, Van began to understand what being a top-ranked titan meant. Flawless firmly believed in his perfection. He believed he deserved to win and he had the skills and experience to back it up. Van still wasn't sure about his own chances, and that was a weakness.

The ref gave the standard speech about keeping it clean while the two titans stared each other down, ignoring him. As they stood toe to toe, Flawless reached out and painfully gripped Van's shoulder. "You don't belong here, *Beer Man*. You're not worthy of being in the same ring as me. You're an embarrassment." His eyes were locked to Van as though expecting Van to agree.

"Screw you, Flawless," Van replied, unable to come up with something wittier.

The ref separated them and they readied themselves for the bell. Van watched Flawless alternate between stretching and flexing for the crowd. Van knew he had a raw strength and endurance to rival his opponent. Titans like Flawless had been pampered their whole lives in preparation for a career in the ring. Van hadn't been raised that way. He had worked for everything he had, which wasn't much. And it had helped to harden something within him, the core of his being. He'd have to hope it was enough. Flawless turned to face him, apparently satisfied with what had felt like an hour of preliminary lunacy, and the bell rang.

After circling the ring a few times, the titans locked into a grapple, feeling each other out, testing each other's grip and strength. Flawless released Van and landed a hard slap to Van's face. Van felt his cheek burning, flushing. He snapped a backhand across Flawless's jaw, wiped the pretty smirk off the titan's face. Flawless kicked out Van's feet, shoved him off balance, then drove him into the ropes. Van bounced back toward the center of the ring. Flawless pretended not to be looking, then turned quickly and hit Van in the chest with a spinning knife edge chop that knocked Van to the mat. Van rolled away just as Flawless's foot stomped where his head had been.

Rather than press his advantage, Scott Flawless turned back to the crowd, flexing and screaming, beating on his own chest. Van climbed to his feet and snuck up on him from behind. He got a good grip on Flawless's hair and punched him in the back of the head three times before Flawless struggled free.

Both titans were breathing heavily as they circled again. The concentrated heat of the lights and the crowd had them pouring sweat. Flawless swung a right hook at Van. Van dodged it. Van threw a left jab at Flawless. He stepped aside scoffing. They seemed to be at a stand-off.

Van was staring into Flawless's eyes when the crowd exploded into an uproar, and something enormous slammed into Van's back. His world flipped upside down and he crashed to the mat amidst a surge of cheers and screams. He peeled his face from the floor and looked up. The ugly mugs of the Landshaker and Eagle were both peering down at him, smiling. They glanced at each other, then back at him, and their boots began to rain down.

Chapter 38

The titans stomped all over Van, seeking and finding every vulnerable place on his body. He covered his face and they hammered his gut. He covered his gut and they worked on his back. They kicked and stomped, harder and harder, pushing Van to the edge of unconsciousness. Van had no idea what was happening. Had the other titans charged the ring? Where was Flawless? Where was the referee?

Van finally managed to grab a leg, and Eagle crashed into the mat beside him, his spikes tearing the canvas. The kicks stopped for a second before a mountain crashed onto Van's stomach. The Landshaker had dropped his full weight onto Van, ass first. Van struggled under the titan's incredible bulk, dying for air.

He rolled over, clutching his gut, as the Landshaker got up to help Eagle. Seemed they'd patched up their differences. Van looked around the ring. Scott Flawless stood to one side, involved in a frustratingly calm three-way conversation with the referee and Venerate Holland. The referee wasn't even looking at the action in the center of the ring. How could he possibly not see what was going on?

Over in Van's corner, Owen Grit fought the Butcher and Hugo Markey. Dim Hurgen had Larvell in a headlock. A flurry of punches from Great Golden Ghost and William the Defeater held Harlan back. It seemed like almost every ONWC wrestler had crashed the fight.

Van tried to cry out, but he had no breath left. He crawled towards the referee. Eagle stomped on his neck, laughing, and followed it with a kick to Van's face. The Landshaker pummeled Van with another body drop, shaking the entire ring, flattening Van and leaving him gasping into the mat.

Van felt a slap in the back of the head, then another, then he was pulled to his feet by his hair. Eagle wrapped him in a full nelson, and the Landshaker began working his midsection with alternating left and right punches. Between blows, Van could see Owen had Hugo Markey on the ground but the Butcher was stomping on Grit's injured knee from behind. Harlan was bleeding from a cut near his eye and trying to get to the ring, but someone on the ground behind him was holding him back. Van could no longer see Larvell.

Scott Flawless turned from the ref and looked over his shoulder, meeting Van's eyes. He shrugged and laughed. Then he turned back to the referee and Venerate, who still looked as though they might be discussing the weather. The crowd was on their feet. Some screamed in outrage and waved fists in the air, some threw beer, others called out the names of their favorites. How the hell could the ONWC get away with this?

More wrestlers were entering the ring now. Dim Hurgen and James Scraps ducked under the ropes, laughing. They carried a barrel. As the Landshaker stepped back, they took position in front of Van. Van snapped his head back and slammed into Eagle's nose with a loud crack, but the titan's grip didn't loosen. He kept Van locked into place as Dim and James held the barrel up over him. It wasn't the Titan's Reach Van had brought to the ring. He had a bad feeling about this.

From behind, Eagle whispered in Van's ear. "We all brewed up something special for you. You're gonna like this."

Richard the Living Portrait stepped out from behind Dim and James and flashed Van a condescending smile. His leather and metal back brace made a squeaking noise as he stiffly advanced. Seemed like all of Van's enemies had become friends. How nice for them. One of the titans pulled the lid off of the barrel, and Van was hit with the smell of piss. A barrel full of titan piss. The crowd was on their feet, but the protests seemed to overpower the cheers and applause. The horrid stench made Van's eyes water, and a wave of anger and frustration washed over him.

Van turned his head to the side and caught a view of the Uplands contingent, sitting placidly in their seats. If they had ever voiced any protest since this had started, they were doing so no longer. They appeared embarrassed. All except Alec, who smiled as though he couldn't have scripted a more entertaining turn of events. Garret leaned over to the brewery president, and Van heard—somehow clearly over the raging crowd—him say, "Maybe a good thing he wasn't wearing the new logo."

Van looked up as the barrel started tipping towards him. He gave one last push back, trying to get away from the grip of Eagle behind him. Then he gave up, resigned to his fate.

But just as Van was preparing for his humiliation in front of thousands of raving idiots, Dim and James stumbled and looked at each other in confusion. Then both stepped back, wide eyed and slack-jawed. The barrel hung suspended in the air between them. The crowd roared like a crumbling mountain. As Van leaned confused and listless against Eagle, the barrel abruptly tipped backwards and poured the entirety of its foul contents over the head of Richard the Living Portrait. He spluttered in horror as the fighting around the ring stalled, and the titans, the ref, and the crowd simply stared at him in stunned silence.

Across the ring, L'Harot'Ni'Set lowered his hands and stepped forward. He gestured sharply and the barrel's lid flew up off the mat and cracked into Dim Hurgen's face. A moment later a blur of muscle shot past him. Sevendhi of Kisket flew across the ring and landed a dropkick directly into the chest of James Scraps, sending him crashing through the ropes and out of the ring.

And then even more titans surged over the ropes. The Wave Rider attacked Great Golden Ghost, freeing Harlan to grapple William the Defeater. Owen threw off the Butcher and clambered up onto the apron, threw himself under the ropes and onto the mat. Harot clotheslined the distracted Dim Hurgen. In the middle of the action, the urine-soaked Richard the Living Portrait was staring down at his clothes in horror. There was a healthy buffer around him. No one seemed to want to get close.

"Motherfucker!" a voice screamed from behind Van and someone crashed onto Eagle. The titan's grip on Van loosened. Van turned and shoved Eagle aside and found Larvell, faced pinched in rage, hands still laced in the hammerblow he'd driven into the back of Eagle's neck.

Van gazed around the ring. Harot was stomping Dim Hurgen's throat. Harlan had Willian the Defeater in a camel clutch. The Wave Rider was beating a turnbuckle to death with the Great Golden Ghost's face. Sevendhi, fighting with one arm in a sling, flew across the ring with a flurry of high kicks. So this was what it felt like to have friends. Now if only Van could leave the ring with a victory to prove himself worthy of their friendship.

Van escaped an attack from the Landshaker, who promptly turned and leveled the Wave Rider. Hugo

Markey was climbing into the ring. That was nearly everyone the ONWC had. Assuming King Thad would keep his nose clean, and that very much seemed to be his style, only Donovan, Jaygan the Dragon, and Creature were missing. The ONWC side still had the numbers, and Scott Flawless was still chatting with the ref, not even in the mix yet. The ref ignored the thousands of voices screaming for him to turn around. Van needed to get at Flawless. That was the only way to end this. But a ringful of titans battled between them.

Van started fighting his way across the ring. He made it no farther than a step or two before the Landshaker seized his head and delivered a punch that rattled Van's brain. "Where you think you're going?" the titan asked, his voice rumbling like an avalanche. He punched Van in the face with a fist the size of a turkey. Van fell to one knee, looking up towards the titan with unfocused eyes. The Landshaker drew back his fist again.

A shout of "BROTHERS FOR LIFE!!!!" resounded across the Coliseum, and in a whirl of bright colors and fury, Panam Manley catapulted into the ring and slammed into the Landshaker. The giant flew backwards, knocking over the stinking Richard the Living Portrait as he went, taking out titans as he slammed back into the ropes, which promptly snapped. The crowd lost whatever restraint they had as the mass of struggling titans fell out of the ring, followed by a pouncing Panam Manley, who paused only to shoot Van a salute before leaping into the wriggling pile below him.

Van looked on in shock. His eyes slowly panned away from the dusty cloud of titan violence that had just been swept from the ring over to Scott Flawless, who stood likewise with a slack jaw. No one stood between Van and him. Panam had cleared the ring and opened the path.

"Fuck, that guy is cool," Van said. Then he ran across the ring towards Flawless. Flawless turned at the last minute, eyes widening. His chest was wide open, and Van drove into him with a two-legged dropkick. Flawless fell backwards, crashing into Venerate Holland and sending him hurtling to the stone floor.

Amazingly, the ref turned away from the fallen Flawless and yelled at Van. "Illegal move!"

Van shot him a dark look, briefly pondering how far he could throw him, then ignored him. The only thing that mattered now was who would be the last standing between Van and Scott Flawless. He gripped Flawless by his perfect curls and smashed his face into the mat. He did it again, and again. Then he leaned in to Flawless's ear. "You were too scared to face me alone?"

"No," Flawless spat, his face upturned as Van still gripped his hair. "I'm flawless. I'm perfect. Stooping to your level for a fight is an embarrassment. You're an embarrassment."

Van brought his face so close he could smell Flawless's wine-soaked breath. "Embarrassments don't win. Let's see how flawless you really are." He threw the titan across the ring, now empty aside from lingering sweat and a puddle of piss.

Flawless got to his feet just in time for Van to slam him into the turnbuckles. When the titan bounded back, Van caught him under a leg, hoisted him over his head, then bodyslammed him to the mat so hard the entire ring bounced. Van reached down, grasped Flawless by the hair again, and punched him in the face—once, twice, thrice—releasing his anger from its humble cage until he lost count of how many times he'd pummeled those pretty cheeks, those comely lips. This titan who represented everything Van lacked—confidence, beauty, perfection—who never doubted his ability to shape the world to his vain fantasies, never contended with the demons that had tormented Van as long as he'd drawn breath, that followed Van from one foster home to another, perched on his shoulder while assholes like Alec Durheed took everything Van wanted and left him the mere scraps of a life.

Van felt others pulling at him, trying to stop him. It didn't matter. Scott Flawless was finished. The titan lay limp in Van's hand, face bleeding onto Van's new boots. Van released him. The titan stood groggily for a moment before his knees buckled, and he crumpled to the mat. Van turned to the ref, who huddled in the corner, and smirked. "Flawless, wouldn't you say?"

Van still seethed, blood hot as dragonfire, as he walked over to his corner and collected his barrel of Titan's Reach. He held it in front of his chest in the bright lights of the Coliseum. The entire crowd stood, cheering, and he felt their power. Then he tilted his head and made a show of examining the red logo at the center of the barrel, the flexing ape that was supposed to look like him. He smiled, hoisted the barrel up over his head, and hurled it into the crowd. The group from the Headwaters Brewery dove out of the way, just before the barrel crashed into their seats and exploded in a burst of wood and eggshell froth. They'd need to do better than repackaging Dotted Steer. Van was in the finals now.

Chapter 39

Van stood in the center of the wrestling gym. He watched dust dance in the sunlight that streamed from a hole in the ceiling. He'd never been in one of these gyms before. He had the feeling this one was rather atypical. White paint crumbled off gray walls. Punching bags leaked stuffing. Old and tattered mats lay strewn about. A single ring with cobwebs threaded between drooping ropes and torn turnbuckles sat in the center.

Owen had kicked out rotting boards nailed across the doorframe to make an entry. The titan stood next to Van, looking around the dim space. "My family's old Empire City Gym," he said proudly.

"Uh, it's lovely," Van replied. Behind him, Larvell walked carefully, trying not to stir up too much dust and ruin his freshly pressed suit.

"No." Owen shook his head. "It's a mess. But it's private and off the books, which means we can use what little time we have to get ready for tonight's match without King Thad's spies lurking around to poison your water."

Van tried not to think about the kind of gym King Thad trained in. Fewer cobwebs, he imagined. King Thad had won by default last night. The OverLord had never shown. Donovan had not been in his corner, and Van hadn't been able to shake the whiff of death that King Thad had carried with him in the tunnels. Thad had danced around the ring, putting on a show of his fearlessness. It was clear he had no worries of the OverLord actually arriving. He'd somehow found the

Nether's price. And paid it in full. So now Van faced the reigning champion for the finals.

Owen was limping around, throwing old planks and mats out of the way, far less concerned than Larvell about the billowing clouds of dust. Van leaned back and spoke quietly to Larvell. "Would you have used this place if Grit were in the tournament?"

Larvell shrugged. "Would have been up to his coach, if he decided to bring one. Usually he didn't."

"I thought you were the coach."

Larvell shook his head. "I'm just a manager. Right now I'm *your* manager." He pointed to Owen. "And he's your coach. Different roles. Be grateful you've got one like Owen, even if it's just for an afternoon."

"Yeah, Van," Owen said, walking back towards them. "Hold tight to that gratitude. Because we've got some serious work to do and it won't be easy. You've got a couple hours to iron out some glaring deficiencies. Your footwork was awful against Scott Flawless."

"Well," Van argued, "there were like sixty titans in the ring."

"And you won't get that excuse again tonight. It should just be you and King Thad. He'll be watching your feet, taking advantage of every misstep." Owen stared critically at Van's boots, as though he could already see mistakes in the way Van was standing.

It was going to be a long afternoon. In an effort to delay the inevitable work to come, Van asked Owen, "So your family owns this place?"

"Used to," Owen replied. He looked around at the clouds of dust, the broken table, then leaned back against the edge of the ring. "We had a bit of a falling out. Or more like a falling away. Everyone was doing their own thing so anything we owned together just sort of"—he looked around—"came apart."

"What was it like...having a family?" Van asked, carefully sitting down on a pile of old body bags. He'd never given the idea of a real family much thought. But then he'd never met a titan who actually had one. They weren't supposed to get things like that.

"It was good, for a time. But we couldn't keep it together." Owen looked down and saw his hands had picked up a layer of dust from the ring mat. He brushed them off on his shirt. "It seemed like even from the beginning, everything was working to pry us apart. My dad was a wrestler and he got all my brothers, cousins, and me started at an early age. And it was fun, for a time, and we worked hard to learn what he had to teach. We'd spend most days in a ring in our backyard. Sometimes people would come and there'd be little showcases. They got a bigger kick out of seeing a titan family than our wrestling, I think.

"My mother held us together. She was the strongest of all of us, despite being half our size. The problem was when other titans, my dad's friends, would come around. Then it wasn't just about putting on a show. They wanted to see which of the kids was the strongest. They'd pick out the strongest two, most often me and my brother Barret, and pit us against each other. Whichever one of us won, they'd heap with praise, raise his hand, carry around the yard on their shoulders. He'd get to sit next to them at the dinner table, get more food, and love it. And the loser would just stare at him getting all the attention. We were trained to be rivals from an early age. Once we were big enough, and my dad got older, the rivalry expanded to include him.

"When my mother died, we tore up everything she'd worked for in a few short years. We turned our family home into a battleground. We'd been indoctrinated with the desire, the ambition. The quest for dominion was all we knew. Soon the weaker cousins and siblings stopped hanging around for the beatings. And those of us who had made our name had no interest in staying around. I heard my father died years ago. I didn't go back then. I haven't been back in years. My brothers and cousins are scattered. Sometimes we meet in the circuit, sometimes even in the ring, and it's just another match. Another titan to defeat."

Owen fell silent a moment, and Van asked, "If you hate this, why do you do it?"

He shook his head. "I don't hate it. I love it. I just have come to peace with the idea that I'm built to destroy. Even if I can't build and keep things for myself, if I can find bad things to destroy, maybe I can be a force of good, whatever that means. And there's no shortage of bad things in our world."

"Now you sound like Kyle." Van still hadn't seen her, not since before the fight with Scott Flawless. He stared at Owen. "Do you and Kyle have any history?"

Owen laughed. "You are full of big questions today, aren't you? I can tell you're eager to get on with your training." He glanced at the gym door, then Larvell, then gave a soft shrug. "Kyle and I have less history than I'd like. I've made an ass of myself plenty of times trying to impress her. But she's always looking at bigger things. She's trying to save the world, Van, not woo a titan husband or win a couple belts. That's why it wasn't a problem for her to toss me aside when I got hurt and you came along." He looked at Van with a piercing expression. "Don't think I haven't seen the way you moon after her. Be careful with that one."

Van tried not to scowl. It was fair advice. But it seemed like there'd been something when they'd last spoken. Some...spark. Probably wishful thinking.

The gym's dust clouds had mostly settled around them but Van was feeling comfortable on his perch. He wasn't ready to stand up and get tossed around the ring, be easily handled by Owen despite his injury. "Tell me about your mother." It sounded like the only happy part of Owen's life.

Owen looked at him sharply. "You're stalling."

"Yeah," Van admitted.

"She was a saint. Stronger than any of us. Stronger than she had any right to be. Which reminds me, I didn't have time to tell you before, but you know the story King Thad fed you about his sainted mother is complete bullshit, right?"

"It is? What's the real story?" Van saw another opportunity to stall. He felt good, reminded of the rare lazy moments of comradery back in the brewery's warehouses.

"His father was the titan Tower Malone. When Thad was born his noble mother was right there in the mix for the throne of the Vantages, which made Thad a possible crown prince. Could have gone a hundred different ways as he grew up, but he got the throne. His mother's not dead, though, whatever he said. She's alive. She still lives in the Vantages with all the rest of his family. They live in a hovel right by the gates of his palace. He makes them stay there. Once he got control of the throne and the family fortune, he took everything they had. Offered them a rundown shack, right where he could look out on them and laugh. The whole family—mother, brothers and sisters. Whole host of nieces and nephews, too. Living in the worst kind of poverty. Every once in a while, one of them will make a run for it, try to get a clean start someplace new. And he sends the guards after them, drags them back. He wants them right there, practically starving at his feet. Dependent on scraps from his table.

"I heard one of his brothers was a talented goldsmith," Owen continued. "He produced some real treasures and got a reputation with the Vantages elites.

King Thad commissioned him to make him his crown. An amazing piece of work, not that I know anything about what makes one piece of sculpted gold better than another. King Thad took one look, pronounced it passable, then had every one of his brother's fingers broken. The brother had his own way to support himself and his family, and King Thad didn't like it. I heard he still wears the crown whenever he goes to visit the hovel and drop off some food scraps or moldy bread."

Van thought back to King Thad proudly and reverently looking at the portrait in his halls. "He said his mother brings him luck."

"Maybe she does, the sick bastard. King Thad likes to put people under his boot and keep them there. And he's patient. He starts small. A gift here, a commission there. Before you know it, you're his slave."

Van shook his head. "I still don't understand how he was able to buy off the OverLord."

"He found his price and paid it. That's what he does."

Van remembered the giant, reeking titan in all black, dragging the coffin behind him. The way the sun seemed to fade, the way everything grew dark. "I never would have imagined the OverLord rolling over for gold. His aims seem...larger." That same smell of death had hung around King Thad.

"Well, if there ever was a ten-man who can figure out what a titan is after and can afford to give it to them on a gold plate, it's King Thad."

"He hasn't tried to buy his way out of tonight's fight yet," Van said.

"He didn't try to bribe me either when I fought him. Of course I lost, both times. He likes to buy titans who think they can't be bought. But he also prides himself as a wrestler, and with good reason. He's not trying to buy you off for the Headlock finals because he doesn't think he needs to. He's seen you fight now a couple of times. He thinks he has your number."

Owen stood and glanced around, clearly ready to begin the training. "And that's why we're here. I didn't have your back at the start of this trip, but that's changed. You survived the last fight because you didn't go in there alone. You were backed by your friends, friends you earned. Now the best way your friends can help you is by teaching you a sliver of wrestling, the tiniest bit of technique and understanding to go with your raw strength and the ridiculous string of luck that's gotten you this far." He looked Van up and down. "We've got one afternoon. Luckily you heal quick."

Van groaned his way off of the old bags, kicking up more dust in the process. "You and me, then?" he asked. He'd have to be careful of the titan's injured knee. He began a laborious climb into the dusty practice ring.

"No," Owen replied. "I found a better option. One who has firsthand knowledge of all your weaknesses. He's running late, but if there ever was a titan who had mastered well-timed entrances—"

Owen cut off and smiled as the sound of breaking boards came from the back door. A moment later Panam Manley walked into the gym. He took off his tinted glasses and looked around. "I love it," he said to Owen, then walked over to deliver one of his complicated handshakes.

Panam shot a glance and a smile Van's way. Then he vaulted up into the practice ring, cracked his knuckles and his neck, and took a fighting stance across from Van. "Hey, brother."

"So manager," Van looked at Larvell, "coach," to Owen, and then to Panam Manley. "And what?"

Panam Manley grinned. "The coach watches and advises, Van. You need a guy who actually gets into the ring with you and beats the hell out of you so you learn the first thing about this wrestling game, brother. And is not at all fueled by jealousy that you're in the finals and he isn't."

Larvell leaned in. "In other words, a sparring partner, Van."

Van watched as Panam Manley pulled off his wild purple and gold shirt, revealing his enormous tanned muscles. "Uh, you'll take it easy on me, right? The fight's tonight."

Panam Manley smiled. "Nah, fuck that, brother."

Chapter 40

Every inch of Van was sore and aching on the grueling walk back to the hotel. It had taken everything he had to hold Panam Manley at bay in the never-ending practice session. The whole time Owen and Larvell had nodded along, as though a humiliating beatdown was just the right warmup for tonight's match. Never mind the pain and tiredness. They seemed confident a couple of hours of rest would square him away.

Panam vanished after the training, which left Harlan, Owen, and Larvell as Van's only protection from the Empire City crowds. The masses flocked around Van, shouting for his attention every step of the way back to the hotel. The city had reached a fever pitch. Revelers clogged the streets waiting on an epic finale to the Headlock and drinking as much as possible before this last party. Hangovers were for tomorrow, and tomorrow Empire City would shrink as tens of thousands of visitors began long journeys home, moving slowly and quietly to soothe their aching heads.

There were rumors that King Thad was buying up all the tickets to the Coliseum, presumably to stack the crowd with fans of his and other important people from the Vantages. He'd had the city plastered with flyers bearing his face. Van pushed his way through the throng to read one stuck to a lamppost. *Come tonight for the coronation of three-time tournament champion King Thad!* They were inescapable. Everywhere Van looked, he saw his enemy, etched face slightly upturned to look up to the sky.

Van didn't think much of his chances. He'd struggled to follow the lessons Grit and Panam had thrown at him even after they'd simplified the concepts at their core. Van was up against a master wrestler, and he wouldn't see a repeat of the chaos that had helped him put Scott Flawless on his back.

When they reached the hotel, Owen and Larvell seemed to understand Van's need for at least a little solitude in the runup to the biggest night of his life. He went to his room alone to lay back on his bed and close his eyes. Against all odds, Van managed to find a calm state of mind. He hung there for all of about thirty seconds before a knock came at the door. He looked up, irritated by the noise, then leaned forward in the sudden hope it was Kyle. "Come," he said.

It was not. It was the *opposite* of Kyle. Alec Durheed crept in, his eyes warily scanning the room's corners.

"What the hell do you want?" Van asked, scowling as he sat up in bed.

Alec stared at Van a long time before answering. "They sent me to try and make peace."

Van barked a humorless laugh. He hadn't seen anyone from Headwaters since last night when he'd ended the match by throwing the barrel of Titan's Reach at them. "They sent you? They don't know shit about shit, do they?"

Alec closed the door behind him. "That's not entirely true, Van. They're damn good at making beer. But you're right. They're out of their depths here. And they," he grimaced, "*we* are being laughed at by everyone who knows you were aiming at us when you threw that barrel into the stands."

"What do you want, Alec?" Van wasn't going to apologize to them, especially not if Alec was the best they could do for a spokesman.

"We wanted to say we're sorry. Sorry we took you for granted and didn't believe in you. It's just...I mean no one saw this coming, Van. Even you didn't see this coming. Or if you did, you certainly never told us."

"Fuck your sorry," Van said. He waved towards the door. "You said your piece, now get lost."

"Look," Alec replied, "I told them the truth, at least as much as I know. I told them I wasn't surprised you hated the whole Titan's Reach thing and you felt betrayed because no one showed up earlier. Probably justified. They feel bad. They really do consider you a friend, Van, and they thought we were all on the same team before you threw that barrel at us. Don't you think you could give them another chance?"

"Why? What have they done for me?"

"You mean other than give you a job since you were old enough to carry a barrel? And pay the taxes that helped keep you in a home and fed since you were a freakishly large orphan baby?"

"I don't owe them anything. It's the law...and it's a cage."

Alec looked confused, but he pressed on. "They aren't really asking for anything, Van. Just...peace. They'd like to know that we're on the same team. If you win tonight, that will be amazing. But even if you lose, what you've already accomplished is amazing, sure. It's something for you to be proud of. They'd like to be proud of it, too."

Van breathed deeply and scowled even deeper. "And they sent you? They don't know anything about me."

"Well, I volunteered. I said we had a rocky past, but I thought you might listen."

"A rocky past. That's one way to put it." Van shook his head in disbelief. "You thought I might listen? To you?" He stared at his giant hands and took another breath. "Stepping out of Headwaters...it's been painful.

But not just in the ways I expected. I knew you all wouldn't support me. I knew there'd be titans waiting to put a hurt on me. And that's all been true. What I didn't realize is how much more clear everything would be when I stepped away from Headwaters, when I could look at my life from a distance, even for a few days."

"Van, I don't know what you're talking about. And I'm not really sure I care." Alec had come too close to the bed for Van's comfort.

"Oh, yeah?" Van rose up off the bed and Alec backed away. Van's shadow trapped him in a corner as Van leaned in, lowering and deepening his voice. "You want me to listen to you? Then you can listen up for a second, too. It won't take long." He took a few ragged breaths, heard the air whistling in his flaring nostrils. "You stole Annie from me. No, don't shake your fucking head. You stole her away and the whole town helped you do it."

"That's not—"

"Yeah, it is, dammit. I loved her and she loved me. And you know that. You might pretend otherwise, but I *know* you know that, you sniveling little rat turd. You and the whole town, you all pretend it was inevitable that she came to her senses and dumped me. But that's just because you never thought we should be together in the first place. You didn't think I deserved her. Maybe if you'd left well enough alone, we could have figured that out. But you didn't, you or the damn town. Instead, you went to work on her. You convinced her. You sold her the story that she was too good for me, the resident loser, a titan who doesn't do anything but work the loading docks. And then once she started doubting how she felt, doubting us, then you swooped in." Van scowled. "I blamed myself, because that's what I do. And I didn't put up a fight, not enough. I owed her better. But she owed me better too."

Alec put his hands up in front of his chest, afraid Van might hit him. "Why would the whole town care about you and her? You act like this was some plot—"

"No, not a plot. Just something that I should have seen coming because of the way you all have treated me since I was a kid. You all acted like I was supposed to be alone, like the idea that I might want a wife, maybe even a family, was some sort of joke. And then you treated her like she was a fool for not seeing that. Eventually she did. You put her under all sorts of pressure. You made sure she understood how unreliable titans are, how dangerous even. It was her place to marry a man of prominence. A Durheed. You helped her understand the shape of her own cage."

"I never said anything to her about a cage. I never made any decisions for her."

"No. You didn't. And yet you still managed to rob me of something that could have made me happy."

"Van, it was her call."

"Yes. It was. But you and everyone else did everything you could to make sure it went the way you wanted." With a last long look at Alec, Van walked back to the bed. "The way it was set up, I was never getting something other people wanted. I see that now. I'll live with it. I've got enough pride I'm not trying to pry her away from your cowardly ass. It was her choice and she was no stronger than I was. But I see it clearly now, and a world in which I listen to your bullshit, let you be the boss of me, that shit is done." He sat down heavily, rubbing at his face. "And that's my piece."

As Van looked out the window, Alec stepped farther into the room and slid past him. Van kept one eye tracking him, not even thinking about why. And so Van was in a position to see Alec's face tighten just before he made his move, saw the blur of Alec's ghostly white hand driving something toward Van's shoulder.

Van shouted, "What the fuck!" and seized Alec's wrist.

They stared at each other, Alec frozen and white. Van dark and angry. Van looked down at Alec's hand. It clutched a long, thin knife, a dirk, its point smeared with a black goo, inches from Van's shoulder. Van glared at Alec's wide, frightened eyes. "What the fuck did you just try to do?"

He could feel Alec's hand shaking under his grip. He squeezed tighter and Alec moaned in pain, trying to jerk free. All signs of the confident emissary, the peace seeker, had vanished. Alec looked like a trapped rat. "He said he'd kill me," he whispered. "Said he'd kill the whole family. Annie and the baby."

"Unless you killed me first?"

"No," Alec stammered. "He said—"

Van reached out his free hand and grabbed Alec by the throat. He picked Alec up and slammed him into the wall so hard the window panes shook and plaster dust rained down from the ceiling. The knife fell to the floor.

He could kill him. He could choke the life out of him right here and just throw him out the window to the stones below. In a town where Judge Cage had passed for a man of justice, who would raise a fuss, especially when Van showed them the poisoned knife?

"…said," Alec wheezed, "said…it…wasn't…kill you."

Van loosened his grip on Alec's throat. He leaned in closer, brought his face right up to Alec's. "Say that again."

Alec took a rattling breath. "He said it wouldn't kill you. Just make you confused. And mess with your memory."

"King Thad." It wasn't a question. "So he gets to throw me around the ring, look like a big stud, and I wake tomorrow with no idea what happened? Don't even remember you were a part of it?"

Tears welled in Alec's eyes as he nodded.

"And what was your price, Alec?"

"He said he'd kill them! King Thad! He said he'd kill Annie and the baby. Said he'd kill everyone in Headwaters." Alec must have seen a lack of sympathy in Van's face, a darkness in his eyes. "I swear, Van, I never would have done it otherwise. We're friends, Van."

Van laughed, amazed that humor could find fertile ground in the black rage he was feeling. It was taking all his strength not to just crush the life out of this insect.

"Please don't kill me, Van. I'm sorry. I didn't mean to take her from you. You could—you could have her back…"

"Don't say that. In fact, don't say anything. Just shut the fuck up." Van threw him on the bed. Alec lay there, face bright red against the white sheets. He breathed heavily, rubbed at his throat as Van stared down at him. "What the hell am I supposed to do with you?"

The idea of killing him seemed to be slipping away. Even in his darkest rage Van wouldn't make Annie a widow, cost Lizzy her father. But when Alec opened his mouth Van raised a hand to stop him. "I said shut up, Alec. It was a…whatever, one of those questions you're not supposed to answer. Just shut up and let me think."

For once, Alec fell quiet. He continued rubbing at his throat, which was already turning an impressive shade of purple. Van should have done that years ago. He also should have suspected that when King Thad couldn't buy him, he'd move on to the people around him. If King Thad had sent anyone else, Van would have missed it. Anyone else, and Van would have stayed on the bed, staring out the window, and things would have ended very differently. Only Van's old mistrust of Alec had saved him.

Alec glanced at Van. One hand nervously gripped the sheets, knuckles white. If Alec was telling the truth, he'd been put in an impossible position. But that didn't mean Van had to forgive him. He could expose him. He should expose him. Alec would lose his job at the very least. And as little as the people of Headwaters seemed to care about Van, no one in the Uplands would forgive an attempt to drug their titan hours before the first Headlock finals they'd ever reached. They'd make Alec's life hell. He'd have to leave. But that would hurt Annie. She and the baby would go with him into exile, to who knows where. Or she'd stay, and raise Lizzy without her father. Fuck. Why had this asshole even come to Empire City?

The image Van couldn't shake was one of Annie standing beside him at the Headwaters beer festival. She held the baby in her arms and looked up into his eyes, a smile on her face that slowed the passage of time. He'd already hurt her enough just by entangling himself in her life. He could never hurt her more. He looked down at the dirk that had come inches from stealing his chance at surviving, maybe even winning, the tournament and picked it up off the floor.

"All right, foreman. Here's what's happening. We're gonna keep this quiet." He snarled at the sudden relief in Alec's face. "But the first time you give me cause, I'll tell everyone what you tried to do today. Here's what you're going to do to stop me from doing that. You're going to be a good husband to Annie, and a good father to that child. And if I ever hear anything to the contrary, you'll regret not having walked into this room and told me exactly what King Thad told you to do." Van reached over and pounded on the wall between the neighboring room without taking his eyes off Alec. "Harlan! Owen!"

The door opened a moment later. Owen poked his head in the doorway; Harlan looked in over Owen's shoulder. They saw Alec injured and shaking on the bed, Van holding a knife. They stepped into the room and closed the door behind them. Alec's face grew three shades paler and he crawled back on the bed against the wall.

"Alec Durheed here," Van said to his friends, "just tried to poison me. King Thad put him up to it. Said it wasn't going to kill me, just make me confused."

Owen took the dirk carefully from Van and examined the black, dripping point, held it beneath his nose and sniffed the black paste. "Could be raventhorn. You see some of that shit in unlicensed bouts. You'd think tournament titans would have more class."

Harlan leaned over to look at the poisoned knife, then simply cracked his knuckles. Van could see Alec's lips tremble.

"Alec and I had a little talk," Van said. "He's gonna be a good boy from now on. But if anything happens to me, you have my permission to tear him limb from limb."

"Understood," Owen said. Harlan nodded.

"Good. Anything to say, Alec?" Alec opened his mouth, but Van waved him quiet. "Actually, forget it. Just get the fuck out of here." Alec slithered off the bed and crept nervously past Van and between the titans blocking the door. Van waited a long moment after he was gone. "Thanks, guys," he said, dismissing his friends, who shut the door softly behind them.

Van held up the knife. All that rage he had held back needed a place to go. He hurled the knife through the window. The sound of breaking glass was an anthem to his anger. He looked around the room, picked up a long mirror leaning against the wall, and smashed it on the corner of the bed. Then he hurled that out the window, too. He gripped the bed and began methodically tearing it to pieces, spraying splinters around the room as he cracked the frame. It wasn't enough. He roared, causing the lingering shards of broken glass hanging in the window frame to fall, then set to destroying everything in sight. He punched the walls, ripped down the lamps, tore the door off its hinges. The whole time he pictured the life he'd been denied. A life where he could have been a part of a family with a woman like Annie. A life where he'd been given paths other than violence and not been guided back into his cage when he'd pretended something different could be his.

Van's knuckles were bleeding and feathers from his destroyed mattress filled the air. At last, he stepped out of the bedroom, walked into the hall, the tide of black rage receding. Larvell stood waiting. He peered past Van into the wreckage that had been his room. "Hell yeah!" he cried. "I'm guessing you're ready to go to the Coliseum!"

Van nodded.

Chapter 41

The crowd roared with an energy Van had never heard before. He didn't care. The lights made the Coliseum brighter than a midday in the mountains. He didn't care. It seemed like every fan in the building was screaming King Thad's name. The weight of the occasion was in the nervousness of every professional pointing Van's entourage this way and that through the tunnels below the Coliseum and then along the confusing labyrinth to the ring. Van didn't give a shit. He spared only a fraction of a thought for the Uplands contingent. He was past caring about them, too. The only thing that mattered was that King Thad had tried to drug him, maybe kill him, and a titan-sized anger had awoken in Van.

He paced the ring like a caged lion, a barrel of Kingsland clutched under one arm, as he waited for the introductions. For Van it had started with Kingsland. It would end with Kingsland. This might be the last time Van ever had to fight, or it might be the start of a legend. And he still didn't know why he was here. Grit fought for a love of the sport, maybe for the memory of the time when his family was together. Sevendhi fought for his country. The Wave Rider for fun; Harot for the titans' cause. Then there was King Thad, who fought for enough wealth and power to put the world under his heel, using every nasty trick in the book along the way. Van needed to destroy him. Maybe Van didn't have to decide why he fought. Maybe it was enough that he stood on the opposite side of King Thad, who had made the Headlock of Destiny his playground, under his rules, and forced everyone else to suffer the consequences.

King Thad's entry into the ring was a blur of voices and lights, screams and whistles, beer flying through the air. He threw gold coins, probably fake, out into the stands as he walked the aisle. The lights sparkled on his crown, his glittering robe, the rings adorning his fingers. His face, upturned and regal, held a mocking smile as he mounted the apron.

Once the titans were both in the ring, Van pushed past the clutch of hangers-on lined up to make self-aggrandizing speeches under the bright lights. He didn't bother waiting. He hurled the barrel of Kingsland at King Thad's face and then leapt to the assault as Thad dodged the attack. The bell clanged frantically as the organizers scrambled to get out of the way of the errant barrel and raging titan.

Van had a jump on King Thad, who hadn't even doffed his fur-lined cape or gold rings. Van punched him in the left eye, once, twice, then grabbed the fur cape and yanked the King off balance. He landed a hard kick to the King's hip, sending him crashing into the turnbuckles and nearly crushing the announcer who had been slow to get out of the ring. Van moved to follow up the kick but stumbled on the referee's foot. He shot him a hard look, not sure if the disruption had been intentional or not.

King Thad had recovered, a broad smile on his face as he stepped forward from his corner, free now of his cape. Van threw a straight right, but the King caught it with ease. For a moment, they stared each other down. King Thad's eyes searched Van's, looking deep. Van gave him a slight shake of the head.

If anything, the ten-man's smile broadened as he realized his plot to poison Van had failed. "So it's a real fight then?" he said. He tossed Van's fist aside and pulled him into a grapple and whispered in Van's ear, "Been a long time since I've had one." He flexed his shoulders forward, his face briefly reddening as he grunted, forcing Van back. "Shouldn't have sent that fool in for such an important job."

Van found his footing and stalled his retreat. "No, you shouldn't have. And from now on that fool is off limits, along with the rest of Headwaters."

King Thad laughed and shook his head. "No deal, Beer Man. Win or lose, I'm going to burn your little town to the ground. I might do it legally or I might not, plenty of ways to skin that cat, but I'm coming after everything you love." He shot a sudden glance back at his corner, which stood empty. "You don't know what this tournament has cost me."

Van followed the glance. Normally that space would be occupied by— "Where's Donovan?" Van asked, brow furrowed in confusion.

King Thad grimaced. A flash of...regret? Fear? "He wanted titans. I gave him titans."

The words slowly sank in. Van found himself pressed back against the ropes. He stared up at King Thad's looming face in horror. "You handed *titans* to the Nether? The price for the OverLord's forfeit was *titans*?" The idea had never even occurred to Van. Losing a fight to the OverLord and being dragged away in that coffin to become a shambling, mindless soldier of the Nether, like the Bearhugger, would be a fate worse than death. Van hadn't been able to imagine something more terrible. Now he could. Being sold to that fate.

The crowd became restless with the titans' stagnating clinch and some booing started to make its rounds about the Coliseum. The referee bobbed into view and tried to break them apart, but both titans ignored him and continued their parley. "Yes," King Thad hissed. "The OverLord proved very persuasive. A hard bargainer. He said I needed to double his *harvest*," King Thad spat the word out with distaste. "He settled for four, said that was the only way he'd step aside and let the tournament play out."

"I don't know who's the bigger monster," Van said, shaking his head.

King Thad abruptly released Van, letting him fall to the bottom rope, then kicked him hard in the gut, twice. He leaned over Van and snarled, "I'm no monster. Just the only one with the wealth to buy the Headlock. The OverLord told me the Titan Wars were coming again and he needs soldiers. So I gave him soldiers. I didn't even need to know his plans. I just needed to know his price."

Van reached up to grab Thad's face, but the titan retreated. As Van took his feet, he shouted at King Thad. "You gave him Donovan! Why? So the OverLord can make an army of undead titans?" Van shook his head again. "An army like that won't stop with your enemies! They'll come for the Vantages too. Your people, your kingdom."

King Thad nodded. "But they'll come for me last. I have the strongest army in the Open Nations. The Nether forces will spread every direction but north, take down everyone else. And then when they arrive at my gates, I'll ask them their price. And I'll have more than enough to pay it." He looked down at his boots, bitterness seeming to twist his lips into a grimace. "I'll admit giving up Donovan hurt. It's hard to train good help."

Van lurched forward and pressed Thad into another grapple. His anger lent him strength and he forced King Thad across the ring to the ropes on the other side. "Who else?" he growled.

"Venerate threw Creature into the bargain. And Jaygan the Dragon was proving disloyal, taking an unauthorized payoff from Grim Tidings. He learned the price of that disloyalty."

Van breathed heavily, thinking. "That's only three. You said *four*."

"I haven't paid him in full quite yet." King Thad smiled. "But I thought you'd already figured that out, Van the Beer Man. *You're* the fourth. He asked for you special." Then he threw off Van's arms and attacked.

Chapter 42

Van had no time to react as Thad launched a relentless attack. He fell into a desperate defensive posture, knees bent, forearm up to protect his head. Thad drove him backwards. A straight right to the face. An uppercut to the ribs. Thad crouched and yanked Van's ankle out from under him, sending him tumbling to the mat, and kneed Van in the side of his head. Van felt as if the whole of the ONWC had entered the ring again, but when he opened his eyes, King Thad still stood alone above him.

Van defended his body from the unending assault as he struggled to find his mental balance. King Thad's confession had rattled him. Suddenly this was no longer just a tournament match, one in which Van might still be patted on the back and told he'd done well just to make it to the championship and lose. Van was fighting for his life. And apparently for the fate of Headwaters. What else could be put on his shoulders? Oh, right, the Nether had been building an army of the undead to restart the Titan Wars and tear the Open Nations to bloody pieces.

King Thad swore and spit and snarled as he landed blow after blow. The calm charisma and authoritative air he usually presented to the world was swept aside as he rocked Van with alternating left and right hooks to the head. He leapt straight up into the air and took Van down with a dropkick to the chest. He picked Van up by the hair, growled in his ear, "You think I got where I am by letting scum like you beat me?"

"I know exactly how you got where you are," Van replied, feeling slick blood on his lips.

King Thad backfisted Van in the head with his free hand. Van crumpled to the mat, and Thad stood still for a minute, gazing at the clump of Van's hair he still held in his other hand. Then he lined himself up and delivered an elbow drop to Van's gut which drove all the air out of Van's body. Van rolled on the mat, writhing and wheezing.

Van heard the chants—*King Thad! King Thad!* They grew louder and louder like approaching thunder. From the corner of his eye he saw Thad climbing the ropes. He just wasn't sure he had the strength to do anything about it. Thad was going to win this fight. And the mat was warm and comfortable. Van wondered if he could take a nice little catnap, just a couple minutes of shuteye to dream of a cold Kingsland Ale. Everything would work out all right. He'd carried his homeland deeper into the bracket than ever before, further than any Uplands titan ever had. Was that enough?

The crowd sensed blood. Their deafening cheers became raucous screams and threats, laced with foulness and violence. But...cutting through the racket like a razor, Van heard the howl of a baby crying. A single wail, sharp and frightened, and then it vanished, perhaps shushed by a mother who held it close. The image of Annie's Lizzy, with brown eyes that matched her mother's, appeared in Van's mind. The child he'd held as he shed a tear, mourning a life he'd lost and a future filled with titans who were going to hurt him. And now he'd learned it wasn't only him they would hurt. Thad had threatened Van's homeland. The OverLord threatened the very existence of the alive and free. That the Uplands seemed to care little for Van, deemed him a misfit and loser, taken from him the one thing he ever desired, didn't matter right now. They needed a champion, and he was all they had to keep the monsters away, to protect them from the dark night.

Van heard the crowd fall silent as thousands held their breath, and he knew Thad had leapt. He clenched his fists, screamed into the mat, and rolled. King Thad crashed into the spot he'd vacated an instant later and tumbled down into his corner. Van fought to his feet. His knees creaked. A sharp pain in his side told him he'd broken at least one rib. His ankle throbbed where Thad had ripped it out from under him earlier.

King Thad also struggled back to his feet, and the two fierce titans squared off again. Van was definitely the worse for wear of the pair, but at least King Thad looked tired now. A moment of inspiration struck Van. "Oh shit," Van shouted, looking over King Thad's shoulder, "Donovan's back."

Thad's eyes bugged out and he turned to look. Van punched him the kidney then followed up with a punch to the back of his head, knocking Thad back to the mat. Van caught his breath as Thad grasped the ropes and pulled himself back to his feet. They glared at each other and began slowly circling.

"Scum! Lowlife!" Thad spat.

"Coward!" Van yelled. "Traitor!"

They grappled, but it was no longer the grapple of two titans feeling each other out. This was a desperate struggle for the upper hand, every ounce of leverage exerted to bring an opponent to his knees.

Out of the sides of his eyes, Van could see Larvell waving his hands at him, Owen hollering for him to keep the King close. But Van was someplace else entirely. In his mind the ropes melted away. Two titans fought alone on a mountaintop, cold wind blasting over them. For once, neither was a champion of anything. Their deep, resounding footfalls echoed across the land; giant oaks and elms shook in the foothills; forest animals burrowed deep in their shelters and drew their families close, waiting for the storm to pass.

Their muscles knotted together as each titan struggled for advantage. Van covered his flaws in technique with brute strength. King Thad leveraged his height, pressed down on Van's shoulders. Each stared through the other. Slowly, so slowly that it took a long time for the crowd to realize what was happening, King Thad's knees began to tremble. He shuffled his right foot backward to steady his balance. Van pressed forward, stabbing his fingertips into Thad's shoulder muscles. He pushed a step forward, feeling the burn in his calves, and Thad retreated again, shuffling his right foot back a few more inches. His forearms started to shiver. Van shook stinging sweat from his eyes, stared into Thad's face, and saw fear there.

Van pressed harder, hoping to end the stalemate. When Thad halted the slow collapse, holding his ground, Van stretched his aching neck back as far as it would go, looked up into the blazing lights, and brought his forehead crashing down on Thad's nose.

At the brutal blow, King Thad wilted, folding into himself, no longer able to endure. Van hoisted the King's bent body over his head and slammed him down to the mat. The King bounced up once, and landed sprawled on his stomach. He tried to raise himself up on hands and knees. Van stood over him and laced his thick fingers together. He raised his hands over his head and, with a roar that carried throughout the Coliseum, he swung them down like a hammer on the crown of King Thad's head. King Thad flopped onto the mat and lay there. He was out cold. The match was over.

The cheers were deafening as the stunned crowd exploded into a booming ovation. People, a good many of them far past drunk, flooded the ring, surrounded Van, screamed and hollered and whistled, slapped his back and tried to hug him as he twisted and spun and tried to free himself. The blinding lights made purple spots in Van's vision. Someone grabbed his arm. He yanked it away. They grabbed it again. Van slowly realized it was the ref, trying to raise his arm in victory. He had beaten King Thad and won the Headlock of Destiny.

The announcer pushed through the crowd and asked Van a question. He couldn't hear. His head spun. He was supposed to say something, right? Something clever. *Flawless*, right? But, wait, that wasn't it. With so many thoughts swirling in his head, Van couldn't make sense of what was happening. So he settled on passing out and crashing to the mat face first, knocking down half a dozen well-dressed people carrying some kind of giant golden belt in the process.

Chapter 43

Van awoke from the darkness bewildered and afraid. He felt crushed, hands tugged at his uniform as he fought his way back to the light. The noise was oppressive—shouting, whistling, people screaming his name from all directions. The lights in his eyes—he couldn't see. He realized he was on his back looking straight into them. He couldn't get up. Too many people, standing too near. Somehow, the ending of the fight had signified the beginning of a scrum that felt just as deadly.

A giant face above him leaned over and blocked the blinding lights. A moment later Harlan pulled Van to his feet. He offered Van no congratulations, no acknowledgement that Van had just won the Headlock of Destiny. He simply turned around and pushed people away, sending them cascading over on each other. A little man slipped beneath Harlan's arm. He was carrying the golden title belt, the grand prize of the Headlock of Destiny. For a moment, Van wondered where the little guy was going, until he smoothly wrapped the belt around Van's waist and clicked its heavy buckle. The ref was trying to raise Van's arm again.

Somewhere under all the feet, King Thad still lay stretched out on the mat. For the moment, he had no guards to protect his body and his dignity. That should have been Donovan's job. But Thad had sold the titan to the OverLord. Now he was at the mercies of the crowd. Van watched a sleazy looking hanger-on slide a golden ring off his royal finger and pocket it. A woman in a tight dress drew her foot back and planted a hard kick into the inert titan's ribs. When she looked up and saw Van had witnessed the action, she smiled and winked.

Van's friends celebrated. Owen and Larvell clapped him on the back, then hugged each other when Van didn't return their jubilance. Through the blinding lights, he could see the titans who had backed him against Scott Flawless spraying beer into the air. Somewhere nearby everyone who'd come out from the Uplands would be rejoicing.

But someone was missing. Kyle still hadn't materialized. Where was she? This was the time for her to appear at his shoulder, whisper encouragement into his ear. Van needed to tell her about Thad handing the titans to the Nether. About how the OverLord had said he was building an army. She'd said the tournament wasn't the ending. She'd know what to do. She'd find a way to…And then Van knew. He knew why she hadn't been here watching. He knew where she was and he knew where he needed to go.

Van shoved a man in a Crater Ale uniform out of the way and headed for his corner, where his Kingsland stood miraculously undisturbed. Just outside the apron, Venerate Holland was congratulating Peters, the brewery president. Van hiked the Kingsland under his arm and jumped down from the ring, landing between the two men.

Venerate gave him a hard look. "You sure know how to negotiate, ten-man." He ran both hands through his oily hair, slicking the stray strands back. "It's time we talked about getting you a better deal."

Van ignored him and started to force his way through tight gaps in the crowd, pushing a path with his free hand, and using the barrel when the hand didn't work.

"I haven't finished with you!" Venerate called after him.

Van paused, then slowly turned back. A few steps and he was looming over the ONWC's corrupt chief. "You got something to say?"

Venerate stared up, cheeks red with anger. "You got a victory tonight, sure, but these matches run through me, and you won't be sneaking another one past."

"No one got a victory tonight," Van replied. He looked off into the distance past the drunken celebration. "I'm not even sure we bought ourselves any time." Van glanced down at Venerate Holland. A part of him wanted to tear the prick apart, right here in front of the clamorous throng. A calmer, colder part of him knew the better way to deal with men like him. He did the one thing that drove them insane—he turned his back and walked away. Behind him, Venerate's voice grew increasingly shrill and then faded away in the distance.

Van moved fast, dancing and weaving purposefully through the tight crowd. He had lost his friends, but he'd find them later. He had a feeling Kyle needed him now. That she'd put herself in the path of the coming onslaught.

Outside the Coliseum, the streets crawled with drunken revelers, just as eager to engage Van as he was to avoid them. He threaded through them, moving relentlessly forward, hugging the Kingsland under his arm, ignoring the distractions, as each step brought him closer to his destination. Van could feel a cold burn in his chest. Everyone around him thought the fight was over. He knew it had only just begun.

The path to the cemetery was easy to follow. Long grooves in the dirt roads, furrows from the heavy coffin the OverLord had dragged to and from the Coliseum, set the course. *You will follow me one way or another, titan,* the OverLord had said. But it wasn't the OverLord that drew Van along the grooves in the road. Something told him that Kyle had not appeared to celebrate his victory…because she'd gone to the Nether.

Soon the dark cemetery loomed before Van. The remnants of the crowd that followed him stopped a comfortable distance away as Van approached it. A tangled, wrought iron fence separated the somber space from the lively streets around it. Rakesh the gambler stood at the gate.

"A congratulations to my titan friend."

"Thanks, Rakesh." Van's eyes remained focused on the cemetery beyond the halfling. He slowly unbuckled the golden title belt around his waist. "Would you hold on to this for me?"

Rakesh reached out nervously to take it. "You walk in the wrong direction. The best parties will be elsewhere. I will happily escort you." His small face was saddened.

"Can't do it. Got someplace else to be."

"I am a world traveler, Van, but even I would hesitate to go where you go. You seek the next opponent. With no rest and no plan."

"I seek a friend who needs help. And I have the feeling the next opponent, the only real opponent, stands between me and her." He tore his eyes from the cemetery's darkness to look down on Rakesh. "I don't know how long I'll be gone. The ONWC won't be happy with this turn of events. And King Thad threatened Headwaters. Can you keep an eye on things for me, keep them safe?"

"The ONWC and King Thad both sit atop a great fortune. Thanks to you, now I do as well. And I have never seen the Uplands. I will happily travel there and keep it safe if needed."

Van let out a breath. "Thanks, Rakesh. You're a good friend."

"But in all honesty," Rakesh continued, "I suspect that job will be easy. King Thad has long ruled by fear. He does not seem so scary now. And the ONWC played fast and loose with this tournament. Their loss will embolden all rivals. They must play defense for a time. Long enough for you to wrap up," he turned and looked back over his shoulder at the cemetery, "what you must." His voice brightened. "And perhaps you won't be long and we will join in a toast with the sunrise."

"Maybe." Van reached out an enormous hand to swallow up Rakesh's tiny one. "Be well, Rakesh."

"And the woman you've spoken of? Annie with her child Lizzy? Any message or deed for her?"

"I've never told you about her."

"Only when drunk, Van the titan. Then you have spoken of her at length."

Van looked past the creaking gate, onto the crooked tombstones and bent trees of the cemetery. "Keep them safe, like the rest. That'll have to be enough."

With a final nod to Rakesh, Van strode past him and into the cemetery. Time seemed to slow as he crossed into the darkness. A chill wind rustled the leaves of the overhanging elms. The lingering commotion from the streets faded as Van walked deeper. A fog had risen to obscure his way, but Van had seen this place enough, memorized it from the nearby rooftops. He knew where the pit was. Right in the center.

He felt an expectant hush in the darkness, like the moment before the bell rang on a match. As he neared the pit, a thin silhouette took form, standing over the black hole, looking down. The Lady Dorothy, ghostly in a white gown. He wasn't sure if he was surprised to see her or not. He wasn't sure if it mattered.

She looked up as Van approached and smiled. "She goes before, in the hopes you will follow." Her voice was calm, almost casual, as though she spoke of another frivolous party where she would trick him into carrying her purse.

"I know," Van replied. "She told me. Said we're going to need each other to find our way out of the darkness."

"Good." She nodded. "She may need more help than she thinks. She is brave, and stronger even than you, but in the land of storms and nightmares attacks come from all sides." She looked down into the black pit again. "Did you win the match?"

"Yes."

"That is also good. I thought you might. Perhaps you'll do okay in the challenges ahead." She folded her arms as though just now feeling the cemetery's unnatural, bone-chilling cold. When she continued, her tone was businesslike. "The journey will be long and perilous. Things in the Nether are not as they seem. Storms rise quickly. Lines are not straight. And you can take nothing with you."

Van nodded. Somehow he'd known there would be rules. Just as there were in the ring. Rules that gave shape and form even as they endured being bent, twisted, and broken. He set the barrel on the ground and pulled the stopper. Then he raised it up over his head and took a long, frothy drink, feeling the smooth Kingsland slide down his throat. Even now it burned, as it had when he was a child. Then he toppled the barrel over to let the remaining golden liquid pour out on the thick, green grass. The ground drank greedily and soon there was nothing left but foam.

Van replaced the stopper and picked up the empty barrel. He turned to nod to the Lady Dorothy, but she was gone, vanished like ash on the wind. Not even footprints remained on the grass where she'd stood. Van, abruptly alone in the deathly chill of the cemetery, let out a long, steaming breath, stepped to the edge of the pit, and stared down on the black emptiness.

The blackness of the pit was so complete it appeared flat, a curtain walling off another place. A place where souls trapped or kidnapped, stolen in storms and in the night, were locked in the darkness. His eyes traced the coffin tracks leading right up to the edge. The OverLord had come and gone through here. And now his prediction would come true, and Van would follow him down.

If all he was to learn about his path was that it would be perilous, that it would be made of twisted lines, so be it. Somewhere down there, a friend needed a champion to stand by her side and face the coming threat. Somewhere down there, the return of the Titan Wars was brewing. Van had long thought his destiny, if he had one, lay in a quiet mountain town. Then for a short time he'd thought it lay in the hands of other titans, trapped together in violence by the cruelties of the bracket. Neither had been correct. But perhaps it was somewhere down there, in the land of storms and nightmares, where Van's destiny hid in a dark cell, waiting to be freed.

The titan tucked his empty beer barrel under his arm, gripped it tightly, and jumped into the black.

THE END

Van's adventures continue in The Piledriver of Fate

Author's Notes

Thanks, as always, so very much for reading. This was a wildly fun book to write and I hope you enjoyed the read half as much as I enjoyed writing it.

This book (and its sequel) never would have happened without the creative contributions of Adam Rose. He's got a brilliant imagination, a brilliant mind, and has been a fantastic friend throughout my life. Without Adam's creative consultation and countless late nights watching old wrestling videos and speculating about how we could turn things up to an 11, I never would have gotten this heavy lift off the ground.

Books thrive on word of mouth and reviews. Please leave a review on your preferred platform or tell a friend about the book if you've got time. Always appreciated.

To learn more about me and other titles, please visit samuelgately.com and sign up for the mailing list.

Cheers.

- Sam

Author's Bio

Samuel Gately is a writer of novels and short stories in the fantasy genre. Most have spies. Samuel lives in Oak Park just outside Chicago with his wife, daughters, and a pair of terrifyingly fluffy dogs.